"You need to kill at least three people to be a serial killer, right?" Will said, his rich voice filling the dome of light the flames had created around us.

"So that's what I'll do."

In the past this sort of thing would have been funny—classic Will, what a weirdo. To the others it still was. But to me everything about him was sinister, from what he was saying to the way the shadows cast on his face hid his true expression. I'd always known he was in a different world to the rest of us, but that world had never been frightening before. After what I'd seen in the last few weeks of that summer, I couldn't even fake a laugh.

"Maybe it won't be exactly sixteen years," Will said, "but at some point in the future. I'll kill three people, all totally unrelated to each other. I'll make them look like suicides so I won't get caught. In different ways, and in different places—ones you wouldn't expect."

He was sniggering now, but I shivered—and not just because the fire was on the way out.

"I'll vanish from January to January one year, no one will hear from me. I'll be off the radar."

THE
KILLER
YOU
KNOW

S. R. MASTERS

REDHOOK

Redhook Books/Orbit
Hachette Book Group
1290 Avenue of the Americas
New York, NY 10104
hachettebookgroup.com

Simultaneously published in ebook in the US by Redhook and in the UK by Sphere in August 2018
First Paperback Edition: May 2019

Redhook is an imprint of Orbit, a division of Hachette Book Group.
The Redhook name and logo are trademarks of Hachette Book Group, Inc.

The publisher is not responsible for websites (or their content)
that are not owned by the publisher.

The Hachette Speakers Bureau provides a wide range of authors for speaking events. To find out more, go to www.hachettespeakersbureau.com or call (866) 376-6591.

Library of Congress Control Number: 2018965619

ISBNs: 978-0-316-48943-0 (trade paperback), 978-0-316-48944-7 (ebook)

Printed in the United States of America

LSC-C

10 9 8 7 6 5 4 3 2 1

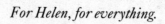

For Helen, for everything.

All of this started the night Will told us he was going to be a serial killer.

He said, "Okay, I've decided what I want to do when I'm older." We looked over at him.

He was the last to answer the question, which meant soon we'd start the long hike home from the electricity pylon deep in the forgotten overgrowth between our village and the next.

What will you be doing in another sixteen years' time?

It was all coming to an end: the night, the summer, the campfire burning on the concrete around which the five of us sat. Most of us secretly wanted everything to go on like this, perhaps for ever, despite saying out loud that we were excited by the mysteries of adulthood. None of us could believe things would ever be as good as this again, whatever problems we had with our parents or each other.

Except maybe Will, sitting there smoking his brother's drugs while the rest of us only wanted to get drunk. Will, milking the moment of reveal for dramatic effect behind a cloud of breath mist and cigarette smoke. Who knew what was going on in his head? Maybe he did think that there would be something better after this.

"You need to kill at least three people to be a serial killer, right?" Will said, his rich voice filling the dome of light the flames had created around us. "So that's what I'll do."

In the past this sort of thing would have been funny—classic Will, what a weirdo. To the others it still was. But to me everything about him was sinister, from what he was saying to the way

1

the shadows cast on his face hid his true expression. I'd always known he was in a different world to the rest of us, but that world had never been frightening before. After what I'd seen in the last few weeks of that summer, I couldn't even fake a laugh.

"Maybe it won't be exactly sixteen years," Will said, "but at some point in the future. I'll kill three people, all totally unrelated to each other. I'll make them look like suicides so I won't get caught. In different ways, and in different places—ones you wouldn't expect."

He was sniggering now, but I shivered—and not just because the fire was on the way out.

"I'll vanish from January to January one year, no one will hear from me. I'll be off the radar."

The others started asking questions, grinning, eager for more.

"Where will you kill them?"

"Won't that be difficult to get away with?"

"How will you fool people?"

They all chimed in, and Will relayed the grim details to drunk laughter and applause—for the most part making it sound like he was improvising the whole thing.

From beyond our circle soft noises drew my attention, cracks and rustling. And looking up, I swore I saw the silhouette of a person standing about ten feet behind Will, at the place where the concrete met the high grass and the weeds. But then it was gone. A trick of the starlight, maybe. Or perhaps too much alcohol mixed up with that sense of foreboding I couldn't shake.

"Then when I'm done," he said, "I'll go back to whatever job I was doing—working in an office or some place. Go out clubbing and get smashed like everyone else. No one would ever know when they're asking me to write a report, or when they're dancing next to me. But I would. That'd be enough. I'll know, and you lot will too, if you remember this—and I reckon you will."

He wasn't wrong about that.

Part I

I'm convinced nostalgia's an illness.

Winter, 2015

…if you took off your rose-tints, I think you'd both see this film for what it is.

I turned off the engine but let the podcast continue, only half-listening to the sound of my own voice coming through the car speakers. Over the road from where I'd parked, my parents' galley kitchen was lit up like a set awaiting actors. They'd hung strange paintings on the far wall and completely changed the colour scheme. The mustard paint was gone. Instead, some interior designer had detonated a magnolia bomb in there.

My dashboard clock read 21.12. Was it too late to go in? Possibly. Hopefully. They were still up for sure—Dad never left the lights on.

Okay, Xan, Jon, I think the time's come to decide whether Steven Spielberg and George Lucas's orientalist classic Indiana Jones and The Temple of Doom *goes into the crusher.*

Orientalist classic? Nice.

So you're on the fence, Adeline?

I switched off the stereo.

I ought to go in. I'd only come home to Blythe for tomorrow's reunion, but it'd be impossible to relax without first finding out more about Mum's diagnosis. Dad had been agitated on the phone last week; all he'd managed to tell me was that there was something wrong with her lungs. When he'd given the phone to her so she could elaborate, Mum hung up without saying a word once he'd left the room.

It was something terminal, it had to be. And if so, morally speaking, I needed to open up a dialogue again—end the stupid cold war of silence we'd been fighting ever since my last visit. Even if it was just to make Dad's life easier.

Yet I stayed in the car, fingering the keys dangling from the ignition. I'd expected this to be difficult—had been dreading it, in fact—but what I'd not expected was the anger that welled up once the lights of the M6 were behind me, and the roads became snakier in direct proportion to just how arse-end-of-nowhere each passing village was.

Blythe. Fucking Blythe. One lane of houses off a main road to somewhere better. A pub, an abandoned bus shelter, and nothing else for miles on either side. This was a place to hide from the world, not a real part of it. A dormitory, and every bare field or barn or dead badger that had been illuminated in the headlights was a reminder of just how isolated I'd been here. If it hadn't been for the friends I'd made, God.

I started the car. It wasn't worth it; I was losing myself, regressing already, preparing comebacks for what Mum might potentially attack me for: blue streak in my black hair, dark eye make-up, nose stud. No, I needed to just go and focus on the reunion. I'd head straight to the hotel and make notes on the podcast—it needed re-editing anyway. This cut made me sound too snarky, too irritable—the friction between the three of us perhaps seeping into my performance. It lacked the genuine affection for the films that had served *Nostalgia Crush* so well over the years.

Besides, I could always try again on my way back to London.

I dropped the handbrake. With my last glance up at the house I noticed an actor wandering on to the illuminated set:

Dad, shuffling across the kitchen. He was smaller than I remembered, and his hair, once the grey of pencil lead, was now white.

It had been over a year, and all that time was visible at once. I tried to bite my nails but they'd been well gnawed already.

Groaning, I pulled up the handbrake and turned off the engine. And when Dad saw me walking up the drive, I put on my warmest smile and waved.

The place had all the charm of a retirement home, which I suppose was appropriate. Dad showed me to a lounge I no longer recognised, the chemical smell of renovation still in the air. Only a minimalist plastic Christmas tree in the corner honoured the season.

"Wow, you really can't come home again," I said.

"Your mum wanted to get the place right while we were still able to, you know?"

Pronounced *Mom* rather than mum here in the West Midlands, of course: the lost United State. I'd been a southerner so long now it always caught me out.

"Where is she?"

"In bed, love. She had a funny turn this afternoon. I'll check if she's up to seeing you. You in a rush?"

"No," I said, and he limped away.

Before I could ask about his leg he closed the stairwell door behind him.

I sat on their pristine white leather sofa and listened to the murmur of conversation in the room above, trying to gauge her mood. Even though the words were inaudible, the Brummie accent's seesaw melody was clear. I had no accent—Mum had made sure of that during childhood. She'd flattened down any sentences that tried to rise up at the end like a kid playing Whac-A-Mole.

That's why you got into Cambridge, she'd once said.

7

Where *was* the graduation picture that used to be on the mantelpiece? Apparently not even that had survived, any personal touch sacrificed to the great, off-white God of Property Development.

I sighed. All this poison wasn't going to help should Mum desire an audience. I needed to stay positive. I took out my phone. An unread message had arrived sometime during my journey up from London.

How you holding up? Is it tonight?

Xan, our podcast's enthusiast, the heart to my mouth and to Jon's brain. The episodes were built upon Xan's passion for some classic movie being gradually dampened by Jon and me, condemning it to the so-called "crusher" unless we found solid reasons for mercy.

Before I could reply to him the stairs began to creak, and shortly after the stairwell door opened again. Dad nodded.

Mother would see me now.

"Do you want a drink, Jan?" Dad asked from behind me.

Mum, sitting up in bed, declined. He left to go and fetch Mum's pills, and I went to give her a kiss. She offered a cheek. Unlike Dad, she hadn't aged at all. She looked well, if anything.

"What did he do to his leg?" I said.

She shook her head. "He tripped in the garden, on one of the branches growing over the path. I told him it wanted cutting." She pronounced the last word like *footing*.

"And what's happening with you, Mum?"

She shrugged. "It's not good, Adeline. They said it was my lungs. All the coughing... They did a scan and then the doctor asked if I'd ever been near asbestos. Well, I haven't, but your grandad used to work on the roofs, and I was always climbing on him when he got back from work. They said it's all scratched up on the inside, and it's going to gradually get wor—"

She started coughing. It sounded painful and I put a hand on her shoulder, but her pointed glance at my chewed nails made me withdraw it into a fist.

"Do you need anything?" I said.

Mum shook her head, then pointed at my feet. "Those boots do nothing for you, love." Leaving no time for me to react, she added: "Are you still with the teacher? Is he here?"

"No," I said, surprised she'd remembered Rich.

"Oh," she said, deflating into the bed and forcing another small cough through her throat.

"Can I help while I'm back?"

Mum thought about this. "Why have you come back, Adeline?" She paused. "I was really hoping it might be because you wanted to apologise."

I bit the inside of my cheek. Last time I'd been here I'd endured a birthday meal of Mum's drunken remarks about my advancing age, about how sad it was that she might never be a grandmother. Then she'd blamed my "problem" on the anti-authoritarian streak I'd inherited from Dad, and suggested that, while Dad had been something of a disappointment, he'd at least been a man. *It might not be fashionable to say*, she'd said, *but women can't get on in the world ruffling feathers all the time.* That had been enough, and I'd kissed Dad goodbye and left for London without another word.

"I'm sorry," I said, because if Mum really was dying, any encounters we shared should at least be neutral. There wasn't enough time in the universe to fix what was broken between us, but a respectful truce wasn't out of the question.

"That's the tone of voice you're going to choose?" Mum said.

Again, I bit my cheek. "I'm seeing some old friends, Mum, and I was worried about you. If you aren't interested in getting on, and if you don't need anything, I'll just go. I don't want a fight, honestly."

Mum straightened up. "Who do you still know here?"

"You won't remember them."

"Your college friends?"

"No, some Blythe friends."

"I knew all your little Blythe friends. Steven. I remember him. His dad had that house at the bottom of the lane. Wealthy man, but he only rented it. It's all done up now."

I nodded, had seen the now extended and updated farmhouse in my headlights at the end of Elm Close when parking up. "Steve's coming," I said.

"See, I remember. And the diddy one, from India. What was his name?"

Now I shook my head. "Rupesh was born in Birmingham, Mum." In my mind I could see the footpath that ran to Hampton-in-Arden, the village next to Blythe. I'd passed the exit earlier, and Rupesh had been the person that came into my mind.

"You know what I meant. And I remember Jessica, too. The red-haired girl."

"*Jen*," I said. "She's the one that's organised it."

"Jennifer. Are you sure? Are they the ones then, the ones you're seeing?"

"It depends who shows up."

"Who else was there?" Mum stared at her fingers like they might hold the answer. "Who was the other tall boy?"

"Will," I said.

"Will. I see his mum around. She still lives in the area."

Mum started to cough again. I returned my hand to her

10

shoulder. Voice soft, I said, "Mum, is it...bad?" When she didn't answer, I asked, "How long do we have left?"

"Adeline, don't be so morbid. You've always been so morbid."

"I'm not being morbid. I probably need to know."

"Shush. Well, yes, it is. But five years, they think, or maybe ten. Could be more. The doctor said I might die of something else before then." She said this with a bit too much enthusiasm.

"Oh."

"You sound disappointed."

"I'm not. I just...I was bracing myself for a last goodbye, you know?"

"No, you're not rid of me yet."

I frowned. "So you're indefinitely dying."

"Yes, if you want."

"Sort of like before, then." And sort of like the rest of humanity.

"Are you going to say sorry properly before you go, Adeline?"

"It was good seeing you, Mum," I said. "I'm around for a few days if you need me."

What sounded like a slightly hammy cough followed me out of the bedroom and into the hallway.

Leaning on the banister halfway up the stairs was Dad. He held a bottle of pills.

"Just having a bit of rest," he said, and gave me a smile that hurt to look at.

I drove east out of Blythe, over the bridge with secret tunnels that in the height of summer you could crawl through if the river was low enough. It was only five miles to the Travel Inn in the next village, Balsall Common. Those five miles might as well have been an endless desert when we were kids.

In my room, I treated myself to a red wine from the mini-bar, then another. I'd held it together tonight, and had made the right call seeing Mum.

Typical of her to contract a terminal illness that didn't kill you, though: maximum sympathy, minimum cost. Dad was seventy-five this year, and the chances were he'd be waiting on her into his nineties. He wouldn't let Mum want for anything, even if it meant killing himself.

I tipped the final mouthful of wine down the sink, barely recognising the owner of such dark thoughts. Was I wishing Mum dead? This was what happened when you came home. You thought you'd built an adult identity for yourself, but two seconds after walking through the door you were a child again.

Had I been this hateful as a kid? Probably, and, being fair, with some cause. I could almost taste the bitterness. I licked my lips. Perhaps it was just the hotel Merlot.

From my bag I pulled out my tablet and lay with it on the bed, hoping to find a film to distract me. I opened my email account. Other than direct text messaging apps it was the only online communication tool I liked to use these days, the increase in misogynist abuse on social media having risen along with the podcast's popularity. A new email from a dating site starting, "Hey babe," greeted me. I deleted it.

I still needed to reply to Xan, so went to find my phone. He'd been standing behind me when I opened Jen's email last year suggesting a reunion the following Christmas. When he asked who Jen was and I told him about my old friends, and about my first real boyfriend, Steve, Xan was intrigued. Then he saw Steve's picture on social media.

"Have a type much?"

It had occurred to me before that there were some physical similarities between Steve and my ex, Rich: long face, dark hair, built for an overcoat. But the additional confirmation of Xan's comment bothered me. In other ways besides looks Rich had reminded me of Steve. His slightly laboured cool had the evocative power of a strong smell or a song, drawing me in despite now being old enough to know better.

The clock on the bedside table read 10.30 p.m. Perhaps I'd get an early night, make the most of the day tomorrow. The reunion wasn't until seven. I was actually looking forward to it now. Before it had been daunting, the likelihood being we'd have nothing in common any more. But after my drive through the villages earlier I couldn't care less: they'd been my saviours once.

We'd all kept in touch from a distance over the years, but I'd ignored one or two invites to actually meet up. Until the podcast I'd never done anything I'd been proud enough to want to show the people who used to know me. It would be exciting seeing them all again. Who were they now? What did they do?

Before I'd left social media, I'd looked at Steve's Facebook profile. The photographs were all sunsets and fields, none featured him. Did he have a partner? Was he married? Rupesh was, I'd seen pictures of both his secular and his traditional wedding ceremonies. He'd never been that religious so maybe he had gone through the motions to appease extended family. Or had his opinions, and his hard-headedness, softened over the years? I hoped not. I'd always liked that about him. Jen was a keen over-sharer on Facebook. I'd seen all her holiday photos and teaching updates, not to mention the dubiously attributed inspirational quotes about creativity that inevitably followed her failed auditions. Her dream had been to act back when we first knew her, and I admired her persistence despite only having managed to score a few bit parts on British TV dramas I'd never heard of. Part of me hoped she would still be trying, and another part, the part that had blocked her posts from appearing on my timeline, wanted her to have found another pursuit that wasn't so demoralising.

I messaged Xan, then lay on the bed with my eyes closed listening to the hum of the fridge.

I'd once looked up Will but nothing about his adult life stuck in my mind. When I tried again recently I found nothing at all. He was a mystery to me. I hoped his life had worked out well, but my memories of him weren't overly positive. To say he'd been awkward and strange was kind. Although, God, he had made us all laugh sometimes.

Adeline, 1997

Some kids around Adeline's age are out in the field behind the back garden. She sees them from the hall window, an Asian boy in a white shirt and a girl with red hair in two plaits. Every so often they cup their hands around their mouths to yell something that drifts over to the house. *Oh Bee, Oh Bee, Oh Bee Wanker, Oh Bee.* They're keen; Adeline is still in her dressing gown.

The two kids in the field hang around the village a lot. They're usually with another one, a boy with strawberry-blond hair who is as tall as an adult and sometimes wears a beanie. The week before, not long into the summer holidays and the Saturday they first moved to Blythe, she'd run into the girl and the blond-haired boy when exploring the surrounding fields. They'd been squashing coins on a train track a few miles from Elm Close, a proper fucking Hovis advert. They'd asked how old she was and when she said fifteen they said she looked seventeen. Adeline assumed they were taking the piss—she had lied: she wouldn't be fifteen until the end of the August—so she'd been snarly with them, told them they'd derail the train.

She should've tried harder. Already too much of this holiday has been spent in her room while the summer burned like touch-paper outside. Maybe in her big black boots, with her fishnets and eyeliner, she *does* look older. Especially out here in the countryside.

Oh Bee, Wanker, Oh Bee.

She dresses: Green Day T-shirt, short black skirt and tights. She grabs her Discman, puts in her earphones and locks up the house. Green Day fizzes in her ears, too: *Insomniac*, the sound of shopping in the Birmingham city centre with Alexa in Cult Clothing and The Oasis, of drinking alcopops down by the canal at Brindley Place. The album was a present from Alexa. Adeline misses Alexa, and her old house, and her old school. She knows she doesn't belong in the countryside. She'd been right all along when she screamed and shouted at her parents when they broke the news that they were moving.

Outside, she turns left from her drive, towards the end of the cul-de-sac. The neighbour's dog startles her by jumping up at the fence and barking with machine-gun-like insistence. She steps back, forced to place one foot into the road. At the last second she raises her head; a silver van jerks to a stop with only half a metre to spare. She holds up an apologetic hand, and the driver, a scowling man with a moustache, shakes his head before indicating to turn into the very house where the dog lives.

Her mouth drops open. Why is he shaking *his* head? It was his dog, his fault she had to step into the road in the first place. The dog runs over to the van but it's tied to a pole in the centre of the front lawn and is yanked back. It turns to snap at the lead with its ugly little head. It's the kind of dog with "bull" in the name, the sort that probably attacks small children. The lead is only two metres long—probably the reason it's so aggressive. Before the man gets out of his van, Adeline sticks up her middle finger and extends her arm, then stomps on, hoping he didn't see but pleased she'd done it. Cruel bastard.

Not much further along is the entrance to an alley between

two houses; a yellow arrow on a fencepost marks the public footpath. The alley smells like hell: dog faeces and compost from one of the nearby gardens. Once through she is in the field with the kids, and her nose fills with the aroma of manure. As shit goes, it's an improvement. She follows the footpath until the girl with the plaits notices her and waves. She approaches Adeline, and so Adeline takes out her earphones.

"Have you seen a dog?" plaits girl asks. She is in dungarees, and with her hair she's a perfect match for the surroundings. She's wearing a lot of foundation for a farm girl, though. *So* conventional. Probably a typical airhead, the sort that shops at chain stores like Mizzle and pretends to like music to impress boys. It might just be bad skin, though; she'll give her a chance.

"I just got attacked by one tied up in a garden," Adeline says.

"Not *that* one," plaits girl says, wrinkling her nose.

"Have you lost one, then?" Adeline says.

"Our friend Steve has. We've been looking all afternoon."

The Asian kid wanders over and smiles at her, says hi. As well as his smart shirt, she notices the boy's black hair is neatly combed into a side parting. "None of us even like it that much. I'm always saying he shouldn't let it off his lead."

"What make is it?" Adeline says.

Plaits girl laughs at this. "What make? I don't know, it's this high and shaggy and a bit grey." She holds her palm flat just above her waist. "It's a real mutant, to be fair. It walks funny because it has something wrong with its back, you'd know it if you saw it."

"It bites you when you stroke it," the Asian kid says and frowns. "It's really old."

"But you know, fuck it," plaits girl says, "Steve loves it, and we have something to do today."

It's the "fuck" popping out from that innocent-looking face

that makes Adeline like this girl immediately. "I can help look if you want," she says. "I honestly have nothing better to do."

"Join the club," the Asian kid says.

The dog's name is Obi-Wan Kenobi, which Adeline doesn't need to be told is a character from *Star Wars*, a film she watched once with Dad. Plaits girl's name is Jen and the boy is Rupesh. By late afternoon, when the clouds cover the sun and the breeze turns cold, they have exhausted the two fields behind Adeline's house, and the fields beyond that which belong to a pick-your-own fruit farm.

In a field of what she reckons is corn directly behind Elm Close they run into the blond-haired kid, Will. His pale skin is sunburned; his belt is decorated with badges bearing the names of mostly U.S. grunge bands. Nirvana is the only one that she's actually heard of, their smiley-face logo with the crossed-out eyes grinning from between Pearl Jam and Soundgarden. He appears to accept Adeline's presence without question, almost not noticing her at all. Adeline has grown used to attention from boys over the last year, particularly the way in which they now look at her. She mostly enjoys it, even if it makes her want to check herself in a mirror to make sure she doesn't have a toothpaste stain on her lips or crusty sleep in the corners of her eyes. Will's reaction is refreshing, and a bit annoying.

"Anything?" Jen says to Will. There's concern in her voice that wasn't there earlier. He shakes his head.

"It'll be fine," Rupesh says, then looks at Adeline. "He's escaped before."

The fruitless search for Obi soon becomes a search for Steve, too. They head further away from the cul-de-sac, deeper into the fields, before coming out near a weird lake not far from the train tracks where she first met them. This is where Will last saw Steve.

On the dirt road up to the lake's edge, Jen asks Adeline where she lived before. She says Marlstone, and tells them about how easy it was to get to Birmingham from there. Then about how much she hates her parents, hates Mum, for moving her here.

"I was thinking of trying to walk the footpath to Hampton," Adeline says. Even though Hampton is small, Dad has told her there's a train to Birmingham from the station there.

"It's too far," Rupesh says. "You can't cycle it either, and it's such a big circle around on the roads it'd take you just as long." His response is decisive, like the matter's closed. None of the others contradict him. In his dark eyes she sees something every bit as grown up as the way he dresses. It's irritating, and she'll prove him wrong when she gets the chance.

"My bike chain's broken anyway," she says.

"I can fix it," Jen says.

Adeline's not quite sure she wants Jen seeing her old bike—she's not ridden it in years. "Is there actually anything to do around here?" she says, smiling her way past Jen's offer.

"*You* could probably get served in The Nag's Head," Will says.

"We always go to Steve's," Jen says. "Do you like films?"

"Yeah, I like films."

"Good," Rupesh says, "because we watch a lot of them."

"Steve's parents have this weird relationship where they never see each other," Jen says. "They work abroad a lot, his mum is always in America, so he *never* sees her. And his dad's barely around, which means we can just spend all day and night at his place if we want. They've got this farmhouse—don't know what we'd do without it, to be honest. And he has all these pirated videos his dad gets from Thailand, stuff that hasn't even come out in the cinemas here. Last summer he hypnotised Rupesh, too, which was fun."

"I wasn't actually hypnotised," Rupesh says, sounding sore.

At the lake they split into two groups and agree to meet

halfway. Adeline goes right around the lake with Rupesh. Will and Jen go left. It's not like any lake Adeline's seen before. It's more like an oversized pond. Heaps of soil and lumps of concrete are strewn at the path's side and in the overgrown foliage nearby, like a building project was abandoned in a hurry.

The lakeside resounds with shouts of *Obiiii*, and ten minutes later they reach the far end. Will and Jen are already there.

"We've found him," Jen says. "He's right the way down the tracks." She doesn't sound pleased. Will is frowning too.

She follows them down another short footpath that comes out at the terminus of an unmarked road. Six concrete lumps, like stubby standing stones, mark the edge of what must be a turning circle. Feral bushes rule the rest of this place. Jen leads them over the road to a gap in the thicket.

"I'm going to stay here," Rupesh says. Now he looks about ten.

Will and Jen share a glance, then Jen nods, touches Rupesh's shoulder and says, "Of course, we'll come straight back for you."

Adeline doesn't ask what this is about. She plays it cool. The three of them reach a footbridge that rises up and over the railway tracks. Jen jumps over the fence at the bottom of the footbridge that separates the path from the two tracks. She walks down the right-hand side and Will hurdles the fence and goes off in the same direction. This can't be safe. She's seen railway safety videos before, but mentioning it would just make her sound like a dweeb. She climbs over, carefully, her short skirt making things difficult.

She stays as far from the tracks as possible. The ballast crunches beneath her. Stray weeds scrape her face from the right embankment. An enormous pylon fills the sky over to her left up ahead. Soon they approach a red shape, the mysterious Steve perhaps? This person is clearly alive, thank fuck, because the way they had been talking made it feel like they were going to retrieve a dead body, like in that film with River Phoenix.

Steve is sitting by the track's edge at the foot of a stony embankment. Will and Jen are in front of Adeline, blocking her view, but she can make out the top of his head, his hair dark like hers. He is leaning forward over his knees.

"Oh no," Jen says.

"It's my fault," Steve says. His voice is soft, composed. He sniffs like he might not long ago have been crying. "This is where we always come, isn't it? He wasn't scared of the trains enough."

Jen goes down on her knees and strokes his arm. "Shhh. It's all of our fault then, or no one's. Come on, let's just go home now, Steve."

He gets to his feet and Will moves aside. Steve is tall, taller than Will who must be nearly six foot. Adeline notices his eyes first when they meet hers. They are amber. He's wearing a red T-shirt with the tyrannosaurus-skeleton logo from *Jurassic Park*. He is holding the bottom half of a dog in his blood-smeared arms. The integrity of the legs—the mop-like grey fur and the black pads of its paws—makes it look like they could still kick if they wanted.

He stops and stares at her, then smiles like nothing is unusual. His eyes are red and sad.

"I couldn't find the rest of him," he says to her, sounding apologetic.

"I'm...so sorry," she says, her chest constricted and brain paralysed. "I...Jen's right, you should go home. Maybe we can come back here. To look."

He smiles, grateful, then takes a step towards her without breaking eye contact. She doesn't want to be any nearer to what he is carrying but doesn't step back. His gaze moves from her face down to her chest.

Is he checking out her tits? No, of course not, why would he?

"I like your T-shirt," he says.

21

"Oh," she says, looking down at the back-to-front Green Day logo. He must be in shock. "I like yours too." He walks by and his grinding footsteps fade. Jen chases him, sharing a concerned look with Adeline on the way past.

Only Will remains, on his knees where Steve was sitting before. The grey and white stones there are stained red.

"Was that where he found him?" Adeline says.

Will ignores her.

"Are you okay?" Adeline asks.

"It's mental, isn't it," Will says, "that this stuff is just inside us all?"

Winter, 2015

"I think all this reunion stuff can be a bit unhealthy, you know?" Rupesh said. He grinned at me from across the table and I smiled back. We were in the private function room of The George in the Tree, a pub at the Balsall Common–Blythe boundary, all oak beams and blazing fireplaces.

"You think?" I said.

He nodded and sipped his whisky. Expecting pre-drink awkwardness, I'd deliberately arrived fifteen minutes late in the hope of avoiding the worst of it. Obviously everyone else had thought the same thing—other than Rupesh. And he'd only had to travel from Blythe, from the same house he'd lived in when we were kids. Not much else about him had changed either. He still dressed smartly and parted his hair at the side, every inch the local GP. Any differences were soft and slight, a tightness of his skin and a confidence in his manner. He hadn't drunk like this, though. Already he was halfway through his second tumbler.

"Just look at the world right now," he said. "Dangerous politicians promising to bring back the good old days. I mean, technically nostalgia is a medical condition, I'm sure you know that. The etymology, it's like myalgia, neuralgia...*Nost*algia. A pain caused by coming home. *I'm* convinced nostalgia's an illness.

The whole world seems worryingly obsessed with the past, don't you reckon? Sometimes I just think, *Get over it*. What's done is done."

"So why are you here?" I said, amused, not sure if he was making a sly comment about my job or was completely unaware of the podcast. He had a point, though.

"I honestly have nothing better to do."

I laughed. "Join the club."

"Plus it's winter," Rupesh said. "Research suggests we're more likely to be nostalgic when it's cold because it warms us up."

A waitress brought my red wine. I thanked her and took a gulp, a little spilling on the white tablecloth.

"I'm also curious about you all," Rupesh said, lowering his voice and leaning forward. "I mean, Steve for example. What does he do now? He was like this golden child, wasn't he? I always saw him going into some high-flying city job. Or maybe something political. That brain, the attitude. When I look on his Facebook profile I can't make head nor tail of what he's doing nowadays."

I shrugged. Yet another club we could join.

"He was very...compelling," Rupesh said. "That was my abiding memory of him—would have made a good barrister."

At first I had dismissed the idea, but there was a definite undercurrent here. Almost like he was trying to bait me into slagging Steve off. "Maybe he is one, who knows?"

When Jen walked in she squealed, and instinctively I got up and met her halfway across the table for a dramatic hug. She kissed me once on each cheek. Her red hair was lighter, and a liberal application of face powder concealed any freckles she might still have. With no such commitment to cosmetics beyond eyeliner—who had the time outside of weddings and funerals?—I felt naked. She looked good. Flustered but good.

"Sorry I'm late," she said. "My car's been playing up the whole journey here. Christmas *bloody* Eve. Typical. I only got in from London half an hour ago, and the bloody taxi was late then."

"Are you back at your parents'?" I said.

"Yes," she said. "*God*, do I need wine."

"Let me go and get you one." Rupesh rose from his chair.

Jen faced him and after a brief pause to absorb one another, they embraced at the same time.

"So good to see you," Jen said. She stepped back and placed a flat palm against his chest like she wanted to check he was real. His hand went to hers just as it retreated, which they engineered into a clumsy hand-hold to avoid embarrassment. This in turn became an even clumsier handshake which they instantly laughed off. "You haven't bloody changed."

"Neither have—"

"Shush," Jen said. "I'll need a drink before we start any of that BS."

When Rupesh returned with a round, the conversation flowed more naturally than before. Jen was still acting here and there around teaching drama at secondary school—although it *was* quite tiring and the kids weren't like *we* used to be. And being a GP was as thankless as it sounded these days, Rupesh confirmed, more so out here in the country compared with the city. I almost forgot about what was causing the crawling sensation in my belly when the man himself, Steve Litt, entered the dining room. We all fell silent.

"Hi, Adeline." I was the nearest to him and he leaned down so we could hug. I pressed my face to his cheek and breathed him in. Remarkably, he smelled the same. Exactly the same. How was it even possible to remember a smell? Where had that information been hiding? Steve moved off around the table to greet the others, but my disappointment didn't last long. When he finished he sat down next to me.

He gave us each a Christmas card and we all thanked him.

That the rest of us hadn't got him one went unmentioned. But then he'd always had a thing about taking such things seriously.

His hair was shorter than I'd ever seen it, making his forehead look high. His shoulders were broader, and he'd grown stubble, trimmed in a line just beneath his cheekbones—the same style Rich wore.

"Merry Christmas," he said to the table. "So it's been a while. Where were we?"

We drank and talked, waiting for Will to arrive before finally giving up and ordering food. He could catch up.

All the while I felt alive and alert in a way that I hadn't in some time, a pleasurable tension in my chest. I couldn't quite get into the conversation, though, and my gaze kept gravitating towards Steve. His hair was pushed up from the sides so it was thicker in the middle. Maybe he was going bald? He caught me staring and self-consciously reached up to check if it was all still in place, a gesture that made me feel surprising tenderness towards him. He was quieter than I'd anticipated, and wore a semi-permanent grin these days that came across as shy. When he laughed, though, his smile was just the same as ever. I could really get used to the way that smile made me feel.

"Did Will definitely say he was coming?" Rupesh said.

"Well...sort of," Jen said. "When I first sent the group email he emailed back to confirm."

"I saw his first reply," Steve said. "But that was last December. He's not been in touch with you other than that?"

"He hasn't actually replied to anything else, no—not since I booked the room. But you remember what he was like. And he said in his email he doesn't use the internet much. I just assumed...You don't think he's forgotten?"

"Has anyone got a contact number?" Steve said, unable to hide his bafflement. Why would Jen assume he was coming if it had been a year since they had been in contact? Unless, like me, she'd not been that keen to see him—extending the invitation only out of politeness.

When no one spoke, Jen said, "I'm sure he'll show up."

I felt partially responsible. When Jen asked for our numbers so she could add us to a WhatsApp group I told her I'd lost my phone to avoid cluttering it with group messages. Will's lack of contact might have been spotted earlier if we'd been messaging more regularly off email.

Jen finished her current glass of wine. "He *used* to be on all the social media sites years ago, but when he didn't get back to me I checked for Facebook and stuff. I couldn't find him, though. I emailed him privately, but he never got back. I did try." She topped up her glass from the bottle on the table. "I never imagined he wouldn't show up. That's the whole reason I arranged this so far in advance, so we'd all be able to make it."

The starters arrived, and I made a plan to try to speak to Steve one-to-one, growing increasingly anxious when I couldn't. Conversation bounced superficially from work to relationships to property. Steve was single—as we all were it transpired, Rupesh having recently divorced—and he had a job in health management that he liked because it was flexible and he could work from home. I needed more, though.

Once the podcast came up, though, that was all they wanted to talk about. Rupesh and Steve both said they had listened to and enjoyed it. Jen had heard one or two episodes, she said, but had some practical questions: "Sorry if this is blunt, but how can you make money that way?"

It was an uncomfortable subject, not least because that very issue was causing some friction at *Nostalgia Crush* HQ that I wanted to put to the back of my mind. I told her about the ethical companies we plugged on air, and the money we received from patrons, happening to mention that a Premier League footballer gave regular sizeable donations. I wished I hadn't. Jen and Steve both gasped using the same note.

"We're really, ridiculously lucky," I said. "I mean, stupidly. Jonathan Ross mentioned us just the once, and, boom, it blew up."

"Jonathan Ross?" Jen said, looking almost hurt before widening her open mouth into an aggressive smile. "And it's your job? Like, full time."

"Only the last two years," I said, worried everything was now coming out like a humblebrag. "But before then, Jesus, if you'd have seen me you'd have wanted to stage an intervention." They all laughed at this. "Seriously, doing a crappy hobby podcast in my friend's basement, three unrelated temp jobs to pay off my billion credit cards."

"Not now," Jen said, wagging her finger. "Now you're living the dream."

"It's not a very useful job in the scheme of things," I said, "not like working for the health service or being a teacher. Mum can't understand how I get paid for sitting around watching films. But there's not exactly much work for qualified philosophers any more, apparently. And it won't last for ever, I know that. I don't even have a pension or anything." It might not even last into next year the way Jon and Xan had parted company last.

"I don't know," Steve said. "I was reading this article the other day, and it made the point that so much of our real life is conducted online these days, podcasts have become surrogate friendship groups for people of our age."

"The cohort that came of age under rampant individualistic capitalism," Rupesh said.

"Of course, none of *us* suffer from such crippling loneliness," Steve said.

We were all laughing a bit too hard at this when the waiter interrupted to ask if our fifth guest would still be attending.

From the others' expressions I could tell we were all thinking the same thing: the reunion of the entire gang might have to wait for another time. I didn't know about them, but I was enjoying myself in the present company, and Will's appearance risked unsettling the balance.

We apologised to the waiter and told him it was probably unlikely now. He left us alone.

"I've bumped into him a few times over the years and we always talked about Elm Close," Steve said. "He remembered everything."

"Fondly?" Rupesh said.

Steve shrugged and looked away. I hadn't considered that Will might actually want to avoid *us*. Understandably he wouldn't have entirely positive memories about how that final summer ended, given what that man did to him, but we'd all parted on good terms before then, hadn't we?

"What Mr. Strachan did to Will wasn't anything to do with us," I said. "Strachan was just a horrible man, do you remember? He always had it in for us."

"*That* was his name," Rupesh said, clapping his hands together.

"Strachan," Steve said. "Yeah, though Will probably wouldn't have even met the bloke if we hadn't gotten involved with him. I suppose Will might hold it against us—well, against me maybe—for egging us all on."

"Well, I wasn't going to say it specifically," Rupesh said, "but that was what I was getting at. Will was in the hospital for months afterwards. He started college a year later than all of us." Steve looked pained. "I just don't ever think we knew how disturbed Mr. Strachan was when we got into all that."

"Yeah, maybe," Steve said.

I knew Mr. Strachan's attack on Will had been vicious, but I don't think I'd known about Will's delayed college start. Perhaps because none of us had really seen much of him after that summer, having all gone our separate ways, I'd never dwelled upon the extent of the attack and its aftermath. After all, none of us saw it happen, we only heard about it later. And we all assumed at the time, knowing Will and his ways, that he'd said or done something to bring it about.

Still, I just didn't believe he held that incident against the rest of us. Something shifted in my mind, and a memory surfaced like a bubble in a rock pool.

"Hey," I said, "maybe he's gone on his murder spree?"

Steve and Jen both laughed.

Rupesh, face paused mid-smile, said, "Rings a bell, what was that?"

"Come on, you remember. We were all sitting around a big campfire and he said he was going to vanish one year and commit all these terrible murders," I said.

"Yeah." Rupesh grinned. "How many was it—three, four?"

"Three murders exactly," I said.

"Specifically three so he'd count as a serial killer," Jen said.

"Didn't he talk about drugging someone?" Steve said.

"Yeah," Jen said, "then leaving them in Loch Ness to make it look like a suicide?" She scrunched her face with distaste.

"He used to say some weird shit." Rupesh was laughing now. "Hanging someone from a fence at a festival, too."

"Yes," Steve said, pointing at him.

"He said he'd hang them with a guy rope from a tent," I said.

"Is that even possible?" Rupesh said.

"Man, that boy," Jen said, looking around her to make sure he wasn't walking in. Her gaze fell to the table. "He used to frighten me sometimes." When she looked up at me I nodded to let her know she wasn't alone.

"Why was that?" Rupesh said.

Jen looked to me, then to Rupesh. "Other than him telling us he wanted to be a serial killer? Oh, I don't know. It was a feeling, things he said. I'm sure if I rack my brain I can give you specifics."

"I know what she means," I said, but like her I couldn't draw up a single specific event that second.

"Good old Will," Steve said, trying to lighten the mood. "He certainly was...different."

"Sounds like a toast." Rupesh held up his nearly empty tumbler. "To absent friends."

After we clinked glasses, Steve said, "Do you remember he wanted to start a campaign to bring back the Roman gods?"

We did, and our laughter filled the little room, drowning out the Christmas Eve revelries in the main bar.

A waiter took away the last of our dessert plates while we talked about all the old films we used to pass the time with when we were kids.

"Of course, they're putting out all these inferior remakes nowadays," Rupesh said, to me mostly. "Sorry, *reboots*."

"A bit like tonight's shindig?" I said, and the others laughed.

"Hey, the night's only just begun," Jen said. "Steve, you were the one that used to get us into scrapes. Can you keep us out of Adeline's crusher?"

"Sorry, I'm retired," he said, smiling. "But, can I just say, I'm really glad one of us ended up doing something like that for an actual living." Steve raised his beer a little as if toasting me.

"Like what?" Rupesh said.

I took the opportunity to down some wine, trying to catch up with the others.

"You know, something creative."

Rupesh straightened up in his chair. "Ah, the *C* word. Sorry, pet peeve of mine. You know I feel pretty creative after seeing five patients in a row who all want antibiotics prescribed for a cold, thank you."

"Oh yeah, I just meant we all watched a lot of films, you know?" Steve said. "It's great one of us ended up making a career out of them so all that time wasn't wasted." He looked to one side. "I was talking about myself really."

"I'm still doing my best," Jen said in a small voice.

"Oh yeah," Steve said. "Of course. I...Don't listen to me." He held up his pint glass, pointed to it and rolled his eyes.

Rupesh finished his drink and ordered another; I ordered water. What was that now, Rupesh's sixth drink? Seventh?

"How are your parents these days?" Jen said. "I remember them so well, they were always so kind to me."

Rupesh's face fell. "They both passed away," he said.

"God, sorry," Jen said, touching his hand now.

"Dad was just over a year ago now. I remember it wasn't long before you got in touch, Jen. My mum died not long after that last summer we had here."

"Mate," Steve said. He nodded, like he understood. "So we're both orphans now."

Rupesh studied Steve's expression. I looked at Steve but he wouldn't look back. Had he mentioned that anywhere online in the past? Fuck. This is what you got for trying to avoid the internet: sanity and awkwardness. Not wanting to overwhelm Steve I resisted the desire to touch him too.

"You lost your parents?" Rupesh said. "Sorry, mate. I didn't know."

"I didn't know about yours either."

"God, Steve," I said, echoing Jen, "I'm so sorry. And you too, Rupesh. Fuck."

Rupesh uttered a bitter laugh. "The information age, eh," he said.

They asked about Jen's parents, a line of enquiry she quickly deflected. "They're both fine. The same. Totally the same."

When the question naturally turned to my parents, I mentioned

Mum's condition but laughed it off with a joke about her making sure Dad was in the ground before she went. We were a sad bunch for sure, but I didn't want to soak up any of Rupesh and Steve's sympathy—particularly as they were bonding over it.

Eventually the ripples of awkwardness from Jen's misplaced foot diminished, and Steve said, "I suppose it's safe to assume Will's a no-show now?"

Jen, who was looking down at her phone, said, "I'm looking up his murders now." That brought some much-needed levity. "Seriously, I am."

Though her blank expression was more than likely just a comedic deadpan, honed at one of the many acting classes she'd told us about attending, I could see a part of her was wondering if there had been something more to Will's words. It was ridiculous, of course. But then why was no one saying anything? And why was I so tense now?

"What would you do—" I started to say before Jen gasped, making us all jump. A surge of irritation coursed up my back and into my shoulders. Such a drama queen.

"No way." Jen brought her hand to her face to cover an open-mouthed grin. "No fucking way, pardon my French." She finished reading, then gave the phone to Steve.

His eyes moved from right to left, his smile morphing into a look of amused intrigue. After taking in what was on the screen, he shook his head.

"What?" Rupesh said.

"I just put in *suicide* and *festival*," Jen said to Steve.

Steve began summarising passages aloud softly: "Festival in Northumberland called Manifest...twenty-one-year-old girl, Ellie Kidd. Police officers are treating as unexplained but not suspicious...Mobile phone video taken by a festival goer was briefly posted on some dodgy message boards before being removed, showed the girl hanged herself from a chain-link

33

fence in a secluded part of a camping area. Found early in the morning. Something about drugs, too."

"From this year?" I said.

Jen nodded. "Yeah, article's dated June the twenty-ninth." She received her phone back and read the article again. "I can't believe people filmed that."

My belly squirmed with a waking disquiet, but Rupesh made a sceptical little humming sound. He was scowling.

"Oh come on, it's a bit odd," Jen said, giving him a playful push. "You don't think that's odd?"

"Does it say anything else?" Steve said. "Anything about a tent rope?"

"Nothing else," Jen said.

"How many people die at festivals every year?" Rupesh said. "How many music-obsessed kids suffer with suicidal thoughts? How many Joy Division fans does it take to top themselves with a light bulb?"

"Holy shit," Jen said. She was looking down at her phone again, her grin bigger. But there was something else present on her face now, wariness settling like frost.

"What?" Rupesh said.

"Nothing for suicide and Loch Ness, but look at this," Jen said, and handed the phone to Rupesh. "Look."

Rupesh studied the screen, muttering, "It would have to be so specific."

We waited. Then his mouth fell open.

"January, this year," Jen said.

"What is it?" I said, slightly anxious now.

He didn't speak, but he gently shook his head while handing me the phone.

The headline read: BODY RECOVERED FROM LOCH NESS. I started to read.

*

My Travel Inn was a short walk from The George, on the other side of the main road. The bar shut at midnight, giving us just over an hour. We occupied a table by a sad-looking pine tree that had already lost half its needles. A television mounted behind the bar was set to a music channel playing Christmas hits. Despite protestations, Rupesh got in the first round.

I chose my seat first having led the way, and Steve ended up next to me. We'd been hurried from The George not long after Jen's discovery and hadn't had time to properly discuss what we'd found. For a long time no one said anything. Jen spoke first.

"So come on, then. What do we all think about Will?" Under the bar lights the age lines around her eyes became apparent the way my own did in the mirror after putting in contacts.

"Listen," Rupesh said, "we've all had a bit to drink, and I've had a great time seeing you all tonight, so don't get me wrong, but it's a coincidence, isn't it?"

"You're not convinced?" Steve said.

"It's just a body in Loch Ness," he said. "The article didn't say it was suicide. It's an odd coincidence, yeah, but that's about it."

The article hadn't even identified the victim, and Jen's cursory search could only find similar articles with similar information.

"Not being funny, Rupesh," Jen said, "but it's a little bit more than odd. It's really weird."

"Maybe." Rupesh leaned back. "Correlation isn't causation, and it would be weirder in a universe this vast if coincidences didn't happen."

"Coincidences like this?" Jen said.

An odd tension occupied the hush that descended on the table, perhaps nothing more than the realisation that the night was over if Rupesh wasn't playing along. That's what this was surely, play? And Rupesh was being a bit of a killjoy.

35

Coincidence was the likeliest explanation, surely? Will just hadn't fancied coming, that was all.

"Come on," Jen said to Rupesh. "It would totally make sense of everything if he was a serial killer."

I laughed, even though there was some truth in what Jen was saying. Yeah, I could see Rupesh's point, humans were pattern-seeking creatures and all that. Pissed pattern seekers right now. But that didn't change the feeling that came with putting these facts together with *what Will had been like*, which maybe wasn't so much any particular detail or set of events, rather it was a colour: a nasty, pale green, like he'd been flagged up by my mind as sour or rotten over the course of all our encounters. Rupesh was a dark purple, standoffish and moody. Steve was a warm red, exciting and comforting like fire. Will had always been green, a sickly, keep-a-safe-distance green.

"I always got on with him fine," Rupesh said.

"He was so creepy sometimes," Jen said. "He didn't talk to your face. He talked to your tits."

"Yeah," I said. "But then, teenage boys."

"Hey," Rupesh said. "I never stared at your boobs, thank you."

"So you agree," Jen said to him. "Will was definitely a serial killer."

"Steve, come on," Rupesh said. "Help me out here."

"He was strange in other ways, too, if I'm honest," Steve said.

"Rubbish," Rupesh said, banging the table a little too hard and apologising when Steve's drink of water leapt from his glass onto the table.

"No, but hang on," Steve said. "We were all probably a bit strange back then, I was going to say. A bit intense stuck out here in the countryside. God, coming here I was worried what you all thought of me, given what I used to be like."

"Remember that game you made us play?" Rupesh said.

Steve looked taken aback, though he nodded.

"The Dedication?" I said. "He didn't *make* us play it."

"That was all of our idea, I thought," Jen said. "And don't you worry, you were fine." She reached over and touched Steve's leg. Before I had time to react to that, Jen faced me. "Maybe it's a girl thing, I don't know, but Will was different. I wish I could explain it better, when I'm not on my gabillionth glass of wine."

"Maybe we should sober up then, think about this again in the morning," Rupesh said.

"It's not just a girl thing," Steve said. "But maybe Rupesh is right and we need to all sober up."

Rupesh shook his head and downed the rest of his whisky. He blinked twice. "It's a blooming coincidence, end of story."

His boozy certainty was annoying me now. I didn't mind a sceptic—I'd loved the great sceptics at uni, you could say they'd inspired my career—but Rupesh was forcibly shutting us all down, a different thing entirely, and I wanted to retaliate. "Playing devil's advocate for a moment, Rup, what if we could remember some more details about the third murder, and then we found those online? I suppose I'm just asking, when *would* you be happy that it wasn't a coincidence?"

Rupesh shook his head firmly and shrugged. "I just wouldn't. It's . . . Why don't you check? Someone come up with something about the third murder?"

We had briefly tried to remember the details before leaving The George but drawn a collective blank on anything specific.

"Like I said, I have a vague sense it was supposed to be local?" I said.

"Anyone else remember that?" Steve sounded doubtful.

"Maybe," Jen said, face overhanging her phone again. "I've got some old diaries from back then, you know. I might've written something about it."

"They in London?" I said.

"I think so," she said, not looking up, "but there's a chance

37

they might be in Mum and Dad's attic. Nothing's coming up about any recent local suicides that I can find. But *Blythe suicide* isn't much to go on."

"Well, drugs will be involved," Rupesh said. "I asked him about how he was going to pull it off and he told us he'd kidnap them, drug them and then make it look like they'd taken a lot of different pills to make sure they got the job done. Look that up. *Blythe suicide drugs*."

It didn't take her very long to shake her head. "Nothing's coming up."

"There you go, then," Rupesh said.

"Unless he hasn't done the third murder yet," Steve said.

"Don't encourage this," Rupesh said.

"Theory time," Jen said with a theatrical flap of her hand. "He told us all this stuff, right? Why would he do that?"

"Because he was trying to make us laugh?" Steve said.

"Or because he's playing some twisted game with us," Jen said. "He gets my email about a reunion end of last year, right? So he thinks: next year. One in January, one in June, and then the last one would be the end of the year, around the time he knows we're all going to be wondering why he didn't show up."

"I don't know," Steve said before Rupesh could storm in, which from his stiff posture looked imminent. "But, you saying that... actually, I think I remember something about him doing something on New Year's Eve." A grin. A shrug.

"Oh, he *did*," Jen said. She began typing something into her phone. "That rings such a bell. Wait. God, what if Will wants us to *stop* him? This is really freaking me out. Okay, well, there's too much other irrelevant stuff when I put in 'drugs' and 'Loch Ness.' Still, this is too weird. We should try and find out what happened to him, why he didn't come tonight. Tomorrow maybe? I'm not going to sleep tonight now."

"Rupesh's right," Steve said. "Even if it kind of fits with what we remember about him, it's just a coincidence."

"What *you* remember," Rupesh said. He slugged his drink.

"You still haven't told me what your criteria for changing your mind is, Rupesh," I said. He glared at me. It cracked me up, which no doubt annoyed him more. "It probably is nothing. I just want to know we're not just dismissing it because it might be a bit inconvenient and embarrassing to have to go and tell the police this stuff."

"Well, you can't tell the police this," Rupesh said. "They'd laugh you out of town. And if he started planning this in December when you wrote to us, it really doesn't give him very long, does it? And let's face it, Will wasn't the most organised."

"Loch Ness was the end of January, that's a month," Jen said.

"Look, this is getting boring now," Rupesh said, "so I'll tell you what you'd need. First, you'd need to find out if Will is around. Because, you know, if you can find him then he hasn't really gone off radar, and that's that. Second, find out what he's been up to all these years, whether he's been in bloody Broadmoor or just minding his own business. Get an idea of how bonkers the idea of him being a serial killer really is, using his life as context. And third, you'd need to connect those two suicides in the real world, outside our varying drunken recollections of something that happened well over fifteen years ago when we were equally drunk."

Rupesh's forehead was glistening and his top two shirt buttons were undone. *He* was definitely drunk, if not a little beyond that.

"There's no variance in our accounts, though," I said.

"Exactly," Jen said. "No one has disagreed with anyone else about what he said."

Rupesh had no response to that, or at least he wasn't quick enough to put it into words.

"Did anyone follow him when he was on social media?" I

said. "Does anyone know anything about what he does for work or anything? Where he lives?"

"He was in a mountain range somewhere at some point?" Steve said.

"Trust me," Jen said, "finding our exact Will Oswald on Google..."

"His mum still lives locally," I said, repeating what Mum had told me.

"Same house?" Steve said. "The one up on the main road?"

"No." Rupesh's eyes were half-eclipsed by his lids. He really was in trouble. "They moved to Meriden. And what, you want to perform a citizen's arrest?"

"Do you know where?" I said.

"Not off the top of my head. I could find out, but not without breaking the law."

At once I understood. "They're patients of yours?"

"Rupesh," Jen said, "what if something really serious was at stake."

"You think this is serious? It's not worth my job."

"Well fine," Jen said. "I'm sure we can find out for ourselves."

"Are you allowed to say if Will's your patient?" I said.

"Would you have access to any information if he was?" Steve said. "Like mental health records?"

"No and no and no and no," Rupesh said, hitting the table once again and surprising himself in the process. He was looking straight at Steve, as if this was his fault somehow. "Sorry, guys, but I think I'm done for the night."

After a moment Steve glanced down at his phone on the table and said, "It is getting late. Father Christmas will just fly past all our houses. It's been amazing seeing you all again." His eyes flicked my way.

"Well, I don't think I could go back to London without knowing for sure about Will," Jen said.

40

Rupesh let out a loud sigh which drew our attention. "You know the truly sad thing about nostalgia," he said, "is that by indulging in it we're openly admitting to dissatisfaction with the present."

"Merry Christmas, everyone," Steve said. We all laughed except Rupesh.

"Funny," Rupesh said. "Anyway, that's what my ex-wife said when I told her I was seeing you all. And I thought I'd share it."

No one spoke.

"Well, I just wanted to see you all again," Steve said.

Rupesh looked like he might cry at that. Instead, he got to his feet, said cheerio, then walked out of the bar, holding up a farewell hand without looking back.

When he was gone, Jen said, "Okay, that was an odd ending." She laughed nervously.

"Shit," Steve said. "Was that my fault?"

"It's not your fault," I said. "I think that ex-wife was very recent. He'll be an emotional fucking powder keg."

"His dad was recent, too," Jen said.

"Hold on." Steve's tone was dark. "He's not going to drive home like that, is he?" When no one replied, he got up. "I'll go and see if he's left yet," he said and ran out of the bar. He came back a minute later shaking his head. "His Merc's gone from The George."

"What if he crashes?" Jen said. "And the police will be everywhere at the moment."

"I can get my taxi to go back past Rupesh's, make sure he's okay," Steve said. "It's sort of on the way. I'm sure he'll be fine. I can text you."

"Thanks, Steve," Jen said. "Listen, are we all around here in the Midlands a while?"

"I was planning on a few days tops," Steve said, "but only if we ended up planning to do something else together." Again, his eyes flicked towards me, then away.

"I have a lot of family stuff on," Jen said, "so I'm back until the New Year. I'd love an excuse to get away. We need to see if Will's at his parents, right?" Steve and I swapped a look. "Just in case."

"I can stay a few days," I said.

We wouldn't need to start recording scheduled podcast episodes again until the New Year, so there wasn't a pressing need to go back. While the other two went to phone for taxis I worked out how long I could realistically afford to stay at the Travel Inn. Podcasting was a career now but it wasn't a lucrative one. One more day, perhaps? I might have to bite the bullet and ask to stay with Mum and Dad. At least I'd already shown my face there.

Steve came back first and sat down opposite me to finish his drink. He smiled. There was, of course, another option.

"Where are you staying tonight?"

"The Premier Inn at Marlstone, Adie."

Adie. How long had it been since I'd been called Adie? That was always my favourite.

Come back to my room.

A little self-tease, of course, but how would he react? I could say come back for coffee and maybe it would be hilarious.

No, tonight was not the night if that was going to happen.

"Am I mad, or was Rupesh a bit hostile towards me?" Steve said. "Honestly, did I say something?"

"You? No, he was cross with everyone tonight. Don't be such a narcissist." He gave me a weak smile.

Jen returned and retrieved her coat from the chair. "They'll be here in five minutes apparently." Lowering her voice, she said, "I don't know about you two, but I'm terrified Will's going to come and murder me in my bed."

42

Steve put his hands on her shoulders and stared into her eyes. I didn't like it. "You'll be fine. We'll all wake up tomorrow and want to thank Rupesh for being so reasonable."

"Ha, fat chance," Jen said. "I am worried about him."

The two of them hugged, then Jen turned to me and we hugged. Last of all Steve put his arms around me and I felt his cheek press against my head. When he moved away I wanted to pull him back.

"I'll let you know if I find those diaries," Jen said. "And if you two remember anything else, you must let me know."

"Yes, Detective," Steve said, and put his index and third finger together at his temple in salute.

"Do you still write your diaries?" I asked.

"No, God. I'd need a warehouse to store that many."

"Would be a lot of literature," I said. "I still can't get my head around how we're all in our thirties now."

Nodding, Jen said, "Time is frightening when you notice it."

Adeline, 1997

There is a knock on Adeline's door Friday lunchtime, a week after the death of Steve's dog. Will is standing on her doorstep in a rainbow-coloured tie-dyed T-shirt that is too big for him. Even slouched over he's the same height as her.

He says, "Steve has this thing he wants to ask you about. I said I'd stop in on my way over to let you know. You should come."

He aims the comment at her chest, and today Adeline isn't wearing a T-shirt with a logo.

Steve's first question to her is: "What's your handwriting like?"

She is just on the inside of the door to Steve's lounge, at the rear of his old farmhouse. The place needs fresh paint and a hoover, or perhaps just demolition. Will walks in from behind her and throws himself down on the three-person sofa next to Jen, freeing generations of dust particles in the process. They're all watching Scooby Doo being chased by a purple ape on the TV.

"More importantly, is it less shit than any of these?" Steve says and holds out a piece of paper to her. He seems more normal now, which she's glad about.

Adeline crosses the lounge and takes it. The same sentence is written four times in four different hands: *Dear Mr. Strachan, Please stop leaving your dog tied up. It's cruel.*

"Yeah, probably." Adeline looks over at the others. "No offence if these are yours."

"I'm offended," Rupesh says from his position lying on his stomach on the floor in front of the TV.

"Offence!" Will says and raises both arms in the air.

"I'm offended," Jen says. "I still don't see what's wrong with mine."

Steve ignores her. Adeline writes down the sentence beneath the others' and shows Steve. He compares them all.

"You were right about Hampton station," Adeline says to Rupesh.

"It's miles, isn't it?" he says, without looking up.

Yes, it is. She had lost an entire sweaty day for just half an hour in Birmingham city centre. It had been getting dark when she walked home through the fields. Full of hate and frustration, she'd carved COUNTRY PUNKS into a wooden footbridge with a scrap of metal she found.

Steve nods, then gets up and leads Adeline outside. They stand together at the end of his drive and he points to the house with the mad dog.

"It's so bad for them being chained up like that all day," Steve says. "They're pack animals, they need friends. It's going insane there, just walking around and around. Even when it's raining he leaves it there. I think it was Mr. Strachan's ex-wife's so that's his revenge."

She explains that the dog nearly got her killed the day she first met Steve. He nods.

"That dog bit Obi," Steve says, "about a year ago when we were on a walk. Bloke never apologised to me or anything, just walked off shaking his head. It messed Obi up. The bite got all infected and he wasn't as friendly any more. Like Strachan's dog passed his nastiness on to him. He never used to wander off on his own before that."

"Well, fuck Strachan then," Adeline says, and Steve grins. His teeth are perfect. She's not in the habit of noticing teeth.

"I think us doing something for that dog will restore the balance in the universe," he says.

"You some sort of Jedi then?" Adeline says, not meaning for it to sound quite as sarcastic as it comes out.

He smiles. "No, actually I just sort of like Aristotle and—" He cuts himself off, looking away a little bit embarrassed. "I just like philosophy," he says in a low mutter.

She moves the conversation on, enjoying the moment of power, even though really she likes the fact he is a bit of a geek. "What is your plan, though?"

Inside, Steve lays it all out: to avoid detection they will all meet up at midnight inside the entrance to the alley to Hampton, which Steve calls Dead Man's Alley. Then they'll leave a note written by Adeline on the windscreen of Mr. Strachan's van. The note will make it sound like a group of local residents is fed up of his cruelty, and written in Adeline's neat handwriting he'll have no reason to suspect it's not true. Paranoid he's bothering everyone, he'll bow to peer pressure and look after his dog better.

Rupesh wants them to just phone the RSPCA, and Will thinks they should slash Mr. Strachan's tyres. Steve, with weariness that sounds like it isn't the first time they've discussed these ideas, explains that the RSPCA have no real powers and that they don't want to end up in prison.

They draw straws to decide who will do the most dangerous part: putting the note on the van while the rest of them keep a lookout.

"Adeline is new to the group," Steve says, "it's unfair to make her do this bit."

"No way," Adeline says, trying not to show how thrilled she is that he considers her part of the group already. "I'm in."

Her self-sacrifice is rewarded with another Steve smile.

The closest thing to straws Jen can find in the kitchen is chopsticks, which Steve snaps into pieces and holds in his fist, the visible ends all level. Rupesh is last to choose a broken chopstick. He takes one look at his, one look at everyone else's, then throws his piece to the floor.

"Cockflaps," he says. "Just typical. I knew it. How am I even supposed to get out my house at midnight, Steve? You lot are all right, you live this end. I've got to walk all the way here from the main road without being seen. And my dad locks the gate."

"I've got to come that way too," Will says. "I'll come and get you. The gate'll be easy."

"What are we going to write in the note exactly?" Jen says. "Just: please be nicer to your dog?"

"Threaten him," Will says. "Got to be tough."

"What about this?" Adeline gestures for the pen. She writes something down, then shows Steve.

"Love it," he says. The others murmur their approval, except for Rupesh who is lying on his stomach watching *Scooby Doo* again.

Dear Mr. Strachan,

Please can you refrain from leaving your dog tied up in the front garden. It is cruel, and it is causing your dog to be stressed and bark all the time. Your lack of consideration has been noted and will no longer be tolerated. If you cannot be humane enough to consider your dog's wellbeing, and consider our wishes, then the next time you hear from us will not be in the form of a note.

Regards, The Neighbourhood

"The Neighbourhood," Jen says. "Nice touch."

"Brilliant," Steve says, almost whispering.

*

That night Adeline listens to her music through headphones and reads, looking up Aristotle in an encyclopedia from Dad's study. Occasionally she sticks her head out of the window to have the night air slap her awake.

At twenty to midnight, she puts on her dressing gown to hide that she is still fully clothed and sneaks out. Thanks to Mum's love of old houses, almost every step caws beneath her feet. In the kitchen she discards the dressing gown in the tumble dryer and leaves the house.

It isn't scary, despite the quiet and the darkness. This street, so dull and adult during the daylight, is suddenly hers—suddenly theirs. She can't see the dog, but all Mr. Strachan's lights are off.

"You came," Steve says, a whisper from the shadows inside the alley.

"Of course I did." She joins him, off the pavement and out of sight. They are close enough that she can smell the soap on his skin, which she relishes over what else the alley has to offer.

From behind them she hears footsteps, and when she turns Jen bustles past her into the alley. Jen's trying to control her laughter and failing. When she gets a grip of herself she says, "I got all the way to the door, then Sparky started following me and meowing."

"Sparky's her cat," Steve says to Adeline.

"Really?" Adeline is straight-faced.

"Sarcasm's the lowest form of humour, Adeline," Steve says.

"I am as low as it gets."

Will is ten minutes late. They watch his distinctive outline approach beneath the streetlight. He's wearing an oversized T-shirt with the *Countdown* gameshow logo on it. Rupesh isn't with him.

"I waited for ages," Will says on his arrival. "I even jumped over the gate to look up at his bedroom and the lights were off. I think he's asleep."

Steve sighs. "Guess we know where he stands." He sounds sad.

"He did say it might be difficult," Jen says, though she lacks conviction.

"Well, we can't leave the note at the front of the house because of the dog," Steve says, "so I'm going to go in through the back garden and put it on Strachan's van that way. There's a big shed there I can hide behind. The van's pulled right up by the house, and the dog won't see me if I can get there. Hopefully."

They follow him deeper into the alley, then once in the field they head left, into woodland that runs behind Mr. Strachan's and, eventually, Adeline's house. At Mr. Strachan's fence, Will gives Steve a boost up with his cupped hands so that Steve straddles the top.

"Wait here," Steve says. "But if anything goes wrong meet me back at mine if you can. Otherwise, we'll catch up tomorrow."

With that he carefully lowers himself down, and his feet gently thud on the other side.

Will's hand brushes against hers and she flinches. Had he done it deliberately? The touch had been too long to have just been an accident.

"Sorry," he says. "It's so dark. You need hunting eyes to see anything."

Hunting eyes. Why would he say that? Adeline shivers.

For a while they stand without saying anything. She chews on her ragged thumbnail. He is right, though, the dark is different here, so impenetrable that Adeline might be alone now and she wouldn't know.

Then a noise disturbs the silence, making her jump.

Wouah, wouah, wouah, wouah, wouah. Mr. Strachan's dog.

49

"He's been rumbled," Will says.

"What do we do?" Jen says.

"Wait," Adeline says. "Just wait. It might be nothing."

The dog's barks start to lose power, becoming more spaced out until eventually they halt after what feels like an age. They wait a while longer, but when Steve doesn't return Will suggests they go back to Steve's. He must have run out though the front. It would explain the dog.

Back in the alley's mouth, they survey the road. Everything appears as it was.

"You wait here," Adeline says. "I'm going to check Mr. Strachan's before we all go past. Just in case he followed Steve out."

Not waiting for any objections, she crosses the road, then turns to look back and survey Mr. Strachan's. The dog is now lying near the house, head resting on its paws facing away from her. Whatever the issue had been, it isn't bothered any more. She walks out into the middle of the road to get a closer look, trying to see if the note is visible on the van's window.

Something moves, a shadow between the van and the left of the house. Her chest freezes for an instant, then she realises it's Steve. He's waving. Up in the house a light is on. She points at the window trying to let Steve know, then wanting to be out of sight in case Mr. Strachan looks out, she approaches the fence as quietly as she can and ducks down behind it.

When nothing happens, she slowly rises to peer over the fence. Steve is leaning over the van. Then something catches her attention, and when she looks up at the house the curtains of the lit bedroom are swaying.

She wants to yell to Steve, to warn him.

The van's headlights come on, illuminating her and the entire drive. Adeline squints and brings a hand to her eyes. They go off, then come back on again.

Hooooonk, Hooooonk, Hooooonk.

The van's alarm. Steve's set the fucking alarm off.

He's running down the drive then, a big smile on his face, and the dog sees him. It charges, snarling, but the lead pulls it back when it reaches the drive. The force is so strong it yelps and ends up on its back.

"My house," Steve says, shooting by her.

He's already halfway across the distance between Mr. Strachan's and his place when she starts running. The others are behind, four soles clapping against the road.

"Did you leave it?" Adeline says when they are all inside.

"No problem," he says. "But that dog is psychic. It was yapping before I got near it."

Upstairs, in Steve's dad's bedroom, they watch the street from behind net curtains with the lights off. Mr. Strachan is out on his drive, patrolling in his dressing gown. His alarm has stopped and the dog's not barking. He goes in without seeing the note.

Even if Mr. Strachan had seen them running away, he wouldn't be able to identify Adeline from behind, not so that she wouldn't be able to deny it was her. They will be okay; their first mission has been a success.

The house is freezing. Steve gets them all musty blankets and starts an open fire using wood he brings in from the outside shed. He gets it going with squirts from a fucking petrol can—the loon. They watch a pirated film called *Grosse Pointe Blank* and Will tries passing around a porno mag he brought down from Steve's dad's bedroom. The film is good, it keeps her awake and distracts her from worrying about getting back home and being caught.

She's on a sofa with Jen and Will. Steve sits alone on his favourite leather swivel chair. Every now and then she checks him out, confident the darkness conceals her secret glances.

51

He looks like the actor in the film. Only Steve is even more handsome. Once or twice she looks over and he is looking right back at her, although there's no way he can see what her eyes are doing from over there.

Adeline spends most days at Steve's. Letting herself into the farmhouse becomes as natural as entering her own home. Mostly the others are around in some combination; occasionally it's just the two of them, which even though she sort of wants, she also dreads, because the thing happening between them makes talking difficult and awkward.

Frightening natural chemistry is what Minnie Driver said in the film the other night. That's a good way to think of it. Makes it seem sciencey, out of her control, like her pathetic behaviour—waking up every morning with him in her head, wearing a specific deodorant because he'd said she smelled nice one day—isn't entirely her fault.

Rupesh had been right: they watch a lot of films. The others all know so much about them that it can be intimidating. They can name all the actors in bit parts, as well as the stars. Steve points out a bunch of actors who all show up in the same films, like they're part of a secret club that hang out together off set, which he just thinks is the coolest thing in the world. Will says something about not wanting to be in any club with himself as a member, which Adeline later realises is actually quite funny.

Since leaving the note—which seems to have done the job as Strachan's dog hasn't been seen since—Rupesh himself hasn't been around at all. She'd seen him out at the bus stop on the corner of Elm Close one afternoon and he'd told her he felt like he let them all down so was suffering a self-imposed exile. She'd told him to stop being ridiculous.

Her birthday falls on a Thursday, the twenty-first of August.

Her parents are both at work, Dad at his toy shop in Marlstone, Mum at the church in Coventry where she administrates part time. Not that she particularly wants their company. When she finally gets out of bed she finds a cupcake topped with a sugar paper fairy on the dining-room table. There is a card with her name on too, and when she opens the envelope a black object falls on the floor. Adeline crouches to retrieve it. It's a voucher for Mizzle. All at once she is struck by a feeling of emptiness, perhaps sensing the chasm between herself and who they think she is. How little they know about her is so sad, despite their best intentions to get it right.

The doorbell rings. She is still in her underwear and dressing gown. The overhang above the front door prevents her from seeing who is outside from the upstairs window. Once dressed, hair dry, she goes down. A clumsily wrapped package with a card taped to the top has been left on the doorstep. Her name is written on the envelope in dreadful handwriting, a question mark at the end presumably because whoever had written it wasn't sure of the spelling, although they needn't have worried.

She tears the paper. It's a Green Day bootleg called *Noize Boyz*. She presses it to her chest with both hands for just a moment before sitting down to read the card. It is signed: *The Neighbourhood*. Adeline smiles at the joke.

That afternoon they go to the fields. They only get as far as the farmhouse entrance before coming to a stop. Their collective attention honed on Mr. Strachan's house, they stand in a line in the afternoon heat like a posse awaiting a shootout. The dog is staring back at them from the edge of the drive, a lead around its neck trailing off in the direction of the lawn—now much shorter than before.

Adeline turns to Steve, who is standing in the middle of them all.

"That fucker," he says.

"Oh dear," Jen says.

"That's a declaration of war," Will says.

Rupesh, perhaps in an attempt to show his commitment now he is back in the fold, steps forward. "Shall I just go to the phone box and call the RSPCA now?"

"I can't believe it," Steve says.

"Let's just keep moving," Jen says. "He'll see us staring."

"It's a declaration of war," Will says again.

Winter, 2015

The next morning my phone buzzed from inside my handbag until I couldn't ignore it any more. It was half ten already, and check-out was midday. My head felt heavy, but when I raised it there was no pain or nausea. It was going to be fine. Nothing a glass of water and a paracetamol wouldn't fix.

I surveyed the room. God this really was the life, wasn't it? Christmas Day in a fucking Travel Inn. On the plus side, it didn't even rank in the top five of my terrible Christmas mornings.

My bag was on a chair next to the television. I got out of bed, counting up what I'd put away the night before. Not an insignificant amount, although my alcohol tolerance was probably at its highest since uni. There were barely any reasons to stay sober on weeknights now I didn't have an office job; the first, second and third rules of *Nostalgia Crush* were that we never recorded before late afternoon.

On my phone a message from Steve read:

Are you still up?

The time on that message meant Steve sent it only ten minutes after we had all said goodnight in the bar. I went to sleep almost as soon as I fell onto the bed, which I now regretted.

Maybe Steve *had* wanted a coffee after all. I began composing a reply, then stopped myself and went back to check the other messages.

Another from Steve read:

> Obviously not...Maybe we should check on Rupesh tomorrow morning? His car wasn't on his drive?? Probably nothing though. Was good seeing you again tonight. X

He'd obviously sent the first text from his taxi. So he hadn't been after a nightcap. Still, he'd managed to manufacture an excuse to see me again, which was something. Rupesh had probably pulled over to sober up once he'd realised how wibbly all the road lines appeared. He'd be fine. But why not check? It was a kind thing to do, and it *was* Christmas morning. As far as excuses to see each other went it was much less of a headfuck than the Will's-a-serial-killer discovery we'd made last night.

Had that really happened? And I'd been half-considering it, too. Had been slightly afraid. Now in the clear light of day it was surely bonkers.

Apparently Jen didn't think so. She'd added us all to a WhatsApp group called *Will Stuff* early that morning, with an introductory message that just said: LOOK. DRUGS! followed by a link to a local newspaper article about the body in Loch Ness. I only skimmed the article—a report on the inquest, the salient points being that the victim was a woman called Sara Kuzmenski and a pharmacy of substances had been found in her system and in the car she left nearby. The length of the article and the lack of detail suggested that the press thought nothing more than a sad accident had taken place. Steve responded with:

> Huh...Interesting.

No response from Rupesh, though. Maybe he *had* crashed? I replied to Steve's first text suggesting that, since I'd be going back to Mum and Dad's anyway, we meet at Rupesh's in an hour.

Balsall Common and Blythe had been bleached overnight. The lanes and the fields between the hotel and Elm Close gleamed with frost; the sky was a grey sheet. I hummed "White Christmas," taking every winding corner slowly despite having the road to myself. The deserted landscape gave me the same sort of contrarian thrill I got from mid-week trips to the shops or the cinema while everyone else was stuck at work.

Rupesh's house stood on Blythe Lane near the entrance to Elm Close. Steve's black estate car was parked opposite, just before a string of white ex-council semis, one of which used to be Will's. I pulled up behind Steve, got out and went around to his passenger door which he opened for me. It was a big vehicle for a man with no family. Inside it was pristine and redolent with the sweetshop smell of new car. The heaters blasted my face. He initiated an awkward hug across the handbrake and wished me merry Christmas.

"I'm surprised you of all people don't have anything planned for today," I said. "No fireplace to lie beside." Something registered on his face. It hit me, what he'd said last night. His parents. What an idiot I was.

"What's better than Christmas morning with old friends?"

"I'm sorry about your mum and dad. I should have known. I wish—" Realising I had nothing insightful or helpful to say, I clammed up.

He came to my rescue. "It's fine, Adie. They were both a while ago now. Dad's love of cake finally caught up with his heart and Mum went just as she would have liked, at high speed in a European city. Car crash, it was instant."

"Jesus," I said. Unable to help myself, I leaned over and pulled his head to my chest. He started laughing. Fuck, he smelled nice. I actually kissed his big forehead, told him how sorry I was again.

"Sorry about your mum, too," he said. "I remember you and she weren't exactly best friends."

"We keep our distance. That works for the most part. I have a safe space in my mind."

When I'd given him his head back, he stared at me and smirked.

"What?" I said.

"Just funny. In some ways, it's like no time's passed at all."

Over the road the solid brown gate at the front of Rupesh's house was pulled closed, blocking any view of the drive. "So what's our plan? I take it the gate was open when you went past last night?"

"Yeah, it was," he said.

"So the fact it's now closed probably means he's home. So he's alive."

"Let's check anyway. He'd probably appreciate it, and I'm worried we got a bit carried away last night. Maybe he felt ganged up on a bit."

"I don't think we did anything wrong," I said.

I wasn't sure how appreciative Rupesh would be about us rocking up mid-hangover, but when it came to yuletide spirit I trusted Steve's instincts over mine—Christmas hadn't meant anything to me for a very long time. Steve obviously wasn't happy about how things had finished last night and I was keen to put off going to Mum's for as long as possible.

We climbed out of the car and crossed the road to Rupesh's drive. Like its owner, the front garden hadn't changed much since we were kids. The lawn needed mowing, and the statue of Ganesh wanted the moss scraping off, but that was about it.

Unlike the surrounding houses, the exterior was bereft of seasonal lights.

Rupesh answered in his boxer shorts and a white Led Zeppelin T-shirt—if I missed one thing about the West Midlands it was its unabated commitment to heavy rock music. The night had brought disorder to his haircut but he was otherwise intact. Steve told him we'd been concerned, and after a momentary hesitation Rupesh invited us inside.

He went through to the kitchen while we stayed in the lounge. A photograph of Rupesh as a young boy and another of him with his parents around the age he'd been when I'd met him adorned the mantelpiece above the fire. I'd only been in the house a handful of times, but I was sure those same pictures had been there back then.

"It looks the same," I said when he came back in. He'd put on a pair of dark purple joggers and held a mug of tea.

"It's strange," he said, "after Mum died it made me so angry that Dad kept it all the same. Then he died and now I can't change it. I couldn't even bring myself to sell or rent the place. Good job too after Becky kicked me out."

"Sounds like it's been a shit time," Steve said.

"Listen," Rupesh said, "I was a bit much last night. I tend to start speaking my mind when I've had a few."

"Honestly, it was fine," Steve said.

"We're just glad you got home safe," I said.

"Yeah, that was stupid. Sorry." He sat back and appeared to take in the empty room. "It's...a problem."

"After *my* dad died I don't want to tell you how much I used to put away," Steve said. If this was too frank Rupesh didn't let it show. "And you had a point. People do look to the past when they're dissatisfied with the present. I'd actually been thinking about it a lot in the run-up to all this. What with my parents, a big break-up...I have such good memories from back then, of being really happy over those summers we were friends. Maybe I wanted a piece of it coming back here."

He'd not simply said a break-up, but a big break-up. That sounded serious.

Rupesh sipped his tea. "Just forget what I said, mate. I was pissed off my face." In the following silence it felt like some sort of equilibrium had been found, and I even started to consider where Steve and I might go next now we knew he was fine. Only then Rupesh said, "I wonder if we were really happy back then. Or did we just think we were happy because we didn't have any obstacles? No bills to pay or boring things to worry about like mortgages or settling down."

"I don't know," Steve said. "What do you think, Adeline? This is your area, isn't it?"

"Don't ask me," I said, but when he wouldn't look away I threw him something I'd said in a few interviews: "I think it's also to do with us knowing how the past ended. All our worries have been concluded. Mostly. We know it all ended fine because we're here to think about it." It was Xan I always had in my mind when I made this point. He loved films that reminded him of his childhood because those were happier, safer times. Safer *places*: because they had borders and could be visited again in memory; everything in them was finished and finite.

"I look back and partly I remember this lovely time," Rupesh said. "Mucking about in the fields and watching films, having all that freedom without any responsibility. But if I really remember it, really try hard, was I that happy? What am I forgetting?"

"I remember being happy," Steve said. "I think. Bored, but happy."

Rupesh gave a gentle, derisive snort. "You were never happy with me."

"I was," Steve said, smile wavering. "I mean, seriously? You don't think I was happy with you? You were one of my best friends."

"Forget it," Rupesh said, "I was just joking. You were fine."

"Was I a bully?" Steve said. His smile had gone completely. "I know I wasn't exactly perfect, Rup, I remember that. I have a lot of regret about how I probably behaved towards everyone, but—"

"You weren't a bully," Rupesh said.

"No," I said, wanting to throw my weight behind this.

"You were just very hard to say no to. But you know... we all had our own issues going on at home that as kids you just aren't aware of. I mean, it must have been weird for you being isolated in that house all the time. Have you ever thought about how abnormal that was?"

"You were going through worse," Steve said. And like a switch had been flicked, his composure returned. "I'm sorry, mate, really. I know I must have made things difficult for you when they were probably difficult enough. I was a massive knob, all those public school edges. It's haunted me a bit, actually. In my mind it's so positive, you know, but I've always known it probably wasn't for everyone else."

Rupesh, now embarrassed himself, said, "Don't worry, mate, what's done is done. I have good memories of it too."

The thing was, despite what they were saying, I only had good memories really—although I got why Steve felt like he did about himself. But I'd found all his confidence thrilling then. It had lanced this nothing village's stultifying atmosphere. What's done is done, my arse.

"What about Will?" Steve said. "How does he remember things, do you think? I sort of wonder if you weren't onto something else last night about him not showing up. Maybe he did hold what happened to him against us? He was a bit off with me when I saw him last, if I'm honest."

"Did you see Jen's message?" Rupesh said.

"Yeah," he said.

"She's definitely keen," I said.

"Have you decided whether or not you are going to pursue 'the case'?" Rupesh said.

"Not yet," Steve said. "But I was just going to suggest maybe asking Adeline's mum if she knows where the Oswalds live now. Maybe pay them a visit. I know it won't prove anything, but I'm curious to see if he's around. If you don't mind, obviously?" Steve turned to me.

"It's Christmas Day," I said.

"Exactly. He might even be home. Today's better than most. Like you said last night, Rup, that would put an end to the idea this is his big murder spree year. Nip it in the bud. At the very least we could just ask them about his whereabouts. That ought to make Jen happy."

"Isn't it a bit confrontational if he is there? Means he probably gave us the swerve last night?"

"Good point," he said. "Although he might've genuinely just forgotten. If he is there and doesn't want to see us we just awkwardly say hi and leave. At least we know then."

"Listen, since the divorce I've not been on great form at work," Rupesh said. "I've not been in our practice manager's good books, so I couldn't really risk looking anyone up on the patient notes system because each time we bring up a patient record we have to log why we are accessing it. It's all monitored to protect confidentiality."

"That's totally understandable," I said.

"Ah," Rupesh said, holding up a silencing finger. "The thing is, last night I wasn't exactly in a vigilant state of mind."

"You looked the parents up?" Steve said.

"Yeah," he said.

"What about Will?" I said.

"I don't have anything interesting to add on that," Rupesh said. "But given your mum's not in good shape, Adeline, perhaps you don't need to go and disturb her."

"You'll give us the address?" Steve said.

"Not exactly. But let's go for a drive. A nice Christmas Day drive, and I can show you the sights, point out what's changed. You know, as a local."

"Now?" I said.

"Well, unless you've got plans?" Rupesh said. "Like Steve said, it should make Jen happy."

I shook my head.

"I've got an empty hotel room waiting for me, so this is better than my original plan to raid the mini-bar and watch crap films," Steve said.

Rupesh fired off a message to the WhatsApp group. Jen responded immediately: she'd been roped into entertaining the children and was desperate to escape. If her car started again she'd be over as soon as possible.

While waiting for her, Steve went to the bathroom leaving Rupesh and me alone.

"If you need to ask me anything about your mum, Adeline," he said, "I've dealt with plenty of patients with similar conditions. They can be challenging as they go on."

"Thank you." I wouldn't take him up on it, though. He was only offering to fill the quiet. As if to confirm this we immediately fell silent.

The buzz of Rupesh's phone came to our rescue, and he smiled when he read the message. "Jen says her car is still being a bit funny so she's *robbed* her sister's. She's only just left."

"I haven't got that message," I said, taking out my phone.

"She didn't send it on the group," Rupesh said.

So Rupesh and Jen were exchanging private messages,

63

interesting. The two had been an item, although I didn't remember them being as serious as Steve and me. But maybe I'd been wrong. It went some way to explaining Rupesh's interest in going along with us about Will now, despite having made such a fuss last night. Or was I just projecting my own motives on to him?

Steve returned, and while we sat waiting for Jen something occurred to me.

"It must have been quite alienating to have been Will once the four of us coupled off," I said. Strange really, because none of us even noticed that back then. "He was the odd one out in more than just the obvious ways."

"I suppose so," Rupesh said. "Are you looking for motives?"

I laughed. "Not really. I suppose I'm just reassessing everything. I think we're more than likely going to end this mystery in about twenty minutes."

"Well, we'll need more than a motive," Steve said. "COM-B."

"What's that?" I said.

"Capability, Opportunity, Motivation. It's a behavioural theory we use at work." To Rupesh he said, "Evidence-based."

"Evidence-based psychology," Rupesh said. "Now there's a thing."

Steve glowered a little, but didn't bite back. Instead, he rearranged his face into a grin.

"Just don't ask me to remember what the B stands for."

Through a ridiculous series of yawns, coughs and comments on unremarkable bits of landscape ("If we go left here you'll notice a nice bit of pothole repair work the council did last year"), Rupesh directed us to the house where Will lived after leaving Blythe without specifically telling us the address—if it made him feel better, why not?

We drove through Hampton-in-Arden, past the train station

that lay tantalisingly beyond reasonable walking distance from Blythe. Funny just how short that journey was in a car.

"Pull up here actually, Steve," Rupesh said from the back seat where he was sitting with Jen. We'd reached a cul-de-sac nestled deep in the suburbs of the next village along, Meriden. "I'm feeling sick."

It wasn't until we were outside the car that I realised this was part of Rupesh's bit, too. He was quite funny. I couldn't believe he'd kept it up this long.

"You go on without me," he said, leaning up against the car. He placed his hand on his forehead. "My temperature's not a healthy thirty-seven, that's certain. Yes, definitely *not* thirty-seven. I'll wait here. Don't want my patients catching this. I'll end up having to treat them."

"Okay, settle down, McKellen," Jen said.

"We've parked far enough from the house, haven't we?" Steve said. "Out of viewing distance."

Rupesh nodded once.

"Is three of us turning up not overkill?" Jen said. "I'll wait with Rupesh. I'm actually bricking it, to be honest. The last time I saw Will's mum she gave me this impassioned speech about being a professional actor. I'm not sure I can face telling her I didn't exactly make it."

"Well," Steve said, "maybe not yet you haven't. We're all still young."

"I'll stay here," she said.

The cul-de-sac was typical of West Midlands developments from the 80s and 90s: identical and neat, with lots of room on the drive. Plenty of those drives were full this morning. The cooking smells made my stomach rumble. It was almost lunchtime.

At the end of the road was a T-junction, and number thirty-seven was at the tip of the right fork. One house stood out immediately. A caravan and a small blue Toyota occupied the drive; both were equally ancient and equally rusted. Weeds poked from every gap in the concrete, and the upstairs window had a crack on which gaffer tape had been stuck from the inside. Gaffer tape had also been arranged into a thirty-seven on the small window to the right of the front door.

On approaching the grand bay window overlooking the drive, it became apparent the occupants didn't use the room beyond as a living space. Inside, tools littered the bare wooden floorboards. Steve pressed the doorbell.

I had no memories of Will's parents when they lived on Blythe Lane. Had I even been to Will's house back then? I'd met all the other parents, but not his.

A middle-aged woman answered the door. She was squeezed into a vintage red dress and wore a shoulder-length blonde wig. This woman I'd have remembered.

"Merry Christmas," the woman said, her voice breathy. She saluted us with a glass of red wine. Her bright red lipstick strayed a fraction beyond the border of her actual lips.

"Mrs. Oswald?" Steve said. "Sorry to bother you, you probably don't remember us, but we're old school friends of Will's from Blythe. We were just out on a walk and thought we'd pop in and see if he was around."

"Oh, goodness, no. Will? No."

"Do you have a contact address for him at all? Or an email?" I said.

Mrs. Oswald shook her head. "We don't hear from that one much these days." She cautiously looked behind her, then whispered: "He's the person non-grata around here."

"Is he?" Steve said.

"Sorry to disappoint you. Would you like a bit of mulled wine, though?"

Before I could speak, Steve gave an enthusiastic *yes* and went inside. I followed and the door shut behind us. I'd expected the briefest of exchanges, a quick blast of information to get us off the doorstep so they could get on with their Christmas. That had been an advantage of today—no time for chatter. Now we were in the Oswalds' bloody hallway.

It wasn't much warmer than outside. The house smelled strongly of incense, but just beneath it lurked a more unpleasant smell, bad feet perhaps. Mrs. Oswald disappeared into the kitchen. Noddy Holder, a fellow West Midlander, was getting over-enthused about Christmas—as he did every year—on a distant radio.

Like the drive, the hallway was cluttered: shoes on the stairs, a coat on the floor. A bookcase filled with DVDs stood up against the wall and above hung a framed photograph of what looked like Marilyn Monroe. Only this woman's nose was larger, and her lips weren't quite as full. The DVDs kept to the same theme: *Some Like it Hot. The Asphalt Jungle. Gentlemen Prefer Blondes.*

Mrs. Oswald returned and handed me a mug of mulled wine. On the opposite wall were more framed photographs of Marilyn Monroe, one with JFK, another dancing with Gene Kelly—his gaze locked on Marilyn, hers focused straight at the camera. I brought the mug to my chest for warmth with no intention of drinking any. Immortalised on the ceramic was a black-and-white photograph of the great woman and the legend: *If You Can Make a Girl Laugh You Can Make Her Do Anything.*

Appraising his own Marilyn mug, Steve said, "I didn't know Will was so into Marilyn Monroe."

Mrs. Oswald laughed. "Oh, I'm afraid that's me. I love our Marilyn."

"You should talk to Adeline about films, she's an expert," Steve said.

When Mrs. Oswald turned to me with a coquettish smile, I

pointed to the tinselled photo frame above the DVDs. "Is this you?" I pretended to sip the wine. What the hell were we doing here?

"A long time ago, yes. A long time ago. They used to pay me to be her. At parties and the like."

"You look a lot like her." I chose my words carefully, *look* not *looked*. Mrs. Oswald's eyes welled up with tears.

"You are sweet, my darling," she said. "Do you two lovelies not have anywhere to be today?"

"The turkey's in the oven," I said.

"Awwww, how lovely. What were your names again?"

"Were you a lookalike?" Steve said. Excellent swerve.

She nodded. "I was Barbara Windsor, too. Not as often, and I didn't like her like Marilyn. Not that there's anything wrong with our Babs."

The door to the front room opened. A stout little man in a pair of denim overalls waddled into the hall holding a spanner in one hand.

"Hello," he said and flashed two rows of uneven teeth.

"These are some of Wonks's friends," Mrs. Oswald said.

Tempting though it was, I didn't look at Steve. Wonks?

"He still has some of those, does he?" the man said.

I smiled politely, assuming this was a stepdad or boyfriend. Unless I'd completely misremembered, Will's real dad had left around the time we'd all been friends.

"We knew Will when he lived in Blythe," I said.

"We haven't heard from him in—what is it now, love?—couple of years," the man said.

"It could be that."

Steve glanced at me and raised his eyebrows.

"Was he here Christmas two years ago?" the man said.

"No, I don't think he was," Mrs. Oswald said. "No wait, maybe he was."

"No," the man said. "Monks was here, but not Wonks."

With that the man walked through into the kitchen to bask in the music, now "Thank God It's Christmas" by Queen. The sounds of rattling cutlery followed, and Mrs. Oswald leaned towards us conspiratorially: "They had a bit of a falling-out, the two of them. They don't really speak."

"Oh," I said.

"He's not had an easy time of it, Wonks. He doesn't help himself." She looked over her shoulder, then up the stairs, then said even more softly than before: "Drugs." Her voice at a more reasonable level, she said, "We did our best to help him, but they wouldn't let him restart university a third time. He wanted to come and live with us, but that didn't work either. What could we do? He lived with his brother for a bit, though, didn't he, Monks?"

A tall figure emerged from the kitchen. It was Will's older brother, whose beer and music and cigarettes Will used to steal. I remembered him, how similar he and Will were in appearance. He probably wasn't much older than us; when he was younger we'd viewed him as a grown-up.

"What's that?" Monks said. His bassoon of a voice was like Will's too.

"Wonks lived with you, didn't he?"

He tutted. "Mum…Yeah, Will lived with me for a bit, not long. In York."

"Any idea where he is now?" Steve said. "We were hoping to catch up with him but none of the contacts we have for him work."

Monks's eyelids narrowed. He took a noisy breath before saying: "I think he's still in York. Last I heard he got a room in a house share with someone connected to his band. See, he doesn't tell us anything, so, I mean, he could be anywhere. Why do you want to know?"

"I told them about the drugs," Mrs. Oswald said through the corner of her mouth.

Monks nodded. "Right," he said, his face stolid.

"What sort of band was he in?" I said, wanting to move things on from the drugs but also asking out of genuine interest. "I can't get my head around him playing music. He didn't play an instrument when we were kids."

"He did," Monks said. "I should know because it was my drum kit he kept smashing. Was a punky band. They were all right, actually. Don't know if they're still going."

"What were they called?" Steve said.

"The Geppettos."

"Should have been The Pinocchios," the man that might've been a stepdad yelled from the kitchen. "Lying git."

"Who are you, again?" Monks said.

"Just some old friends," Steve said. "From Blythe."

"Oh." He sounded suspicious, but to me he said, "I think I remember you. You look the same. Hair and everything."

"Thanks," I said. "I think."

"You all still around here?" he said.

"My parents are," I said.

"I remember you, yeah," he said. "You lived on Elm Close. You were the little punk?"

"I was indeed."

He appeared satisfied and mooched off in the direction he'd come from.

The full mug of wine in my hand was starting to cool. I asked where the toilet was and Mrs. Oswald directed me upstairs. On my way up Steve began to make our excuses. He'd clearly seen enough. Will was off the radar as far as his family were concerned.

I threw the wine down the sink in the bathroom, then turned the tap on to remove any evidence. On the way out I saw a wooden name plaque on one of the bedroom doors: Wonks. I pushed my fingers against it experimentally and it opened with a click.

There were lots of reasons not to go in, lots of grown-up, sensible reasons. But given I'd come this far it was fitting I did the Velma Dinkley bit. Plus, Steve would get a kick out of it; his face when I told him about this on the way back would be priceless. I was Jessica bloody Fletcher.

I went inside slowly, taking care not to give myself away with a misplaced foot on a creaky floorboard.

Even though the curtains were open, the small window and the overcast morning meant my eyes needed to adjust to the darkness. From what I could make out it was still a typical messy teenager's room: shelves jammed with CDs and badges, magazines poking out from beneath the immaculately made bed, a few random posters on the wall (the Nirvana logo with the smiley face, the Pixies' *Trompe le Monde*, Jack Nicholson as The Joker). Strange, and sad, it was preserved that way—*and if you'll follow me upstairs, we have the final parts of our Marilyn Monroe exhibit, and also our very special 90s Teenager exhibit—* though nothing obviously murderous was lying about.

On the CD shelf, next to *Dookie*, were spines marked "The Geppettos." I picked one of them out. The cover was a black-and-white cartoon of a half boy, half donkey; the band name and DEMO were printed in the top left-hand corner. On the back was a track-list with a small photo of the band and some contact information. The photograph was only big enough for me to make out three shapes with messy hair, all of them potentially Will.

If they were still going the website might be up. We could call the telephone number on the back, too. It might even be Will's. If not, we could at least ask his band mates about what had happened to him.

I took a picture of the website and number on my phone.

I turned back to the door and stopped. The wall on this side of the room was not obscured by furniture or curtains, but neither was it bare. I stepped closer to make sure I wasn't imagining it, which I definitely wasn't. Hundreds of different models and porn stars, all in various stages of undress, were displayed here on posters and calendars. They filled every space from floor to ceiling, a wonderful wall of objectification. It must have taken a long time because nothing really overlapped. And the wall faced the bed too, grim. I took another picture, wanting the others to understand.

Perhaps the display alone might have simply upset me. But many of the women, probably over half, had been defaced. A blonde lady in a red-spotted white swimsuit had two tiny holes where her eyes should have been. Another model had tears and biro marks where her nipples once were. And of course some ladies had suffered the indignity of having been poked through either the front or back of their crotch, depending on which direction they'd been facing.

The whole thing was so grim. Why had Will's family let it stay this way? Had his bedroom been like this in Blythe? And if so had any of the others seen it? The thought of the boys in particular, sitting around in Will's room and not even finding such a strange display in the least bit unsettling made me feel incredibly lonely in a way I'd felt only too recently.

Silly bitches all over the internet think they can't be found?! Careful bout shit you say.

I stepped out onto the landing and released a long breath I'd been holding unawares.

At the bottom of the stairs another Marilyn Monroe winked at me. Maybe the whole family were fucking serial killers.

*

72

"So the question is," Steve said on the walk back to the car, "does she dress like that every day, or is it just for Christmas?" I couldn't laugh. I still felt soiled. Was I overreacting? Plausible perhaps, now free of that strange house. "And what was all that Monks and Wonks stuff?"

The other two were waiting for us in the back seat of the car, engaged in what looked like a thumb war, for Christ's sake. They let go of each other when we climbed in.

"Well?" Rupesh asked before the doors were even closed.

"Well," Steve said, "they haven't seen him in what they say was years, and they don't know where he is. But it doesn't mean anything really."

"Still," Rupesh said, "not a brilliant start for the sceptic camp."

Steve recounted the other things we'd discovered, and wasn't able to resist mentioning the mum's Marilyn Monroe obsession, like it might be extra proof.

"Oh, she had that when we were kids, don't you remember?" Jen said.

"I don't think I ever went to Will's," Steve said.

"Did you go in his bedroom?" I said, mainly to Rupesh.

"Yeah, I must have done."

"Was there anything weird about it? Do you remember what he had on his walls?"

"No, not really. Maybe some band posters, I don't know."

"I never saw it," Jen said. "Thank God."

"Did he have any women on the wall?" I said.

"Maybe, he was a teenage boy. Why?" Rupesh said.

"Well, I just saw Will's old bedroom," I said, "and, you know, if I was on the fence about all this stuff I'm definitely wobbling now."

When I showed him the picture I'd taken, Rupesh said, "I'd have probably remembered that."

"So that *is* weird to you?" I said, relieved to hear it.

"Yeah," Rupesh said, though I could hear his caution. "I

mean, you come across some bizarre things in my line of work, but the defacement is, well, not nice."

I looked at Steve whose mouth hung open. "That's a man with women issues," he said. "Dare I say, Mummy issues? It's strange he's kept it all up, he's been back since he was a teenager, right? They said that."

"He's definitely been back," I said, and told them about the CD.

"Will was in a band?" Jen said.

"There was a phone number on there," I said, scrolling to the photo.

"Shall I call it now?" Steve said.

"Do it," Jen said.

Steve took out his phone and I recited the number. After a while Steve shook his head.

"It's saying it's not recognising it."

"There's a website, too," I said, having already started looking. The Geppettos' stark internet presence came up on my screen. It had three links: *Shows*, *Listen* and *Contact*. The *Contact* page offered the same phone number as the CD, plus a basic web form for emails. The *Listen* link was broken. The only image anywhere was a banner with the donkey-boy hybrid at the bottom of the page.

"I'll send a message later," Steve said. "When I'm on a laptop."

"Hang on," I said. I was looking at *Shows* now. "They're still gigging, and they've got a bloody gig on Boxing Day. A Fuck Christmas extravaganza, apparently. And the night after, but that's up in York. Then they've got some in the New Year. We should go to one."

"That's an idea," Rupesh said. "Hey, Will, great gig, killed anyone recently?"

"That's *exactly* what we'd say."

"Where is the Boxing Day one?" Rupesh said.

"Manchester."

"It's not that far in the scheme of things," Steve said.

"It's like, what? An hour?" I said.

"I'm working that evening," Rupesh said.

"Oh, come on," Jen said. "We have to go."

Steve started the engine. "If I don't get a response to the web form it's at least another lead. We can have a reunion road trip."

Rupesh sighed and leaned back in his seat.

When we drove away I noticed something in the wing mirror, a person emerging from the end of the cul-de-sac where we'd just been parked, someone who had the same general shape as Will's brother. I couldn't be certain, but if it was him did he see the four of us? He'd probably have some questions about the story we'd spun back at the house if he had. I didn't mention it. Wouldn't matter now.

Back in Blythe, we pulled up outside Rupesh's house. He had work commitments later on that night, while Jen needed to show her face at home for the big family meal.

"Rup, do you still think we're chasing a wild goose?" Jen said.

Rupesh shrugged. "I don't know what to think. I'm still a bit hungover."

Steve turned to face them both in the back seat. "We've fulfilled a lot of your criteria this morning."

"Yeah," Jen said. "If this doesn't count as off the radar... And does he seem stable to any of you based on that room? On the uni story."

Rupesh made a noise like a creaky door. "Sort of. You still need to connect these two suicides to each other for me. Just keep me in the loop, yeah?" He held up a hand. "It's been good seeing you."

Jen and Rupesh both got out of the car and we watched them walk up the drive.

"I think I need to go and sort out my accommodation," I said, not quite ready to face Mum yet.

"Hope it isn't too stressful." He touched my shoulder, and I reached up and touched his cheek briefly. In this harsh light I saw wrinkles I'd not noticed before. How strange that I should feel tenderness for him again, protective of him even, like I held a secret belief that Steve Litt should be immune from time's effects.

I left the car and spun to wave him off from the pavement. He rolled down the window. "Honestly, do you think I was a bully, Adie?"

Rupesh had really got to him.

"You know what I thought of you," I said. "Stop fishing."

He contemplated this and finally nodded, satisfied for now at least. I meant the sentiment too, but there on the pavement with him about to depart, something else came back to me from that time. No, he hadn't been a bully, not that I saw. Arrogant and thoughtless at times, though, yes. He'd abandoned me after that first summer, hadn't he? Without even a goodbye. And I'd done all sorts of stupid things that year out of anger as a result. He'd made it up to me, of course, sent me a home-made Christmas card, then a letter, all before that second summer started. But at my grotty new comp in Balsall Common I'd been so irascible all year that I'd made no friends, and instead spent every night alone watching films.

"Oh, have you got your parents a gift?" he said. And of course, I hadn't.

"Shit. No. Thanks. Fuck."

"Christmas is important, Adie," he said, and wound up the window.

And that was the Steve I remembered. The one who never forgot important dates and their relevant gifts and cards. Christmas. Anniversaries. Birthdays. The first time we ever kissed, hidden in a maize field not far from where I was now standing, had been on my fifteenth birthday. Such a powerful memory. He bought me the most thoughtful gift, then pretended it was from all of them. I'd sat with him on the baked soil between the stalks that afternoon, a strange energy filling the space between us. For once I'd not been nervous; not worried about my hair looking greasy, or if I had any spots around my mouth. I'd been drunk too, which helped. I remember Steve's long eyelashes. As pretty as he was handsome. We'd laughed at first, when we realised we both had our eyes open. Then we'd kissed more forcefully, and while I'd been there before with boys, the pull of him had been new. I'd put my hand under his shirt, felt his heart beating through the skin, and we'd fallen and banged our teeth together. But we kept going. And if we hadn't been interrupted... who knows?

Steve's car pulled away from the kerb, and when it had passed me I noticed someone had fingered the smiley-faced Nirvana logo in the dirt down in the left corner of the rear window: two crosses for eyes and a tongue poking from the wavy mouth. I shivered, remembering Will's bedroom. Then, imagining perhaps some kids just like us having been the culprits, I let myself smile. They really did love heavy guitars around here.

Rupesh, 1997

At the entrance to Elm Close is a post box, a phone box and an old boxy bus shelter. The shelter is set back from the road and surrounded on all sides by an overgrown bush. Rupesh, out posting a letter for his dad, is close enough to read the graffiti on its dark wood panels when cigarette smoke draws him closer and from inside someone with a deep voice calls his name. Recognising the voice, he peers inside. Will is sitting in a shadowy corner smoking.

"Not seen you in a while," he says.

A good few days have passed since Rupesh's no-show at Dead Man's Alley and he's been avoiding them all in the hope that they eventually forget he didn't turn up.

"I've been busy," Rupesh says, and sits down beside Will, still clutching the letter. Will offers Rupesh the cigarette. He notices all the dirt under Will's fingernails and recalls Will telling him he only brushed his teeth once a week.

"No thanks," Rupesh says.

Will doesn't act like he holds the no-show against Rupesh, which is something. He starts off on one about Kurt Cobain, how he's more famous than ever now he's dead and how well death sells. Maybe he's already forgotten? He wouldn't put it past Will. He hopes they haven't all been talking about him behind his back. That they don't all hate him now.

In the middle of Will explaining how if he were a rock star he'd just start off his career pretending to be dead, Adeline appears in the shelter entrance and says: "Why is there a bus stop if there are no buses?"

Both he and Will jump.

Once Rupesh has finished chastising her for scaring them, he says, "There used to be one, but everyone drives out here, don't they? It never got used."

She nods, happy. "So what happened to you the other night?"

Cockflaps. *She* hasn't forgotten. Now he's going to have to explain himself.

"I did warn you I wouldn't be able to get out," he says. "I could hear my parents. They were still up. I was all ready to come out, too."

It's a lie; he'd fallen asleep early with no intention of going outside. Steve sometimes goes too far—and that Strachan thing had just been ridiculous. Why so late? Why so...well, adventurous? Every gang needs someone like Steve to pull them all together, sure, to find places for them to hang out and come up with things to do, but why make it all so stressful?

He knows why, though. Steve's seen too many films, especially ones with gangs of kids coming together to beat some shared enemy against the odds. Those sorts of films are fine, but best watched rather than lived. Rupesh prefers stories like Sherlock Holmes or Batman, brilliant individuals who are sort of better than the rest in some way, and are only really troubled by other brilliant individuals, like Moriarty or The Joker.

Will offers Adeline the cigarette and she takes a puff. She hands it to Rupesh and this time he also takes a puff, even though the cigarette feels odd in his hand. When he gives it back to Will he narrows his eyes at Rupesh.

"Where have you been then?" Adeline says.

"Oh just, well, busy with life things," he says.

"Bullshit," Adeline says. "You've been avoiding us, haven't you?"

She smiles and so does he. He can't help it. "Fine, I just was worried you'd all be annoyed with me."

This isn't quite a lie, though it isn't the whole truth either. He really means that Steve will be annoyed with him. The thing is he never expected the thing to happen if he just said he couldn't do it. Rupesh's role in the group is to balance Steve out. It's like what his physics teacher Mrs. Kaur once taught them about *moments*, how a construction crane needs a counterweight at the back to stop it toppling forward. Usually, if they weren't all doing it together the gang did something else. Not this time, though. Now he's the odd one out.

Adeline is rolling her eyes at him. "No one's annoyed with you, are they, Will?"

"No one cares," Will says.

It's Adeline that has changed things in the group. Shifted the dynamics in some important way he needs to get his head around. It's obvious why: she is really fit. It's obvious too that Steve fancies her, and probably Will too—although he is harder to read. Does Rupesh fancy her? He is unsure. While her whole monochromatic Gothy thing is attractive, there is something hard about her he doesn't like. He probably does fancy her, even if she could be a bit blunt sometimes, a bit sweary, a bit frightening. Not like Jen, who is always so sweet to him. With Adeline around powering Steve's enthusiasm, resisting its excesses is going to be that much harder.

"Anyway, it's my birthday tomorrow and you need to come and celebrate," she says.

"Steve says he has *plans*," Will says with a trace of world-weariness.

"We're meeting at Steve's after lunch. If you're not there I'll come and hunt you down and drag you out."

Yeah, she's scary, Adeline. But it's nice she gives enough of a stuff to make a fuss about him being there to celebrate her birthday.

Still, the next day he's nervous about seeing them all together again when he makes his way down Elm Close. He's running late, as he always is, and that won't help with Steve's hypothetical grudge. Passing Mr. Strachan's the road is fragrant with freshly mown grass, and when he looks over at the neat lawn the dog isn't there.

He lets himself into the lounge where they are all engrossed in a conversation about a film they'd watched without him. Adeline raises a hand when he comes in, but the rest don't notice. Or they're ignoring him. Not a good start.

"Sorry about the other night, guys," he says when there is a gap in the chatter. "Like I said to these guys, I was all set to go but it was just impossible."

Jen, whose back had been to him, turns and utters a joyous cry of his name. It probably means she doesn't hate him—a real relief. Of all the gang it's Jen's opinion that matters most to him. Without a doubt he definitely fancies her. He's not her type, though, he's realistic about that. She always likes the most conventional-looking actors in the films they watch. Even if through some miracle she did like him, there are all sorts of complications around what his parents might think about him having a girlfriend which he didn't necessarily want to find out about. Not to mention that joke she once made when she was angry with her parents, about the best revenge on them would be to start going out with Rupesh because he was Asian. Plenty of reasons existed to help him not waste too much energy on fantasising about getting together with Jen Sherman. Still, her reaction buoys him.

"You didn't really need me anyway, did you?" he says. "I've not seen that dog since."

"We thought you'd fallen asleep," Steve says, and the others laugh. He doesn't like that laugh one bit. The anxiety that had evaporated on seeing Jen drenches him once more. From his tone alone he can tell Steve hates him for not showing up. He's playing it cool, but he's annoyed.

They *have* been talking about him. Jen probably thinks he's lazy. A coward even.

Rupesh has spoken too soon.

Strachan's dog is back on the front lawn once more. Like he's been waiting for them all to be together again to make his next move.

Out in the field behind Elm Close they sing a half-hearted Happy Birthday to Adeline, the mood in the group low. Will's claim that it's a declaration of war isn't far off the mark. That's how it feels. Rupesh doesn't like Strachan one bit—whenever he sees Rupesh he always scowls at him—and though Rupesh could take some satisfaction in Steve's plan failing, he doesn't. In fact, he is unsettled by this development. While it's one thing for Rupesh to challenge Steve, it's another entirely for someone like Strachan to do it.

Jen passes around some vodka, which perks them up, and Steve says they should just enjoy the rest of Adeline's birthday and not let Strachan ruin it. He instigates a game of Jurassic Park, a souped-up version of hide-and-seek he invented last year where the seekers are "velociraptors," and if you are caught you are "disembowelled," then become part of the raptor pack. It's ridiculous, really; though if Rupesh's going to going to get back into Steve's good books he'll have to throw himself into it this year. And of the things Steve makes them do it isn't the worst.

After Steve's outlined the concept and the rules, Adeline says, "You lot are fucking mental. How old are you?"

"It's really fun," Rupesh says. Only he notices Steve flash him a side-eye, undoubtedly because the last time he'd played he complained about it the entire time.

"Drink some more of this," Jen says and hands Adeline the repurposed plastic water bottle. "I know what you mean, but trust me, it's a laugh. And this is as good as it gets out here."

"It's so great the corn's this high," Steve says.

Trying to sound helpful, Rupesh says, "Actually, it's not corn, it's maize."

From a pile of rubble that might once have been an outhouse—the "base"—all of them except Jen scatter in different directions.

Rupesh hates it deep in the maize. You can't tell the *shhhhh* of the leaves from the sound of someone approaching. Once he is alone down one of the rows he turns back on himself and waits for Jen to leave. When she's gone he sits on a pile of bricks at the base and waits for the others to finish running around. He's technically won now. If Steve doesn't work out what he's done, he might even congratulate him. In fact, is it enough to make up for the no-show? No, dream on. He'll have to make a bigger show of things than just being here when they all arrive. Make it look like he's been wandering around out there the whole time like the rest of them.

With some reluctance he re-enters the maize down one of the rows. The *shhhhh* sound seems to follow him, like the stalks have lined up to applaud his decision. It's creepy. He slows down, and quickly understands that all the leaves are at ear level, meaning that it only sounds like they are responding to his presence because he is close enough to hear them. The explanation is good, yet his heart still pounds.

He tries to distract himself, focus on that end goal of not having to worry about Steve making him the butt of the group joke. Yet out here the plan seems stupid. It had been the alcohol thinking for him. Steve's not going to see him playing the game enthusiastically as equal to him not showing up. That just isn't how Steve's idea of fairness works.

An idea with such chilling plausibility overwhelms him. He'll probably make Rupesh do something awful to Strachan. Two birds, one stone. *The next time you hear from us will not be in the form of a note*, they'd written. Whatever that might be he'll want Rupesh to do it to level it all out. Even bloody Steven.

His panic is broken by the sounds of nearby voices. He crouches on the floor and looks through the stalks. Five, maybe six rows across to his right, he sees movement. He watches and waits.

It becomes apparent that whoever is over there isn't on the hunt, so must be hiding. With a few stealthy steps he crosses two rows in the direction of the voices.

It's Adeline and Steve. Of course it would be those two. Of bloody course. He can hear them, an intimacy in their back and forth. She's thanking him for a CD and Steve is making a weak effort to convince her the gift was from all of them. Steve probably set up this whole afternoon to get her out here alone.

There is a long silence, then Steve says, "What?"

"Nothing," she says.

"What?" he asks again, laughing.

"I was imagining what would happen if I actually just kissed you," she says. "What your face would do."

"Do you want to kiss me?"

"I want to see what happens to your face."

He shrugs. "Do it then."

It's not hard to guess what happens in the following silence, especially when Adeline breaks it with, "You're not meant to open your fucking eyes. I'll look silly."

Rupesh doesn't want to hear any more. He's happy for them,

he supposes, even if the inevitability of Steve once again getting exactly what he wants without any effort is so boring it's crushing. Just once couldn't he have to jump through the same hoops as the rest of them?

Just once couldn't it be that easy for Rupesh?

He is walking backwards through the stalks, too wrapped up in his thoughts and trying to be quiet to notice Jen standing in the row he has just joined. By the time he does it's too late. Clever girl. She puts one finger to her lips, then with her clawed free hand she strokes her fingertips across his lower belly.

"Rar-r," she says.

His plan to win the thing no longer matters. Jen's touch ripples through his body. All he can think to say back is, "Rar-r."

Now a raptor, Rupesh whispers to Jen that Steve and Adeline are close by. He almost relishes interrupting them now with Jen at his side.

Together they stalk, and are within two rows when Jen halts. Adeline and Steve are clearly visible from here, and the sight is quite something. Adeline's on top of Steve. They're kissing. Worse, they look like they might be trying to—

Rupesh turns to Jen, offering a look somewhere between disgust and shock. She only has eyes for them, though. And now the softness and playfulness have gone, replaced by a look Rupesh can't fathom. Jealousy, maybe. Is that what he's seeing? Cockflaps. That would just be perfect. And why wouldn't Jen fancy Steve? He's more her type than Rupesh.

Finally she snaps out of whatever hold the scene has on her. She gestures for Rupesh to wait further down the row, which he does, knowing that she plans to flush them his way.

He hears Jen leap through the stalks, hears Steve yell to Adeline, "Run, save yourself," then the sound of pounding feet heading his way. A flash of black and white in his peripheral vision, and he leaps through the two rows and grabs Adeline around the waist. She screams, delighted, and the two of them fall to the floor laughing.

After catching her breath, the four of them, all raptors now, fruitlessly search for Will before they eventually find him back at the base, smoking a victory roll-up on top of a pile of bricks in the rubble.

"You took your time," he says.

Will had clearly stolen Rupesh's plan.

Hours later, tired and thirsty after multiple rounds of the game, they head across the field to the stile onto Elm Close not far from Steve's. Jen offers Adeline the water bottle filled with the remaining vodka and Adeline shakes her head. Then she offers it to Rupesh, who casts a quick glance Adeline's way, then shakes his too. Jen looks puzzled by this, which had been Rupesh's intention, then shrugs and drinks some herself. If she fancies Steve now, then maybe he'll just fancy Adeline.

Steve is leading the way, and Will is trailing behind them. Jen drops back and hands the bottle to Will, who responds with a simple, "Cheers, ears."

Oh great, maybe she fancies Will now. Good work, Rupesh. His thoughts are fuzzy, and not in a pleasant way this time.

Up ahead Steve has slowed down, and when they catch up they see why. A police car is parked outside Mr. Strachan's. Steve urges them to be cool and keep walking. Mr. Strachan is standing by the silver van on his drive with two police officers, a man and a woman. The windscreen is cracked in a spider-web pattern and at the centre a brick protrudes from the glass. Jen turns to Will and sees he is grinning. Mr. Strachan is pointing in their direction and the officers watch them all file towards the farmhouse before making their own way over to them.

Cockflaps.

*

The police take all of their addresses, and the following evening they interview everyone individually with their parents present. Mr. Strachan's claim is that he saw "a youngster" running off in the direction of the fields after hearing the windscreen smash. He has also shown the police the note left on his car earlier in the holidays.

Rupesh sits nodding through the whole process, head pounding with what must be a hangover, not wanting to speak in case he blurts out that it's Steve they want really. He's the instigator. He's the reason any of them have to do these things. If it weren't for him then Rupesh would just stay indoors.

The police are kind, though. And it's clear they don't actually think Rupesh has anything to do with it. Once they have gone his dad tells Rupesh to maybe give those other kids a wide berth for the rest of the summer, and that he knows all about that troublemaker Mr. Strachan, whom he'd trust about as far as he could throw him.

That night Rupesh is in his room listening to Foo Fighters, his headache fading but complicated thought still a great effort. It's nice of Will to have made him a copy, although the album's a difficult listen because at the end of each track Will's taped himself talking about each song, offering his wild theories about what he thinks the songs mean. The forty-five-minute album takes up both sides of a ninety-minute tape.

The door opens slowly and his mum walks in. Rupesh turns off his Walkman.

"Hi," he says.

She stares out of the window at the fields behind the house, saying nothing. His mum mostly does this when she is lonely, although today it could be to talk about the police visit. Only after a few minutes does the taut sensation in his middle start to ease and Rupesh turns the music back on, leaving her to it. Eventually she moves from the window, kneeling down by the bed where Rupesh is lying, and takes his wrist. This is less common, but still something he is used to. She runs her long fingernails down the lines on his palm, a pleasant sensation, and one he finds particularly comforting today. She rarely touches him.

She does this for a long time, then after coming to some understanding with the universe, tells him there is no doubt. It's there to see in his palm. He will soon come into great wealth. Her brown eyes are filled with kindness and wonder. She smiles at him and he smiles back.

When the door finally closes he gets up, pulls out a briefcase from under his bed, and pops the two number locks. Inside is a red exercise book that his dad bought for him. On the front is written: *Property of Rupesh Desai, Keep Out Please.*

Using a biro that holds the page of his last entry, Rupesh writes down the date, then: WINDOW 5 MINS, PALM 20 MINS. Then he returns the book and the briefcase, and starts getting ready for bed.

Winter, 2015

Armed with a bottle of fizz for Mum and a flower that squirted water that had been in a sale bin at the petrol station for Dad, I rapped at the door despite knowing it wouldn't be locked. How many times over the years had I heard that Blythe was statistically one of the safest villages in the UK?

Dad answered wearing a red jumper with a reindeer pattern. "Oh darling, it's you." He swept me into his arms, so bony beneath the wool. "Come in, the Queen's speech is on soon. You know how your mum loves the Queen's speech."

She was sitting right in front of the television with a blanket over her lap.

"Hi, Mum, Merry Christmas," I said, handing over the bottle of Prosecco.

"Oh," she said. "Well, give it to your dad. I can't drink it at the moment with the meds I'm on. Thank you, though, I'm sure we can think of a use for it, can't we, Paul?"

"I'm sure we can," Dad said, and took the bottle from me. In a voice Mum wouldn't hear, he said: "Two presents for me then."

The Queen began her yearly message with textbook regal professionalism. It was just as dull and irksome as I recalled, but how long could it be? Ten minutes? Fifteen? God, what if it went on for an hour? It couldn't be an hour, surely?

"You don't normally do the royals," Mum said.

This was exactly the kind of test I needed to face down. Such comments were the missiles that Mum threw without even thinking, and they inevitably ended any peace between us—so often hitting the perfect, reaction-provoking targets in the past. But at some point, if there was ever to be lasting peace, one party, *the stronger party*, had to be bigger and rise above it. I wasn't fifteen any more.

"They're sort of interesting." This was me, rising above it, though I did have to add, "In their way."

Later in the evening Dad made me dinner and offered sherry. Seizing the opportunity, I declined the drink, bemoaning having to go and locate a cheap bed and breakfast so that I could spend more time with my friends.

Dad took the bait. "You should stop here, love." He'd already poured me a shot, and was out of breath from the short walk to the kitchen and back.

"The spare bedroom's full of rubbish," Mum said.

"I can sort that," I said. "But I don't want to put you out. I don't know how long I plan to stay for, to be honest."

"You can stay as long as you need," Dad said.

Job done, a glass of sherry in hand, I climbed the stairs, hearing Mum say to Dad: "Are you not going to sort that room?"

"Adeline's doing it," he said.

She would kill him; it was just a matter of time.

After clearing the boxes, curtains and blankets from the bed in my old room, I took out my tablet and tried to find Xan online. When I couldn't, I decided on an early night.

I didn't sleep much. I never slept well in strange rooms, especially ones with spiders on the ceiling. Alone behind closed eyelids, the idea that gangly, drippy Will might actually have been serious started to take root. Suppose he had really murdered two people? And if he had what was next?

My phone had been off the whole afternoon, so when I plugged it in the next morning all the backed-up messages began to ping. The others had agreed to meet at Rupesh's at lunchtime. Jen had uncovered something interesting that she wanted to discuss.

While I ate breakfast I Skyped Xan.

"Addy," he said, his face taking a moment to come into focus on the screen as his camera got to grips with the light levels. Just the sight of his big bald head and bushy beard made me grin. He grinned back.

I could tell from the posters on the wall behind him that he was in the studio not at home—probably yet another argument with his boyfriend—no doubt editing their *Temple of Doom* podcast. He was nothing if not predictable.

"Have you jumped Cusack's bones yet?" he said.

I laughed. What was there to say? Nothing really, not yet anyway. I redirected the conversation by telling him about all the Will stuff, which I'd known he'd get a kick out of.

"Fuck, Adeline," Xan said. "Can you imagine the press we'd get if you solved a bloody murder? We could do a whole separate podcast about it. Like *Serial*, right? But with a proper ending. I mean, everyone knows someone who, if the police turned up at their door and said, 'Do you know such and such person because they just killed a bunch of people?' they'd say, 'Yeah, I do, and, you know what, that doesn't surprise me.' Once in a while, one of them must actually be the real deal. Someone must have been Fred West's mate and thought, Bloody hell Fred's a crack, but I wouldn't leave the kids with him. Hey, and maybe if we do a crime podcast and it takes off, you won't leave me for the BBC."

And there it was. He'd managed a full minute without mentioning it. Since November we'd been in discussions with some enthusiastic BBC commissioners who wanted to make the podcast into a half-hour radio programme: a more streamlined *Nostalgia Crush*. But Xan, the least cautious of us usually, had been sceptical, predicting they'd want a generic film review show using our brand. Right down to some of the words they chose, Xan was right. But in the pub afterwards, when Xan got up to get a round in, Jon and I had started mulling over some of the *other* things that had come up in the meeting. Contracts. Wages. The possibility to work on other BBC programmes.

"I'm not leaving you for anything yet," I said to Xan. "You're the one who's made a decision."

"I can read the writing on the wall, Adeline," Xan said. "And it says *monogamy, mortgage, babies*, all in your lovely handwriting."

"Monogamy and babies?" I said, feigning disgust.

"Your words. Especially when you're drunk. Come on, don't tell me there's another reason you went back for this reunion?"

It was my own fault for drinking with him. He had a way of unpicking me. I wasn't anti those things, it was more that I wanted them alongside other things—and specific versions of those things.

"I don't want babies qua babies," I said. "You make me sound so conventional saying it like that."

"Qua? Did you just *Latin* me? Listen, Cambridge, there's nothing wrong with being conventional about a few things. You breathe air, don't you? You drink water? You travel by car and not on a hobby horse. Some conventions are fine, they're a good laugh. And the BBC is a good convention. They're long standing. Reliable. I just don't think that's why I do podcasting, you know? I'm just not that interested in making a career of it if it's not what I want to be doing."

"It's the art for you, yeah?" I bit my tongue about the fat inheritance he'd been living off that no doubt kept the wheels of individual freedom lubricated. "I'm not that keen to go back to working in an open-plan office making tea for people I barely like, so I just want to think on it. We can still do the BBC thing and *Nostalgia Crush*. It's not out of the question. You're the one making it a choice."

"You'd have split priorities, and that'd be unfair to the donors."

"Well, Jon thinks we could make both work, and that you're just doing this to spite us because you haven't liked a film since *American Beauty*."

"If I am doing that I'm doing it unconsciously," Xan said. "But really, who wants another contemporary review show? I mean, I just don't see the point. Decent opinions take time to form, you can't just watch a film once and have anything meaningful to say about it. The social-media age is so fucking present-obsessed."

"Woah, hang on," I said. "The whole point of *Nostalgia Crush* is that these old classics aren't always as great as—"

"Oh shush, you," Xan said. He cast a dismissive hand across the screen at me. "I knew you'd say something like that. Weren't you meant to be turning your brain off?"

A soft knock on the door was followed by Dad peeking into the room.

"There's a man here for you?"

"Me?" I said. I wasn't expecting anyone, but could it be Steve? "Thanks, Dad," I said, and with a nod he began to retreat. "Xan, I have to go."

"Is it your man?"

"I don't know. I'm going to hang up now, but it doesn't have to be like this whatever Jon and I decide."

"You think about it."

I ended the call, and went downstairs. Steve was probably at a loose end, maybe wanting a private meet-up before seeing the rest of the gang.

Only it wasn't Steve. Instead, standing at the door, was Will's brother.

Jen, 1997

It's early afternoon and Jen is trying and failing to nap on her bed. Her sister, Andrea, is back from university and dominating the house. Her music channel blares in the lounge, "Stupid Girl" by Garbage now. While Mum and Dad are at work there is absolutely no escaping her—in any room. Jen's shattered. Last night Andrea was on her phone to her boyfriend until three in the bloody morning. It wasn't only the jab jab jab of her ha-ha-has that kept Jen awake. It was also the festering anger over her lack of consideration.

There's no chance of her sleeping now either. But revenge will at least make her feel better. She sneaks into Andrea's room, steals two pocketfuls of vodka miniatures from her bedside drawer which she decants into her trusty Volvic bottle, then heads out into the sun to find a drinking partner.

The gang haven't really spent much time together since the brick incident, and she hasn't seen Adeline at all. But over the road, Adeline emerges from Dead Man's Alley. She doesn't see Jen, and walks straight past her own house towards the mouth of Elm Close.

Where is she off to? Only two people live that way: Will and Rupesh, and it's not going to be Will, the only one that appears even a little bit immune to her charms. What is she up to?

Jen calls her name, and catches up with her at the corner of Elm Close. "Where have you been?"

"Grounded," she says. "I just tried calling on Steve. Has he been around?"

Jen understands now that Adeline doesn't know about Steve's Dad coming home. It's rare Jen knows something Adeline doesn't these days, and it makes her stand a little straighter.

"You mean you don't know," she says, watching her face for a reaction.

"I don't know a thing. I was going to go and ask Rupesh if he knew." Adeline's caterpillar eyebrows draw together. She's genuinely worried. "Where is he?"

Putting aside the fact she is going to Rupesh first instead of her, this means that Steve didn't go and say goodbye to her properly, which actually is quite slack—especially given what they'd seen Steve and Adeline getting up to out in the fields. As much as Jen is enjoying being in the know, she does like Adeline. Okay, it is a bit annoying that she just swooped in and knocked Steve off his feet so quickly. And that the whole group, especially Rupesh, has been affected by her, and without making any effort, just by looking different and being a bit opinionated, she won them over. But there's no pleasure to be taken from Steve's coldness. She sympathises. Boys can be so thoughtless sometimes. Bloody girl power.

"Well, his dad had to fly back to meet the police," Jen says, "because, you know, I suppose legally Steve shouldn't be left on his own as he is. And he was really annoyed, so he paid for Steve to go back to school early."

She can read her expression and now something else dawns on Jen. Adeline didn't know about his school.

"He's gone back to King George's."

"King George's?" she says.

"The boarding school."

"What? He boards?"

It's all there to see in her expression, all the pieces falling into place. There will be no after-school or weekend meet-ups. Not now she lived here, out in the middle of nowhere. She'd be thinking about all the girls at his school that might fancy him, how he'd forget all about her. She is undoubtedly feeling what Jen has been feeling all summer.

"Poor Steve," she says. "At my last school we had boarders. We all felt really sorry for them, abandoned like that. Why didn't he tell me?"

It doesn't surprise Jen that Adeline went to posh school too—she couldn't even fix a bike chain—although it is the first time she's mentioned it to her. A bit shameful given she is supposed to be a punk or something.

"How did you find out?"

"He told me before he went. Sorry."

Adeline shakes her head, sighs, looks like she might start crying. Neither of them say anything for a while. Jen then says, "Aw," and takes Adeline into her arms. "He's an idiot."

If she is crying, she does so quietly and without moving, although her mascara hasn't run when she pulls away.

"Do you want to do something?" Jen says, holding up the plastic bottle. "I have alcohol."

"Thanks. But I think I want to lie down. I saw Will around in the fields somewhere," she says, with just a hint of sarcasm.

"Cool. See you at school maybe?" Jen says. Although she doubts this, because her lunchtimes are always busy with either choir or drama club. She's sure she'll see her around, though. And if not she'll make friends easily enough, although she couldn't count on Rupesh and Will because they both went to Arden school in Knowle. Did she even know that? She'd have to start from scratch.

"Hopefully," Adeline says.

She heads over to Rupesh's in the hope that maybe he wants to get drunk. At the start of the summer she'd hoped to get off with him. Now time is running out. There's always been a spark between them, though she never would have thought it might take this long. Adeline has somehow messed things up, though in what way is hard to say exactly. Like when Jen had offered him the vodka after that stupid dinosaur game—usually he'd say yes to that, but because Adeline had said no so had he.

Her mood's not improved one bit when Rupesh answers the door and says: "Hey, Jen. Where's Adeline?"

Why does she bother?

"How would I know?" she says.

"I saw you both from the window."

"Oh," she says. "She felt ill. I'm bored—do you want to do something? I've got some more vodka, we could..." He's already shaking his head.

"I have to do chores tonight," Rupesh says.

"Fine," she says. "I suppose I'll see you around." Although she doesn't suppose this at all, because if last year was anything to go by they might not see each other until next summer.

She ambles home, in no rush to spend all night being ignored while Andrea and Mum talked about all the great times Mum had when she was at uni.

Is Rupesh not interested in her at all now that Adeline is around? Or is there a way to win him back? Her usual tricks—starting thumb wars, playfully touching him on the shoulder when they're joking around—aren't working. Her friends at school wear more make-up than her, and maybe that's what she needs to try. Adeline doesn't wear much more than whatever she does to her eyes, though.

Or maybe it's not her fault at all. This is Rupesh's mistake. He doesn't realise what's staring him in the face. Well, forget him. She'd go to school, get with a boy there. A different sort of boy, one that noticed her the way Rupesh used to. That boy Dan Evans is always smiling at her. He's big, and she doesn't like him the way she does Rupesh, but there's a sort of dangerous quality to him, and if Rupesh found out somehow maybe he'd realise—

She screams when Will steps out from Dead Man's Alley just as she is about to cross the road.

"Sorry," he says. He's amused by her reaction.

"You scared the life out of me," she says, laughing herself.

"*You* scared me," he says, although he doesn't look scared. He looks the way he always does, calm and like part of him is elsewhere, particularly his milky blue eyes which in clear daylight give the impression they're not connected to a person.

"Do you want to do something?" he says. "Flatten stuff at the tracks?"

She hesitates a moment, then decides, yes, she doesn't mind doing something with Will. He's spoken more to her this summer than anyone else has.

He almost looks quite cool today, tufts of his blond hair poking out from his Nirvana beanie. Almost handsome in a funny way.

"Do you want to get drunk?" she says.

He shrugs. "Always."

Trusty Will. His lips are a deep red, in need of some lip balm maybe. What would it be like to kiss them? A swirl of confusion and curiosity passes through her at that fantasy. One thing is for sure, it would definitely get Rupesh's attention.

The two of them find a bald spot in some long grass up on the embankment set back from the railways tracks, much further down from where Steve found Obi. Behind them a pathway appears to head off into the weedy jungle in the direction of the pylon's base. They sit close enough that their shoulders touch and get through half the drink in a few delightful minutes.

Will points to a dead animal a little way up the track. "I've been watching that squirrel, right, and it doesn't move at all when the train goes over. I always heard the suction would pull you up, but it obviously doesn't. I reckon you could lie under a train and it'd just pass right over you."

She's not noticed before, but his finger is so long, like it would need extra knuckles to work. Her head is swimming with the vodka and everything he says and does is funnier and stranger than usual.

"You're not a squirrel," she says. "You'd die."

"I'm not scared of dying. It's like sleep. Or before you were born."

"For ever, though. Can you imagine that? For ever and ever and ever."

"We all have to do it." He shrugs. He is always shrugging. Jen's mum often says of her work colleagues that they are the personification of things: the personification of stupidity, the personification of thoughtlessness. Will is the personification of shrugs.

"Some people live on, though, don't they?" she says. "Shakespeare. Uh, Freddie Mercury. Marilyn Monroe."

"You sound like my mum." Will plucks a bit of grass, rolls it in his root-like fingers, and throws it forward. "Galaxy of the stars."

"What are you on about?"

"Don't worry," he says.

Jen knows that Will's mum is a member of the Knowle Players, and was once in an episode of *Brookside*, and even though she doesn't exactly understand what that expression means, she thinks she understands it on some level. It conjures images of handprints in cement, and of Greek legends, Andromeda and Perseus, immortalised in the night sky. She is about to ask more when a high-speed train appears in the distance and soon screams by them, close enough for her to feel the rush of the displaced air.

When it is gone she looks over and Will is staring at her. First at her chest, then briefly at her face. Then he looks at the tracks.

"That was loud," he says.

Her bra is slightly visible at the armhole of her tank top so she adjusts herself. But why bother? Let Will look if that's what he wants, did she really mind? He is the one here with her, drunk with her.

She lies back on the grass and, unable to get comfortable, she says, "Will, can I lie down on your lap."

"If you want," he says.

She puts her head there and closes her eyes. There is a faint, wee-like smell coming from his trousers that she knows is just damp, like how the towels in the bathroom start to smell if they're not put out to dry. It would be off-putting normally, but now she feels close to Will and doesn't mind. Still, she flinches when his fingers touch her forehead. Eyes open, she sees them disappear above her sight line and feels them slowly press into her hair. She is tense at first, with him touching her that way, but actually the sensation is nice when she concentrates on that. Little tingles of pleasure scatter across her back when his nails score her scalp.

Will's mum is probably too busy acting to do all the cleaning and drying her mum does. She should maybe speak to her one day about how she ended up in *Brookside*, whether the Knowle Players have teenage members.

The fingers stop moving through the rows of her hair. Something cold and dry presses on her mouth.

He is kissing her. Will is kissing her.

She tries not to react, holds her breath. He has managed to

lean over and put his lips to hers upside down. Is this what she wants?

His tongue squirms forward and she isn't able to stop it going into her mouth. She can taste the vodka, and cigarettes, and something like peanuts. He is overeager, doing it wrong, or maybe it's because he's upside down. He is too deep and she thinks she might gag.

She sits up, takes a deep breath.

"You okay?" he says. His voice is low and calm.

"Sorry, I wasn't expecting that," she says. But she pours as much smile into her delivery as she can so as not to upset him.

She reaches for the bottle and there is a quarter left. She swigs all but a tiny drop, then offers this to Will. Immediately she feels the sickness and resistance ebb.

"Can we do that again?" he asks.

She doesn't say no. She smiles at him. Wanting to be kind, if only to reward him because he is the sole one that has recognised her, that has seen there is something special about her. And it's not like he is ugly. And it is not like she didn't enjoy it when he stroked her hair.

"You don't fancy Adeline then?"

"Not thought about it," he says.

He moves beside her again and leans in.

"Gently," she can't help but say. And he does go slower this time, but still his tongue feels like an invasion. She doesn't want to be kissing him. It should be Rupesh, and this isn't right. But there is a chance he'll tell the others about this, and that she did something wrong in some way, and that will be awful. So it is only when his long fingers enclose her right breast that she breaks the kiss and forcibly takes his hand away.

What to say to him now? How to make this less terrible for both of them?

"Can we just do what we were doing before?"

Shrug. No emotion registering on his face. "Yep."

On her way to his lap she lets out a sigh that is disguised by the noise of them shifting positions. It takes a long time for the sensation to feel relaxing again. A long time before she is satisfied he doesn't hate her, and allows herself to close her eyes.

When she opens her eyes again two eyes are looking back. The light has changed, it is getting dark. There is drool on her cheek and Will's fingers still move back and forth in her hair. Another thing—there is an insistent pressure on her neck that she only fully understands when it pulses against her.

She sits bolt upright and wipes her mouth. Winces. The vodka; her head. A different pressure acting on her, like a fist is pushing against the back of her left eye.

"What's the time?"

"Dunno," he says.

"How long was I asleep?"

"Dunno. A couple of hours."

Hours? A couple of hours? They had come here early afternoon. If it's starting to get dark it must be...nearly teatime. He's just been sitting there stroking her hair and staring at her all this time.

On the walk home she can't bring herself to say anything to him. He occasionally rambles, at one point about the fields having Roman things buried in them, about the Romans living for ever. She can't listen to him, though. He should have woken her up.

When they say goodbye she goes to her room and hides under her bedcovers. Her head thumps and crying makes it worse. Downstairs plates clank and doors bang: Mum and Andrea making dinner together, happy bloody families. Why had she let Will kiss her? Why had she even gone with him in the first place? Stupid, stupid girl.

Winter, 2015

Will's brother delivered his answer to how he knew where I lived—*Everyone knew where* your *house was*—without any apparent clue as to how creepy it sounded. Still, his opening line was enough for me to want to hear what he had to say: "So what has Will done this time?"

It wasn't my house to invite him into, and as Dad was pottering around in the kitchen within earshot I suggested we walk and talk rather than conduct whatever business he imagined we had in the doorway.

Outside it was chilly, coat weather really, although I didn't appreciate my mistake in not bringing mine until it was too late—and I didn't want to go back either in case he read it as a sign that I expected his stay to be long.

At the end of the drive he gazed over at the house where Mr. Strachan once lived, shaking his head.

"And I remember who lived there, too," he said. "That wank stain has a lot to answer for. I don't think he was quite the same after all that, Will."

"I know, awful," was all I could think to say. "You reckon it changed him?"

"Oh yeah. See, his whole attitude was different after that. He just withdrew. Hit the booze and the drugs big time."

"And did Strachan ever explain why—"

"Never. Copped to it without ever explaining. I can only imagine Will said something to him that day that made him flip. Left him with a permanently damaged eye, you know."

"Jesus."

We turned left, heading towards the mouth of Elm Close. At some point I planned to go and walk along the old footpaths, see how they'd updated Steve's place, but something about Will's brother, his resemblance to Will perhaps, made me want to stay visible and keep to the main road.

"What made you ask if Will had done something?" I said.

"Just worried about you, mainly," he said. He had this tic of taking a sharp, noisy breath through his mouth before speaking. "Why did you show up at ours? On Christmas Day."

Doubtless he had come here with some agenda and I didn't want to end up hoisted on a lie.

"Well, we'd actually organised a reunion that Will didn't show up to. We were sort of trying to find out what happened to him, actually."

"Right," he said, appearing to mull over the implications. "So he's not...done anything to you?"

"No," I said. Then to keep honest, I added: "Not that we know of."

"It's just, I went to catch up with you yesterday and there were four of you in that car. Just, when people start coming asking about Will in big groups I worry. Especially when I saw it was you."

There was an opportunity here to learn more about Will that I could share with the others later. "If you don't mind me asking, what worries you? We were still thinking of trying to track him down. Is that a bad idea?"

"See, Will's not good with boundaries. He gets these obsessions. Especially about...well, if you're pretty." I didn't react to his compliment, didn't like the flirtatious edge he'd tried to add again. "After his trouble at uni he lived with me for a while, signed on, smoked weed, looked for work. Remember him getting sick a lot because he never ate right. I'd been at York and he was at the poly, and I had this housemate, pretty like I say, and he latched on to her, because she was nice to him. Gemma moved out after six months. He didn't know it was because of him—that she didn't really appreciate his appearances in her room for late-night chats. She had this problem saying no, to be fair, thought she was helping him after what he'd been through. That's just how he was with women, never understood the rules very well."

We reached the end of Elm Close and turned left down Blythe Lane. I folded my arms to keep warm.

"Then he went through this stage of never being around, staying in his room all the time. I just thought it was Will being Will. Next thing I'm picking him up from a police station because of something that happened at Gem's. When I asked him about it in the car, he told me that he'd argued with her at her house because he'd overheard a conversation she'd been having slagging him off. See, I didn't even know he'd been in contact with her, which was weird anyway, given why she'd left. It didn't make sense. So I pressed him, and he said he'd carried on being friends with her, going around to hers for chats, and that's when he'd overheard her saying bad things to someone about him. Didn't make sense. Told me he'd confronted her, and I'm like what did he hear? How did he hear it? How did he find out where she lived?

"It only came together once Gem came to speak to me about it. See, he'd been going to hers all the time, and she'd been too polite as always, but eventually told him that her boyfriend wasn't happy about him turning up and that he had to stop.

"One night he comes over all agitated, and she says he

definitely has to stop. And he starts yelling at her. Accuses her of thinking all these things about him, hysterical, crying. He broke a mug against the wall by her head, and her boyfriend, who was in the other room, had to restrain him after calling the police. Thing is, the stuff he said turned out to be things she and the boyfriend had actually talked about the last couple of nights. Really specific things, sentences and everything. She says the window had been open that night, and later she'd found mud on the floor of her wardrobe."

"Shit, that's terrible," I said. He might have been folded in there all night while they slept, stewing hatefully in the dark, waiting.

Monks gulped air with another pharyngeal hiss. "He and I fell out over that. He moved out and to be honest we haven't spoken since. I kept tabs on him for a while, but he wanted nothing to do with me. He fell out with Mum and Roger, too, and they lost track of him. He kept wanting money, and Roger always thought it was drugs because of the stuff that happened at uni."

We were approaching the pub we all used to know as The Nag's Head. Outside a sole smoker sat on the stoop. I told Monks I was grateful for his concern about us, but once more reassured him that we wanted nothing more than to establish why Will hadn't come to the reunion despite saying he would.

"I'm surprised you got a response at all," he said. "Hey, while we are here, do you want to get a drink? Talk a bit more. Catch up on the old neighbourhood."

Having not spoken to him before yesterday, I declined, telling him I wanted to get back because of the cold.

"Pub's got a fire," he said, doing nothing to ease my doubts that the whole appearance had been a pantomime to get me to go for a drink with him.

"No thanks."

The walk back was a little awkward. I tried to make small talk, asking about his real name.

"It's Michael," he said. "Mike. Monks was... It's a long story, but basically our sister, Liz, couldn't say Michael, so she said Monks."

I don't think I even knew there was a sister. Had she been at the house during our visit?

"Can I have your number?" he said when we reached my parents' drive. On seeing the reaction on my face, he quickly clarified. "I'll let you know if Will gets in touch with us. You never know? And, Adeline, could you let us know if you do hear from him? I think Mum is going to be over the moon that you heard from him recently."

Once we'd swapped numbers, I said, "We noticed his band are still gigging. They have one tonight in Manchester."

"Really?" he said. "See, that's good to hear. He kept going on about leaving them to do a solo project. They were quite serious at one point. Got played by John Kennedy once. You going to go?"

I laughed like it was the maddest suggestion in the world. "Is he definitely playing with them still?"

He shrugged. "I couldn't say." Before going back to his car, he said, "I didn't mean to scare you or anything."

"What do you mean?" I said.

"He's harmless really, I just... I just never want what happened to Gemma to happen again."

"I understand," I said, once more picturing Will crouched down inside that wardrobe listening to the intimate late-night sounds of two lovers who knew nothing of his presence.

We all sat at the far end of Rupesh's open-plan lounge around a large table, tea and coffee on the go. The cold from earlier that day had burrowed into my bones and I sat with my knees up to my chest on one of the dining chairs while filling in the group about what Mike told me.

When I was done, Steve said: "I haven't heard back from the web form yet. The number was a dead end…"

He trailed off and no one spoke, each of us lost in thought.

"What did you want to tell us, Jen?" Rupesh said.

"So okay." She sat up straight. "The loft is a complete state so I haven't found my diaries yet, but on Christmas Day, well, it was just boring as hell, a lot of kids running around, and you know, everyone *can't* take their eyes off the toddlers. So I started flicking through some of the articles about the supposed suicides again. The one at Manifest had more written about it because the press picked up on some comment the coroner made at the inquest about the girl taking Paroxetine. Apparently it can cause suicidal behaviour, and she wasn't prescribed it—so he made a recommendation about online drug loopholes being closed. He actually linked it to her suicide. Anyway, the girl had a prior history of mental health problems: depression, suicide attempts, addiction; she was well known to mental health services. So on a whim I searched her name and *mental health hospital*, and, hey presto, turns out she was something called a Peer Support Officer at this hospital, Wallgrove, in guess where? York."

Jen brought up the article on her phone and placed it on the table for the rest of us to see. I leaned forward. A photograph occupied most of the screen: five women standing in a line, grinning in front of a modern building. HOSPITAL STAFF RAISE £2000 FROM PEDOMETER CHALLENGE, read the article's headline. Beneath the picture was a caption listing the women's names.

"It's the same Ellie Kidd," Jen said, "same face in the photo they used in the articles about her inquest."

"York's a big enough place," Steve said, but his expression was both impressed and concerned.

"I mean," Rupesh said, "I've worked and studied there." He didn't sound convinced either. The coincidence was too strange.

"I'm sure everyone's got connections to a uni town like that," Steve said. "Still, it's hardly evidence *against* Will."

"But hold on a minute," Jen said. "So there wasn't as much on the woman who died at Loch Ness. Her name was Sara Kuzmenski and the report on the inquest revealed a history of mental health problems too. Anxiety, depression. They love mentioning mental health issues, it's in everything for both women. Her brother commented at the inquest that she'd tried killing herself before, although in the end the coroner said he couldn't speculate on why she'd gone into the water so ruled it as *found drowned*, with drugs and alcohol a possible factor. Reading between the lines the family seemed to accept it was a suicide. They found weed, alcohol and anti-depressants in her body and in her car, and her mum said she loved nature so it made sense that she would travel to the Highlands. But here's the thing: Sara was from Boston Spa." No one spoke, and so she added: "Near York. The inquest was even done by the same coroner's office. So not only are these two suicides linked by what we remember, but both are living in and around York and suffer from mental health issues severe enough that no family or coroner asks questions when they take their own lives in odd locations. Wouldn't you say that having previous mental health issues might make them obvious candidates if you wanted to make a murder look like a suicide? Add to that Will's connection to York..."

"It's an independent connection," I said, looking over at Rupesh. "Which means he's not on the radar, we have an independent connection..."

"And as for the character profile you wanted for your three criteria, Rupesh," Jen said, "Adeline's story and that wall at the parents' house are pretty—"

"Off the wall?" Steve said.

"Fucked up," Jen said. "I think if you want a motive, then Will being mental gets my vote."

"Is *being mental* a motive?" Rupesh asked, raising his eyebrows at Jen.

She looked hurt. "What I mean is he's got some type of head issue. Maybe he hates women. No murders are ever random—that's what they always say on crime shows, anyway. It means your criteria have all been met. There's more too. Some idiot left a horrible comment that Ellie Kidd was a known druggie and that the article didn't include the fact that the inquest said she was high on GHB. I've seen friends take GHB, back in the day anyway, and I tell you what, if you wanted to give someone a drug to get them in a state where you could make it look like they'd hung themselves, you could do worse."

"True," Rupesh said. "GHB could do that."

"It would be interesting to see if GHB was one of the drugs Sara had in her body."

"I think it would show up on a routine toxicology test," Rupesh said, thinking aloud. "Saying that, something like Rohypnol wouldn't, and that could make someone pliable too. I don't know about Ketamine. If it was GHB surely the coroner would have noticed the connection. Or maybe not."

"I suppose the GHB is hearsay," Jen said, "but I was thinking about maybe getting copies of the inquests. Checking the GHB thing. And also checking to see if Sara was on Paroxetine. I mean, think about it, if you wanted to trick a coroner into thinking your victim was prone to suicide, stuff them with some drug with suicidal thoughts as a side-effect. I looked online and you can get inquest details, but only certain people get access. It's basically up to the coroner, but Rupesh, with your background surely—"

Rupesh cut her off with a laugh. "I'm not doing that."

Jen pressed her lips together and stared at him. Then she said, "Okay, well anyway, Will was into drugs, right? I mean, he'd know which drugs to use to get someone out of it enough to set up a suicide. Hey, maybe he was even their dealer."

"I don't know about that last part," Rupesh said. "It's all interesting. Interesting, too, that we know Will had dependency issues, which may have put him in direct contact with a hospital like Wallgrove. Same with the Loch Ness lady. The three northern connections is something. It's a fun jigsaw. But how would you feel going to the police with this? And say they then take us seriously, not that I think it's likely. So we send the police out to Will and we've got it wrong. How is that going to make him feel about us? How are we going to feel about doing that to Will? Especially if, from all we've learned so far, he's actually quite vulnerable."

"Or worse," I said, "imagine dragging this all up again for those girls' families if we're wrong?"

"Imagine if we're right, though?" Jen said.

The room fell silent.

Rupesh went to get Jen some water at her request. When he came back, he said, "Of course, if he is doing this gig in Manchester, he's not off the radar, is he? Then we're back to square one, ish."

"Well, then we need to go," Jen said. "Only problem is I can't. I want to so badly, but I've got bloody Gamestock."

"Gamestock?" Steve said.

"You heard," Jen said. "Bloody Gamestock. This stupid thing my older sister makes us do with the extended family *every year.*"

I'd forgotten Jen's older sister, mainly because by the time I'd met Jen, Andrea—that was her name, wasn't it?—was a university student, an otherworldly thing to be at the time.

"I'm so sorry," she said, "but I'm already in their bad books

111

for spending so much time with you lot. But you guys have to go, someone's life could be on the line, right? If he's still got a third planned. I'll try and get the diaries down from the loft, too, before next time."

"Got to say, Jen, it's impressive, how much you've found out already. You considered becoming a detective?" Rupesh said, and Jen beamed. "I would come, but I'm working tonight."

To me, Steve said, "Do you fancy it then?" The others couldn't see his quick suggestive eyebrow lift, a gesture just for me, sealing our partnership.

"Yeah," I said. "I suppose we have to."

"Keep us updated to let us know you're safe," Jen says.

"Sure, but we'll be fine," Steve said. "It's a public place. I'm not worried."

Steve, 1998

Steve kneels at the base of a laurel hedgerow bordering the farmhouse's front garden, pretending to look busy in case his dad decides to check up on him through one of the windows. What he's actually doing is resting his legs, lost in a slow fume about the injustice of this particular set of chores. Dad can dress it up as a "deal" all he wants, but this is a punishment really.

He snips off one of the remaining stray branches missed by the electric hedge trimmer using a pair of rusted shears, agitating a wasp that flies at his head. He swats at it and growls before throwing the branch into the darkness beneath the bush.

At first that brick through Strachan's windscreen last summer had seemed like the perfect response to the dog being back in the garden. It hadn't been Steve, but he was proud of whoever had taken it upon themselves to level things up. Only then the police had got involved, and Dad had to cancel meetings and fly home from Singapore. Life hasn't been easy since then, and after being sent back to school early he'd then been made to stay at school during half-terms, and with two depressing host families for Christmas and Easter. He'd had to plead with Dad to avoid a similar fate this summer—which is why he's now having to tidy this mess of a garden before June ends.

He's been making some progress, especially since GCSE

exams finished, but when he agreed to the chores he imagined being able to find more short cuts. He throws another cutting beneath the bush. Hiding waste this way saves him having to pile it up and carry it over to the burn barrel, but it doesn't save much time.

He wished Will would come back. He'd shown up the afternoon Dad wasn't in, and taking a trick straight from Tom Sawyer, Steve had got him to cut back all the conifer bushes in the back by telling him how much fun it was to use the hedge trimmer. He'd also thrown a tenner his way, mainly because Will didn't get pocket money and he felt bad he'd done so much. It's slow going and with only a few days left until July there's every chance Steve might not get it all done. Whether or not Dad will stick to his promise to send him away if the garden isn't in tip-top condition, despite all his efforts so far, he doesn't want to find out. Especially as a far worse threat was raised in the aftermath of last summer: moving back to London. It's in his interests to keep Dad sweet and as far away from this idea as possible.

Steve's calves are starting to go numb. He stands up and his knees click. Over the top of the hedge he can see all of Elm Close. The back of a car is just disappearing onto Adeline's drive, and shortly after the girl herself emerges from the driveway. She walks towards the farmhouse, and Steve checks his T-shirt for sweat stains—a habit born of having a surname, Litt, that rhymes so well with pit. This year some kids at school had taken to calling him "The Pits," though he hoped that was more about his attitude than his smell. After meeting Adeline last year he'd felt the need to compromise at school less. People he genuinely liked really existed so why bother pretending any more? He'd turned against some of his friends—acquaintances at best, really—and their daft opinions. Had stood up to teachers he knew were talking rubbish. Seen himself as a sort of

Socratic superhero, righting wrongs in the wake of not giving a fuck. The others hadn't seen him this way, though.

Adeline wears the remnants of her school uniform, an untucked white shirt and grey skirt that hangs down to just above her bare knees. She also wears a smile that is either apprehensive or confrontational, either one likely there because they haven't spoken since last year. She is just as pretty as he'd remembered and his heart punches the air. A day hasn't gone by without him thinking about her.

"If it isn't Steve Litt," she says, coming to a stop on the other side of the hedge.

"Afternoon, Adie Thomas," he says, tugging at the reins of his grin without success.

"So here you are," she says. "I've seen all the others but was wondering if you'd deafed us off. They said your dad was back."

"Yeah, he's taken some holiday to keep an eye on me. I'm still working off my Strachan debt from last year." He glances back at the house to make sure he isn't being spied on.

"God, really?"

"Annoying too, because I told him when we moved here he should get a gardener, but he said no and that he wanted a big garden he could work in to relax more. I knew he wouldn't. But no one listens to me. What happened with your parents when the police showed up then?"

She shrugs. "Dad defended me to the police. Mum tried bloody shopping me. They argued." She gives a double thumbs-up.

"Seriously?"

"Strachan gave the police that note, and when they asked my parents if they recognised it, Mum was all like, Hmmm, let me think about it, that writing does look a little bit familiar. Then she *grounded* me." She puts air quotations around grounded. "Like we're in some fucking American sitcom."

"Wow." They're getting close to talking about how last

115

summer ended, which he isn't keen to do. They'll need to at some point, but he's not sure he can really explain just how fast it all happened, and that even if he had found some small way to get a message to her it wouldn't have come close to capturing what it was he wanted to say. Even putting it like that makes it sound too intense and like a romantic movie. She's here, though, still talking to him. Perhaps the Christmas card he'd sent her had done the job.

"So are you still doing exams then?" he says. He glances at her skirt, then can't help but drop his gaze further down to her legs before looking straight back up to her face. It is hard to keep your thoughts straight around her because your mind just wants to try to comprehend what it is seeing. She is just so striking, raven hair and pale skin—by far the most *extreme* looking girl he's ever seen.

"Literally just finished my last one."

"So great, are we all finished now, then?"

"Yeah. The others were going to come call for me after tea. Suppose you can't join us, though."

"You should come to mine," Steve says.

"What about your dad?"

"He's out tonight."

Steve has big plans for the gang this summer, and he wants them to get back into their rhythm again as soon as possible. Nothing he wanted to do could really start before Dad went back to work properly next week but perhaps tonight would be a good warm-up.

His attention is drawn to the drive next to Adeline's: Mr. Strachan is out in his front garden washing his silver van.

"Our old friend is out," Steve says, and she turns before he can add: "Don't look."

He's in a tight white T-shirt, and for an older guy he looks quite strong—his chest solid and arms thick.

"Looks like he's been working out," Adeline says.

"Didn't have you down as being into muscles?" he says.

"I'm not. He's probably one of those saddos that spends all their time in the gym, like lack of muscles is the reason his wife left him and not the fact he's a thoughtless div." Steve can't help but laugh at this.

Strachan glares at them. He can't have heard, though.

When Adeline heads home she walks down the middle of the road to avoid getting close to Strachan's. Not entirely sure why, Steve begins counting in his head. He has reached five when she looks back at him, smiles, then looks back to face the direction she is heading once more. It's a law, isn't it? The law of looking back. The sooner someone does it the more they like you. Whether he's just invented it or heard it somewhere before, it feels true. And now tonight can't come quickly enough.

There is no way he won't be finished with the garden now.

That evening in Steve's lounge they half-watch a film while catching up on what happened to them over the previous year. Adeline stuns Steve by knowing the name of an actress with just one line.

"I got a subscription to *Empire* for Christmas," she says.

Both Will and Rupesh are taller, and Will now has a wispy moustache—just like Strachan. While Jen doesn't appear physically bigger, she somehow occupies more space than she did before. Gone is the uncertain girl from last year. This is superstar Jen, lead in all three school plays that year and fresh off the back of a relationship with some dim lunk who in school status terms had apparently been a catch. Her hair is short, making her look older.

Adeline had mentioned earlier that her path rarely crossed with Jen's during the school year. That Jen had been an insider at the school in a way Adeline hadn't wanted to be. Steve could have guessed this would happen. He'd known Jen had an established friendship group, a group of girls who are told off daily for wearing their skirts too high and too much make-up—conventional girls, not girls Adeline would have much time for. Also, with Adeline being as set as she was on going to Marlstone Sixth Form, what would have been the point in making an effort for just a year? That's how he'd felt when things had started to turn against him at King George's this year.

The way the gang are with one another it's like only a week has gone by. It's obvious now they are all together that the group needs the five of them, that the group has its own special dynamic.

When the film draws to an end, Steve asks: "Any of you lot notice something about the road, by the way?"

They have noticed many things it turns out, but none of them know what he is talking about.

"Strachan's dog," he says. "It's not there any more. Even that pole is gone."

He looks around to see that they are all looking around too, searching for a confession.

No one says anything, though, and Steve says, "Whichever of you did that, well done."

It's another week before Steve's dad goes back to work. Steve finishes the garden in time, although his dad has thrown in the added hassle that he is expected to keep the garden in good shape now it's been completed. Small print, he says.

The first afternoon he has to himself he calls on Adeline but she's not in. Rupesh is away with his family in India. Not wanting to speak to Jen's sister, he calls in at Will's.

"I saw them all go out earlier," Will's older brother, a Will-a-like in a Metallica T-shirt, says. "The really fit one was going on about the train tracks?"

"Thanks," Steve says, trying not to get too close to the open front door, which was emitting a warm, mushroomy stench.

"She got a boyfriend?" Will's brother asks. "The Wednesday Addams girl. She's well nice."

Steve shrugs. He's pretty sure that Adeline wouldn't be interested in this bloke, though older boys are always a threat when it comes to girls. Most of the eligible girls at King George's go for older guys because they can drive and buy booze.

"Yeah, she's with someone," Steve says and leaves.

As expected he finds the others out by the train tracks. Are they trying to flatten things on the tracks again? Funny given Adeline was always so snarky whenever it was suggested last year. He sneaks up along the embankment through the grass in order to jump down and surprise them, tough work but worth it so he can eavesdrop on their conversation.

"I just had a thought," Will says. "You ever wondered why people eat bogeys but not ear wax?"

"Oh, God," Jen says, exasperated, her upper body collapsing onto her legs dramatically. "I'm soooo bored. Adeline, speak to him."

"Me," she says. "What can I do?"

"He was really off with me when I asked him about how long this is going to last," she says.

Steve had been off with her a little bit. Only because he'd been both disappointed that it wasn't Adeline and because he had made it clear he'd seek them out once he knew it was the right moment. He can see through the grass that they are on the stony embankment opposite. Jen throws a stone at a plastic bottle they've set up on the opposite side of the tracks. It bounces off the plastic and the bottle stays upright. Not coins then, but not much better. They're so useless at amusing themselves.

A high-speed train rushes by where they are sitting and

not one of them—Adeline, Jen or Will—so much as flinches. Something weird is going on with Jen and Will—they're sitting unusually far apart.

Adeline throws her stone next and misses. "I don't know if he'll tell me," she says.

"Of course he'll tell you," Will says.

"He bloody *loooooves* you," Jen says.

God, is he that obvious?

"No he doesn't," Adeline says, looking away from them. Steve can see she is smiling.

"He's probably just being cautious because of what happened last year," Adeline says.

"Do any of you want to confess to that while we're talking about it?" Jen says. She's looking at Adeline.

"Don't look at me." She can't help but laugh. "I thought it was Rupesh."

This cracks everyone up, including Steve, even if it isn't outside the realm of possibility. The obvious candidate is surely Will, though? Will who'd all but suggested it was what he was going to do mere hours before it happened.

Another train shoots by.

"We don't need Steve to have fun," Adeline says after it has passed.

"Why don't we go down to that fruit farm and free all the bees from the hives or something?" Will says.

They look at him with incomprehension.

"I don't think the bees are trapped," Adeline says.

"They come in and out as they please," Jen says.

"Bad idea too," Adeline says, "I'm allergic to them."

"How bad?" Will says.

"Think *My Girl*," Adeline says. "Mum used to scream when they came near me as a kid so I assume it's bad. Don't really want that, thanks."

"We could go looking for Sparky," Jen says. "He didn't come home last night or the night before."

"Cats do that," Will says. "He'll come home when he's ready. I heard one cat walked a thousand miles to get back to his old house. In fact, I think that's what that Proclaimers song was about." He starts to sing in a high voice with a bad Scottish accent.

"This place is a bit of a Bermuda triangle for animals," Adeline says. "Mum says Mr. Strachan thinks someone's kidnapping animals. Well, he said gypsies are, to be precise, although I think he's just a bit racist. A couple have gone missing in the village."

"Don't say that," Jen says. "Sparky'll come back."

"Yeah. Of course," Will says. "Pointless looking, though. If he doesn't want to be found he won't be."

Spying an entrance point for himself, and eager to join in, Steve stands and says: "Maybe Strachan's the one doing the kidnapping."

They all look over, shocked. He can see on Adeline's face that she is wondering how long he's been standing there, how much he heard.

"Good news," he says. "Dad's back to work. I have no idea if things will be as free and easy as last year. He might decide to pop back home a bit more often now, but my place is your place again. And once Rupesh is back we can get started." He sits down between Will and Adeline.

"Started on what?" Will says, playing with the laces on the red Converse he wears all the time.

"My big plan for the summer. But don't worry about that for now, I'll get to that when we're all here. Listen, I'm serious about Strachan, by the way." He throws a stone and knocks the bottle over first time. "Not the animals, but did any of you get an assembly about a man going around in a silver van trying to pick up kids?"

121

"Yeah," Jen says, "we had a couple, didn't we?"

Adeline nods. "Someone from our school said she'd been approached by a guy in a van who'd told her that if she came with him he had a load of perfumes in a warehouse. She was a bit of an attention seeker, though, and it happened right after that first attack so…"

"A few kids at my school said they'd been asked stuff by a bloke in a silver van after our assembly," Will says. "Like one kid said he'd been asked for directions, but he'd put his map on the passenger seat and asked him to get close to show him."

"You think it's Mr. Strachan?" Adeline says.

"Well, you know who else has a silver van?" Steve says. "And think about it. First one happened in between Marlstone and Solihull, near Catherine-de-Barnes, right? The second one in Balsall Common. There's a lad at school whose dad's a copper and he says there's loads of stories they're keeping quiet about so people don't panic. One over at Hatton, he said. One in Marston Green. All on country roads, kids walking home. Offered things, asked for directions." He nods at Will. "Knowle. And my assembly said the guy had a moustache."

"Ours was a beard. And, to be fair, people could be chatting poppins," Will says.

"Even if half of them are made up," Steve says, "you draw these sightings on a map and they form a perfect circle around Blythe. This kid showed me."

Adeline laughs. "What?" he says. "I'm serious. And when he gets kids in there they don't even tell, they're too ashamed."

"He's not the spider in *Arachnophobia*," Adeline says. The others appreciate the reference.

"You all laugh if you want," he says. "Silver van, living in the middle of all the sightings, barely ever in, often out at night, I've watched."

"Cruel to animals," Jen says.

"Exactly. I'm just saying I'd watch yourselves out in the fields is all. Shit, I'm wasted here."

"So what you got in store for us?" Jen says. "Is it in the fields? Is it busting Mr. Strachan?"

"Maybe, maybe not," he says. "You'll have to be patient."

They get bored of the train tracks and walk back to Elm Close for teatime. Steve walks Adeline to her back door after the others disperse.

"So can you tell me about your master plan?" she says.

"I don't want to spoil it. It's odd too. I'm not sure everyone'll be up for it."

"Why not?"

"It might have some strange…" He considers his words, which appear to be floating above him. "Terms and conditions."

"Does it involve sex?" she says.

Steve jams a hand into his pocket to conceal the rush of blood to his knob. "Well, it doesn't at the moment." He grins, and for just a second he holds her gaze, then looks down.

"What *does* it involve then?"

"No, I need to tell you all together. At once," Steve says. "You might think it's bad, then I'll lose my enthusiasm."

"I don't think I have that effect on you," she says. "And I can keep an open mind."

"Okay, and if it does involve sex?"

Adeline shrugs. "Depends who it's with."

Steve nods. "Well, it doesn't," he says, "although that's good to know. I'll tell you this, though. It's a game."

When he walks away he counts to five in his head. He's about to look back when he sees that Strachan is heading over the stile at the end of Elm Close with that ugly dog of his.

He's carrying what looks like a trowel. It's probably just for picking up after the dog, but he's not seen Strachan with it before. Curious, is he up to something? Burying evidence. With nothing better to do, tea being another frozen pizza or lasagne he'll only need to microwave, Steve follows Strachan for a while. He's not entirely sure about this whole him-being-a-kidnapper thing. Given all the evidence it isn't out of the question either. And worth being vigilant about.

He follows him for ten minutes or so, not sure what he'll see. Then Strachan vanishes in the middle of the maize. Steve checks up ahead and the footpath is clear. It's getting cold anyway, and he should probably eat before the others come over to watch films. He turns back to go home and after just a few steps Strachan steps out from the crops in front of him with the dog at his feet. Steve jumps but manages to stop himself from crying out.

"Something I can help you with?" Strachan says. And like the dog is an extension of him, it growls too.

"No."

"You following me?"

"You wish," Steve says, screwing up his face to look hard.

Strachan considers this. "You better watch yourself this summer," he says eventually. "I know you're the little ringleader. I see them all following you around, fuck knows why." The combination of Strachan's swear word in front of him—out here alone man to man—and the diminishing of Steve's authority rocks him.

"You should watch yourself, too," he says. It's weak, a crêpe-paper threat.

"I've done younger'n you," he said, his face so calm that it had to be true. Steve is taller than Strachan but feels much shorter. "You understand?"

Steve is still trying to get control of his thoughts when Strachan shakes his head and walks by him.

*

124

At home Steve tries to watch a film to calm down. He can't concentrate, though.

Watch yourself. An idle threat it might have been, though it doesn't quite have that feel, not after how last summer ended.

What if Strachan isn't done with them yet? Perhaps he has more in store for them this summer. Things that might ruin everything Steve's been planning, daydreams that got him through boring lessons and long, lonely evenings all last year.

Watch yourself.

Of course Strachan doesn't see things as fair and even, how can Steve have been stupid enough to believe that? It's obvious. Hadn't he seen that look Strachan gave Adeline and him?

Strachan's been out talking to Adeline's mum too, on the charm offensive. Then the other day there had been Will. Steve saw them talking over the fence briefly before Will shuffled off. Will who is vulnerable to manipulation, easily distracted and loyal. These are Strachan's war games, building up to something more substantial.

Steve's feelings about things like this are often right. Just look at Dad and that garden. That's what the others perhaps haven't worked out about him yet. He thinks about these things more than other people, worries about them. It means his instincts are more finely tuned to the world.

And what he now knows is that taking Strachan lightly is a mistake they can't afford to make.

Winter, 2015

We took Steve's car, setting off to Manchester from Rupesh's just after 4 p.m. into an uneven downpour. Our conversation barely grew beyond small talk when it wasn't about Will. I did manage to find out about his big break-up by simply asking him outright.

"It's not very interesting," he said. "Her name was Emily and she was in the year below me at Cardiff. We met when I was twenty-two and we broke up when I was twenty-nine. Seven years of what was mostly a good thing."

"Were you in love? Don't answer that if you don't want to, by the way, I'm just being—"

"What can I say? It was easy. We both fell into it after a night out and neither of us had any reason to end it."

"A fine old British tradition."

"Well, when I met her I was just done with all that fiery teenage intensity. Everything was just like, *whoosh*, covered in napalm, do you know what I mean? It was exhausting."

I nodded, though I'd never stuck around in a relationship once the crackling and smoking stopped. In fact, I'd not been in *any* relationship much longer than a year.

"Honestly, at the point we met I wanted a friend," Steve said, "not, like, a sparring partner, which had been my type.

126

Too much manic pixie dream girl nonsense on my part. Emily was younger than me, very easy going, quietly ambitious."

"Am I included in that?" I said, immediately hating how self-obsessed it sounded. Steve didn't appear to mind.

"Not at all," he said with a laugh. "I think you set too high a standard. Nothing ever lived up to it."

"Good save," I said.

"I'm serious."

It was a good thing Steve was looking at the road because I could feel my cheeks burning. "We were just children, really," I said.

"Some days we were children," he said. "Some days we weren't."

I took a second to compose myself, wanting to tell him that I felt the same way. Instead, I asked: "So what went wrong with Emily?"

He thought about this. "She decided she liked the smell of napalm in the morning. She got this job at a London advertising firm and was out pretty much every night after a few months there. I thought I was being a really cool boyfriend, Mr. Twenty-First Century, just ignoring how upsetting it was that I never saw her. And she was asking all these questions. Have you ever done coke? What are your thoughts on threesomes? Just randomly throwing them in like we did this sort of theoretical stuff all the time."

He sounded so conservative. What on earth would he make of the last ten years of my life?

"I can see your face, Adie," he said, "but you have to understand Emily to understand why those things were odd. She didn't drink more than two glasses of wine at the weekend. She'd never been to a festival or taken drugs. She'd had sex with one person before me. And I was sort of in a place where I'd done all my experimenting—do you know what I mean? I already felt like I'd lived a good few lives."

I did sort of know what he meant. I'd had no real interest in the childish drinking societies I'd been invited to join at Cambridge, already having experienced drinking and all the fun that came with it both at sixth form and before then, with the gang.

"In the end," he said, "she cheated on me with a bloke from her office. In her office. Literally fucked him in a supply cupboard. Honesty is often the worst policy."

It wasn't an entirely conscious decision to put my hand on his leg, but I couldn't help myself around him.

"I'm sorry she cheated on you."

After some time had passed, he said, "At least it was final, I suppose. Unlike us, drifting apart."

"Oh, come on," I said. His smirk was meant to let me know he was being playful, but fuck that. "You moved away."

"And you never kept in touch."

"Bullshit, Steve. I was besotted with you."

"Besotted?" If he was taking the piss I couldn't tell. "That's how you felt?"

"You seriously want to go here? You stopped writing to me," I said, shoving his shoulder playfully but not really playing at all. Apparently I harboured a little bit of anger after all that time, funny.

"That's not true, you stopped writing to me."

I was about to launch into another protest, then restrained myself. Perhaps it had been my fault. It had been so long ago. And maybe sixth form had distracted me from Steve.

"Well, how will we ever know for sure?" I said.

"Do you still have those letters I wrote to you?"

"No," I said. "I might have burned them in a rage. You?"

"I keep everything."

After queuing in traffic, getting lost in the city centre, then parking a mile from the pub, we hit yet another queue on the stairs down to the venue's cellar bar. Lots of people wanted to fuck Christmas this Boxing Day, it seemed. From below wafted the smells and sounds of live music: alcohol and body odour, power chords and drums. If the font size on the posters lining the stairwell was anything to go by, The Geppettos were tonight's second band.

We were about to descend when my phone began to buzz in the pockets of my jeans.

Jen.

I showed Steve the inside of my index finger and left him in the pub to take the call outside.

"Is he there?" Jen said. "Have you found him, Adeline?"

"Not yet."

"I got my diaries. I found them. And I think he really bloody did this, you know." Hysteria accompanied everything she said like the crackle on a record.

"We just got here," I said, and trying to settle her down added, "You not doing Gamesfest?"

"Gamestock. Well, I had to be doing something useful, you know, thinking of you two out there on the case. And it's addictive, this research. Andrea had a big go at me for not being a team player, Jesus, they're downstairs now. I'm thirty-three and she's thirty-six and we're arguing like kids. But listen, this is serious."

"What was in the diary?"

"I detailed the whole night a few days after," Jen said, "must have been a lot going on. But here are the important bits." She began to read the entry aloud. *"Will went last and said he'd be a serial killer. He told us this thing about being a murderer and making them all look like suicides. WHAT A PSYCHO! It was funny, though. I said he should put badges of bands he likes on each body so we'd know it was definitely him, and he said that was a great idea. Thing is, even though he was joking, it wouldn't surprise me if he did it. Ha ha.*

"And then hang on, there's another bit: *The scariest thing was Adeline said if he wanted to do one in Blythe then maybe the last victim should be one of us! Will said that was a great idea, said he'd save the method as a surprise! Great, why did she have to go and say that? I'm blaming her if he kills me, which he probably will given his general WILLNESS™.*"

I had no memory of suggesting this to Will, but even so, it wasn't clear to me what Jen thought this showed.

"That's interesting," I said. "Maybe we should meet up and discuss it tomorrow."

"Don't you see? The last place is definitely Blythe like we thought. There haven't been any suicides around here recently. And Adeline, the last victim might be one of us. What if that's why he agreed to the reunion and never showed up?"

I was about to disagree, but something hit me. A single mental image that had been nagging for attention which I'd dismissed again and again. The smiley face on Steve's car. When I told Jen she gasped.

"He's fucking with us," she says. "You need to be careful. Maybe just come home, we'll go to the police."

Now we were here, in the safety of a crowd, we were surely fine to see it through. She was probably overreacting. Nonetheless, she'd unsettled me. Less of a jolly adventure when it was your head on the block.

"There's other stuff in here too," Jen says. "Things that reminded me why I feel the way I did about him. Like, I'm convinced here he basically murdered Sparky, my old cat that vanished. Isn't, like, animal murder a total sign of being an actual murderer?"

I laughed at this, if only to feel better. It was in crime films at least, although that wasn't proof of anything. But hadn't I experienced something with Will and animals back then? It came back to me then, on that busy side-street in Manchester.

I'd found him burying a fucking rat or something in the fields that day I'd found out Steve had been sent back to school. And when I'd asked him about it, he'd shrugged it off with some nonsense about doing his bit to be helpful or something.

"Fuck me," Jen said when I told her.

"Is there anything about any badges in the articles," I said.

"I doubt it, but I'll check again," she said, and I could hear a voice yelling in the background. "Literally, can you hear that? That's Andrea now…I'm coming…We need to meet first thing tomorrow."

"Definitely," I said. "Anything we find I'll text you about too."

"Great, good idea. Hey," she said, her tone abruptly shifting, confidential now, "can you imagine if we actually stopped someone being killed? You, a famous podcaster."

Not quite knowing what to say to this, I just said, "I'm not famous."

"It would make a good podcast, wouldn't it?" Jen said. "We'd probably all be famous."

"Maybe," I said. She sounded like Xan now. "I'll speak to you soon."

I found Steve inside and he handed me a glass of wine. I downed half of it and explained what had happened. And when I was done, I asked him if the Nirvana logo I'd seen drawn on the back of his car was his handiwork.

And of course, he shook his head.

131

Will, 1998

Problems, problems, problems—they never end at home. He's grateful now to be outside after the morning he's had, happy to be going down to the fields with his spade on his shoulder and some cigarettes in his pocket and the sun toasting his cheeks. He'll find a place to dig and just space out for a while. It's really the only thing that he likes to do when the others aren't around. Rupesh will be home from India today, then they can all get back to what they do best.

He's never realised before how important Steve's place is to the group. Jen, Rupesh and Adeline's parents don't like kids coming over—they're all so strict. And while Mum and Dad aren't strict, the total opposite really, they have their own issues—and he definitely doesn't want the gang inside his house, seeing all Mum's *stuff.* She'd been having one of her low mornings, and he couldn't just leave her sitting at the kitchen counter alone while she was wearing one of her wigs. Especially not the black one. Was she Elizabeth Taylor, or maybe Audrey Hepburn? Not that she looks like any of them, really, she just looks like Mum in a—

So he'd spent the morning reassuring her, talking about all the usual things she has to talk about to get back to normal again. All the stuff about Liz, the stuff Dad and Monks won't talk to her about any more.

A rat in a cage, that's how he'd felt. Not now. Now he is closing in on Dead Man's, and once he's found a good spot he'll—

"You again."

The voice came from his left. It's Mr. Strachan, standing on the other side of the hedge. His hedge. What does he want? He'd said hello the other day, too, told him his tie-dyed T-shirt was blinding him. Wanted to know if he had a pair of flares to match.

"Hello."

"You off to bury the bodies?"

"No," he says, far too quickly, and he keeps walking. It's a joke, though, because it's a funny thing to say to someone carrying a spade, not because he actually thinks Will is about to bury anything. "Looking for Roman stuff."

"Really?" Strachan says. "And what do you know about Roman stuff?"

Will stops. He knows a lot about Roman stuff. He knows lots about history. About castles and forts and Pyramids and mental half-animal, half-human gods. He knows some locals think that Blythe might once have had a very small Roman outpost, or even a settlement. Locals like Rupesh's dad, who told him he wanted to go out to the fields with a metal detector when he retires. He's a bit different for a doctor, Rupesh's dad, and as well as history he likes UFOs and Nessie and stuff like that. Will likes him, thinks he is a—

"Good God," Strachan says, "are you catching flies in your mouth or are you thinking?"

He must be thinking, because he prefers to catch flies with those long strips of yellow paper, although he wishes he had one of those electric bug zapper things.

"I heard there might be coins out there," Will says, and shrugs.

"Did you?" Strachan says.

133

"My friend's dad says some people at The Nag's Head have found stuff...artefacts." He's pleased with himself for remembering this word. "He says no one has ever properly investigated round here. Thinks local people want to keep it to themselves so they can find and claim anything valuable."

"He might be on to something there," Strachan says. "Do the farmers know you'll be digging up their land?"

"No," Will says. "I didn't know—"

"Don't worry, kid, it never stopped me," Strachan says with a wink.

Strachan seems all right. They had all hated him so much last year, yet here he is talking about the Romans with him like he didn't get a brick through his windscreen and a note left on his van because of—

The dog! That's why they hated him. He was mean to it, leaving it outside like that all the time, the wazzock.

"What happened to your dog?" Will says. Shit. He shouldn't have said anything. Now he's made it obvious.

"He's inside. Safe. What's your name? I see you about a lot, you and the other Famous Five."

He should lie really. But Will's terrible at lying under the cosh.

"Will," he says.

"Right, Will, pleased to meet you," he says. "Do you know my name?"

Will shrugs.

"It's Bill. Which is short for William, like you. Will, I don't think some of your friends like me very much, do they?"

He shrugs again. Up until now he'd have sworn he didn't like Strachan. Now he's not sure.

"Have you seen Roman stuff then?" Will says.

"I might have," Strachan says. "I can show you if you want."

He's about to say yes, because he'd quite like to see an adult's collection of Roman stuff, see if it's like any of the rubbish he's collected over the years. This is how they get you, though. The paedos and the nonces. And he nearly fell for it.

"Not now," he says, and starts to walk off.

He hears Strachan mutter, "Suit yourself," and tut.

He hopes he didn't get it wrong. Steve might be right about Strachan, though, and if he goes off with him…well, that's how these things happen. They get you alone in their house, on your own, away from safety. But if Strachan's not a paedo, then maybe he'd been a bit rude walking off like that. He has his spade; he could have chanced it. Would have been a good weapon had Strachan actually tried anything. He vividly pictures himself striking Strachan with it—not down onto his head with the flat part, no. Heads are made for things to land on them from above. No, he would keep the spade low and shovel up into the pocket between Strachan's lower jaw and his Adam's apple. One quick blow, that's all it would take. Then he could stand over him while he choked and spat, grabbing himself and struggling for breath, bring down the—

He looks up. Steve is outside his drive at the end of Elm Close looking over at Will. He's wearing yellow gloves and tidying up the overgrown hedge for his dad again. After a second he waves. Will waves back but quickly darts down Dead Man's. He's not in the mood for Steve today. He might end up having to do gardening again, and that electric hedge trimmer hadn't been half as fun as Steve made out.

Nearly at the end of Dead Man's he stops. It occurs to Will that there're more questions he wants to ask Strachan. About what he thinks Romans might've been up to around here. And why no one's found anything here at all. And really, while he's got the spade, there isn't anything to worry about. Plus if he is up to anything funny then Will can be the one to catch him at it. He'll be a hero.

Back he goes, peering out from the entrance to Dead Man's to check for Steve. The coast clear, he runs back down the road and into Strachan's drive.

At the front of his lounge Steve is standing like some sort of ringmaster while the credits to the *Scooby Doo* film they watched last year play behind him on the television. Steve's raring to start the summer for real with whatever scheme he's dreamed up, though what a cartoon dog had to do with it Will hasn't a clue.

"So we are going to play a game called The Dedication," Steve says. "Loosely based on what we just watched. Sorry, probably didn't need to see the whole thing."

They all groan, including Rupesh whose arrival late afternoon had prompted Steve into calling this gathering.

In the film, Shaggy is left a mansion by his late uncle. The rest of his stuff—gold and jewels and all that—has been hidden in different places, and the only way for the gang to find it is to solve these silly clues hidden over the estate. Turns out the silly clues are the extent to which the film is relevant to Steve's game. He could have just called it a clue hunt and they'd have got it. Then again, this is the whole point of Steve—his showmanship. Keeps things interesting.

Rupesh has a trench across his brow already.

"So, basically, each of us will have a turn being the Puzzlemaster," Steve says.

"The...what?" Will says, sniggering, setting the others off.

"You heard," Steve says, taking it in his stride. "The Puzzlemaster will then set the others a task—"

"You've got to come up with a better name," Jen says.

"Shush, let him finish," Adeline says.

"Thank you, Adeline," Steve says, his face stern. "So each one of us will take a turn at being Lord Puzzle—"

Even Steve can't keep a straight face this time. Will falls on his side and squeaks, "Lord Puzzle," between breaths. Jen rolls her eyes.

"The rest of us then have to solve each puzzle," Steve says, "with the ultimate aim being to get to some final point where Lord... the person setting the puzzle will be waiting."

All of them look at him blankly. Then Rupesh puts his hand up. "I don't understand," he says.

"Okay, so it's like that film? Let's say I'm the person setting the clues."

"Lord Puzzle," Will says with a grin.

"Yeah, so I'm Lord Puzzle. I basically leave clues for you. So one might be: *Go to the place where someone threw a brick through a car window.* Obviously better and a bit more mysterious than that—but not too mysterious, we want everyone to understand it. And so you'll all trot off to Mr. Strachan's based on that clue, and there will be another clue waiting for you there. And so on and so on, until the final clue takes you to me, Lord Puzzle."

"Do we have to trot?" Will says.

"Trotting's optional," Adeline says.

"What happens when we find you?" Rupesh says.

"Well, it's sort of a race," Steve says. "So the first person to me gets four points, the next three, down to the last person who gets one point."

"Why isn't the first just the winner?" Jen says.

"Well, they are the winner, but of that round," Steve says. "But each of us has a turn at being Lord Puzzle."

"How do we decide who's Lord Puzzle?" Rupesh asks.

"Well, my trusty assistant, Adie, over here managed to find the perfect solution to that very problem," Steve says, pointing. Adeline holds up the broken chopsticks in one hand and gives him the middle finger with the other; he's *her* fucking assistant.

"Oh, cockflaps," Rupesh says. "My favourite."

It's an interesting idea, a big game that lasts longer than an afternoon. There are problems with it too, though, and Will has questions.

"If we're all following the same clues what if we bump into each other?"

"That's part of the game," Steve says. "You've got to try and avoid seeing each other so you can get ahead in the race."

"Okay," Will says, nodding. "Can you, like, destroy a clue when you find it, to like, make it harder for the next person?"

Jen tuts, but Adeline's giggling. She's always laughing at the stuff he says, although he reckons sometimes it's because she feels sorry for him. She's all right Adeline, and definitely has the best taste in music. Maybe a bit up herself. You can tell she's one of those that's just used to people falling all over themselves for her, so Will doesn't like to give her much. You had to resist that sort of thing. Give 'em an inch et cetera, that's what Dad says about women. Will's clever enough to know Dad is talking about Mum mostly, although Dad probably thinks what happened to Liz wouldn't have happened if he'd been stricter with her. Kept her from going out all the time.

"That would make it impossible, not just hard," Rupesh says.

"Yeah, don't do that," Steve says. "It'd be a nightmare. Also, if you're setting the puzzles, try and think big, okay? We don't have to be confined to Blythe. I'm imagining each person's Dedication will have its own day, so there shouldn't really be people bumping into each other as different people will solve the puzzles at different times and will try different routes to get places."

"What about joining forces?" Jen says.

"Why would you want to do that?" Steve says. "Points can't be shared."

"People could help each other solve the clues maybe, then it could be a foot race."

"What if we both reach you at the same time?" Will says.

"Again, it's a race," Steve says. "You actually have to touch the puzzle setter to place."

"Can you sabotage people in other ways?" Will asks. "Like cutting brake lines on people's bikes or whatever?"

"For God's sake, Will. Stop trying to sabotage people," Jen says.

"It's really up to you," Steve says. "But, you know, within reason. Not sure anyone is going to want to stay friends with someone who cuts their brakes."

"Fair enough," Will says.

"How many clues do we do each?" Adeline says.

"It's up to the person setting the clues," Steve says. "I'd think three or four would be the least amount to make it a good round. Also, the person setting the clues will probably have to think of a way to let all the others know at around the same time to make it fair, and take into account where various people live. Like maybe phoning them or something. Or leaving a clue that can only be opened at a certain time with everyone there. Everyone happy so far?"

"Casual," Will says. Although it seems to him that the gang won't be spending much time together during this game. Then again, they'd be out in the fields, wouldn't they? So he can bring along his spade and kill time that way.

The others nod too, except for Rupesh who looks like he's tasted something sour.

"Am I the only one that thinks it's going to be a lot of hassle?" Rupesh says. "I mean, is it really going to be fun, or is it going to be a lot of hard work? Coming up with clues, walking around all over the place."

"It'll be fun," Jen says. "All of us out in the fields sneaking around."

"Not with Moonshine about," Will says.

"Who?" Steve says.

Will's tried this name before, at school. It didn't take. With this lot it might. "Moonshine. You know, the guy in the van. Because it's a silver van."

"Oh, Strachan, you mean?" Steve says.

"If you like."

"Don't say that, Will," Jen says. "Don't be creepy." A spear of injustice pierces his belly. That's so unfair: what he'd said is creepy, but he isn't *being* creepy. Why is she saying that if it isn't true? To wound him, is why. To remind him that she hasn't forgotten the afternoon when she went mental at him, when all he'd done was try to be kind, let her sleep even though his back was hurting just because she'd told him she'd been up all night because of her sister, and she'd looked so pretty too, in the sun, her hair and teeth and lips—

"We're not letting him ruin the summer," Steve says. "He probably won't attack near here anyway. I showed you the map."

The map, yeah. Steve's map based on what his mate's dad supposedly said. Whatever, never mind: it doesn't bother him really. He's not scared of being kidnapped. It's just more of Steve being Steve. Making things dramatic.

"If you're all with me so far, the next bit is the real decider, but it might be a bit controversial. At the moment the game needs some consequences."

"Stakes," Will says.

"You hungry?" Rupesh says.

"The game needs stakes."

"Exactly," Steve says.

"I'm vegetarian," Rupesh says.

"Like a prize or a forfeit or something," Will says.

"Totally," Steve says, looking to the others. "I've got some ideas of my own. I thought I'd open it up to suggestions first, though."

After a long silence, Rupesh says, "Can't we just have a prize for the winner?"

"What prize?" Steve says.

"I don't know," Rupesh says. "Like, one of your films or something? You've got enough of them."

"Oh, Rupesh," Jen says, "you're sweet." She reaches over and rubs his shoulder.

Will isn't sure what to make of this. It makes him cross, although Jen is always poking and hugging and stroking people. Not him, mind.

"The prize has to mean something if it's going to work," Steve says. "If you can think of a present, Rup, that will make you do your best to win if you're behind on points in round four then I'm listening. I'm just not sure anyone's going to be that fussed about a second-hand, pirated copy of *Shakespeare in Love*, no matter how much they like Gwyneth Paltrow." He looks at Will here.

"If the prize was actually Gwyneth Paltrow," Will says. He's joking around, but he's nervous. It's clear Steve has a plan, and he doesn't always like Steve's plans.

"So my idea," Steve says, "is that the loser gets banned from coming round here."

Kaboom. Through puckered lips Will emits a soft *oooo*. Jen blows air out of her cheeks. Rupesh looks terrified.

"For ever?" Rupesh asks. "I mean, that would be like being thrown out of the group."

It's a critical point, and it's unclear what any of the others are thinking. They're all hesitant to commit, it's a big decision. Thing is, this is what they've been after: a bit of excitement. And Steve's delivered his bit.

"I'm against that in theory," Adeline says. "But the stakes do make a difference to how fun it'll be. And actually, I'm assuming that we'll be staggering out these rounds." Steve nods. "So by the time we've finished, maybe there won't be much of the summer left anyway. And who knows what'll happen after that? We'll all be at different colleges."

"Also it's not quite that harsh the way I think we could do it," Steve says. Taking a seat in his chair, he explains there will be three possible outcomes that the winner will have to draw from a hat. One of the outcomes is that the loser is banned from the farmhouse. With it simply being in there the stakes are high, but the chances were it wouldn't happen. The second option is that the winner gets final veto on the films they watch from Steve's dad's collection, while the third option is that nothing at all happens. Nothing. Everything stays the same.

"Well, I'm definitely not going to lose, so I'm in," Will says.

"Fighting talk," Jen says. "Well, I don't see how we can kick anyone out, really. So, yeah, I'll say yes just to get on with my life."

"You know, you have to hold us to it, Steve," Will says. "No sympathy. Otherwise it's pointless. If I lose and get banned, out is out. Banned is banned."

Rupesh still looks like he's agonising, like he really believes there will be a scenario where he, not anyone else, will get kicked out of the group. "I don't have a choice, do I?" he says. "It'll end in tears."

"Brilliant," Steve says, getting to his feet. "So, let's all vote. Anyone that doesn't want to do The Dedication, raise your hand?"

No one holds up their hand.

Content with the result, Steve brings out a bottle of his dad's whisky.

"Now we're talking," Will says, and reaches up to get the bottle from Steve when he's close enough.

"No," Steve says. "Chopsticks first." The hardness in Steve's voice makes Will scowl.

142

Adeline holds out her hand, and as each person takes their chopstick they have a sip of the whisky. On this occasion, everyone partakes. When Rupesh removes the second-from-last piece, and it appears to be the shortest, he looks like he might start complaining. Only then Adeline draws hers, a shorter, stubbier thing, barely an inch long. Seeing it, Rupesh throws up his arms and starts singing "We Are the Champions."

It's dark outside, and they are all a bit drunk and deep into *Ghostbusters*.

From nothing Rupesh says: "Why's it called The Dedication?"

It's a good question, one Will's not even considered—just another of those big words Steve and Adeline liked to chuck around to show off to each other. Funny word, too, Dedication. Brings to his mind a church full of people all singing hymns. Or marathon-types, legging it around even though no one is chasing them.

"To show your dedication to the group," Steve says.

Makes sense. Total sense. The least "dedicated" is the one that loses. Actually, that is a point, another one he hasn't considered. If the loser gets banned from Steve's, then how—

"What about you then, Steve?" Will says. "You going to ban yourself if you lose?"

Jen and Rupesh both emit a little "oh" because, yeah, it is a good point. Steve just offers a laugh, fake and full of itself. "I'm not going lose."

And it seems everyone is just fine with that. Just in case, Steve adds: "But if I do I'll think of something."

Will isn't fine with it, and he's surprised Rupesh hasn't immediately started firing at this easy target. Nothing Steve could think of could match the punishment of losing the farmhouse. Pretty funny Steve's nearly managed to get away with that one.

He's about to say something else when Steve says to him: "So I've seen you and Strachan chatting a few times."

Will's not sure what this has to do with his point. But now he's noticed Jen, lying with her head on Rupesh's lap. He doesn't know where to look, or on what to focus.

"You and him best mates now?" Steve says, not letting it drop. He sounds a bit annoyed. Probably because he hadn't planned on anyone picking holes in his big summer plan.

"Nah," Will says. "He asked where I was going the other day, and so I told him it was none of his business. Probably wanted to paedo me."

"Will," Jen says, disapproving. Adeline laughs and so does Steve.

"Just be careful round him," Steve says. "I'm serious. He might be out to get us for last year."

"I don't think he cares any more," Will says.

"No, he does," Steve says. "Honestly, he does."

Winter, 2015

Once we pushed our way downstairs, me in the grip of a dread drowning in wine, it became clear we couldn't get much further than the entrance without a fight. Almost a hundred people were rammed into a room designed for half that number.

The first band, a post-rock outfit named All Lay Down Before Me You Extraordinary Apes, finished playing to luke-warm applause. The house sound hadn't reached the end of the first song when an amplified voice filled the room:

"Hello, we're The Geppe*two, three, four*—" The band started to play.

They didn't sound too bad, a bit thrashy and shouty and, well, snotty really—not a style I associated with Will Oswald. Monks had been right. I gestured for Steve to lean down, which he did, and I yelled, "Can you see him?"

He stood on his tiptoes and shook his head.

"I'm going in." I managed to apologise my way through the dense crowd to the front of the stage. On my way, someone pushed by in the opposite direction, knocking me off balance. When I'd steadied myself, I spun around to reprimand him, but glimpsed only the back of the man's chequered shirt and the side of his face before someone stepped into the space he'd left behind. For a moment I was convinced I'd seen Will rather than just some tall guy in a beanie, and my heartbeat quickened. I was relieved when I scanned the room and saw plenty of other Wills staring towards the stage—the place where the real Will would be.

This is rebel heeeeeeeeell! This is rebel heeeeeeeeell!

The tide of the crowd brought me out near the outward-facing PA speaker on the left of the stage, and the singer's snarls jabbed at my eardrums.

This is rebel heeeeeeeeell!

All three Geppettos wore rubber masks. The front man and guitarist, in skinny jeans and a bright orange vest, wore a Pinocchio mask and had the microphone jammed up beneath it, the cord trailing out of the neck hole. The bassist, the nearest Geppetto, bounced around pulling Nicky Wire shapes in a Goofy mask.

The drummer was a Cheshire Cat. It was impossible to tell if it was Will under there. My version of him was based only on the picture I'd built over the last few days: a composite of his younger self, a few glanced-at photos on social media from years before, and my imagination. This drummer could be Will—a Will with tattoos and thick arms and a forceful stage presence. I wouldn't know unless the mask came off.

So I stayed at the front for the next twenty minutes until The Geppettos ended their final song, a two-minute blur introduced as "Your Last Friends." The crowd applauded and called for more, but the guitarists left the stage—bloody masks still on. The drummer soaked up the adulation by coming to the front of the stage and pumping his fists. My gaze was drawn to his feet. Red Converse All Stars, a Will Oswald trademark.

The drummer threw his sticks in the crowd and walked off, vanishing behind a black stage divider.

The throng began to dissipate as the next band, another outfit requiring copious stage changes, provided a bar break.

I turned to find Steve and couldn't see him. When I looked back a bright rectangle had appeared in the darkness to the right of the stage into which the band had vanished. Someone had opened a fire door onto a patio, lit up by an outside wall light. Two band members I recognised as the bass player and the front man, now without masks, were carrying out their gear.

And the drummer? Perhaps he had opened the door in the first place, and now he was getting away.

I climbed up onto the stage and was almost at the fire door when I came to a stop. The drummer was sitting on the edge of the stage to my left, hidden behind the stage divider, Cheshire Cat mask still on.

"Will?"

The Cheshire Cat just stared, watching my approach. It had to be him. I smiled, reached forward, then hesitated. There was going to be another Cheshire Cat under there. And another one under that. This was a dream. I was going to be in bed in London, the reunion yet to happen.

I grabbed the Cheshire Cat's right ear and pulled. The mask came off without any resistance.

"My name's not Will," the drummer said.

He wasn't Will either, nor was he another Cheshire Cat. A grey-haired man of about fifty looked back at me, old acne scars on his cheeks where unblemished skin should have been.

"But you can call me what you like," he said.

"Sorry," I said. "I thought you were a different person."

"I am a different person," he said.

I gave him a weak smile and went back to the fire door. Not wanting to be rude, I turned back and said, "You were good," but the drummer had gone. I really was in fucking Wonderland.

Outside it was drizzling. The patio was part of a beer garden at the side of the pub. The bottom of a steep road finished right outside the garden's front gate, accounting for the puzzling fact that having descended steps to get into the cellar, I was now back at road level. The singer and the bassist were packing guitar cases and amplifiers into the boot of an old Estate. I approached the singer.

When he noticed me, he flashed a gappy grin.

"I liked your set," I said. The man's grin widened. "You've not got a CD, do you?"

"Oh no, I'm sorry, we're not really…We don't record any more. I was going to say we aren't a proper band." He spoke with a soft Irish accent.

"We're not," the bassist said, and walked by, presumably to get more equipment.

"What I mean," the front man said, "is that we used to gig and carry CDs, but now we just do this for fun. And basically all our old stuff's online. I can give you an address if you want?"

"I actually looked you up before," I said.

"Really?"

"Well, the thing is, I'm not sure, but my friend and I, who's inside somewhere, we think we used to be friends with your drummer."

"Danson?"

"Is he the Cheshire Cat?" I said.

"Yeah, that's him."

"No, not Danson. Our friend was a boy, well, a man, called Will. Will Oswald? He had blond hair and—"

"Oh right. Yeah, of course we know Will." For the first time he stopped smiling.

"We were hoping he still played in the band."

"Afraid not."

The bassist emerged from the venue cradling a huge bass amp. He loaded it into the back of the car, slamming down the boot before going back for more.

"What made you think he was still playing with us?"

"Just something we heard from another friend. We've been having a little reunion of sorts and couldn't get in touch with him."

"Right. Have *you* not seen him in a while?"

"We haven't actually."

"Well, I don't know if you knew but to be honest with you he wasn't that well the last time we saw him." He was avoiding eye contact now, and I could sense his discomfort.

The bassist reappeared with another load of gear, and I saw him shoot the singer a look.

"Sorry, what's your name?" the singer said.

"Adeline," I said.

He held out his hand. "I'm Gaz Geppetto. Do you want to stick around and I'll catch you upstairs? I don't know how much you want to know..."

"Would that be okay? We'd be grateful for anything you can tell us," I said. Then added, "What do you drink?"

Steve was already in the upstairs bar waiting. We ordered a round, and sat at a table in the corner where Gaz joined us. He sipped his pint and said, "That's my favourite bit of the gig. You know, it's funny you turning up here. I was thinking of Will recently." He grimaced and became intrigued by the patterns on the table top all of a sudden.

"I actually thought I saw him earlier until I saw how many other identical-looking men there were in the room," I said.

"I did invite him to come to a show. So maybe. Man of mystery, that one." He didn't sound convinced.

"How did you meet him?" Steve asked. "We didn't even know he played drums."

"He just auditioned for us when we started up in...2010. Up in York."

"That where you still are?" I said.

"Yeah. We were all ex-uni there. He could do the job, you know, bang, bang, bang. And he was really good at coming up with stuff for the band image and that. The Geppettos was his idea. He loved that bloody Disney *Pinocchio* film, and he came up with the masks idea too. He wanted us all in Pinocchio masks, but Rudo, bass man, and me voted him down and just settled for general Disney masks. He was totally mad." He took a sip of his beer. "But that was kind of the problem after a bit."

"What do you mean?" Steve said.

"He was actually, like, mad. It started small and we tried ignoring it, right? Drinking, drugs, general fucking weirdness. Drummers are rare so you sort of find ways to make excuses for them in a way you wouldn't with normal people. Rudo calls them Drummer Sins. They're half the weight of a regular sin."

"How bad was it?" Steve said.

"He was a just a bit obsessive at first. I don't know. He got into the habit of not being happy with his count-ins. One-two-three, you know. He'd stop us every song, sometimes twenty, thirty times to get it right. The fucking count-in. We ended up doing them ourselves, like The Ramones. Really odd. Sort of killed the fun a bit. He got sick a lot too, always getting flu and ear infections, didn't look after himself and kept missing practice. And we knew he liked to go wild, but then he starts turning up to practice off his face, forgetting all the bloody things we spent hours learning. In the morning and daytime we're talking here. I mean, he was playing songs half speed because he was tripping his tits off talking about the drums being fucking marshmallows. And yeah, it was funny sometimes, all things considered, but you know, after a few years it was just out of control. He was talking a lot more bollocks; he was missing stuff all the time."

"What sort of stuff was he saying?" I said.

"Oh, I can't remember. We had an argument about whether George W. Bush was a fucking lizard once. It was stuff like that, Nessie's an alien, abductions, conspiracy theories. Pretty relentless."

Steve looked at me. Gaz took a massive gulp of his pint. I brought my own glass up, then stopped and brought it back to the table. I needed to slow down.

"Anyway, the whole thing came to a head because we had this BBC radio session booked, probably about three…no it can't have been." He stopped to do some arithmetic. "No, it was probably only two years ago, now I think about it. Feels like ages. We had a few festivals booked, and we were going down to promote it. Was a big deal for a little band like us. And we turned up in the van to pick him up and he just wasn't there. We were going mental. Ended up missing the fucking session.

"In the end we got Danson in, a mate of my dad. Will wasn't answering his phone or replying to emails or nothing. And we had a great time at the festivals with Danson, and he was looking for a new band. So when we finally caught up with Will like a month later we just said it wasn't working and that we'd moved on."

"How did he take it?" Steve said.

"It was amicable enough. I think he was expecting it. Thing is, we found out from one of his housemates later that he'd had a sort of episode in a supermarket the morning of that session, attacking people and yelling and all this. He hadn't shown up because he'd been fucking sectioned."

"Shit," I said.

"Yeah. He was in a hospital for a good few weeks, and they knew him there, too. He'd been in and out, and we had no idea. I mean, we were mates for three years, you know, but never close enough to talk about his life or whatever. So we'd just got pissed off with him, which, looking back on it, was shitty of us. We didn't realise he was having, like, real mental health problems. Not that I think I could have done anything, all things considered."

151

Gaz took a long gulp, which finished off his pint.

"Does Will still live around York, do you know?" Steve said.

"The last time I saw him was randomly in town, and he was living in like some sort of supported housing thing. He looked a bit thinner, a bit knackered. He asked if I wanted to buy his drum kit. Actually, I remember him saying he was thinking of going back to Birmingham."

"When was this?" I said.

"Year and a half at least."

"Did he say where in Birmingham?" Steve said.

"No, we only talked a minute. All things considered, I was happy he seemed to have some plans, but maybe I was trying to make myself feel better. Him being not too far away in Birmingham was why I pinged him an invite tonight, but he never got back to me. Was a bit hopeful of me really, it was an old number."

Gaz went to great lengths to clarify that on the whole Will had been a top bloke, despite everything. I felt bad that we had brought it all back up.

"I don't suppose you can remember the hospital where Will was placed, can you?" Steve said. By that point Gaz had finished up his pint and was looking ready to go.

"Yeah, it's the mental health place near the big graveyard," Gaz said. "Wallgrove, I think it's called."

Under the table, Steve bumped his foot against mine.

"Sorry, I'm dancing around what I want to say here," Gaz said, his voice even softer than before. "The reason I reached out to him with an invite... The thing is, this might be bollocks, and this is real friend-of-friend stuff, but I don't want to *not* tell you, just in case, right. Surprised me you asking after him tonight, if I'm honest."

"What is it?" Steve said.

"Someone, not that long ago, actually. They said... they said Will was dead."

Part II

Why's it called The Dedication?

Winter, 2015

I regretted my third glass of wine on the drive home, but it had felt necessary once Gaz left us. Given how difficult it had been to find Will, the idea that he might have fucking died had a dreadful logic to it. The revelation accompanied us in the car, an unwanted passenger. I'd been just about ready to go to the police and tell them Will was a murderer.

Our response had to be thought through now, and we needed to work out how we could find out for sure. Especially as we faced the awful prospect of having to tell Will's family he was dead.

What did this mean about all the things we'd discovered, too? Had everything really just been a coincidence? I felt sick. A realistic possibility was that we'd manufactured all of this.

I read Steve the diary entries Jen had sent us in the group chat half-heartedly, photos of the actual pages marked with her wild handwriting. It was too much to deal with in that moment and he was quiet, distracted. Without explicitly saying so we knew everything had to wait until tomorrow, when we were back with the others.

I gazed at the passing cityscape while Steve muttered something about having introduced Will to *Pinocchio* after he wanted to drop out of school. He quoted a song lyric, about little beliefs growing up into trees. I opened a window and pushed one cheek towards the rushing air, wanting my head to open up and the night to wash out the inebriation.

When Steve pulled off the M42 he signalled left at the roundabout, towards Knowle and Blythe. To the right of the roundabout was a large Premier Inn.

"That's where I'm staying," he said, pointing while he waited for two cars to pass.

I had no interest in going home, no interest in sleeping in that forgotten bedroom alone, all the mixed-up thoughts about Will pulling me to and fro.

"Is it cosy in there?" I said.

"It's pretty standard budget fare."

"Are there spiders?"

"Not that I noticed." He looked down at my leg, where my hand rested, palm down. Conscious of my tatty fingernails I hid both hands between my legs.

Voice wavering a little, I said, "Can I see it?"

It had happened, again, after all that time. In a hotel room of all places. Sex with Steve Litt. And though it had been a blur of clicking teeth and uncomfortably misplaced body weight, the whole thing rushing by before we found any real rhythm, it was still the best sex I'd had in years. I barely slept, the night full of detailed imaginings of how it would all go wrong from here. At around five in the morning, bored and bothered, I gave up trying to sleep and decided to go home. While I was dressing, Steve stirred.

"You're not leaving, are you?" he said.

"I should get back before my parents wake up. I don't really want to answer *those* questions."

He insisted on driving me home, ignoring my protests. Once parked outside the house, he said, "I'm sorry. I got a bit self-conscious tonight. It's been a while."

"I had a good time," I said, and kissed his cheek. "See you soon."

I stepped out of the car, and entered my parents' house through the unlocked door. The smell of paint made me feel oddly nostalgic.

Adeline, 1998

Adeline will take them to Brindley Place, by the canals in Birmingham city centre. The location of the other clues isn't as important; they'll be left along the way. It's that final destination that matters. She will reclaim it from her past life, before Blythe, and bring it into the present.

She tells the others to be home around 11 a.m. on Monday, two days after Steve announced The Dedication. At 9 a.m., Adeline leaves her house and heads for Dead Man's Alley. The field where she'd caught Will burying that animal is now filled with maize, already above head-height. Amidst the crops the stillness never fails to bring on a gut-level disquiet that today is much worse. Perhaps it is because of all the chat about Strachan, or whoever it is, trying to kidnap kids. Or it may just be its association with Will. She's glad that today she will be safe in Birmingham when Will starts prowling for her clues. Prowling, yes, that's the word. With his *hunting eyes*. That little expression has stuck with her since getting to know Will better. He's hilarious sometimes, but she just finds him...He's like milk on the turn.

Down in a sliver of pines where the land dips is the footbridge where COUNTRY PUNKS is still scratched into the handrail. She places a blue, steel petty-cash box belonging to Dad in the little pocket under the far step. She leaves the key in the lock and a folded note in one of the tiny plastic draws—technically the second clue of her Dedication.

Train your sights on Hampton-in-Arden for the next clue,
A crack in a STATIONary wall will reveal all to you.

This clue is her toughest, but it will impress Steve if she sets a high standard.

The rest of the path to Hampton, particularly one nasty section after the beehives, has been cut back since last year, making the route easier. When she finally reaches the phone box in Hampton, she takes out a scrap of paper with their numbers on, ready to call them in order of closeness to Dead Man's, which means Will is first.

She picks up the receiver and pauses. In a way if Will lost it wouldn't be the worst thing, at least she wouldn't be stuck out in Birmingham with him alone if he arrived ahead of the others. Perhaps she ought to phone him last? No one would know.

But that isn't right. And it's unfair, too, because his odd phrases and animal burying were only part of the story. What really bothers her about Will, if she's honest, is the way he reacts to her. She doesn't register to Will the way she does with the others. With Steve certainly, but also Rupesh and Jen—they sense and respond to her arrival and her departure, and her general existence, in a way that Will doesn't. It makes her want to poke Will. Or even poke herself, just to check she isn't invisible. And while she's never been the most popular, beautiful girl in school—was in fact an utter dweeb when she started senior school in her braces and glasses—she's grown accustomed in the last few years to being able to *affect*. So much so it is strange when it doesn't work—annoying, even. Like he's doing it deliberately to make a point.

She calls Will first, though. Then Rupesh, Jen, and finally Steve.

On the dead man's path it won't smell so nice,
So give your nose a rest beneath the nearby pines.

"Amazing," Steve says after hearing it. She hangs up, unable to keep the pleasure off her face on the walk to the station.

Her train is just two minutes away when she arrives. The place is deserted, there's not even a member of staff behind the counter. This is good, because it means getting a mysterious *permit to travel* from the free machine on the platform—a licence to guilt-free fare dodging.

She stands on tiptoes to slide an envelope into a crevice in the platform wall, leaving the end poking out ever so slightly so it is visible to someone who knows where to look. This clue will get them onto the train, which Adeline does once it comes to a halt. She leaves her next clue under a large black rock by the lake at the centre of the National Exhibition Centre, a giant complex of warehouses for conventions and large concerts. The station here is called Birmingham International, even though it's nowhere near actual Birmingham. She then catches a train to Balsall Common, going back the way she came through Hampton. She leaves a clue under the railway bridge just outside the station, hidden behind a light on the wall. Then she climbs back on board a train to Birmingham New Street, real Birmingham, the ratio of grass to graffiti inverting outside as the train closes in on the city.

It is as she pictured it, the sun and the bustle, a sense of important things going on all around her. The canal here isn't the same as the industrial-looking ones visible from the train at the city centre's edges; here the red-brick buildings on either side are home to pubs and restaurants that boast of their views over the water.

Two shy skaters, maybe a bit older than her, walk by twice, key chains jangling, before coming over to her to ask if she wants to come and watch them do some tricks at the library.

"I've got to wait for my boyfriend," she says, although she thinks they can read that this is BS. They are nice about it, though, and wander off apologetically, leaving her alone. A year ago she'd have bitten their hands off—good-looking, scruffy boys were half the fun of the city. Now she has no interest; they'd wandered into the wrong story. Today is all about the game. And Steve.

Who will get to her first? If it's Steve—let it be Steve—they will have the kind of forced alone time that often leads to interesting things. She needs to be cautious, though: last summer had been painful and nothing that has happened in the last few weeks has cleared up why it took him until Christmas to write to her, nor where it is their *friendship* is going. There is still that unmistakeable pulling sensation when they are near, yet it's like he's fighting against it.

It isn't Steve that first walks down the footpath towards her, it's Jen. Of course, Jen. Super-keen Jen, here ahead of Steve.

"I won?" she says, beaming and out of breath.

"You won," Adeline says.

Jen shakes her head. "Steve was ahead of me the whole way, but I lost him at Birmingham International."

Great.

"I thought he'd be here," Jen says. "Your clues were fucking great."

"So glad they worked."

"So am I. I was worrying about following the canal the wrong way and ending up in Scotland." Jen looks up at a clock on the tower referenced in Adeline's final clue. "Three thirty? Bloody hell, that was a mission."

161

Steve arrives next, ten minutes later.

"You got here before me," he says to Jen, then gives Adeline an apologetic look suggesting he'd been on the same page as her about the two of them being alone here.

Will is next, racing to get to Adeline despite no sign of anyone behind him. Will reaches out to touch Adeline, and she thinks his hand is going for her shoulder, but it comes in too low, and just for a moment his palm slides against her breast.

"Oh shit, sorry, Adeline," he says on the way past. It's an accident, of course, and Adeline tries not to dwell on it. Hands on his hips, his face red and his back rising and falling along with his breathing, he looks at her with a slanting smile.

"Two points," Adeline says. "Despite all your effort."

"Which unsurprisingly," Steve says, "means Rupesh is the first loser. Was he actually behind you?"

Will shakes his head. "I didn't see him at all. Just didn't want to come last."

They sit on a stone wall at the side of the canal, talking about their various encounters on the journey to Brindley Place. To Adeline, some of Jen and Will's comments sound a little like complaints. But Steve seems to think it was spot on, says it gives them all a lot to live up to.

While they wait for Rupesh, clouds cover the sun. Adeline grows anxious, the clock hands approaching 5 p.m. She wants so badly to show them some of her favourite shops, make their epic journey worthwhile. But when their conversations begin to lull, Adeline gives up hope. It's too late; the shops will be closing. They need to head back soon if they want to avoid walking on the footpath in the dark.

Bloody Rupesh. Yeah, maybe he'd got lost, confused by one of the clues. But he never wanted to do this in the first place. He probably never left his house.

They decide to walk back to New Street Station slowly. If he's on his way still they'll run into him. Not that Adeline or Steve believe they will.

"He saw that first clue and just didn't fancy the walk to Hampton station," Steve says. "I can just see it."

Only then does it click in Adeline's mind: Rupesh and trains, trains and Rupesh. That first time she hung out with them, when Obi died, Rupesh wouldn't come all the way to the tracks with them. He'd stayed behind. And in fact, now she considers it, whenever they go to the train tracks it is always without Rupesh. Is he scared of trains? Is that why he isn't here?

She puts this to the others, just as they are ascending the ramp into the shopping area above the station.

Will comes to a stop, his hand moving to his mouth. "Oh shit," he says.

They all stop, and have to congregate against the ramp barrier to avoid the stream of other pedestrians.

"Fuck," Jen says.

"What?" Steve says.

"I didn't even think," Jen says.

"Me neither," Will says.

"I thought his parents just don't want him close to the tracks," Steve says. He turns to Adeline. "Some relative of his got hit by a train in India. That doesn't mean he won't go on an actual train. As a passenger, yeah?" Steve stares at Will and Jen, waiting for them to say something to disprove him. They just look at each other like they are both in pain, but they don't contradict him.

To Adeline, Steve says: "He just didn't fancy it. There's no excuse. Fuck him." With that he turns from them all and continues up the ramp.

*

163

They reach the Hampton end of the footpath around 7 p.m. Darkness is coming. When they finally exit Dead Man's Alley almost two hours later, Steve turns right on Elm Close, away from the farmhouse.

"Where are you going?" Jen says when she catches up.

"I want to see if he's home," Steve says. "You can all go back to mine and wait if you want."

"What are you going to say if he's there?" Jen asks. "It's getting late."

"I'll just ask him why he ruined Adie's Dedication."

"It was fine," Adeline says, although it's nice he's so annoyed on her behalf.

Jen looks to Will, Will back at Jen. With a shrug, Will says to her, "Let's just tell him."

Steve isn't interested or doesn't hear. He carries on, determined. The gate is open at Rupesh's house, and Steve walks down the drive with the rest of them trying to catch up. A statue of an elephant with human hands sits watching their approach from the immaculate front lawn.

"Steve, will you just hold on a second?" Jen says.

But Steve rings the doorbell while she's still speaking. Will and Jen immediately start arguing quietly. Rupesh's dad answers, an overweight man with a kind smile. It's hard for Adeline to imagine this is one half of the force that Rupesh is so reluctant to disobey. He goes to find Rupesh.

Steve faces the three of them and gives them an unattractive, told-you-so smile. When Rupesh appears his expression is hangdog. Suddenly Adeline wants to protect Rupesh, to intervene and get Steve away from him.

"What happened, mate?" Steve says.

Rupesh steps out onto the porch and pulls the door behind him so it's almost closed. "My parents won't let me—"

"Seriously," he says, trying to be light-hearted Steve,

laughing at what Rupesh is saying but sounding slightly mad. "You might end up getting thrown out of the group for good."

Rupesh shrugs, not knowing where to look. "I'm sorry, I couldn't come."

Adeline tries to call Steve off, but he cuts her short with a silencing hand.

"No, you worked really hard to make a great round for us, Adeline. And we waited around for hours for—"

"It wasn't hours," Jen says.

"For at least an hour," Steve says without missing a beat, "and you were here all along. Are you going to do any of the other rounds?"

"I'll do the others. I just couldn't do this one," Rupesh says.

"Because your parents won't let you play by the train tracks?"

Rupesh's eyebrows shoot up, and his jaw falls open. "What?" he says. He looks at Will, then Jen. "No. I just—"

"And you're scared of your parents? Let's be honest, that's why you didn't come, isn't it? You saw the train station clue and just went home. I mean, you're sixteen. You can make your own decisions, Rup, you don't have to do everything your parents tell you."

Will lets out a long, agitated sigh. "Tell him," he says.

Steve doesn't hear now. He's enjoying this. He thinks he's got everyone on side. He's not even in the same space as them any more.

"I just think before we go to all the effort of the next rounds we should know what's happening?"

"Rupesh, lovely." Jen's tone is so at odds with Steve's that everyone looks at her. "I think if Steve knew about what me and Will do, then he'd probably shut up. Don't you think, Will?"

"What, me? Shut up? Are you on *his* side?"

"There are no sides, Steve," she says. "Just get your head out your arse for a moment."

Steve looks like he's been slapped. He starts shaking his head.

"Rupesh?" Jen says.

Rupesh nods. "Can I just come over after I've done the washing-up?" he says to Steve.

Steve holds up both hands, his abdication. "Fine. I have no idea what's happening now and I'm just going to *shut up*, I think. Seems like it's what everyone wants. I'm just angry for Adeline and…"

She can hear shame in his voice now: his painful return to reality. It makes Adeline reach out to him and touch his arm. He looks down at her hand, surprised. Not knowing what else to do, Adeline nods, trying to convey that she sympathises with him whilst urging that they now leave.

After a moment, he nods back, and the four of them head to the farmhouse.

The lounge smells of microwave pizza and ketchup. Steve is folded up on his throne. Rupesh sits on the dusty sofa with Jen, Adeline on the floor next to Steve's chair.

"I don't want to talk about this again, ever," Rupesh says. "It's just embarrassing."

Steve says nothing. He's trapped, knowing something is coming that will make him seem like an idiot, but unable to work out just how big of a one yet.

"I don't like trains," Rupesh says. "Medically."

Will laughs at this, which surprises Adeline, though Rupesh doesn't seem to mind.

When no one says anything, Rupesh adds: "That's basically it. My legs shake and I get sick if I'm near them. I feel sick just hearing one."

Jen reaches up and rubs Rupesh's back. "Just tell them why, and they'll understand," she says.

"Basically it's my mum," Rupesh says. "She's fine most of the time, but sometimes she goes off work because she has these sad spells, and then we've got to be extra nice to her because where we lived before she used to disappear for these walks."

Adeline's heart is a cold stone in her chest. Steve is staring at the wall. This is going to be bad.

Rupesh continues: "Dad used to take me with him when we went looking for her, and we'd always find her. In a café, or sitting in a cemetery. She said sometimes she needed to find her thoughts. Anyway, one time she went missing and Dad was so worried, and when he came home I could just tell something was wrong. And he'd basically found her down at the train station, which at the time I didn't know what it meant. I overheard him telling my grandparents on the phone that she'd had this Russian novel in her bag and I didn't know what that meant either. I just knew that something bad happened to Mum involving a train."

"How old were you?" Adeline says.

"It's been all the time I've been alive," Rupesh says. "But this was when I was probably six or seven. So then every time I went past the station or heard the train I got scared. I've worked it out since. In that book a woman throws herself in front of a train. And since then we've found her at road bridges and at cliff tops. That's why Dad moved us to Blythe, to be away from danger. And I still get weird with trains. It's silly. Sorry."

No one says anything else. Rupesh, who has been staring at the floor while talking, lifts his head to look at Adeline.

"I understood the clue and everything," Rupesh says. "It was great. But even seeing the word stationary made me feel funny. I sort of worry if my legs go or I pass out I'll fall onto the tracks."

"It was our fault," Jen says. "We should have told you not to involve trains, should have made something up. But, Rupesh, none of us even connected it until we were in Birmingham waiting for you."

"Sounds horrible, mate," Steve says, turning away from the wall to address Rupesh. "And sorry, you know, about earlier."

"I would have told you, too," Rupesh says. "It's just, well, a bit pathetic."

"It's not," Steve says, and like that the atmosphere in the room begins to return to normal. Then he says, "It's only the first round, anyway."

"There's still plenty of time to catch up," Will says.

"Exactly," Steve says.

Jen stops rubbing Rupesh's back. She's about to say something when Steve stands up and leaves for the kitchen.

"That's so unfair," Jen says once he's gone. "We've got to void the first round."

"Well," Will says, "I suppose getting Adeline to do it again would be harsh, and the game wouldn't be fair unless everyone got their points from this round."

"I don't mind," Adeline says.

"Fuck the game," Jen says, whispering now. "That's just horrible. I don't know if I can stand to be around you lot right now."

"It's okay," Rupesh says. He touches Jen's hand. "I'll make do with one point. I'll catch up. Can we just...move on?"

Jen tries to smile for Rupesh. They look intimate to Adeline. Romantic even.

"You're next, though, Rup," Will says. "That means you'll be slinking into round three on one point."

Jen gets to her feet. "I'm going. Rupesh, I'll walk you back if you want."

"Thanks," he says. He stands up, offers the three of them a bashful smile, and he and Jen leave.

Once he's gone Will says to Adeline, "This has all gone a bit weird."

"Yep," she says.

"I thought your round was good," he says.

"Thanks," she says. "I was a bit worried some of the clues would be too hard."

He makes a noise of agreement. His right foot is up on his knee and he plays with the laces.

"I wonder what it's like to want to kill yourself," Will says.

The remark has barely sunk in when Steve returns. "Where are the others?"

"Home," Will says.

"Listen, sorry, but I just remembered, Dad's back tonight so I need to get this place clean."

Will rises and makes his way to the door. Adeline gets up too, but when Will turns his back to them Steve gestures at her with wide eyes and a shake of the head—*don't really go.*

"Do you want a hand clearing up?" she says.

"Thanks, Adeline," Steve says.

Will studies them both before giving them a wonky, closed-mouth smile. He roams out, raising a hand by way of goodbye, his back to them.

They don't clear up. Steve suggests they watch *Grosse Pointe Blank* again and Adeline doesn't resist, even though she must have watched it twice in the intervening year and can quote whole sections by heart. At first Steve sits in his chair, a distance that from the sofa feels much further than it really is now that the others aren't in the room. Adeline doesn't mind. She is just happy to be alone with him finally.

Fair is fair, he has made his move, so she should make the next. She asks for a blanket because she is cold, then insists that he should join her because it would be more environmental than starting the fire—although in reality she's terrified he'll set the fucking place alight the way he handles that petrol can. He does, and, not long afterwards, they are holding hands under the blanket, and then not long after that, kissing, mouths open. Her hands push under his clothes to find skin. It happens so easily; why has it taken this long?

But he breaks the kiss when her hands try to explore beneath the waistband of his boxers. He smiles and turns to the film, pulling her close.

"I thought you were brilliant today," he says, watching the television. Dan Aykroyd is telling John Cusack that they should form a union.

"Thanks," she says.

"I was just pissed off that Rupesh ruined it. Was I too harsh?"

"Are you still annoyed now?" she says.

"No. Not really. Yes." He laughs at the little journey he's just taken. "It's unfair, isn't it?"

"For him," she says. "He's been through a lot." She's abrupt, irritated by the sudden end to the kissing. She wants to go back to it.

"I just can't help but feel he does it deliberately. Not what he told us. Just, why is it always him that's doing things like this?"

Adeline goes to the bathroom, and when she returns he is looking out of the window.

"You'll never guess what I just saw? Will coming out of Mr. Strachan's drive."

"What's he up to?" she says. There's no one there when she looks.

"Exactly."

It's really cold now, and all at once she's aware of how grim the farmhouse actually is. While it is always neat—Steve often tidying up rubbish and burning it in the fire while they are all still there making mess—when was the last time it had been cleaned properly? If his bedroom is dirty like this maybe it's best she doesn't ever see it. It's not on the bloody cards today.

They watch the rest of the film but don't kiss any more. It is like his mind is somewhere else. She hopes she hasn't upset him. Perhaps he is just embarrassed still, trying to deal with the secrets the others knew and he didn't. When she kisses his head and says goodbye, he looks up at her, shocked. But he doesn't protest, even though she wishes he would. Just a little bit.

Winter, 2015

By the time I rose from bed the gang had agreed to meet at Rupesh's in an hour's time, before he went to work. Mum and Dad were already up, Dad down in the garden doing God-knew-what given the time of year, Mum shut up in her room with the television on. I made them each a cup of tea, then got ready, getting round to Rupesh's ten minutes early.

Rupesh was in the shower readying himself for a quick departure to his session at the out-of-hours clinic once we were done, and it was Jen who showed me to the lounge. Surprising, as her car hadn't been on the drive.

"Engine's still playing up so I taxied it here," she said. "What are you thinking about this then? How much did this bloke say, how much detail?"

"Not much," I said. "It was third-hand information. We managed to take a phone number for this friend of a friend of his before we left, and Steve's chasing the guy."

When Steve arrived, though, he told us the number was a voicemail bust. We all sat around the dining table again with the hot drinks that Rupesh, now in his work suit, had prepared.

"It's not much to go on, is it?" Jen said. "If it's just a rumour. There's nothing online for a dead Will Oswald and if we apply to the General Records Office it can take months. But anyway, let's say he is dead, isn't it still just as weird that these suicides happened the same year he dies? He could have done them before he died, presumably?"

"Problem is that we don't know *when* he died," Steve said. "Might've been before any of these suicides, which rules him out. This Gaz guy last saw Will a year and half ago; you heard from him, when, December? And even supposing he was alive for the Loch Ness one, we don't even know for sure that one was a suicide, not unless you've found anything since?"

"It's an obvious suicide," Jen said with a wave of her hand. "They just couldn't say it with certainty, probably because of how Will made it look. I'm not convinced by this at all. Don't you think his parents would know by now if Will was dead, or that there wouldn't be something on the internet about an unclaimed body being found or something? I've looked for that too, and there's not."

"That's a good point," Rupesh said, and she flashed a grateful look his way.

"What we know so far is that he was definitely off grid for whatever reason," Steve said. "Maybe he was living under a different name? If he had nothing to identify him on his body, and no one knew his real identity, it's possibly they might not have got around to it identifying him yet for whatever reason. I don't know how long these things take. Do you?"

"There are dental records and DNA analysis they can do," Rupesh said.

"But those things take time, presumably," I said. "And rely on there being existing records, so in theory it's possible he's sitting in a morgue somewhere unclaimed."

"It's possible," Rupesh said. "I mean, Will might have had some troubles but I wouldn't have thought he's in the standard cohort for an unidentified, unclaimed corpse. But in theory it's possible. Except how did this person find out he was dead in the first place?"

We all thought about this. He was right, he couldn't have died in such obscurity if someone knew he was dead. It didn't make sense.

"Unless," Steve said, "the fallout with his family was bad enough that whoever dealt with his funeral arrangements kept it from them, perhaps at Will's request."

"He might've left instructions in a will," I said.

"This is all complete speculation," Jen said. Her tone sounded increasingly agitated. "There must be a list of unclaimed bodies? How big can it be? Can't we phone the coroners in York?"

"If he died in York," Steve said. "We don't even know that. We don't know he was unclaimed either. We could try those lists, yeah, I suppose. But if he's been disfigured? Or doesn't look like we think and we misidentify him."

"Come on," Jen said. "Isn't it just as likely this is rubbish and the man you spoke with got the wrong end of the stick somehow?"

"Of course," Steve said. "He gave the impression the guy he got it from was reliable, though. But yeah, maybe reliable in the musician world means turns up to practice on time. I mean, I'll keep trying this number—but I'm just a bit uncomfortable now about pressing on with all of this Will being a murderer stuff. I'm not going to lie, I only half believed it anyway, and it was a bit exciting before. Now I don't really want to have to tell Will's parents that in the process of deciding whether or not he was a serial killer we actually found out he'd died and nobody had told them. That's not really what I signed up for, sorry if that sounds awful. This has just gone from odd to sad too quickly."

"You want to just forget it all then?" Jen said. "You don't think we owe Will's family this?"

"If I'm honest," Steve said with a quick glance my way, "no. We don't know what was going on in that family. I'm sure there's a reason Will lived his life the way he did. Things that drove him that way."

My instincts were with Steve, perhaps because he and I were there last night, live at the scene of Gaz's revelation. I hadn't yet shaken that feeling of shame—a bunch of middle-class professionals essentially contemplating whether our old friend was a murderer in part because he'd had the misfortune to slip down into the borders of the underclass.

"What about all the stuff I found?" Jen said. "What if those bodies have badges on? We still need to report that to the police. This isn't over. And Adeline, come on, the thing— the *face*—on the back of your car? That's like...a calling card. Like The bloody Joker or something."

I shrugged. "There *are* a lot of Nirvana fans in Birmingham still, I suppose. Steve's car was in the car park at a hotel. Could have been anyone."

"So now we all believe in the coincidence fairy?" Jen says. "Nothing's changed." Her eyes were darting left and right, addressing us all.

"Let's just take a breather and think this through for a while," Rupesh said. "Jen, you're right that nothing's changed about what we've found. But I do think we should consider what all of it means if Will has passed away."

"He could still be after us," Jen said. "And we're meant to just pretend all that didn't happen?"

Wanting a break from her glare, my attention wandered up to the dresser leaning against the wall in the centre of the lounge. Its shelves were packed with knick-knacks, decorative plates and little ceramic models with a Hindu and Indian theme. That was when I noticed something out of step with the other items, tucked away on top shelf: a green Nessie figurine in a tartan hat smiled out at the room. I found its benign presence briefly soothing.

"I agree with Rupesh," Steve said. "And all this speculation

175

on Will's mental state ending with him having died some death his family aren't aware of... I don't know."

"I feel irresponsible," I said. "It doesn't feel right."

No one spoke. I concentrated on the dresser, not sure what more there was to say.

When I turned back to the table, Jen was looking out of the window shaking her head, arms folded. "So what happens if he is dead," she said, "but then I find out those badges are on the body?"

Steve looked at me, and I looked at Rupesh.

"Why would you do that, though?" Rupesh said.

"Just imagine we decide to find the families of one of the victims," Jen said. "To stay on the safe side. And they told us those badges were—"

"Well, don't do that," Rupesh said.

I agreed; we didn't want to be like those lunatic Reddit detectives that start harassing the real-life subjects of true-crime documentaries, the ones that Xan laughed at and admired in equal measure.

"Theoretically, theoretically," Jen said, "what I'm asking, guys, is if it's not Will and it's not a ridiculous coincidence—and all the rest is the same—who else knew about his murder spree?"

Again we all looked at each other.

"Dead or alive we'd have a problem," she said. "So what do we do next? Do we try and find out if Will is really dead, which I don't believe, or do I look for the badges and then decide which of you three is doing this?" Rupesh frowned. Steve's mouth was ajar, dumbstruck. "Are you serious?" I said.

"If Will is dead, yes, I am," she said.

Rupesh stood up sharply. He glanced at his wristwatch. "I need to get going, sorry. This is getting a bit silly now. For what it's worth, I think it's a coincidence."

"Obviously I don't think it is one of us," Jen said, "that's not my point. I'm just saying this isn't done."

"Maybe you have a point, Jen," Rupesh said. "But I really need—"

"We're not the only ones that know," Steve said. "Someone else was there that night and probably heard what Will said, too. That's if we're actually going down that road."

It took us a second. But he was right, someone had been out there that night. We'd seen and heard him.

"Strachan," Jen said.

Steve nodded. "If Will was our first suspect based on his *history*, what about a guy who went to prison because of Will?"

"And we all had history with him," Jen said. Rupesh sighed.

"Maybe," Steve said. "It's worth considering, isn't it? I wonder what he's been up to all these years, whether he remembers us?"

Straight away I knew who might have the answers.

As we were leaving, Rupesh grabbed me in the hall and indicated I should hang back. Once the others were gone, he said, "Listen, I wanted to speak with you about something. I contacted a friend of mine who works on the Fibrox trial up at the Radcliffe in Oxford."

I wasn't following him, so he added, "Your mum's illness. Now, she may not fit the inclusion criteria, and of course she may end up in the control group and be given a placebo. But if she gets the actual medication they're trialling it could add up to ten years. And to me it sounds like she might be a fit." His expression was solemn, and he was avoiding eye contact.

"Thank you, Rupesh," I said, staring at him, overwhelmed. "That's so sweet."

"Of course, it might not be that useful, and your mum might not want to do all that travelling. But I thought I should tell you. I'll let you know what he says anyway."

I couldn't help it; I hugged him, and though he remained stiff, he did hug back.

"We all have to go one day," Rupesh said, "but I know sometimes even a little bit more time can make a difference."

I pulled him closer, then let him go, ready to leave. As if he wanted to balance the emotions in the room, he then said, "Of course, I remember how things were with your mum, Adeline, so don't feel you have to use it."

"What?" I said.

"Well, I remember how it is with the two of you. I know it's been difficult."

"Of course," I said, no idea where this was leading.

"What I'm saying is that I know relationships with parents are complicated. So I won't judge, or be offended, if you don't take up the offer. I mean, in medicine we have to make life and death decisions routinely—"

I twigged what he was saying and heat surged into my face. "Rupesh, I don't want Mum to die," I said, sounding more defensive than I'd intended.

"No, well obviously. What I mean to say is it's a quality of life issue, and these things aren't clear. But it happens a lot in medicine, so don't feel bad...Just do with that what you will, that's all I'm saying."

A silence fell between us, as I rifled through all the things I'd said about Mum to the others that might give them the impression I wanted her dead.

My eye was once more drawn to the green Nessie model up on the dresser, and my thoughts took a different direction.

Rupesh sounded glad for the change of subject when he asked: "What's caught your eye?"

"Just admiring your Nessie," I said and laughed. It was good to laugh. Made things more comfortable.

"It was Dad's," he said. "I think he actually thought the monster might be real, if you can believe that. A man of science, yet he thought you couldn't dismiss all those eye-witness sightings."

"It just looks a bit out of place."

"Oh right, yeah, well most of that stuff was Mum's. But yeah, Dad loved Loch Ness. He even bought a cabin in Inverness."

With that, Rupesh looked at his watch again and hurried out of the door.

Something was different about the lounge when I got home, but it wasn't obvious what it was until I saw Dad sitting at the top of the stairs, having a "little rest." He'd packed away the plastic Christmas tree and put it in the attic. On his own.

"It wasn't a problem. You know your mum can't tolerate Christmas outstaying its welcome."

"Dad, I know you think you're thirty, but you can ask for help. That tree is really heavy."

He dismissed me with a *pffft*.

"Where is she?" I asked.

"Your mum?" he said. "In bed, love."

I went up and let myself into her room. Shutting the door behind me, I went to her bedside. She said nothing but watched me with some apprehension. She was sitting up, the page of a glossy magazine open on an article about the royal baby.

"Mum," I said.

"Yes."

"Mum, I need to ask you about something. This is really important, so can you look at me please? Thank you. I want to ask you about Mr. Strachan. I need you to tell me what happened to him after he was arrested."

She tutted and turned to look out of the window. "Why would I know anything about that?" Her voice was only just louder than a whisper.

I took a deep breath, waited for her to make eye contact with me again, then said, "You know why."

Rupesh, 1998

The others are all waiting for Rupesh outside the front gate of his house.

"Okay," he says, closing the gate behind him before taking a deep breath. His chest is so tight. "The first clue is, 'Look near the grave from 1974.'"

No one responds at first. Then at last Will makes a sound like he's intrigued.

Steve says nothing but does *that face*, the one where he squints with his mouth open like you've just said the most disgusting thing in the world. Like he's saying, *That's not a proper clue.*

It's not a proper clue, though; Steve's right. He only made it up on the walk back from the graveyard ten minutes ago. He barely slept last night, and spent so long in bed this morning he only really had time to come up with one clue before needing to hide the thing somewhere. The graveyard isn't far from the house, just opposite The Nag's Head on Blythe Lane.

"So are we all meant to leave together, from here?" Steve says.

"No, of course not," Rupesh says, realising that if they did, they'd all reach the clue at the same time. "Go back home, and then leave at exactly eleven."

"I live further from the graveyard than Will," Steve says.

"Not really," Rupesh says. "From here it's about the same."

"And we'll all see each other?"

He hasn't planned this far ahead. He can be such a cock-flap sometimes. Now he is just confirming all the worst things Steve must think about him.

Adeline saves the day, suggesting they all leave at slightly different times, like she had done with her round. Even though this has its own problems, it seems to satisfy Steve. They walk off, leaving Rupesh standing on his own. He feels sick. The whole rest of his Dedication still has to be invented, and he's only got fifteen minutes until they set off.

The clue he'd spent all morning on—the one in the graveyard—is not that much better than the first.

BARNey Rubble would like it here.

More than likely it will be the best one, though, and only because it borrowed a trick from one of Adeline's clues. Will they understand he means the old barn out in the fields behind Steve's? They might equally focus in on the *rubble* part. What if they think he means all the bricks scattered around the lake, or the base?

The trees from the gardens on either side of Dead Man's Alley rise up and block out the light. Rupesh shivers in the shade on his way to the stile at the end. His nose fills with that horrible dark compost smell. His clue will have to do, it's too late now. He's so fed up he can't give it any more thought. Fed up of being made to do things he doesn't want to do. Fed up of that look on Steve's face when they are supposed to be having fun. If it weren't for Jen he'd just give up completely. He won't jinx it by dwelling, but Jen's been paying him a lot of attention since the summer holidays started. He still likes her a lot, too, and if, *if*, either of them are banned from Steve's, they really would be in trouble given both their parents' attitudes.

Rupesh climbs the stile and with great relief steps into the field where he first met Adeline. He's in the sun again, and he instantly feels happier. It would be so nice to lie down and go to sleep somewhere.

This field is never used for crops, and other than it being home to the footpath it seems to serve no purpose. He walks through it to the next field, one filled with maize. He follows the footpath through the stalks. They tower over him, and the effect of the leaves rubbing together sends a familiar spike of fear through his belly. He quickens his pace. Why does it feel like someone is following him? Nothing to worry about really. It's just because he can't see or hear anything but the crops, that's all.

He reaches another stile and tries to jump over it to the safety of the next field, one with a much shorter crop, but in his haste he misplaces his footing. He stumbles, misses the wooden step on the other side, and tumbles onto his arse in a bed of what he thinks is barley.

He looks back at the maize field, breathing hard and sweating. What a cockflap. No one is there. He grins. He laughs. This is because of that dumb film they watched last night, the one about a clown living in the sewer, that's why he is being so pathetic. That clown had been in his head all night, its laugh and its big, yellow teeth. And all that stuff about that man, kidnapping kids. Now it's the summer holidays he'll know kids won't be sticking to the roads. That they'll be out in fields like this, vulnerable.

He shakes off these notions. He's too old to be this scared about kids' stuff. It's something about these friends, and being out of school for such a long time with them, it makes him feel much younger.

On the stile behind him, a trembling cobweb links the space between the ground and the wooden step. That bloody clown had been a spider at the end, and Steve had found that disappointing. Rupesh hadn't. And looking at the stile he understands why it creeped him out like it did: what is a cobweb if not the physical manifestation of a brilliant predatory intelligence?

He's about to get up when something glints far back in the shadowy recess beneath the step. Rupesh crawls forward to get a closer look but the object is obscured by grass and weeds. Brambles and nettles prevent him from going around the side, too: he'll have to put his hand under there if he wants to get the thing out. He'll have to go *through* the cobweb.

This is just the sort of thing the clown in that film would want him to do. Hadn't its eyes glinted in the dark? Rupesh looks around and sees a stick, which he uses to try to retrieve the mystery object. It's heavy, and it takes a few drags of the stick. Eventually a brown wallet emerges, its leather strap open revealing the silver snap fastener that glints once more in the sunlight.

Rupesh picks it up. It's heavy, heavier than his dad's wallet, certainly. Inside are two twenty-pound notes, a fiver's worth of coins, and a whole stack of credit cards. He takes out one of the cards and recognises the name embossed at the bottom in typewriter font: Mr. W. Strachan.

Right in the spider's lair.

He must have dropped it when he was out walking that dog, the one that had started all the problems last year.

This is so weird, and not just because he'd been thinking about the silver-van man.

He would soon come into great wealth, that's what his mum had said to him again last night. Okay, so she is always making that prediction, and it has never come true before. And a broken clock is still right twice a day. Still...

He looks at the wallet. Yes, weird. And out here on his own a little bit frightening, too. If he turned now and saw someone standing watching over him, there would be no way to control it: he'd scream like a baby.

The barn is a giant rust-red insect hiding in a dip between two fields. It houses only three bales, long past their best. Rupesh sits on one with the wallet on his lap. He needs a clue—in more ways than one. They will be here soon enough, time is ticking.

He absently plays with one of the wallet's zip pockets, there's something squishy inside which he shouldn't really investigate further. He glances around, then slowly pulls open the zip and peers inside. The bright red foil and the words *Strawberry Flavour* make him retreat immediately. He doesn't want to think about Mr. Strachan doing *that* at all, no. How old is Mr. Strachan anyway? In his sixties at least. Jen somehow discovered his wife left him because he worked too much, so maybe he has a girlfriend now?

Rupesh stands and begins to pace around the bale, forcing himself to focus. After running through a few possible clues and next destinations, he considers the wallet: is there any way to include it in The Dedication?

The only problem is that then Steve will take charge. He'll end up making Rupesh do something he doesn't want to do with the wallet, like set it on fire, or throw it in the lake.

What does Rupesh want to do with it, though?

Whatever Steve doesn't.

Ha! Isn't that just too true.

He does delight in that tiny amount of power he still has over the cosmic force of Steve Litt: the power to disappoint him. It's never deliberate, not really. But everyone else is too scared to go against him. It isn't that he dislikes Steve. He finds him funny and clever, sees all the other good things that draw the others to him. It's just all that intensity feels dangerous in one person, it reminds him of the times before his mum gets properly bad. When she spends all day experimenting with recipes she won't let anyone eat, or starts bleaching the ceilings.

He puts the wallet down on the hay bale. No, he won't use it. Maybe he'll mention it to Jen once the game is over. Or possibly Will. For now he just needs a clue, any clue, before time runs out.

Off in the distance a high-speed train roars by. His pulse quickens and his legs weaken, but he quickly asserts control again, repeating *no, no, no, no* inside his head. He's been trying to overcome his fear through willpower alone, and this particular mantra works well. In the last six months he's managed to walk quite close to the tracks where they found Obi. Providing a train doesn't pass as he's approaching, he can get almost up to the footbridge at the lake's far end before getting nauseous. But if his mum ever wandered beyond there he'd be stuck.

Maybe he should try to leave the clue up at the train tracks today. That'll be funny, a big fuck-you to old Steve. It'll also be a big fuck-you to Adeline, though—even if there is a definite difference between *going near* the track and being *on* an actual train. She might not see it that way. Even if there is a small chance some of them might think he's really brave, he just knows Steve will do that face. And he'll say, *I thought you were scared of trains.* Not that the train track is an option anyway, even if he could use it to score some points against Ste—

Voices drift over on the wind. How long has he been at the barn? They are coming.

Cockflaps. Steve won't like this at all. He should have got up earlier. Why didn't he get up earlier?

An idea strikes, and it's too late to resist. He takes out from

185

the pocket of his jeans the pen and pad of paper he brought along for writing clues. He scribbles something, tears it from the pad, then puts it beneath the wallet on the centre of the bale:

TAKE ME HOME PLEASE!

Steve having the wallet is better than Steve finding him here.

He runs from the barn and crawls beneath a gap in the hedge, moving away from the voices and up out of the dip. When he reaches the highest point he sees three of them. The dark hair is Adeline's. The dungarees are Jen's. Will is lost in his own world behind them.

Why are they all together, and more importantly, where's Steve? Was he coming to the barn the way Rupesh was now trying to leave? Through the field where they'd played that game last year. The one behind Steve's house that he would know better than anyone.

This isn't just cockflaps. This is megacockflaps. There has to be a third way back to Elm Close. There has to be. Without another thought, he climbs over a fence into a grassy field he doesn't recognise.

For a while it's going well, the roofs of Elm Close are visible on the horizon. Then he ends up in another maize field, the wrong maize field, and he can't find his way out. He walks between the rows where there is no footpath, destroying countless spider webs. Bits of long-dead insects stick to his shirt and his face. A fuzzy leaf slaps his cheek and another actually cuts his arm. Time ticking away, he begins to run. He imagines the clown stepping from behind the rows ahead, holding out a balloon. Or worse: Mr. Strachan, a grin on his face, about to share his secret life with Rupesh in the worst way possible.

186

It feels like he might have an asthma attack, and he hasn't had one since he was ten.

Eventually the maize ends at the edge of some woodland. Despite the fence being covered by a thorny bush, he climbs over and falls to the floor beneath the trees. When he gets to his feet a bramble's tentacle is attached to his arm below the shirt sleeve. He tries to yank his arm away, but the skin tents in multiple places—like in a horror film.

Thorn by thorn he frees himself, then makes his way through the woods in the direction that feels right. How long has it been now? Ten minutes? Twenty?

He emerges in the field behind Steve's house. Once over the stile onto Elm Close, he looks up and doesn't see any of them outside Mr. Strachan's looking puzzled and annoyed. Maybe it will be okay. He walks towards Mr. Strachan's, passing Steve's house on his left. Now all he needs is a clue and a next destination, just something to buy more time that he can leave in the bushes in front of Strachan's house.

"Hey," a voice says. Rupesh jumps, then turns. Jen is at the end of Steve's drive. Heat floods his body. "Are you okay?" She is frowning at his arm.

"Yeah, fine. I—I just got a bit lost."

"Was there meant to be a clue for us at Mr. Strachan's?"

"There was supposed to be," Rupesh says. "I sort of messed up, though."

"Shit," Jen says.

"Yeah," Rupesh says. He looks to the farmhouse. The rest of them are all looking out at him through the lounge window.

The shame of walking into the farmhouse is even worse than the time he was caught stealing sweets from a woman's handbag at a school fête when he was ten. Then he had just been honest when his dad confronted him. Poured out a confession in the hope it would lessen his punishment. It had worked, and his dad remarked on how he admired his honesty. If he just holds up his hands now, tells them the truth, they'll be nice to him. Especially now they know about his mum.

"Why are you *here*?" Steve asks. He is in his chair, a cat away from being a Bond villain. The others are still standing at the window.

"I messed up," he says.

Steve looks at the others, and they all look back at him.

"I was trying to do this thing. I was. I just got lost."

"So, I don't understand," Steve says. "Where did you get the wallet from? And what if someone else had found it and taken it? Also, none of us would have known which of us was the last to find that clue. So what was your plan? It would have been left there all day with that cryptic note on it."

Steve is smiling, and he really does look amused not angry. Rupesh is cautious. He bites his lip, casts his gaze down. "I found it on the way to the barn and I thought maybe I could use it as a clue."

"Oh," Jen says. It's an encouraging tone she uses, and Rupesh is grateful for it.

"Yeah, and then I couldn't think of a way to do it, even though I thought about it for ages. Then suddenly I heard you all coming and I just panicked." He tells them about running away, and about the maize field. He even throws in how scared he was about the clown jumping out at him.

Steve says, "I thought you'd gone all master criminal on us and stolen it when you did Mr. Strachan's windscreen in last year."

What is Steve up to? Rupesh tries to mirror his smile, injecting his own with some puzzlement. "Ha, ha. As if." He pushes on past the comment. "I just found the wallet under a stile."

"I believe you," Steve says. "The receipts stashed in here are all recent anyway."

"Seriously," Rupesh says, "I just couldn't think of anything quickly enough."

"I get it," Will says, crossing the room and throwing his long body down on the sofa. "It would have been good if you could have used it as a clue."

"Yeah," Jen says. "I say it should get points for creativity."

"I thought the one of you that got there last would realise and collect the wallet or..." He trails off because he might be getting away with it, and wants to bring the discussion to a close before Steve asks anything else. He finishes with more honesty. "Anyway, I didn't think it through."

Steve is studying him, that little smile still there. "So, if you hadn't found the wallet, right, what would we all be doing now?"

Rupesh needs to swallow, but suddenly he can't remember how. As always, Steve just knows things. Like when Rupesh is using his undeniably strict parents as an excuse to get out of doing things he doesn't want to do.

He doesn't have an answer. He is seizing up, panicking. He begins to rub his arm, actually making the pain worse in the process, hoping sympathy might save him.

"Can't he just do his round again?" Jen says. "He can pick up where he left off."

"Well, he can if he's actually planned something and wasn't making it up as he went along," Steve says.

"I did have something planned," Rupesh says.

"Is your arm okay?" Adeline asks. She looks concerned.

"Oh my God," Jen says. "You're bleeding."

Rupesh looks down. He's somehow managed to get a proper wound going and a rivulet of blood has run down the length of his arm.

"Kitchen sink," Adeline says, standing up.

"I'll do it," Jen says, leaping to her feet.

It's such a relief to be out of the lounge; it feels like the room's gravity is different. Jen cleans out the kitchen sink and fills it with warm water. She rolls up his sleeve. He knows it's spineless, and he hates himself for doing it, but he says softly: "I can't do another round again. What if I mess up? What if...?"

What a cockflap. He stops talking, refocusing, trying to sound like he hadn't been panicked and scared in the fields. *No, no, no, no.*

It works. Jen uses kitchen roll to wash his arm and appears to take great pleasure in the act. She would make a brilliant nurse, or doctor even, a brilliant carer of any sort. But Jen would be able to do anything she wanted, she's so warm and clever. Why is he being so pathetic, so *wet* in front of her?

Jen changes the subject to what they should do about the wallet. She thinks they should take it back to Mr. Strachan, money and all, which Rupesh agrees with.

The two of them return to the lounge. Jen is carrying the broken chopsticks.

"Uh oh," Will says.

"Rupesh wanted to do his Dedication again," Jen says, "but actually I don't think that's fair on him, so we should all just draw chopsticks for the points and move on."

There is silence, no one speaking because really the decision is Steve's. Without even the slightest sign of the annoyance and disappointment he'd shown after the first round, he simply shrugs and nods.

"It's not ideal," he says, "but I suppose... Yeah. Why not?"

Jen isn't expecting this. None of them are.

"I mean, it's not like Rupesh gets any points for this round anyway whether we do it or not," Steve says. "Let's just draw the chopsticks. I'm easy."

Jen shuffles them, then brings them around to each person in the room except Rupesh. Adeline wins, followed by Jen, then Will, with Steve picking up the shortest piece and a single point.

Steve stares at his stub with a lopsided grimace. "Actually, Rupesh, Will and I think you should do your Dedication again."

They all laugh. It's good, and Rupesh's tension and shame float away. This is why they all hang out together. Why he loves spending time with them.

Steve reaches underneath his chair and brings out an A4 pad. He starts writing something, then holds it up to show the group. It's a league table.

Jen — 7
Steve — 4
Adeline — 4
Will — 4
Rupesh — 1

"I'm falling behind," Rupesh says.
"Don't worry," Steve said, "still plenty of points to play for."

They're halfway through a film when the discussion starts about what to do with Mr. Strachan's wallet. Do they keep it and get revenge on him for reporting them all to the police, or do they give it back and just feel good about doing the right thing? Steve pauses the video and now insists on a vote.

Jen and Will vote for the wallet to be returned.

Will voting this way is weird. He hated Strachan. Steve pulls a face at this too.

Adeline votes against. "I just don't like him," she says when asked. She's chewing on her thumb, tapping her foot quickly against the floor. She's been a bit distant all afternoon. "Why should we help the bastard?" Something's up with her reaction, too. It's too forceful.

There is a way to regain Steve's trust here, an easy way that will hopefully wipe the slate clean as far as his round is concerned. Rupesh votes to keep the wallet. This gets as many surprised looks as Will's vote, although Steve can't keep the impressed look from his eyes. It's worked. And Steve has no idea. Besides, giving it back will mean interacting with Strachan—and that's the last thing Rupesh wants. Their last encounter with him had ended with Rupesh chucking a brick through his windscreen. He'd drunk too much vodka that day, and been eager to make things right with Steve so much that doing that had felt like a better solution than whatever Steve might make him do to balance things himself. Only then, as he'd begun to sober up, and the reality of those police visits hit home, he decided it was best to stay quiet—and the others all seemed to think it was Adeline or Will, thank goodness.

Steve nods, then looks up like he's considering all of their choices. He's yet to vote, and having waited to have his say has the chance to decide.

"Honestly, I don't like Strachan," Steve says, "but he's beneath us. He's not worth the hassle. And not like this. This is all a bit...too convenient. Like it might be a trap. A wallet right out on the path where we hang out. Nah. It's just too out of our control."

"What?" Adeline's face twists with confusion.

This is turning into a strange afternoon. What's happening here? Is Steve so into disagreeing with Rupesh that he's going to give the wallet back to spite him?

"And anyway, we've got The Dedication now," Steve says. "We're done with him. I'll throw it on his lawn tonight, he'll think he dropped it there, dozy nob head."

Adeline gives a loud sigh and stands up. "Fine. Do whatever. I'm getting a stomach ache so I think I'm going to go home."

"What about the rest of the film?" Steve says.

Will gets up too, there are leftovers at home and he wants to catch *Countdown*. Before Adeline gets to complete her storm-out everyone leaves the farmhouse together, which Rupesh is fine with because he still doesn't entirely understand Steve's reactions to his failed Dedication and the wallet thing.

Jen peels off at her house, briefly leaving Rupesh with Adeline and Will.

"Are you okay?" Rupesh says to Adeline. She has one hand on her stomach and her mouth is a hard line.

Her look softens. "I'm fine, thank you."

"Didn't expect Steve to want to take it back to Strachan," Rupesh says.

"No," Adeline says. "Who knows what's going on in his head?" Her expression tightens further, perhaps with pain, although it also appears a bit regretful.

They stop opposite Adeline's. He's not sure she's right. Steve might be easier to read than she thinks. What if the reason that he's okay with Rupesh messing up everything is because he doesn't care if Rupesh is banned from the house?

"Adeline," Rupesh says before she crosses the road, "what'll happen if I don't get enough points?"

"I don't know, Rupesh," Adeline says. She sighs. "Just do your best."

"I think he'll stick to the ban if it comes to it," Will says. "He swore he would."

Adeline frowns at Will. "Do you honestly, really in your heart, think Steve is going to make someone stay away from us?"

Rupesh and Will exchange looks.

"Do you not understand anything about him?" she says. "About how useless his parents are, and how we're practically his only family. He won't hold anyone to it."

"You're well grumpy today," Will says. "Are you on your period?"

She groans, shaking her head. "Do you have any idea what a

horrible little fucker you sound sometimes? What's wrong with you, Will?"

The smirk he used to deliver the line is still there, frozen while the rest of his face expresses actual terror. She is balling her fists.

"Sorry," he says. He holds up his hands. "I'm sorry."

"I don't care," she says. "I've had enough of your shit today. Both of you. All of it."

She stomps across Elm Close, then pauses at her drive and glances up at the house. Then she looks back at them. When they just stare she makes a shooing gesture and says, "Fuck off."

The two of them trudge up to Blythe Lane. Before turning right, Rupesh has a last look back and catches a flash of black hair and black boots: Adeline, disappearing down Dead Man's Alley.

It's not fair that Adeline lumps Rupesh in with Will: he didn't say anything weird. This is partly why, after saying goodbye to Will, he heads back to Dead Man's Alley to find her. She would never have said that normally. She is blunt sometimes, and harsh when necessary, but it usually feels right at the time. Something's definitely wrong with her today.

Adeline hasn't gone far. She is sitting facing Rupesh on the stile step where he'd fallen earlier. She glowers at him, eyeliner running down her cheeks.

"I was worried about you," Rupesh says and stops in front of her.

"I'm fine," she says. He hears warmth in her voice. She isn't going to tell him to fuck off. She sniffs and lets out a throaty moan.

"Do you want a tissue?" he asks.

"Not if you've used it," she says.

"No, it's clean." He reaches into his pocket and pulls out a small pack of tissues, a habit born of his mum's earliest troubles. Often, in the aftermath of an incident, she would cry quietly to herself, and that was when Rupesh would bring out his pack for her. "Such a useful boy," she would say. He really liked being a useful boy, and he *really* liked it when she cried. Because if she didn't cry, and instead just sat there staring out of the window, they knew they would be out again the following day, looking for her up high, or where it was noisy.

Adeline thanks him and takes one from the pack to blow her nose.

"I never like to be shy of a tissue," Rupesh says, then winks. This makes her laugh, and Rupesh can't believe it. Had he ever made Adeline laugh before? He tells her about why he carries them, and Adeline's expression grows sombre. He should have kept quiet.

"How is she now?" she asks.

"She was better when we first moved here, but it's got a bit worse recently. She's started talking about how fast the traffic is up on the bend where the footpath ends on the main road. Dad's got this mad plan to buy a house up in the Highlands somewhere to keep her away from roads and trains and…but she'd still have ways to do it." He pauses. "Sometimes I…" Is he going to tell her this?

It feels natural enough, and somehow right, yet he shouldn't. It's too revealing. That he sometimes wonders if it would be better for all his family, including his mum, if she actually just did it, because then at least they could grieve and eventually get back to normal, is not an out-loud thought. Because if he tells her that, he might end up telling her he sometimes *hoped* she'd done it those times before. Which is worse, he knows. No, he should stay quiet. "No, nothing," he says.

"I'm sorry, I feel stupid for crying when you're going through something so much worse."

"Everyone's problems are different, but they're still important."

"I think your pain is probably worse than mine," Adeline says, the last part of the sentence becoming clogged up with emotion. She buries her head in her lap, a moment later holding out a palm to Rupesh. He dutifully hands her a tissue. "I'm being pathetic."

"Do you want to tell me?" he says. He is surprised by how confident this sounds, how adult. His instinct is to soften it, but when he does even that sounds grown up: "You don't have to. I can just sit here and be your vending machine if you want."

She laughs again. Twice in a minute.

"I caught my mum having an affair," she says, then sighs deeply.

"Oh," Rupesh says. She doesn't say anything else. How do you reply to that? Suddenly the little stones near his feet need moving around. He uses the end of one of his laces for the job. But he has to say something more than that, so he tries: "Are you sure?" Is she sure? What an idiot.

"Yes, definitely sure," Adeline says. "Dad's been away at this toy convention thing and I told Mum I was staying out at Jen's last night. I was actually at Steve's. But then Steve decided his dad might be coming back, which I've no idea why he cares about, but anyway. I got home and that fucking prick from next door was—" Her voice had been gaining in pitch, and now she breaks off before regaining control once more. "Was fucking her on the sofa in the lounge."

"Mr. Strachan? Are you sure?" He can't believe he's asked it again. How could she not be sure? Mr. Strachan is rather specific.

"Yes, I'm sure. I walked in and he was fucking her from behind over the...over the stupid leather sofa that Dad hates but lets her have because—"

She looks like she might cry again; instead, she growls and bangs a fist against her thigh.

"I hate her, Rupesh. I fucking hate her. And there's nothing I can do because it would just destroy my dad. He'd kill himse—Oh shit, sorry. That's not what I meant. It is what I meant but I just..."

"How do they even know each other?"

Adeline takes a deep breath. "It's fucking Will's fault. They met because of that brick through his windscreen. He's been sniffing around our garden ever since, and Mum's been all: Bill's just showing me his hydrangeas or whatever the fucking fuck. She's such a bitch." She punches her leg again.

Rupesh lifts his head from his miniature quarry without making eye contact with her, and the stile sparks something in his mind that can move them quickly away from her misplaced anger at Will.

"That's why you didn't want us to give the wallet back," he says.

She shakes her head, mulling something over. "It's my fault the wallet was here in the first place," she says. "It was lying on the table when I ran out of the house, and I knew it wasn't dad's because he's got a Popeye one from the shop. So I just grabbed it and came straight out here to get some air and decided to hide it under the stile. Fuck him. I knew I should have chucked it in the corn. Or buried it. And then, get this, yesterday—and literally this is the only time she's mentioned the whole thing—Mum asks if I've seen it. So I'm like, have you asked Dad? And she's all, well Mr. Strachan is really worried and it's a criminal offence, blah blah blah. I said I didn't have it but to be honest maybe it's better Steve gives it him back. I just want to forget this as soon as I can. Your parents are doctors: do you know if you can bleach your mind? Do those little mind zappers from *Men in Black* exist?"

"That's all she said to you?"

"Yes, well, then she said yesterday: I'm sure you'll do what you want, but think long and hard about how it would affect your father. I mean, what the actual fuck?"

"What did you say?"

"I asked her if she loved Dad, and she looked at me like I was an idiot, and she said: *Grow up, Adeline.*"

They listen to the *shusssing* maize without talking. Rupesh is angry and sad for her. Above, an aeroplane coming in to land at Birmingham Airport whines, one final exertion at the end of a long journey. Unlike the trains, he doesn't notice the planes now, although when they first moved the sound made him think of going to India, the home of his grandparents. When Grandad had been here last, six months ago, he'd asked what kind of person moved his family to live in the middle of all these fields if they weren't a farmer. His dad never talks to Grandad about his mum.

Adeline thanks Rupesh, telling him she feels better having talked it out loud. He asks her if he is the only one who knows, to which she says yes. It's funny Steve isn't out here with her now, handing her tissues and reassuring her.

"I'm sorry I shouted at you earlier," she says. "Will deserved it, but not you. He can be such a little weirdo sometimes."

Rupesh nods, then feels like a traitor. "He's okay, really."

Adeline isn't impressed, and Rupesh wishes he could tell her what he knows about Will. There is every chance she would change her mind if she knew that, like both of them, Will has his own things going on.

That the Oswalds are drunk all the time isn't even the start of it. Neither is the disgusting house, oil and mud darkening the walls and carpets, weeks-old mould growing in tea cups left in odd places. Or even the ice-cube tray he'd found in their freezer last summer, each block home to an entombed spider. No, the real trouble starts when you notice the complete lack of family pictures around the house. Instead, black-and-white photos of random people that he didn't recognise hung in their place. Will's mum explained them by saying: "We're theatre people, my love," which made no sense at all to Rupesh. She also has this expression, "Galaxy of the stars," she yells when talking about a famous person she likes. It's creepy there, and it's no wonder Will likes to come over to Rupesh's, where his dad actually finds Will's oddness charming, often talking to him about history and conspiracy theories and the supernatural, topics that don't really interest Rupesh.

Of course, Rupesh discovered there was one family photo at the Oswalds.' He came across it when searching through an ancient pile of old *Beano*s stacked up in the corner of their dusty dining room. In it three yellow-haired children smiled out, one clearly Will, one obviously his brother, and a third, a girl with pigtails who looked a lot older.

"I didn't know you had a sister?" Rupesh had joked, based on the assumption the girl was a cousin or a friend with a likeness—his family have a ton of such pictures. Will hadn't laughed, though. Instead, he'd walked over and snatched it from him. He'd looked at the picture then, and after a while said, "I thought I'd lost that." Then, he left Rupesh on his own for a long time, came back with a red face, and asked Rupesh not to mention the photo again.

Will told him a month later about his sister, Liz: a hit-and-run outside a nightclub. She'd been fifteen. No arrests. He'd listened and nodded, and once more agreed not to mention it ever again.

"I'm getting cold," Adeline says. She looks back in the direction they came from. "I'm not that fussed about seeing *her*, though. I'm happy not to speak to her ever again."

"I'm sorry it happened," Rupesh says.

They both stand, and when Rupesh looks up after brushing off his trousers Adeline is coming towards him with her arms out. She hugs him, and it is lovely, the smell of vanilla and leather all around him. He rests his head on her shoulder.

"Thank you," she says.

When Rupesh emerges from Dead Man's Alley Jen is out on her drive washing her dad's car. She smiles at him, and he smiles back. Then Jen notices Adeline behind him, and her smile falters. He waves, but Jen is already turning away, getting back to her work.

"Do you get the feeling she doesn't like the two of us hanging out on our own?" Adeline says, winks, then wanders off.

His hopes rise as he thinks about what that statement might mean. Then, as usual, concern edges in too. How will Jen react to seeing them? He should go over. Make it better.

He might make it worse.

Instead, he allows himself to savour the moment of hope Adeline gave him, just in case he never gets the chance to feel this hopeful again.

Winter, 2015

A fleeting panic crossed Mum's face before she decided on her plan of attack. It would mark the very first time we'd broached the subject of her affair, at least directly, since it happened.

"Bill, our old neighbour, you mean?" she said.

In no mood to mess around, the memory of it riling me again, I said, "The man next door. The one I walked in on you—"

"Why are you thinking about him?" She stopped and listened. "Where's your dad?"

"Downstairs, clearing Christmas."

Since that day I'd been her accomplice by omission. I'd never told Dad what I'd seen, not out of loyalty to Mum, but because I couldn't see any good coming from it for Dad. He was such a simple man that he'd stay with her anyway. The information was useless; it had only the power to upset him. The times I'd wanted to tell him, in the heat of arguments just to spite her, had been numerous over the years. I'd always resisted—a thankless restraint.

"Something has happened, with the friends I was seeing, and it's connected back to that time. His name came up and I wanted to know if it's possible he might have been involved."

She shrugged and turned a page in her magazine. "If he's still around he'd be very old, Adeline. He was older than me and your dad. He'd be in his late seventies now, if not his eighties."

"Do you know how long he was in prison? Do you know when he got out?"

"Adeline, it was a long time ago now. He used to have a lovely magnolia tree in his back garden, you know, and the new lot just ripped it up. Something about the roots."

"Have you heard from him since then?"

She paused and sipped her tea, gaze fixed on the magazine in her lap. "Do you think he's like his mum or his dad?"

"Who?"

"George," she said, gesturing to the two open pages of royal baby photos.

Years ago I might have lost it with her completely, and I had sympathy for that younger version of myself. Nothing to be gained by that approach now; I told her I didn't know and went to my room to mellow out. Let her stew and I would try again later.

Out came my tablet, which I prodded for information on Mr. Strachan. Like Oswald, it was a real googlut—irrelevant William and Bill Strachans clamouring for my attention. Strachan Blythe, Strachan Prison, Strachan Midlands: nothing useful at all. I was scraping at the bottom of this barrel when a soft tapping was followed by Mum opening the door and stepping inside. I'd not seen her vertical since I'd been there.

"What is it you think he's done?" she said, pressing her back up against the now closed door like it might provide additional sound proofing.

"It's nothing, Mum," I said, grasping for a lie that did the necessary job. Then it came: "We got some anonymous messages online, stuff not many people from outside Blythe would have known."

She shook her head while keeping her eyes down, like she was disagreeing with the carpet. "He wrote me letters."

"When? Do you still have them?"

"I didn't keep them," she said. "I didn't want anything to do with him, that man. Started off friendly enough, a couple of months after he went to prison. I had a feeling he was up to something, so when I wrote back he—" She began to cough.

"You wrote back?" I said, wanting to get up and stroke her back or something. But it passed on its own.

"Not for long," she said. "He was after something, I could tell. He kept asking, every letter, about all you kids. Why was he asking about you kids? How you were, what you were doing. Nothing about me, really. I sent him less and less. To be polite. I hoped he'd get the message. And then he started on about that boy, Will was it, the one he beat up? Oh, he regretted what he'd done, and they'd been good friends, and that he wanted to make sure he was all right. All this about how he never lied, pleaded guilty to do right by the boy. I knew what he was up to, though. I wasn't born yesterday. Keeping track of the one that put him away. So I just stopped writing."

"How long did this go on for?"

"Oh, on and off, a few years, I don't know."

"And you stopped because he wanted to know too much about Will and us?"

"Something was off about it," she said. "Your dad never liked him much, but I'd never really seen what he meant. Until then."

Much like with Will, nothing she'd said about Strachan meant much in isolation. Yet when you'd braced yourself for nothing yet found something, the effect was powerful.

"He came to the house once," she said. "It was funny him turning up one of the few times your dad wasn't in. I wondered if maybe he'd been watching us."

"When was this?" I said.

"Five years," she said. "Ten. Your dad had sold the shop by then. I didn't want to be in the house with him so I went to

The Centurion. He wasn't in a good way, Adeline. He had this burn on his cheek he said someone give him in prison—stank too, like mothballs. He told me he was struggling to find work and I told him about that fruit-picking place—they always want help there."

"What did he want?"

"To see me, he said. But he was on about you all again, about Will."

"What did you tell him?"

She tutted. "Nothing. I told you, I knew what he was up to. He was after his address."

"Did he seem dangerous to you? Like he might harm Will if he found him."

"You wouldn't know it, not obviously. But then you never can tell, can you? It was obviously all under there before waiting to come out, his criminal side. Do you think he'll cause you trouble?"

"No, I don't think so," I said, not entirely sure if her concern was genuine or whether she was relishing being at the centre of the drama. "It's just a bit of a mystery—but maybe you're right, if he's got an old grudge he could just be using the internet to mess with us from afar."

She stared at me for a long time, taking in my face, looking thoughtful. Then she pointed to her own right nostril and said: "Do they let you wear that at work?"

I laughed; how could I not?

I touched my nose stud, and said, "I'm sort of the boss."

"That's something," she said, then very quietly added, "It was an accident."

The change in tone meant I didn't really need to ask what she meant.

"He'd come over to share cuttings. Your dad was so busy then."

I waited for more but that was it. She wasn't blaming Dad, I knew that, though I could have swallowed that remark whole were she explicitly apologising. It stung, Dad ignorant and unassuming through it all—peacefully unaware of the apology due to him.

"Well, that is the downside of living somewhere beautiful," I said. Mum was still coming to grips with the reality I'd discovered five minutes after arriving in Blythe. "It's lonely."

"It was one bad moment, Adeline," she said, opening the door to leave. "But I don't suppose you've ever had one of those."

I napped that afternoon, the lack of sleep from the last two days finally catching up with me. By the time I woke up, it was teatime. Retrieving my phone, I trawled through messages: Steve, Jen, and over twenty on the group chat. Jen asked if she could call me, Steve what I was up to that night. This was now moot: the others had already agreed to meet at Rupesh's at 8 p.m. Half an hour's time. Jen had something incredibly important she needed to share with us—again.

I grabbed another bite of cheese and bread—all I could find—before heading back.

Again, I was early, only this time Jen wasn't there. Rupesh and I sat in the gloomy lounge waiting for the others.

"Do you know what she wants to tell us?" I said.

"I was going to ask you the same thing," he said.

"I have some news of my own too," I said, and repeated to him what I'd learned from Mum.

"Well," he said, "another odd coincidence, certainly. I still wouldn't go to the police based on that. And I don't personally remember Mr. Strachan being there the night Will told us, if I'm being honest." He reached into his trouser pocket, then handed me a piece of paper. Written on it in his doctor's handwriting was an email address. "Listen, more importantly, my friend contacted me. He said you should get in touch with him. Like I said, he's not promising anything but it's worth a go."

I thanked him, but now I was somewhat taken aback by his lack of enthusiasm for what I'd told him. And what did that mean? If Will really was dead, and Rupesh didn't think it was Mr. Strachan, did he think it was someone in the group?

Clocking the daft Nessie figurine again, and aware of a brewing awkward silence, I asked, "When did it happen? Your dad."

"It was only last year, actually. At the start. About six months later my marriage collapsed. Roll on New Year already."

"It's funny, isn't it?" I said, gesturing to the model.

"What is?"

"Well, that body being at Loch Ness and your dad having a cabin there."

"Not really." Rupesh frowned, then shrugged. "Coincidences don't really interest me. Real life is full of them."

Once again I was stumped by his total disinterest.

The doorbell rang and he went to answer it. He returned with Jen, and not long after Steve arrived. While Rupesh was at the door dealing with him, I asked Jen about her earlier message.

"I need to tell you about what I've found," she said. "It's better I show you all anyway. But also I need a favour. My car needs a new EGR valve and I've managed to find one cheap, but it's over in Derby—I'd go myself but I still don't trust the car—I'm keeping Knowle Cars in business this Christmas, I tell you."

"Can't you just take it to a garage?" I said. It wasn't that I didn't want to help. It seemed like a lot of hassle, though. But then, Jen has always been hands on. And if I was honest, my reaction was just a manifestation of my envy.

"And pay an extra few hundred pounds for the work? I don't think so. I'll pay for the petrol and everything. We can catch up too. We'll have lots to talk about."

She grinned at me and so I nodded. In her hand was a laptop bag I'd not noticed before. She took it over to the table just as

Steve walked in. She brought out the laptop and started to type and click, her eyes darting back and forth wildly. While she did this, I told them about Strachan. Rupesh didn't appear to be listening, his troubled gaze was on Jen.

Jen's response to my story was, "Wow, that's so weird, isn't it?" She didn't look up, though. "Just hold on while I find this. Sorry."

I turned to Steve, hoping for something more. "In my mind that sort of makes him the prime suspect now, no?"

"That's what I thought." I smiled back at him, relieved.

"Everyone gather round me and brace yourselves," Jen said.

My grip on my mug tightened and the others took their places at the table.

Jen spun the screen around to face us. "This is a bit shocking, I'll warn you. It took a while to find but I knew some horrible website would have it somewhere."

A video was playing on the screen, shaky mobile phone footage of mud and grass, the sound of muttering.

"This isn't—" Steve said.

But it was. Fuck, it really was. The mobile footage from the Manifest suicide. I wanted to leave the table, but it was impossible to look away.

The camera rose and was looking up at a huge steel fence from about ten feet away. The muttering continued alongside the crackle of the wind in the phone's feeble microphone. There was maybe one other person there, or the person with the camera was so excited he had to talk to himself. The camera came around a bend in the fence and for just a second a small crowd and a police car were visible in the distance, before the camera dropped and began to film the ground again.

It now swung back and forth at the end of an arm, occasionally giving a glimpse of a grey boot. For a blessed moment there was a chance that they'd seen the worst already.

Now the audio changed, the microphone adjusting as the camera rose again. The screen briefly filled with a section of a police car. Then there was the steel fence once more. Only now, in the middle of the screen, was a hanging girl. She was suspended low on the fence, feet touching the floor, knees bent. As if the angle of the head and the way the hands fell weren't grotesque enough, the camera started to zoom in towards the face. That close up the camera couldn't focus, but it didn't matter, because Jen now paused the video. She scrolled back a few seconds and paused it again.

"There," she said, pointing to a specific place on the lapel of the girl's leather jacket. "That's a badge, isn't it? That's a fucking Nirvana badge. Isn't it, Steve? It's the smiley-face logo. Is *that* good enough for everyone?"

"Oh, Jen," I said.

"I'm going to need something stronger than coffee now. Fuck," Steve said and got up.

The video started playing again, but Jen's demonstration was over. Only I couldn't stop watching. The girl's short hair moved in the wind. Something was wrong with her mouth. She didn't look peaceful or serene or whatever other shit people made up to make death seem better. This girl was inanimate. Fucking dead. And even though the camera quality spared us some detail, the blurry badge on the girl's lapel was without doubt a Nirvana badge. I knew because it was exactly like one I'd seen just the other day on the shelf at Will's.

Only Jen wasn't done.

Rupesh brought out his whisky, for which we all were grateful, and Jen held up a photo on her phone.

"Just in case anyone is still sceptical," she said. "This is the shower in the en suite of my room last night. Don't know how long it's been there, but Mum says I'm the only one that's used it since I was here in the summer."

The image showed the top corner of a shower cubicle door. Jen had to zoom in for us to see the details, but even from the initial shot it was obvious what we were being shown, a small finger-drawing in the grime: the smiley Nirvana logo.

"Fuck," Steve said again. "Seriously?"

"Well, I didn't put it there," she said. The hand holding the phone shook. "Someone is fucking with us. Someone who was in my house. Will. Strachan. Whoever. This is real."

No one said a thing. Rupesh stood up and held her. He encouraged her to drink from the tumbler of whisky she'd put down by the laptop.

"Did you call the police?" I said.

"I wanted to talk to you first," she said. "I can't really explain it without you lot, can I? But we need to go now, right? Show them this stuff."

With so much to take in it was hard to know what to focus on. That the death was connected to us now was getting harder to deny. Add to that what Jen had seen…someone was definitely fucking with us.

Rupesh sat back down with a sigh. "Listen, I don't want us to fall out. Obviously something is going on here, so hear me out first. The badge is unsettling, fine. It's just…" He sat up straight and put his glass down on the side table. "I work with the police, okay. I work with them a lot. I know them down at Marlstone. I'm on first-name terms with more than one of them. I know how this sounds but, come on, I have a professional reputation to think about. So before we race into anything, I want to just put that on the table."

"That's pretty spineless," Jen said. "Our lives might be on the line."

"Come on now, listen to me. We don't know that for certain. Your diary is just one source, he might not be coming for us."

"So fine, our lives or someone else's are on the line." She raised her shoulders to make a what's-the-difference gesture. "Forgive me if someone breaking into my house is clouding my judgement."

"If it's someone else's life at stake then I don't think our moral responsibility is as black and white as you're making out. People die, I see it a lot. Want to save lots of lives, give all your money to schistosomiasis, thousands saved in—"

"Death or not death," Jen said. "Seems pretty clear to me. Rupesh, I could die."

"For the sake of your reputation, Rup—" I said.

"Hear him out," Steve said, holding up his hand in a patronising halting gesture.

"No, it's not that. Look, I can't stop you," Rupesh said. "I'm not the police police. But that badge...It was at a festival. People at festivals wear badges."

"So who did the two Nirvana logos?" Jen said. She sat down on the sofa set at a right angle to Rupesh.

"I can't answer that."

"Do you think I did it?" Jen said.

"I didn't say that. Look, it's not like it was the logo of some obscure band like...Academy Morticians or something. Who hasn't heard of Nirvana?"

"Did Adeline do it then?"

"Because you didn't seem that convinced it was Mr. Strachan," I added.

"Maybe what Rupesh is trying to say," Steve said, "is that we need to get our evidence straight before we go to the police."

"I was saying what I was trying to say, thanks, Steve."

Steve held up both of his hands. We were all edgy, pushed to this place of certainty where there was no room for scepticism about the fact something was going on. Only the exact nature of the fuckery was still up for debate.

"Another thing," Rupesh said, "if we all just show up at a police station with this wild tale I think it's unlikely they will take us seriously."

Jen sighed. "Why do you come on so hard with the sceptical stuff? I don't think we *all* want to go anyway. I was thinking just a few of us go and put it to them, you know? Steve, you'll be able to put it best."

"Me?" Steve said. "You're the one with all the information."

"If they start questioning me the way he is," she pointed at Rupesh with her head, "I can't guarantee I won't lose it."

"I mean, I could," Steve said, "I don't mind, but will you at least come with me?" He gave me a barely perceptible glance midway through speaking.

"I'll go," I said. "We can do it tomorrow. I'd suggest we go now, but I think we stand a better chance of them taking us seriously tomorrow." I raised my empty tumbler.

"So you are going to go?" Rupesh said.

"And what if they don't believe us, like Rupesh says?" Steve said. "What then? Especially if lives are at stake."

"Then we have another conversation," Jen said.

We drank more. It seemed like an appropriate response.

When Steve and I went outside to wait for his taxi it was close to 11 p.m. I was drunk, and not wanting to make the short walk home in the dark I had an idea his taxi might drop me around the corner. From inside, we thought we heard Jen yelling at Rupesh. Before we'd left the house Jen told me quietly that she was going to stay to talk to Rupesh before going home, which I hadn't questioned. She'd clearly been angry with him, which combined with her general edginess had now come to a head. I couldn't blame her for losing it with Rupesh.

I made a show of being fine walking home alone, even though we both knew this was pantomime. I didn't really want to be alone at all. Not with what we now knew.

"You know I've got some old John Cusack films on my laptop back at the hotel," Steve said at the end of the drive.

"Really? I'm a big fan."

"I know. Maybe you want to go home, though, we've got a big day tomorrow."

"You're right," I said. "Thing is, I'm not tired yet."

We got through ten minutes of *Say Anything*—by which point I'd consumed another small bottle of tart red wine—before I took off Steve's jeans and climbed on his lap, loving his look of surprise. That was where I stayed for a while, this time insisting on bliss.

At around five in the morning I once more abandoned trying to sleep and called a taxi to pick me up from Steve's hotel. A combination of having slept most of the previous afternoon, the alcohol and my aversion to new beds had meant I'd been wide awake all night.

I left him a note, trying much harder this time not to wake him up. My head hurt from the booze, and I didn't have it in me to be charming during the lift back that Steve would indubitably try to give me if he came around. At home I checked the house, and even under the bed, before downing two paracetamols and slipping beneath the duvet.

Steve picked me up from my parents' later that morning. It was the twenty-eighth now, and New Year was edging closer.

"You seen my message yet?" he said once I'd taken my place in the passenger seat of his Octavia.

"No?"

He handed over his mobile phone.

"What am I looking at?"

"Our mate Gaz's friend just rang me back," he said. "Think it's safe to say Will isn't dead. Or if he is then it's unrelated to what Gaz heard on the grapevine."

The page on the screen was a social media site for posting music, one I'd never heard of. Two tracks had been posted under an image of a donkey. The EP title was *Last Will*. The artist was Will Geppetto RIP. To the left of the main image was a biography.

Will Geppetto passed away peacefully in a contented deep sleep state. A number of cassette tapes were discovered beneath his bed containing his final dreams. They will be posted here in his honour. RIP old friend.

"Basically, this guy told me someone else he knew had seen a page dedicated to Will online somewhere," Steve said. "He was a bit of a doofus by the sounds of it, a stoner maybe, so it took a while to get the story out of him. But actually the most useful bit of information I got was what he said right at the start of the conversation."

"What do you mean?"

"His opening bit was that he didn't know a Will Oswald, but knew who I meant because I'd mentioned The Geppettos in my message. Apparently, everyone in York knew him as Will Geppetto. So I just looked up that name. And turns out, after weeding out things like *Will Geppetto reunite with Pinocchio at the end?*, the only match was this page, which, unless I'm mistaken, looks like the name of a side-project. So the guy obviously found this somehow and thought Will had died, and because no one actually gave much of a toss about Will, everyone took his word for it."

I threw my head back on the seat with a sigh. "This is so odd," I said. "I was convinced Mr. Strachan might be a genuine suspect."

"I suppose he still might be," he said. "We don't need to think about it. We just tell the police everything, leave it in their hands. I suppose Mr. Strachan wouldn't even be on our minds if we hadn't been distracted by this Will-is-dead stuff."

"Yeah," I said. He was right, although that in itself bothered me. Why hadn't we considered anyone else before that moment? Because Will was such an obvious candidate. Was that why? I thought about Rupesh, how dismissive he'd been yesterday, and ran that theory by Steve for good measure, throwing in all the details about Loch Ness I'd found.

"Do you genuinely suspect him?" Steve said.

"I can't keep any of my thoughts straight. It's as likely as any of this madness, isn't it?"

He considered this. "It might not actually be that much of a coincidence," he said. "I remember Will and Rupesh's dad actually used to bond over all that supernatural stuff. Will probably threw Loch Ness in as a murder site back then because of Rupesh's dad."

"Yeah, perhaps." Something about what he'd said had thrown me.

He caught me staring at him. "What?"

"It's nothing," I said. Where was I going with this? "Just, you sound like you've given this some thought. Will's choice of locations."

"I've given all of this a lot of thought, haven't you?"

"I suppose."

"I've been wondering if he chose those places back then not just because he liked music and the supernatural, but maybe because of his love of history as well. Manifest wasn't far from Hadrian's Wall, Loch Ness had Castle Urquhart. It also makes sense that his final one would be in Blythe, you know? As it's our historical site. Am I overthinking it?"

Maybe he was. And maybe I was. Because now I'd opened

up the door to suspecting the others, I couldn't close it. And if it could be Rupesh, why not bloody Steve? Why not Jen, who was luring me out alone later that afternoon?

He was right about us not needing to think any more. Perhaps the time had come to let someone else do that for us.

When we pulled into the car park at Marlstone police station that afternoon it was almost empty. Steve silenced the engine. He took my hand in his and squeezed.

"We're doing the right thing," Steve said. "And if nothing comes of this it's at least off our conscience."

He squeezed again.

Like many of the older buildings in Marlstone, the police station was built in a time that valued function—and something of the 70s still haunted the inside. A smell of lemon detergent hung in the air, and noticeboard posters warning about sexting and cyber-crime mingled with those warning of seemingly eternal dangers like swimming in quarries and playing on train tracks.

We were the only two in the waiting room, and a man greeted us with a smile from the front desk.

"This is going to sound really strange," I said.

"Oh, my money's on it not being as strange as you think," the man said.

Only while we explained, uttering phrases like, "this was over fifteen years ago," and "really they might just be suicides," it appeared from his changing expression that the money was ours.

He took our names, and Will's, then asked us to sit down, addressing us with wariness dressed as professionalism.

"They'll be looking us up," Steve said. "They'll look up Will, too, and hopefully he'll have some old record, maybe connected with his stay at Wallgrove, and they'll be more inclined to listen to us."

215

Twenty minutes later two uniformed officers, male and female, came out and introduced themselves as PC Massey and PC Clarke. An odd expression flashed across Steve's face when they arrived. He eyed the male officer in particular with some puzzlement, then glanced at me to check how I was responding. A reaction to them just being PCs, more than likely. They weren't bringing out the big guns yet—but that was fine.

They invited us into a small office not far from the waiting room. It was so close I was glad no one else was present—the flimsy door didn't seem enough to contain our revelations. Steve and I sat on one side of the table with the officers opposite. PC Massey, slender and severe-looking, asked the questions; PC Clarke, heavy-set, youthful yet balding, took notes, rarely looking up from the clipboard resting on his lap.

We began with our drinks on Christmas Eve, our shock that such similar crimes could have played out in the same year, a year in which none of us had seen or heard from our old friend Will.

"So you haven't seen Will in how long?" PC Massey asked.

"I've not seen him since we were kids," I said. "Not in real life."

"I've seen him, both in real life and not," Steve said. "In the flesh once or twice a few years back now."

"Could you give a physical description?"

"He has blond hair and is about six three," Steve said. "His parents live locally and might have a recent picture."

We explained what we knew about Will's mental state, what Monks had told us, and about York, the independent connection between Will and the two suicides.

"York's a famous city," PC Massey said, playing devil's advocate for sure, just doing her job. "My brother was at uni there."

"Sure," Steve said, "I've got connections to York. Everyone probably does. But that doesn't matter, does it? This just establishes Will had the opportunity to do it. And that from what we've found out he was there around the same time as these girls."

Then we brought out Wallgrove and the badges. Yes, the badges, they seemed interested in those.

"How do you know the bodies had badges on?" PC Clarke asked, interrupting, for clarification.

"Well, we don't," Steve said, perhaps a little more irritated than he should have been. "We were hoping that was something you could look into on your system. All we know is one of the bodies definitely had a badge on it."

"Can you clarify how you know that?" PC Massey said.

"Our friend is taking a sort of Scooby Doo approach—well, I suppose we're all guilty of that to some extent—but I think *she's* getting into the detective role a bit too much." Steve sounded nervous. He was talking quickly, was all over the place. "Anyway, we heard there was a mobile phone video of the poor Manifest girl, and our friend managed to find and bring it up on a laptop, which was obviously a bit of a shock at the time."

"You viewed a video of one of the deceased?"

"It wasn't like we had much of a choice," I said, not liking how that sounded in the police woman's voice. "And I should add it wasn't just any badge. It was a Nirvana badge just like one I saw on the shelf of Will's old bedroom. Although admittedly he had a few different ones too."

It was going well enough, they were engaged at least, not laughing. Then PC Massey, a note of concern in her voice, asked: "Did you approach the victim's family at all? I only ask because that might be something an amateur detective might think to do in a case like this."

"No," I said. "None of us thought that was a particularly good idea." Except Jen had, of course.

PC Massey was now frowning at PC Clarke, who continued to keep his gaze down.

"So you considered approaching the families?" PC Clarke said.

"Well, maybe not *considered* it," Steve said. "Discussed it. We discussed a lot of things before coming to you."

"You shouldn't go anywhere near those families," PC Massey said. She wasn't on our side at all. She wasn't even close.

Of course, they would be convinced by the smiley faces. They were the proof that someone was messing with us. They were threats, surely.

"Did your friend phone the police when she found the second smiley face?" PC Clarke said.

"Well, no. She wanted to discuss it with us first," Steve said, snapping at him once again.

"I don't know about you, but if I really thought someone had come into my shower and left a hidden message there I'd be straight on the phone," PC Clarke said.

PC Massey agreed: nod, nod, nod.

"Well, she didn't know for certain," I said. "She didn't see them do it. It's strange, though, isn't it?"

"It is," PC Massey said. "But the psychologists tell us people have a tendency to see patterns when they're looking for them. And Nirvana are a pretty popular band, even these days, though I never got it."

"Is there anything else you think we need to know?" PC Clarke said.

Rather timidly, Steve said, "Well, we think we know when and where the next murder is going to happen."

"That's if it is a murder," I said.

"Okay," PC Massey said.

"Our friend's diary said it would be somewhere in Blythe," Steve said, then described the area for them.

"I see," PC Clarke said, for all the world looking like he was pretending to write things down. These two were going to have a really good laugh about this when we were gone.

"And you said you knew when it was going to happen," PC Clarke said.

"New Year's Eve, we think," Steve said.

"Is this from the diary?"

"No, actually. That's something we just remember," I said.

"If we're being totally honest it might be any time in the next three days, too. That is unless it's already happened and we haven't heard."

There was a movement in PC Massey's head that might be a supressed shake. And I was right there with her. It was obvious now what was wrong. We'd misjudged the power of the evidence. Through the lens of knowing Will, it appeared so flawless initially. But there was no possible way of conveying Will to them. What he had been like and why this story made so much sense. There were things about Will that could only be learned through a childhood spent with him, a zoned-out, animal-undertaking, mad-comment *colour* to our friendship with him, which made all this other stuff plausible. We'd been sitting here filling in the cracks of a wall that hadn't been built.

"We're actually worried he might've, you know, kidnapped someone already," Steve said. "That is if he's not coming for us. Is there anything you can do?"

"Do you have any idea why it might be now?" PC Massey said. "Any insight into his motivation?"

"His motivation is that he said he'd do it," Steve said. "He's a man of his insane word. Perhaps he's snapped. Or maybe he was never sane to begin with, we don't know. Maybe he always wanted to do it but it wasn't until he met these suicidal people in hospital that he found a way to do it and get away with it. No one will even notice. He'll be doing them a favour, that's how he'll see it. I don't know."

"It might be the reunion that started it," I said. "We all committed at the end of last year and that's around the time he went AWOL."

"I think you ought to be careful speculating on your friend's mental health," PC Massey said, now making direct eye contact with me. "And Adeline, earlier you mentioned your profession was a podcaster." Yes, I had said that, and often did these days, Xan having convinced me to be proud of my job while it lasted. Now I wished I'd kept my mouth shut.

"Mm hmm," I said.

"You're not recording a podcast about any of this, are you?" PC Massey asked.

"No. No, not at all. I do podcasts about old films."

"Right," PC Massey said. "Well, just wanted to check. I know these true-crime things are quite big at the moment." She gave PC Clarke a look and he grunted his assent.

"Look," PC Clarke said, "being honest with you, we're limited in what we can do when a crime hasn't actually been committed."

"But what we're saying is that a crime has been committed," Steve said, gesturing to the clipboard on PC Clarke's leg, finally showing some frustration.

"Yes, we understand that. But because more than one force would need to be involved it will take time to speak with them."

"What about the break-in?" Steve said.

"Well, your friend is free to report that, of course," she said.

"Can you do anything?" I said. "At all. I mean, what if he's coming for us?"

"I would suggest you remain vigilant, but no, at the moment I don't think so." PC Massey held my gaze. "I understand why you're all reacting as you are, given the things you've found and talked about. But this could be coincidence. That's the reality of it and what we would struggle with. Your friend might be avoiding your reunion because he doesn't want to see you. I know that might be something you don't want to think about, but it's also something we have to consider. And we see a lot of suicides in our work, lots of unwell people who unfortunately take their lives in all sorts of imaginative ways. There are even websites we've seen dedicated to such things, extremely sad. We'll do our best given what you've told us. But without any more evidence..." She trailed off and looked at PC Clarke.

"So that's it?" Steve said.

"Thank you for sharing this information with us." PC Massey stood up and held out a hand. "If you've nothing else to add, then I think we'll process what you've told us and be in touch if we need to. And let us know if you can think of anything else that might be helpful, anything more...specific. I'd probably lay off the Scooby Doo stuff, though, especially with regards to the victims' families."

I cringed. Steve gave me a look that I knew meant mentioning Strachan wouldn't help our cause right now.

"Isn't it possible one of your mates is just winding you up?" PC Clarke said. He was fighting a smile, the bastard.

The glare Steve gave him would have caused others to at least react. PC Clarke didn't flinch.

Walking back to the car, Steve said, "They weren't even taking us seriously. I don't know why I ever expected they would. The stuff he was coming out with. I know why, too."

Specifically *he*?

Before I could delve into the gender politics of Steve's remarks we'd reached the car. Once inside Steve started the engine before I'd had time to put on my seatbelt, and by the time I'd done that we were almost out of the car park.

"That policeman, Clarke," Steve said. "I knew him at school. His dad was a copper, I remember he'd always be making up wild stories about what his dad had got up to. He was the one that told me about all these other supposed kidnappings going on around the Midlands, do you remember?" I didn't. "We used to take the piss out of him a bit. Wind him up and let him go, your dad ever shot anyone? That sort of thing. He recognised me, I could tell. He really didn't like me much back then."

"I thought you seemed a bit edgy in there."

"I wasn't edgy. I felt like an idiot. I knew I could have said anything in there and he'd have been against us." He struck the steering wheel with his palm. "I bet he saw my name and knew it was me before we came in. Thought he'd get a bit of revenge."

"Come on, that was a long time ago," I said. "I doubt he remembered you." It was a weak thing to say given everything we'd already been through in relation to our own past.

"You don't know him," he said and sighed. "Will you tell the others what happened?"

I nodded and took out my phone.

When I picked up Jen from her parents' giant mock Tudor in Marlstone that afternoon she'd been hitting the coffee hard. Or maybe the coke. She gesticulated like a conductor, fired off words like a prom-night teenager.

"We have to get more evidence then," she kept saying once she'd shown me the location of this car part on the map. "Rupesh is going to think he's right now, and that I'm just completely mad. He never sees the danger. He's too innocent, that's always been his way. I think it was his mum, he just got into the habit of having to believe things would be okay because the chance was one day she would kill herself, you know? It's so sad, but when you love the guy it's hard to try and get that through to him. You know?"

Did I know? Perhaps. What I hadn't realised fully before was how Jen seemed as bothered about Rupesh's reaction to her as

222

she was about the murders, if not more so. The reason for this became a little clearer later in the journey, when she confessed: "You know we slept together? Yeah, the morning you came over and I was already there. Felt weird. But good weird. Weird, though."

Not knowing what else to say to this really, I told her about Steve and me.

"Shut the farmer's market," she said. "Well, that shouldn't surprise anyone really. You could tell when he walked in the other day that you two are soulmates."

"I don't know about that."

"Well, you don't see it from the outside. Like iron filings and a magnet, you two. It was always like that."

"It is quite comforting in a way, isn't it?" I said. "To know that some things don't change."

Jen contemplated this. "It is. But it also sort of makes me feel like a made-up person. Like if we all just fancy the same people we did when we were fourteen it's obviously out of our hands, isn't it? We think we choose all these little things that make us who we are but it's all decided really. Will just probably knew all along he was going to be a serial killer. You know, you think you can change things, you try really hard, but maybe you can't."

I asked her what her thoughts were about Mr. Strachan, but I could have guessed her response.

"Do you not just feel it, Adeline?" she said. "It's Will. It just is."

Forty minutes later we entered a village not unlike Blythe, positioned right in the middle of dense countryside at the outskirts of a big city. It was slightly larger, but like Blythe there was neither a train station nor any obvious bus stops, and all the cottages were red-brick semis that probably once housed staff for the large mansion we'd passed at the village boundary. Jen directed me in between her jets of chat.

223

"I really do think that this would make a great podcast," she said. "Us tracking down Will, him being dead, then not. The police not believing us because one of them has a grudge against Steve—stay straight here. Not to mention your Strachan stuff, that's a whole episode right there. You know? And then me finding all those clues."

"I suppose," I said. I couldn't imagine it being anything but a chore. The podcast was where I vented, where I let loose. Less than an hour in the car with Jen and I was shattered.

"I know *Nostalgia Crush* is successful," she said, "left here, but this could be a big deal, like internationally. Maybe it's even a documentary or something."

"Not a feature film? You could play yourself."

"Ha, fat chance. Some actress I am. One paid role in ten years. My agent dropped me, that's what I didn't tell you in front of the others. I'm too fucking old now."

"You know, Laura Linney was thirty-four when she got her first big acting role."

"You're sweet," she said. "But who? I mean, I know the name…Anyway, it's the next right here. One thing I've realised is that being an actress…that's a fourteen-year-old's dream. Why am I still chasing a fourteen-year-old's dream? Because I once made a promise to myself to see it through. So I'm keeping a child's promise. Funny, when you think about it. You inherit all these childish beliefs and promises, and you have to really be on it to keep them in their place. No, I'm done. If I'm going to make it it's not as an actress."

I didn't ask about what "making it" consisted of, and how that coexisted with putting aside childish things.

"We're practically here. Find somewhere down this road to park. Of course, we need to find Will really. To make the ending work. Preferably before he harms anyone else or us. That's important, isn't it?"

"Yes, but what else can we do?"

"I have some more ideas. But it is important, Adeline, isn't it?"

"Yes."

She smiled. "We'll be okay here, pull over."

We'd pulled off the main road opposite a farm, and were parked on a tributary inside a housing estate. Lots of the houses we'd passed had looked posh; the ones here, however, were run-down and shabby, I guessed council or ex-council.

My first awareness that something was wrong was when Jen insisted I come with her without giving a reason. When we were still walking two minutes later, and Jen kept consulting her phone for further directions, my unease began to swell. Why hadn't we parked outside the place?

We finally entered a gate to a pebbledash maisonette with a rusting fridge on the front lawn and music pumping from an open upper window.

When she said, "You trust me, don't you?" my breath caught.

"Jen, what are we—"

"Don't worry. Remember, this is important. And follow my lead."

She knocked on the door and before I could move—run for the hills from whatever insanity I'd stumbled into—a young man of about nineteen, acne still on his cheeks and around his mouth, answered the door in an England football top.

"Hi, are you Chris?" Jen said, her voice eerily professional all of a sudden. "Chris Kuzmenski?"

The man smiled after appraising us and apparently deciding it might be his lucky day. "Yeah."

Kuzmenski. Fuck, the name of the Loch Ness girl.

I couldn't move or think or breathe. She'd hunted down the family. She'd hunted down the family and dragged me with her. What did I do now?

"My friend and I are doing a podcast—"

225

Fuck. Fuck.

"—about a man we think might have been a serial killer. My friend here is actually already quite a famous podcaster, and—"

"Wait up," he said, his smile shifting, reforming into something more reflective of the fact it wasn't his lucky day at all. "You're that fucking nutter from Facebook," he said.

"Listen, Chris, this is really important. We need to know something about the body of your sister. Lives might be at stake here and—"

"You fucking are, too. You look older than your picture."

Even given the circumstances Jen took this like a slap to the face. Regaining her composure, she said, "That was just a standard journalistic approach."

"I'm giving you five seconds, no three, to fuck off now. Get off our drive or I'm calling the fucking Bill."

"I'm so sorry," I said, but he was already closing the door. And despite his bravado he actually had fear in his eyes.

"Please, Chris, help us," Jen said. The door slammed, but Jen wasn't done. She pounded with her fists.

I grabbed her arm and spun her towards me. "What the fuck are you doing, Jen?"

"He has to tell us, Adeline," she said. "If the police won't help us it's the decent thing to do."

"Have you lost your mind?"

Stupid fucking question. I did the only thing I could think of, and walked away. She called after me, but there was no way in hell I was taking part in any more of this.

I went the wrong way. Got lost. Panicked when I thought of all that was at stake if the police arrested us here having done what we'd just done. It was nearly ten minutes later than I came across the car finally. Jen was sitting on the bonnet. She was crying.

"I'm sorry, Adeline," she said.

I got in the car, and wanted badly to drive away without her.

But she got in with me without a word, and we drove off, all the while my eyes alert for flashing blue lights.

She'd baited him with a glammed-up younger Facebook profile picture. Like some sort of predator on the groom. Sent him a friend request, which he'd accepted, then told him she was an actress looking to build her followers. Only she'd asked too many questions, spooked him, then when she'd continued asking more, he stopped communicating altogether.

"Jen, that's crazy," I said. "You have to see that's like, like stalking. And to bring me in without telling me."

"I knew what you all thought," Jen said. "I knew you'd try and shut it down. None of you were taking it seriously enough. I was the only one." She was crying hard again now. "You're like Andrea, you all think I live in a fantasy world."

"Wait, none of us think that," I said. "But what you just did...fuck."

"I know. I am off in my own fantasy world, thinking we'll solve this bloody case and do our own podcast about it or whatever. This is who you're dealing with, Adeline. What is wrong with me? I'm such a fucking saddo."

"You're not," I said. If the dam was coming down I didn't want to be under it when it finally happened. "I'm sure you thought you were doing the right thing."

She nodded. "Yes, lives are on the line, Adeline. And Rupesh was being so...so Rupesh. God, that kid's face tonight. He wasn't much older than my sixth-formers."

"I think we need to all maybe take a step back from this," I said.

"Yeah," she said, sounding calmer now.

"Just think about what we do next."

We drove in near silence. Time dragged.

*

227

When we pulled up at Jen's parents' again, Jen hugged me, then kissed my cheek.

"Don't confuse growing up with giving up, you said to me once," she said. "Do you remember? It always stuck with me: you thought if we just concentrated hard enough we could stop ourselves from becoming like the grown-ups we knew, with their nine-to-five jobs and mortgages and... At the time it made perfect sense, but now I can't remember what we were so scared of."

She left the car and went into the house.

I was taking out my phone from my bag to let the other two know what had just happened, and didn't notice someone leave the house and come over to the car until I heard a knock at the window. I lowered the glass. It was Andrea; she had older and heavier set versions of all Jen's distinctive features.

"What happened?" Andrea said.

How to answer that one. The truth. Some of it. None of it.

"She's crying her eyes out in there."

"Well, to be honest, I'm a bit stumped," I said. "She just got very upset and wouldn't say why to me. I just dropped her home. I'm an old friend."

"I remember you," she said. "From Blythe. You were the little Goth. Sorry to grill you, it's just we're a bit worried. She's been locked up in her room most of Christmas, been on her phone the rest of the time."

"We've just been catching up," I said, then added, "though she's not seemed herself."

"Take it you know about what happened to her, right?" Andrea said. "She told you about the school."

"No."

"You know her engagement broke off in the summer, and now she's on gardening leave from the school. They suspended her at the start of term."

She'd been engaged. Why hadn't she said anything? I couldn't help but ask. "They suspended her? God, was it serious?"

"Oh yeah. She held back some kids in after-school detention for doing a play about how great Islamic State were. So she showed them a bunch of videos of actual beheadings she'd found online, other stuff too, apparently, to scare them. Make them see sense. Didn't work out very well for her."

"Fuck me," I said, and Andrea gave a grim laugh.

"You can say that again," she said. "Is everything okay, then? There's no trouble? She won't tell us anything if we ask her."

I put her mind at ease, that we were just some old friends who were equally concerned, then I drove back to Blythe. It wasn't until I got home that I saw Rupesh and Steve had been messaging the group. I phoned them both to fill them in on what happened, then headed over to Rupesh's.

It was nearly 7 p.m. Rupesh had been working at the out-of-hours centre again, this time to cover the twice rolled-over Boxing Day holiday. He hadn't even changed out of his work clothes, yet he was already on the whisky. Outside it had begun to rain.

"Now I hope you might understand why I was tempering my enthusiasm for all this somewhat," Rupesh said, the three of us seated in the lounge following my more detailed version of the Jen fiasco. "Jen and I have been speaking a lot off group and I've been getting increasingly worried. Some of the things she's been saying… I feel stupid, actually, she kept telling me her plan was to find some of the relatives but I kept ignoring it, thinking it was so patently absurd. I thought, well I hoped, she was just working through things. Do any of you know about what happened to her recently?"

I told them what I'd found out from Andrea.

"Exactly," Rupesh said. "And if she wasn't in a good way before, this hasn't helped."

Steve sighed. "So what do we do now? The police aren't interested, Jen is on the cusp of getting us all arrested. Presumably none of this changes what we've found. What next, we just wait to see if Will kills someone in Blythe or comes banging on our door?"

"It's not crossed your mind it might actually be Jen doing some of this?" I said. "The smiley faces. I mean, at every stage she's led the way on this and we've followed her enthusiasm."

Steve looked crestfallen and Rupesh puckered his lips.

"Well, it had. But I don't think so," Rupesh said, still apparently weighing it all up. "No, I don't think so. But hey, I have something to tell you both, and I think it might bring us closer to finishing all this—which I think for Jen's sake might be a damn good thing."

He topped up his whisky, then leaned forward so that his elbows rested on his knees—a storyteller's pose.

"That first night we met I found Will's parents' address in our surgery's system but I didn't find any more records for Will. Nothing locally, nothing on the national spine. I mean, you can opt out of the national spine, but it was curious that nothing about his mental history came up at all anywhere. Curious but not impossible. Especially if he was going around under a different name."

I already knew what he was going to say. "You looked up Will Geppetto?"

Nodding, Rupesh said, "I couldn't look it up on the spine as we don't have access at the hospital. The company that run the out-of-hours in Marlstone, though, use their own bespoke database. It's not as useful as the spine, but the security is piss-poor, and as I was sitting there between patients, I put in Will Geppetto after you sent your message. Your Manchester friend said he'd considered moving back to Birmingham, well *hey presto*, a single entry, from this summer. Obviously I can't tell you the diagnosis, only that it wasn't relevant to what we're interested in, a typical out-of-hours, coughs and colds sort of thing. But there was an address. In Sparkbrook."

There was a silence while this information sunk in, then Steve said, "Will lives in Sparkbrook. After all this."

"We have Will's address," I said.

"Presuming he didn't lie," Rupesh said, "but we've got nothing to lose just showing up and finding out."

"Hold on," I said. "Show up?" After that afternoon I was pretty much done with doorstepping.

"Well, what choice do we have if the police aren't interested, other than doing nothing? And I presume, given that you've all convinced me into taking this seriously, that isn't an option." He waited for a response but neither of us spoke. "I don't want to confront him necessarily, but I do want to look him in the eye now. And okay, so suppose he is really a murderer. Perhaps us lot showing up at his house might be enough to throw him off doing this hypothetical third one. Put a doubt in his mind about the fact we're on to him."

"We could maybe casually mention his killing spree the way we all brought it up," I said. That would be the most non-confrontational and obvious way to do it. "You know, ha ha, remember when you said this, what a laugh. Just unsettle him."

"Something like that, yes."

"I don't want to be the killjoy here," Steve said, "but might showing up shift the focus onto us? Isn't there every chance he's set this up and is expecting us, even?"

"Yes, there are risks," Rupesh said. "I've thought this through and if we're not walking away then our choices are limited. Maybe we send him an anonymous note telling him we know his plans. Well, he knows we all met up, doesn't he, and he knows that we are the only ones who could know about his murders? Therefore we're implicated directly, which is high risk if he is actually a killer.

"Or suppose maybe we watch him and wait to catch him in the act, maybe try and film him doing something. Again, very high risk, time consuming, and actually might lead to nothing at all. None of us are trained in surveillance. I can't even imagine how we'd go about doing that in a serious way. And suppose the only act left to catch him in is the murder itself. Then we're implicated at a murder scene, and we've saved precisely nobody, putting our own lives in jeopardy in the process.

"No, turning up, telling him we were thinking about him and wanted to see him, having a drink then subtly bringing up the murders is low risk, it allows us to see his reaction, and it allows us to feel like we actually tried to intervene should this all turn out to be more than a collective fantasy."

"I thought you said morality wasn't black and white," Steve said. He was squinting, like he was going over some complex equation in his head.

"I think doing things this way is relatively low risk where our safety is concerned and might change things," he said. "It's a calculation. But whatever we do I don't want Jen coming. Between us, I'm worried how she might react."

No one argued with this, although Steve said, "She'll be pissed off we cut her out. She's already texted the chat saying she wants to meet up as she's got more ideas."

"We'll tell her we tried to call but couldn't get through or something," Rupesh said. "I don't know. That we wanted to act straight away."

"And what do we tell Will when we show up?" Steve said. "How did we get his address given he's obviously gone to a lot of effort to keep off the radar?"

For the first time Rupesh had no answer. Twice he looked like he might respond and twice he said nothing.

"Aren't you worried he'll assume that, as a GP, you looked him up on your records system?" Steve said.

"We could blag it," I said. "Just say we found him on the internet. Or that the Geppetto guys gave it to us. I mean, if all the stories we've heard about him are true then I doubt his memory is one hundred per cent."

"If he really did it, then he'll have been actively keeping himself off public records," Steve said. "He'll want to know how we found him."

"Steve's right," Rupesh said.

"This is something we need to think about a lot more," Steve said. "It's great we have the address but I think there are too many things that could go wrong. I'm actually a bit scared if I'm—"

"What about if we just say I saw him walking on the street on my way past," Rupesh said. "We'll tell him I've been doing locum work in Sparkbrook and I saw him walking into his house. So our story is that three of us are all going out for a curry, and when I tell you about how I once saw a Will looka-like walking into his house, you two say it'll be a laugh to go and see if it really was him."

The thoughtful silence that followed grew longer, and the window for objecting gradually closed. It was a good plan, and it sounded exactly like the sort of thing we would have done. Sparkbrook was right in the Balti triangle, of course we'd go there. And any locum work Rupesh did wouldn't be easy to verify should Will have doubts. It was good.

"What if he's not been around?" Steve said. "And you say you saw him on a day he was away?"

"I'll say it was a few months ago," Rupesh said, "keep it vague. I mean, we know he's been there since the summer, so presumably he must have been there at some point during that time."

"I think it'll work," I said, my energy renewed at the prospect of it all being over soon. Wishful thinking, yeah maybe, but everything would be so much easier if we found him.

"It will," Rupesh said. He downed his remaining drink, put the glass on the table, then stood up. "Let's do it then, before I change my mind."

"Now?" Steve said. "You don't want to think about this more, perhaps without the whisky?"

"He could kill someone tonight," I said. "Of all the evidence we have the New Year thing is the flimsiest part of everything we've gathered."

"No, I remember it," Steve said. "It was definitely New Year."

"Well, I want this over," Rupesh said. "With or without you two."

Five minutes later Steve was behind the wheel of his car, rain lashing on the windscreen as he headed out of Blythe towards Birmingham city centre.

Jen, 1998

She does all her best work in the dark. Under the quilt, in the hot blackness. It's where she's always gone when she needs to think, where she writes her diary by torch light. It's also where she came up with her Dedication, and where she is now. In her hand is the cordless phone.

Through a series of patient steps she manages to get all of the gang on the same phone call and when they are all on the line finally, Steve says she's a genius. It's called conference calling, and she heard about it from Gilly Ellis at school. She found instructions on the computer using the web—her family are the only ones in the road with access. It was great for things like that, as well as looking up song lyrics, like Alanis Morissette's "You Oughta Know." Now she knows what *go down on you in a theatre* means.

What the web didn't say is that conference calling is hard work. Without seeing people's faces you can't tell whose turn it is to speak. There are a lot of pauses, so Jen takes control.

"I'm going to be quick," she says. "Follow the river from the bridge down to the big bend that always floods at ten a.m. tomorrow. Your first clue will be waiting there."

Wanting to be dramatic, she hangs up straight away.

She lies in the dark, excited. Rupesh played along so well;

he's not a bad actor himself. The next part of her plan, the one to save him, is even better than the conference call. It's been a week since Rupesh's round and she's had lots of time to think it all through. She still hasn't quite figured out how to make sure Adeline doesn't overtake her while she can't earn any points. But in the dark, nothing is impossible, and as she runs through her Dedication in her mind once more things begin to fall into place.

At 9 a.m. she sets off from the house in a cagoule and welling-ton boots. Andrea, back from university again, gives her a look like she's mad when she passes the lounge.

Outside the rain spatters on her head. In her right hand is a plastic bag. She doesn't mind the rain really, and doesn't even care about how she looks in the cagoule. Given she has to see Will today it feels safer covered up.

Not wanting to be alone with Will if he finishes her round first is one of the reasons she sent Rupesh the location of the second clue before anyone else. Of course, the main reason is that she wants a chance to be alone with him. He'll never make a move, though, and the thumb wars and playful punches are getting stupidly out of hand. If things don't occur fast enough you have to take things into your own hands. That's what Ade-line did with Steve, and look how that worked out.

And of course, Rupesh is losing and really needs to win this round. Both she and Rupesh need access to Steve's place for the rest of the summer. There's no way she wants her parents seeing her with him out in the street or the fields if they were going out. Dad's a Conservative councillor, Mum an admin-istrator for the local Tory MP, and both have loud views on immigration. They always say they aren't racists, but they only ever refer to Rupesh and his family as the Indian lot, and she's heard her dad mutter about *mixed* couples on the telly more than once. And while in a way she'd love to stick it to them by getting with Rupesh in full sight of the village, the likelihood is they'd find some *non-racist* way of stopping them hanging out full stop. She has to be practical.

She'd love to see Rupesh win the whole game too, just to shock everyone into realising how great he is.

At the end of Elm Close she turns left. She walks along Blythe Lane, past the pub and the cottages that look like they're made out of melting marzipan. It's a mile to the river, and there is no footpath beyond the pub. It's a main road and the cars pelt past her, spraying her even more.

Further down the lane beyond the pub, there is a mansion with a wall all around the garden. A net curtain up in one of the top windows twitches. Who lives there? One day, when she is a famous actress or singer, she'll buy it. Everyone tells her she'll go far, and that you have to follow your dreams. The teachers at school and her parents. Adeline, too, for whom she acted out a scene of *Romeo and Juliet* last year—although maybe she'd just been stringing her along. Who knew with her? That's the difficult thing with Adeline. She can dish out the praise, give great advice. Jen can see why the others like her. But Adeline is playing tricks too, the sort boys don't see happening because they're a bit stupid. Short skirt tricks. Arm touch tricks. Laughing at bad joke tricks. There's no room for Jen when she is around.

But she'd said something sensible that day that stuck with her, about how Jen just had to make a promise to herself to not give up if she wanted to make it. Ignore any doubters, commit to it every day afresh, and don't confuse growing up with giving up. Praise and advice from Adeline is the real thing.

But if Adeline comes last in the game, it wouldn't be a problem any more. She is the newest in the group so it would probably be the fairest way for things to go.

The final stretch of road to the river has flat, empty fields either side. At the bridge she leaves the road. It takes ten minutes to reach a sharp U-bend where rubbish often catches causing the river to flood. Here she takes out the first of three plastic boxes from her bag and places it under a bush near the river's edge. It's yellow, bought from WH Smith in Marlstone by Mum the day before.

Her clue is written in a bit of a Shakespearean style, *Macbeth* fresh in her mind from the Drama Club production at the end of term. It's more romantic to think of The Dedication as being like a quest from the old days, rather than some stupid thing based on bloody *Scooby Doo*.

She waits in the disused bus shelter. It's hopefully where the others will all end up if her first clue is good enough.

Will wanders past first, and for a moment he stands in the bus shelter's mouth, looking around to make sure it's safe to continue on. She can smell that dampness wafting from him, hear his breathing and his muttering. Shit, if he turns around she'd be trapped in here with him.

Then he's gone, running in the direction of the river.

Just thinking about Will makes her cringe. She had just tried being nice to him last year, and he'd taken it the wrong way. And she'd been drunk too. She doesn't know what he'll do when he finds out she likes Rupesh. Even now, despite what happened last year between them, he hasn't learned anything. When he talks to her, Will acts like his chin is attached to the floor by an elastic band, his gaze always dropping from her eyes to her breasts. And as much as she wants to talk to his mum about acting, she doesn't want to have to ask him. Or go to his house.

Through a gap in the shelter wall Jen watches the others leave Elm Close one by one. Steve's first, jogging. Then it's Adeline. She looks over at the bus stop. Can she see her? After a moment she continues on.

"So, what's all this about?" Rupesh says, his voice behind her at the entrance.

He is in a black coat that looks like it's made of rubber. He looks so silly, except for his beautiful, raindrop-dappled face.

"This is about you not getting kicked out of the group," she says, reaching into the bag and taking out a pink box. She opens it and takes out the paper slip inside. "You'll need to remember this clue in case anyone asks."

"Why are you doing this for me?" he says. He's holding the little note she gave him the day before, slipped into his hand when the others weren't looking.

"You have one point, you need help," Jen says, and once he's read the clue, she puts it back in the pink box and leaves it hidden beneath the bench.

By the lake, just off the muddy footpath in a patch of overgrown woods, a yellow salt bin has been abandoned. Jen's plan is to hide the third clue inside—if it will open. Otherwise she'll put it underneath.

She thinks of this whole place, the lake and the muddy surrounds, as being Will's—because this is where she once found him digging holes, searching for Roman ruins he'd said, based on some mad theory he had. She doesn't like coming here really, but knows it's a great place for the game, and she wants very much for her round to be one of, if not *the*, best.

They stomp across the scrub to the salt bin. A train hoots in the distance. Jen looks over to Rupesh, who gives her a little nod just to let her know he's fine. When they reach the bin, Rupesh steps to one side and pulls up the lid, only his feet slip and he loses his balance, ending up slightly behind the bin on the floor.

"Oh, rank," he says.

"What?" Jen says.

"Don't come around."

Only she does. It's not disgusting, not really. It is just sad. It looks like some animal, maybe a sheep or a fox, has died. Only its dirty bones remain. Lots of them, little bones and big bones.

"That's more than one animal," Rupesh says. His face contorts in disgust.

"How can you tell?" Jen says.

"Skulls," he says.

No wonder Will likes it here, this graveyard for animals. The other week he said to her that animals didn't have souls. What did that even mean? A shiver rattles her bones.

"Could one of them be a cat?" Jen says. It's silly; she knows Will has nothing to do with this really. More likely it was something to do with one of the creepy fishermen that lurked around the lake sometimes, perhaps one of their dogs died or they'd dumped some strange, unwanted bait here.

"I don't know. I don't think so," Rupesh says.

She takes out a red gift box from the plastic bag. "I can't leave it here now," she says. They scramble through the foliage, back to the path from where the yellow bin is only partially visible.

"Leave it here," Rupesh says. "Just off the path. They'll find it."

She bends down and tucks the box underneath the leaves of a shrub, one red corner just visible. She stands a moment longer, staring into the woodlands. Then she feels a tug, and realises Rupesh is holding her hand.

"It's fine there, come on," he says, and when he squeezes, she squeezes back.

It's another half an hour to the fruit farm, located almost exactly halfway between Blythe and Hampton. On the way along the footpath they see Mr. Strachan approaching with his horrid dog and dash into the maize to hide from him. He snorts up what sounds like a giant wad of phlegm and spits it on his way past them. It lands somewhere near where they are standing and they both grimace at each other.

"Do you think he's really doing what Steve thinks?" Rupesh says when he's gone.

"I can believe it," Jen says. "He's pretty rancid. But who knows? Steve has too much imagination. To be honest, Will scares me more than him."

"Really?" he says. "Will's okay."

"Yeah, well I don't think so. There's things about him I know that you wouldn't like. Things he's said to me."

"Oh," he says, looking very worried now.

From the footpath you could walk straight through the perimeter bushes into the back of one of the fruit farm's orchards. The air is pungent: mud and wet straw. Running parallel to the footpath on the other side of the bushes are twenty tatty wooden boxes lined up in a row. Beehives. They're like the filing crates in Mum's back office.

She kneels to place another gift box behind the fourth beehive along, the whole while remaining so nervous about that lip at the bottom. No bees leave or enter while she's on her hands and knees, although they are close, she hears them buzzing nearby, in the trees and the grass.

Once she's made the drop she leaps to her feet and back to Rupesh who is waiting over by the gap in the bushes looking wary, not unusual for him, though this time he has a specific reason.

"Jen, isn't Adeline allergic to bees?" he says.

"Oh, is she?" Jen says, allowing the actress to take over.

"Will said she told you while I was away?"

"Oh yeah, I remember." Of course she does, that's the whole reason she's chosen this place. It's only fair, after all. It had been Adeline's thoughtlessness that had cost Rupesh his points in the first round—her saying she didn't know is a load of rubbish. Surely she'd noticed Rupesh never came with them to the tracks? Now she'll probably come last and Rupesh will come first—a good trade. "But yeah, like, I've got a cat allergy but I still have cats."

"Will said it was like *My Girl*," Rupesh said. "That kid dies."

"Films aren't real life, Rupesh. Don't worry about it." She walks past him and hopes he'll follow. Would he care this much if it was anyone other than Adeline? If it were her? She hears his sceptical hum, *his* sound, like bees buzzing, but then she hears him jogging to catch up.

It will be fine. There weren't even any bees there.

The two of them walk side by side at the edge of the maize field behind Steve's house.

They are counting the rows. One…two…three…four… five…

There is still a light rain, and they are all going to get soaked going into the rows to retrieve the clue, if they weren't already. But it's too late to do anything about it now.

Thirteen…fourteen…fifteen.

They stand not far from where the base was that day.

"You wait here," Jen says. "Just shout when you can't see me any more."

"Okay."

Jen enters the maize, her almost empty bag in hand. Thankfully the fibrous leaves are far enough apart on either side not to touch her, and they've prevented the ground from getting wet. It's always eerie in here though, with the hissing of the maize and the forlorn calls of the crows above. She's grateful Rupesh is nearby.

"Stop," Rupesh says.

When she turns she is surprised at how far she's come. She

242

can't see Rupesh either, but can just make out the light where the rows end. She reaches into the bag and pulls out the final box. It's blue, the colour of the imaginary sky in all her planning. Ironic given the rustle of the stalks in the wind and the patter of rain on the leaves. She crouches, sets the box down on the soil, and checks one last time that the final clue is definitely inside.

"What's this clue?" a voice asks.

She nearly screams. She loses her balance and falls onto her bum. It's just Rupesh.

"Sorry," he says. "I thought you'd hear me coming. I forgot it's impossible, isn't it?"

Agreeing, she hands him the box and he reads from the paper strip inside. She's a bit embarrassed, and a bit annoyed.

"*Beware raptors*," Rupesh says.

"We're going to jump out at them," she says. "We'll hide and wait a few rows across. Tell me when you can't see me any more," she says and steps into the next row, then the next, then the next.

"I can barely see you now," he says.

Jen sits down. "What about now?"

"No, only if I really looked hard, or if I was crawling along the floor."

He comes through the row then, sitting opposite her on the dry floor, mirroring her, his legs crossed so that their knees are almost touching.

"I'm glad you're here," she says when the wind and the rainfall intensify in tandem.

"I'd have been too scared to sit and wait in here," Rupesh said.

"I never planned to do it this way if you weren't with me."

It's the words, *with me*. They affect him, his posture stiffens. She's chosen these words deliberately, too, hoping they would have that power, confident they might.

He's going to say something, she can read it in the uncharacteristic hardness of his expression, jaw tight, eyes askance.

"Do you want me to read your fortune?" he says.

"Maybe," she says. "I don't know. Does it hurt?"

"No. Well, it's not meant to. Depends what it says, I suppose."

He reaches and takes her hand, bringing himself closer. He runs his finger down the lines on her palm, and pleasure pulses up her arm and through her whole body, and after a few seconds another shiver runs up her back, this one so wonderful she can't help but moan a little. It's so embarrassing, and he feels her tense up, and asks if she's okay.

"This is your lifeline," he says, the pad of his index finger sliding across a groove in her hand. "Yes, it's going to intersect with your wealth line, which means you'll come into some money at some point in the distant future. Just before your fiftieth birthday."

"Do you really know what you're doing?"

"Of course," he says, and his fingers move to her wrists and the sensation is so intense it's almost unbearable. She fights the urge to drag her hand away. "And your fate line meets your lifeline here, which probably means you'll meet the man you marry around the age of thirty."

"Oh good, plenty of time to get my career in place first."

"Your career line looks good, actually," he says, and his smile gives him away.

"Career line? You're making this up." She leaves her hand with him, though, and for a while he just continues stroking and doesn't say a thing.

She closes her eyes, moans again, then isn't at all surprised when she smells his girly scent nearby, hears the creaking of his rubber coat, and feels his cold lips on hers. Inside she burns.

They fall onto their backs, and kiss so much her lips tingle.

They're still kissing when Steve reaches the clue. They hadn't noticed his approach, and Jen is still stupefied from what's just happened. But Rupesh takes control, and jumps out at Steve when he takes the paper slip from inside the box.

"Fucking hell," she hears, followed by the sound of a scuffle.

"Hey, it's just me," Rupesh says.

"What are you doing?" Steve says, agitated. Jen gets up and steps through the rows.

Rupesh is on the floor, the open box nearby. Steve stands over him ready to attack.

"You okay?" Jen says.

"Yeah," Steve says, though she wasn't asking him. Rupesh has a cut on his cheek.

"Did you hit him?" she asks Steve.

"Sorry. I just...It was just instinct." To Rupesh he holds out a hand and helps him up, apologising. "You got here first then, Rupesh?"

"Yeah," Rupesh says. He is glaring at Steve.

"That's...good," Steve says. "Well done. The comeback's on, then."

Jen nods, then explains that they'll have to set the box back up and wait for the next person to come.

They don't have to wait long before the next person arrives. Adeline. Ha. She knew that stuff about the bee allergy had been an attention-seeking lie. Here she is, no later than she would have been had she left the clue any place. Typical.

They all pile onto her without mercy. Adeline screams. Jen accidentally knees Adeline in the side, and apologies. Adeline doesn't even appear to have noticed. All four of them lie on the ground in a heap. The fact she's here doesn't matter now, she's still only got two points.

"You found the clue okay then?" Rupesh says. They get to their feet.

"Yeah, it was right there at the entrance to the beehives," she says, then looks to Jen, "which was good as I probably wouldn't have been able to get it if it had been any further in. Did you forget?"

"What?"

"I'm allergic." Adeline's smiling, but her face reminds her of a fish caught on a line. There's pain underneath. She's annoyed her. Good. Fair is fair, at least she knows how Rupesh felt now.

"Right," she says. "I'm sorry, we did talk about that." Then she realises what she's said and quickly allows actress Jen to take control. "Rupesh and me did, the other day, didn't we? But we thought it wasn't serious, you know. It's not like it can *actually* kill you…"

Rupesh doesn't back her up, instead he just makes that sound.

"So hang on," Jen says. "Steve, why was the clue not where I left it?"

"I couldn't let Adeline go in there with her allergy," he says, his little smile directed only at Adeline. Ugh. "Have you not seen *999*? That's serious."

"So you helped Adeline?" Jen says. "Isn't that a forfeit?"

"When did you and Rupesh talk about Adeline's allergy?" Steve says. "Were you discussing it with relation to the game? Because that's not really allow—"

"I didn't mention the game," she says quickly, overwhelmed by the sensation that Steve somehow knows about her plan with Rupesh. He couldn't possibly, and yet, the way he is smiling now makes her think he does.

A long time passes where the only sound is the rain on the crops. Then they agree they need to take their final places for Will, and Steve starts doing the game maths out loud: he and Jen are top with seven points, and Will and Rupesh are both on five points.

They form two camps on either side of the fifteenth row, three rows across, waiting for Will to claim his one point.

From where Jen and Rupesh sit they can hear Adeline and Steve whispering, giggling.

"Did he really hit you?" Jen says.

"Yeah," Rupesh says, and laughs. "But it was instinctive."

She finds his laugh painfully lovely, and she reaches up to stroke his still bleeding cheek. Sometimes she hates Steve, even if his stupid schemes allow for things like this to happen.

When she lowers her hand Rupesh clasps it in his. She leans over and kisses him again. She doesn't want the others to get here. She wants to stay in the maize for ever, fuck the future, and her parents, and stupid sixth-form college.

But no, it would end, wouldn't it? Everything comes to an end, no matter how much you want a pause button or a drug that slowed down time.

A melancholy like nothing she has ever felt before overwhelms her. And she clutches Rupesh's hand so tightly in hers he says, "Ow," and in irritation she throws it back to him.

"Fine," she says.

"Just a bit tight."

She is getting cold now, her teeth are starting to chatter. Beads of rain collect at the end of her nose that she can't be bothered to wipe away.

After what could have only been half an hour but that felt like twelve, they give up and return to Elm Close. Will hasn't shown. The rain has stopped finally, and outside Steve's house they say their goodbyes. They are about to head their separate ways until the evening when Will emerges from Mr. Strachan's house and starts down towards them.

"What is he doing there?" Steve says.

"Have I missed it?" he says when he reaches them.

"Yes," Adeline says. "We've been waiting out in the fields for you."

"We're freezing," Jen says, her voice a little shrill.

Will's gaze drifts down to where she and Rupesh are holding hands once again. She considers letting go, allowing him to find this out more gently. But then another raindrop falls from her hair and down her nose, making her itch. Now is as good a time as any.

When he sees their hands something flashes on his face, some electrical pulse in his funny little head.

He looks up and shrugs. "Soz. I lost the time, and when I found it again I realised I'd probably missed it all anyway. I'll make it up."

There is a collective sigh, though Will and Steve are staring at one another now.

"Why are you at his place?" Steve says.

He shrugs.

Jen can't believe this. Will and Mr. Strachan? Where had this come from?

"He was just showing me some stuff he's got," Will says. "He's all right, to be fair."

"You know he's probably grooming you?" Steve says.

"He's not like that." Another shrug. "He's all right."

"I just give up," Steve says, and walks back to his house. "I'll see you all later. Will, you get one point."

No one else knows what to say to him. Jen should be furious; he's wasted her time with this round. Strangely she doesn't care. That he sees her and Rupesh is enough. Without ceremony they drift apart, Jen holding Rupesh's hand right up until the point that they will be visible from Jen's house. When she turns back, she sees Will still standing there, watching them.

Winter, 2015

It was hard to tell from all the way across the road, and through the gap I'd made in the fogged windows of Steve's car, but the lanky man exiting the end-of-terrace looked like it might really be Will Oswald. He was wearing a blue cagoule and a beanie, but the gait and height were a match enough for me. We'd been parked on the street opposite his house painstakingly going over our approach when Rupesh noticed him leaving.

"What do we do?" I said from the passenger seat.

"Follow him," Steve said, sounding uncertain. "Or wait."

We watched Will walk to the end of the road and disappear down an alley.

Steve took my phone from me and scanned the already-open Google maps. "We can try and drive on down the road, we might be able to catch up to him on the other side."

When no one offered a better plan, he handed my phone back and started the engine. He took the next left, then a right, getting deeper into the maze of conjoined houses.

"What exactly are we doing?" I said.

"Let's just see where he goes," Rupesh said.

After almost ten minutes of keeping a distance, ducking in and out of car parking spaces, the man we were following arrived at a main road. When we reached the same junction in the car he was no longer visible, having turned right. Not much further down the road in that direction was a pub called The Centurion—the same name the pub in Blythe went under these days.

"So if he's in there, what's our plan?" I said.

"We're just out for a curry," Rupesh said, "and popping in for a quick drink before we eat. This is perfect, we can just *accidentally* run into him. It's even better than my stupid locum story."

To me, the pub didn't exactly look like the sort of place any of the three of us would voluntarily opt to enter on a night out, but on the inside it wasn't so bad. It was quiet, and the few men propped up at the bar didn't give us the Wild West eyes when we approached.

I could see across to the far end of the room now and the man we'd been following, the man who was without doubt Will Oswald now he was out of his beanie and coat, sat at a table facing our direction but gazing down at his pint.

"It's him," I said through my teeth. "It's actually fucking him."

"I know," Steve said. "Let's just get the drinks in and be normal."

Once we'd been served we followed Rupesh to a table near Will, but before we could he looked up.

"Hello, hello," he said in a baritone untouched by time. He appraised us without cracking a smile. Was that the look of a man surprised by the appearance of three old friends or the look of a killer working out what his next move should be? I swore I could see his fight or flight responses warring behind his flat expression.

"Will Oswald," I said.

"I can safely say I didn't expect this tonight," he said, his brow creasing.

Immediately I was decoding what he said, working out if this might have a double meaning.

Then he addressed Steve, his expression a fraction more severe: "What are you doing here?"

We sat at Will's table without being invited. I held my wine two-handed and close to my chest, my shield. This was him, Will Oswald: the Holy Grail, the Ark of the Covenant, our fucking McGuffin. His hair was still blond and unkempt, his manner just as slow and indecisive as it was in my memory. So much was different, though: cheekbones jutting from skin so white capillary networks were visible, corneas waxy and reddened— the right eye in particular, which didn't quite look out at us in the same way the left one did. Strachan's legacy.

"How have you been?" I said.

"Better," he said. Did he mean he'd *been* better, or that his life was better now than at some previous time?

I began spinning him the story we'd settled on in the car. If he thought it odd he gave nothing away. We'd decided to bring up the visit to his parents, but not the trip to see The Geppettos, reasoning that Will would be more likely to see the former than the latter—it couldn't have been him I saw in Manchester. And we didn't want to make it obvious we'd been hunting him down.

"How they all doing?" he said. "I don't see them much these days."

"Yeah, they seemed good," I said. "We weren't there long, just popped in on the off chance while we were out walking. Your brother mentioned your music stuff to us. I had no idea you liked punk. You weren't into it when we were friends." Feeling brave, I added: "You were into, like, Nirvana and all those grunge bands."

"My crowd at sixth form, at Arden, were big into skating and weed and all that. They listened to a lot of punk so...I don't remember much of that time, you know?" He laughed, the first crack in his icy front. "Maybe overdid it a bit."

"We probably knew a few of the same crowd," I said. "It's

251

funny, we were talking about all the old times. All the stupid things we did. Do you remember much of it?"

"I remember watching a lot of films." We all laughed at this. "And that game," he said, gesturing towards Steve with his pint.

"The Dedication," Rupesh said.

"You did one with balloons," Steve said. "It was brilliant."

We moved on to his absence at the reunion. Will's reply was to shrug. "I don't think I got an email from anyone."

"You replied," Steve said. "We saw it."

He shrugged. "Don't think so. To be fair, I've not been on the internet a lot lately." He looked at Steve. "I decided to go a bit AWOL from life."

"Everyone wanted to know how you were doing," I said. "No one could stalk you on Facebook."

Steve laughed at this. Will didn't. He nodded earnestly. "Got rid of that. I decided all that stuff's bad for people. What is it even? Just adverts, all of it."

He turned things on us, asking about us and our lives, and we obliged as much as we could.

"You still doing therapy?" he said to Steve.

"My degree, you mean?" he said. "Been a while since then. No, I'm in health management now. Sell-out."

No smile at all from Will. Then he asked about Jen, at which point Rupesh promptly swung the spotlight back around.

"What about you?" His tone almost patronising. "What occupies your days?"

"Not much at the mo," Will said. "I suppose I'm unemployed."

Already a picture of Will was developing that contrasted with what I would have expected from a man committing a complex series of murders. His appearance, where he lived, everything he was and wasn't saying. He barely looked able to feed himself. But then perhaps this explained his actions partly. Poverty, status anxiety—I'd read *The Spirit Level*. Were the killings an expression of his need to reassert power over the world? It was hard not to feel both sorry for him and guilty about rocking up here to harass him.

When I reached the end of my drink, I went to the bar to get the next round, aware now of that corset of anxiety clutching my core. Rupesh came with me.

"I don't know what I was expecting," Rupesh said, "but I haven't a bloody clue. Do you?"

I shook my head.

"We need to move the conversation on somehow," he said. "Just get something out of him."

The barman needed to change one of the barrels, and when we turned back to the table in the corner Will and Steve were talking. Hopefully Steve was drawing something from Will, charming him. But by the time the pints were poured, and we were back at the table, their conversation had petered out and Steve looked glum.

Rupesh was right, it was time to go for it now.

"Hey, do you remember the big campfire we had before we went off to sixth form?" I said.

"Vaguely," Will said.

"What about your murder spree?"

"What?"

Shit. Too much. I sensed the others' tension. Ignoring them, I kept my attention on Will and focused on maintaining a jolly expression. He looked blankly at me. No smile, no frown.

"I remember that," Rupesh said from somewhere on Mars. "That was hilarious."

"You know," I said. "You said you wanted to be a serial killer, bump off three people." I forced myself to laugh.

It was so transparent, so obvious now it was out in the open. But *he* didn't see that. Hopefully.

"Oh yeah," he said. He gulped from his pint, then gave a long *ahhhhh*. "That's what I've been doing this last year, actually."

A correct reaction was crucial now; we needed to respond in a way fitting to the various versions of what might be reality: laugh without restraint in case Will was just joking, not overdo it such that a Will that did actually commit those crimes would now become suspicious of our real intent.

I couldn't see Steve or Rupesh to rate their acting, but it sounded like their combined laughter managed to hit the sweet spot. A line I'd heard somewhere floated by, not entirely right for the situation, but I grabbed it gratefully: "Good for you, it's a growth industry."

"I probably said a lot of random shit," Will said. "People are always saying that about me."

"But this was your magnum opus of random," Steve said.

"You don't remember that at all?" Rupesh said.

Steady now, we needed to be careful.

"Nah," Will said.

"Nothing about a drowning at Loch Ness?" Rupesh said. "Or hanging someone at a festival?"

I couldn't imagine this insubstantial man having the strength to string up a drugged body.

"I remember burying your dog," Will said to Steve. "What was she called?"

"He," Steve said. "Obi."

"Obi, yeah."

"And I remember that other dog."

Steve didn't appear to know how to react. Something about Will's manner interested me. He was jousting with Steve, just as Rupesh had the first time we had all been at The George. It was a polite joust, but the lances were still sharp.

"Which dog?" Rupesh said.

"The dog we thought we were rescuing," he said. "Mr. Strachan's."

"That was a bad time," Steve said.

"Yeah, it was," Will said, and it fell quiet again. Before I could ask him what he meant by *thought we were rescuing*, he finished off his drink, then said to Steve, "You getting the next one in?"

"Sure." He looked at me, then Rupesh. "What you having?"

"Lager if you're heading to the bar."

"I am." He paused to finish his own drink before getting to his feet.

Once Steve was gone, Will pulled out his beanie from his pocket and put it back onto his head. He stood up.

"You're not going?" Rupesh said.

"Yeah," he said. "Think I'll go to the pub round the corner. Nothing against you two. I just don't think a reunion with *him* in is for me."

"Steve?" I said.

"I'm happy you're all doing well," he said, glancing over at the bar.

I had to stop him, slow him down, so that Steve could get back and fix it.

"I'm just trying to move on, if you get me," he said.

"What did you mean about the dog?" I said, trying to stall.

"We just got him wrong," Will said. "Strachan. Ask him." He gestured to the bar where Steve was looking over, puzzled.

"What did we get wrong?" Rupesh said.

"Sorry, it was nice seeing you." He holstered his hands in the cagoule's pockets, turned and walked towards the exit.

This was it, our last chance to do something. I panicked.

"Will." I tried injecting as much joviality into my delivery as I could. He turned back, halfway between the door and the table. "Don't kill anyone, okay?"

He stared at me, his face stony. Heat coursed to my cheeks: it sounded so absurd. Yet there was something else underneath his expression again—recognition of the call back to his earlier joke maybe. Or more than that?

With a half-smile, Will nodded and said, "Okay," then left the pub.

"Tell me he's gone outside for a cigarette?" Steve said, returning from the bar. That he hadn't bought a round again suggested he already knew better.

"He left us," I said, still watching the space where he'd last been. I told him what Will had said, and Steve seemed to wilt.

"What did I do?"

"Dunno," Rupesh said. "He asked us to ask you about Strachan's dog."

"That's crazy," Steve said. "It's nearly twenty years ago, for fuck's sake. If anyone should—" He cut himself off and shook his head once. "I don't know what he means. That's just...crazy."

"It is crazy," Rupesh said, and got up. "Come on, if we hurry we can get back before him."

"What do you mean?" Steve said.

"He said he was going to another pub," Rupesh said. "Let's go look through his windows at least, see if we can't see something incriminating. I told you, we've done the hard part. I want this over tonight."

We didn't see Will on the drive back to his house and parked around the corner. The rain had stopped but there was a cold wind blasting through the street. Steve knocked on the door and got no reply. All the lights were off.

Ratty net curtains obscured the front window, so Rupesh tried the gate to the right of the house and it opened.

"I'll just be a few seconds," he said.

What the fuck was he doing? "Rupesh," I said.

"I need to see something," Rupesh said, and left us standing at the front of the house. No one else was around, which was fortunate given that our frequent nervous scanning made us look suspicious as hell.

"I don't know what he thinks he's going to find," Steve said. "I think we should go. Reassess."

"Something's got into him," I said.

"Jen?" Steve said. I shivered and folded my arms. "Do you want my coat?"

"No, I'm fine."

Steve stepped forward and pulled me to him, rubbing my back with his hands.

We leapt apart when the front door rattled, then opened. Rupesh's face appeared in the gap.

"What the fuck?" I said.

"Back door was open," he said and shrugged. "Come on."

Steve and I looked at each other, then around the street once more.

"Shit," Steve said.

We left the lights off, but the incoming streetlight made it clear the place was long overdue a renovation: the wallpaper was coming away in places, stains marked the ceiling, and the stink of damp permeated every part of the house. Most of the rooms were not just sparse but empty. Investigating each room our footsteps echoed on the hard floors. Only a teabag on the kitchen draining board and a mostly used tube of toothpaste in the upstairs bathroom indicated anyone might live here. We reached the bedroom last, and inside were five cardboard boxes full of clothes, arranged around a mattress and some blankets in the room's centre. The walls were bare, no cut-out models or band posters here.

Sounding frustrated, Rupesh said, "There's nothing, is there?"

"What about that?" Steve said, pointing to a pair of women's knickers on the floor by the mattress.

"So he has a girlfriend," I said. "Good for him."

"You don't think him living like this is weird?" Steve said.

It wasn't so much weird as incredibly sad. This was a man

whose family owned a property, albeit an unkempt one, in a highly desirable suburb just fifteen miles away, and here he was on the floor of what was probably subsidised housing of some sort given he was unemployed.

Downstairs again, Rupesh went back to the kitchen. The seconds passed and I grew more and more anxious as the likelihood of Will getting home increased. We really needed to leave, this was voyeurism now.

"What are you doing?" I said. The *thunk* and *chink* of cupboards and drawers being studied reverberated through the house.

"Just one last check," Rupesh said.

"I'm going outside," I said to Steve. "I'll meet you both by the car."

I had no intention of being arrested tonight. There was being a team player, but now Rupesh was in the throes of some testosterone-fuelled madness, and was going to take us all down with him.

"I'll drag him out," Steve said, leaving me in the hallway.

I wasn't going to wait. Not with the BBC thing and the rest of my life all about to happen. I opened the door and went to the car, relieved Will wasn't out there waiting for us like a serial killer in a film.

The car was locked. Fuck. I stood by the bonnet, hoping the car in front would give me some cover should Will stroll by. Where were the others?

Wanting to be as far from this place as possible, I took out my phone and texted Jon. I'd shore up the future right now. Finally give Xan what he'd been badgering me to do since we last spoke.

My hands trembled. Had he had any more thoughts about the BBC? Please? Hurry because I think I've just fallen down the rabbit hole into—

"Adeline?"

A low voice spoke from the other side of the road. Will stared at me from the opposite pavement on my right like a stray dog. He crossed the road, moving towards me.

"What're you doing here?" he said, passing through the gap in front of Steve's car while I stepped up onto the pavement.

Nothing came, and now Will was in front of me. He grabbed my arm just below the shoulder, hard enough to bruise. "What are you doing here?"

I cried out in shock and pain, and tried pulling away from him. He tightened his surprisingly strong grip.

"Will, get off her," Steve said. He and Rupesh had finally decided to come out of the fucking house, Steve's knight-in-shining-armour act marred by the unsettling waver in his voice.

Will released my arm and darted towards Steve.

"Why are you here?" Will said.

Steve smiled weakly in the absence of a fast enough answer. It was a total giveaway. We were fucked.

"We came to talk to you," Rupesh said.

It was too late. Will, a match for Steve in height and size, grabbed him by the collar of his coat, shoved him up against the wall and brought something out of his pocket with his left hand. It wasn't obvious straight away what it was, not until he brought it to his mouth, drew out a blade from the Swiss Army knife with his teeth and pressed the point to Steve's throat—all in one fluid movement.

"Shit, Will," I said in what was close to a scream. "What the fuck are you doing?"

Steve said nothing. His neck muscles were taut as he strained to get away from the blade.

"I'm sorry if I wasn't clear last time," Will said, "but I don't want anything to do with you, okay?"

Last time? He meant the pub, didn't he? Because that level of grudge didn't bode well for our situation.

"I don't want you in my head," Will said. "I don't want to see your face. I don't want you in my life."

"That's fine," Rupesh said. "Just let Steve go, Will, and we'll get in the car and go, okay? This is our mistake."

Without looking away from Steve, Will said, "How do you know where I live? All that shit about going for a curry, like you'd be caught dead in a place like the Cent'. How did you find me?"

"It's my fault," Rupesh said. "I work as a locum round the corner, at the health centre, and I saw you a couple of months back as I was driving through here to the Stratford Road. Said to these guys it would be a laugh if we showed up and it was really you."

"Then we saw you coming out when we got here," Steve said, "and thought we'd follow you to see if it really was you before knocking on the door—"

"*SSSSSSSssssss*," Will said, thrusting his flushed face into Steve's. "You talk and all I hear is *sssssssssssss*. I saw you. And her. In Manchester. Why are you following me?"

It *had* been Will in the audience. I scanned the street, the windows overlooking this scene. Where the fuck were the neighbours?

"We wanted to catch up with you. But if you don't want to see us, we'll go," Steve said, trying to slide away, in the direction of Rupesh. "Sorry we even—"

"*Sssssssssssss.*"

"Will, put down the knife and we'll just go," I said. I had to do something. Steve sounded genuinely terrified.

"You should all know better," Will said.

"We'll go," Rupesh said.

"We won't come back," Steve said. The knife had actually cut him now, and there was blood trickling down his neck.

"But you always do, don't you?" Will said. "You're always there. No matter where I move, or how much I stay offline. I don't want a fucking reunion. I don't want to even think about you, any of you. None of it means anything to me any more."

I noticed the gap between his spread legs just as the blood began to mark the collar of the white T-shirt under Steve's cardigan. I stepped forward and kicked Will there as hard as I could. The knife fell to the floor and he folded over in near silence. Steve stepped away and shoved him over. He looked down at Will, now on the floor with his knees pulled up to his chest, eyes and mouth tightly closed, withdrawing from his agony. Steve reached up to his neck and brought his bloody hand before his eyes. He was going to attack Will, that's how it looked, anger possessing his face. Only Rupesh stepped forward then, ushering us to the car.

"Come on," he said. "Now."

Steve allowed himself to be led away, but he never took his eyes from Will.

"Anyone have any doubt about him now?" Steve said once we were back out on the main road.

No one said anything. The rain was falling once more. Outside, the outer suburbs of Birmingham flashed by in an orangey blur of streetlights.

I was still in shock ten minutes later. Beside me in the driver's seat Steve kept reaching up to touch his neck with a shaky hand.

"Man," he said, "that was so stupid." He was angry with Rupesh, but trying to reign it in.

"Do you want to go to the police?" I said. "He attacked you. Even if it doesn't stick it might keep him from—"

"We just hunted him down and broke into his house after telling the police we suspected him of a murder," Rupesh said.

"Then we left him on the street after attacking him," Steve said. "I think I know whose side I'd be on right now if I were them."

I didn't know what to say. Maybe that was right; maybe Will would even call the police about us. None of this included what Jen and I had done earlier that day. Who knew whether that kid had reported the two of us to the police?

It had been Will at the gig in the audience. What did that mean? That he'd not been hiding after all; that he had responded to Gaz's invite then seen us and not shown himself?

Or had he only owned up to having seen us in Manchester to put us on the back foot, an invention to make it seem like we'd been stalking him rather than vice versa? We'd caught him by surprise at the pub tonight, interrupted his plan, so perhaps he'd lied his way out of it by acting upset with Steve. He'd obviously seen me at the gig as I'd seen him, and when we hadn't mentioned that part, we'd shown him we were holding something back, that we had an agenda. So he'd used that to his advantage, inventing outrage about us being there when actually he was there following us. Watching us the whole time, perhaps from the start. Playing with us, like he'd been doing with the Nirvana logos.

"What about you, Rup," Steve said. "Any thoughts?"

"Yeah," he said. "Take me home please."

After dropping Rupesh back, an awkward moment passed in the car when it felt like Steve was working up to inviting me back to his hotel. As much as I wanted to, I hadn't been sleeping well in the hotel, and really I needed a good night's rest after all that had happened. We needed our wits about us.

But did I want to be alone tonight? Really?

In spite of my exhaustion I got a taxi home early the following morning.

The house was quiet and still dark. I crept upstairs and tried to catch up on sleep. My mind was feeling around for mental purchase still when I saw the envelope marked ADELINE at the end of my bed.

Inside was a single sheet of paper with the smiley face drawn in thick black marker pen.

I went back downstairs and found Dad reading in his office.

He said he'd found the note in the black letterbox attached to the outside wall, which meant it could have been dropped there any time after the previous morning when it was last checked. Or at any time during the night.

It was the following afternoon when we could all finally meet at Rupesh's. I spent the morning awaiting the appearance of the police at my door for one of the three or so crimes I'd been involved in the previous day. Steve met me at my parents' and we walked over the road. I told him about the note.

Jen's car was already on the drive, apparently fixed now if it had ever been broken in the first place. Maybe she'd even gone over and stayed the night.

I told Rupesh and Jen what I'd told Steve but neither appeared that interested. Jen held herself with the air of a cowed child. Rupesh looked like he'd been up all night.

"Jen and I have been talking about all this," he said, "and think that we need to take a step back." He glanced at Jen.

She nodded. Steve turned to me.

"I know how you feel, Rupesh," I said. "I want to go the police with all this; I'm terrified, frankly. But they're just as likely to arrest us if Will's put in a complaint about last night. Especially if it's that same cop."

"Only problem is we might not get this step-back option if Will comes after us now," Steve said, and I murmured my agreement.

"I think I've seen enough," Rupesh said.

"What does that mean?" I said.

"I know how this sounds, but the chemistry in this group…" Jen said. "I think we're a bad influence on each other."

"Maybe we are," I said. I pulled out the picture from my pocket and held it up. "But bad chemistry doesn't explain this, which is a problem."

"Listen, at this point no one has directly threatened us yet," Rupesh said.

"Well, Will did cut me last night," Steve said.

"Fine, you know what I mean, though. That could have been unrelated to all the things we've had in our head, just speaking objectively. Someone is playing some sort of game here, that's certain, but if I'm perfectly honest I'm not sure it was that bloke we saw last night. If anything… if anything at this stage I feel like it's more likely to be one of us than him."

"I left this note myself?" I said.

"Look, that doesn't mean I actually think it's any of you," Rupesh said. "I just didn't see what I expected last night. I need time. My feeling is that for now we stay vigilant, like the police said. But I'm a little bit scared of us when we're together now, of myself around you, at least as much as I am of whoever might be doing this. I feel like I can't think straight."

"Okay," Steve said. "That sounds… I mean, whatever everyone wants to do I'm happy with. But again, I had a knife put to my throat last night, so forgive me if I feel like there's some safety in numbers. Adeline, what do you think?"

"I'm confused, too," I said. "And tired. But my instinct is not to scatter right now. Seems crazy."

"Maybe we just go our separate ways for now," Jen said, looking at the floor. "And wait. Just in case the police show up to ask us anything, maybe it's best we are all in different places."

"Yeah, I think so," Rupesh said, so softly it was almost a whisper.

We got the message: the two of them had made up their minds long before we'd arrived.

"Yeah. Okay," Steve said, looking at me when he spoke. "But if anything else happens we need to meet up."

"Let's see," Rupesh said, and the room fell quiet.

I lay on his chest in bed after a short, intense fuck that was over before we'd even considered using a condom. It was stupid, but I was too pissed to really care. This was a celebration of our relationship continuing beyond the nightmare of the last few days. Steve had bought a bottle of wine from the hotel bar when we couldn't take any more of the mini-bar rubbish. I ended up drinking most of it, and the bitter taste hadn't been much of an improvement. Until my second glass I'd considered sending it back.

Steve was quiet, staring up at the ceiling while I stroked the hair on his chest, sleep already lurking nearby. His smile, usually close to the surface even when not present, was buried deep now.

"Are you okay?" I said.

He thought about this. "I can't work them out. We should be banding together now."

"Maybe," I said. "I think Rupesh wants to just pull Jen out of the firing line, though."

"Yeah, you could be right. Makes me wonder, though, all this stuff, about the past. About memory. Maybe our gang wasn't what I remember it as. Maybe it was only ever you and me really. When it came down to it. They're so...messed up. Locked in their own little thing. I sometimes think I just projected what I felt about you onto them."

"Well," I said, and closed my eyes, "it's you and me now."

Like it had been me that made his first claim, he said, "No, we needed the others for context. Other people are context, aren't they? And you need context. You can't just be in a bubble on your own. I feel we've all been through so much, we should

265

all be together at the moment. When I was a kid I always wanted a gang, you know? Like the kids in all those films we watched. It makes me sad thinking of that now. Feel a little pathetic." He gave a laugh that was close to being a sigh.

"We all feel a little pathetic once we hit out thirties and see the dreams of our youth for what they are," I said. "It's like seeing the handwriting you had as a kid."

"You're right," he said. I could smell the wine on his words, not unpleasant and, mixed with his aftershave, heady. "You lot were the best, though, my tribe, my pack. I'd have thought at the time we could have knocked at the devil's door together."

"Everyone's just a bit scared, Steve, I think. I'm scared." I nuzzled his cheek.

"I just feel that Rupesh is still acting odd towards me," he said. "Don't you think? Like right from the start, like he's holding on to to some grudge. I've been trying with him, I really have. Backing him up even when I didn't necessarily agree with him. If he saw how I remembered him then maybe he'd chill out. But you can't force that kind of thing, can you? Force someone into seeing what you mean to them. This is so Rupesh, too, wanting to drive us apart at a time like this." He paused, then added, "I can almost believe what you were saying before about him."

"I understand," I said, although now, hopelessly inebriated on his scent and the drink, I wasn't sure I did. "You know, permanence isn't the same thing as importance." This was something I'd said on the podcast once, and it felt right now. "What happened then was still important, then. If he remembers it wrongly, so what? We remember it right."

It worked because he kissed my head and went quiet. I reached up and caressed his cheek, feeling my exhaustion in the increased weight of my arm. In some complicated way that I wanted to unpick when sober, he'd been hurt over the last few days. Perhaps like we had done with Will, we still believed Steve was a version of himself that perhaps wasn't real any more, invincible and strong. But this was a Steve Litt with his edges knocked off, who burned in the sun and shivered when it got cold like the rest of us.

"Sorry, I'm killing the vibe, aren't I?" he said. "You know, I just wish he could see who I am not what I was."

"Well, I can see it."

I kissed him softly, then sat up and pulled his head onto my lap. I ran my fingers through his hair, the style unable to withstand my exploration, giving way to reveal the widows peak he tried so hard to cover. I leaned down, neck muscles straining, and kissed the thin patch on his crown. And that was where I fell asleep.

I awoke sharply to the sound of knocking at the door. It took me a moment to understand where I was.

"Still in here," Steve shouted.

His voice made me wince. I raised my head from Steve's chest and waited for my body's first indication as to how bad the hangover was going to be. Incredibly, I'd slept through the entire night uninterrupted. That probably meant something, perhaps that I was home, finally. Yes, wouldn't that be nice? Home in this beautiful man's arms. But today was going to be a write-off, I could already tell from the way my brain wasn't quite keeping up with where I wanted to look.

"Sorry," someone said through the door.

The bedside clock had been unplugged, so I rolled over and reached for my phone. My head ached with the suddenness of the movement. When the screensaver cleared I saw ten missed calls. Immediately my insides began to coil. It was Mum's mobile, she'd tried calling during the night, starting at 4 a.m.

Dad. It had to be Dad. I pictured him at the top of the stairs, head in hands, breathing heavily. Something had happened to him, why else would she be phoning? She never phon—

The pain in my head swelled and the room started moving independently of me.

"Everything okay?" Steve said.

"No," I said.

I threw back the covers and ran to the toilet. I got the lid up in time and vomited mostly wine into the bowl. It took ten minutes for the nausea to pass, during which time Steve had come to check on me and I'd demanded he leave me alone, not wanting him to see me this way.

I felt no better once it was over, if it actually was over. I called Mum, but a male voice answered.

"Hello, darling." It was Dad.

"Dad? Thank God, I saw Mum's number and thought something had happened."

"Well, I'm afraid it has, my love, it's just your mum's phone had all the charge. She's had a fall, Adeline. It's quite a bad one, on the stairs, and she's hit her head."

"Oh God, Dad. My phone was on silent. I'm so sorry. Where is she?"

"We're at the hospital, in Marlstone. I don't want you to worry about it, she's in the best place now."

"Is it serious?" I said. But the answer to this was obvious. I didn't need to hear Dad's response. So I asked something else. "How did it happen, Dad?"

"She said she thought she heard someone in the house. She's always hearing people in the house. She must have missed the top step, I've done it myself. I just heard her shout and—" His voice cut out and sorrow stabbed my heart.

"I'm coming now," I said, and when I hung up Steve was already dressed.

Part III

Time is frightening when you notice it.

Will, 1998

Will's morning wasn't going to plan at all. First he was late to meet the gang because Mum was in the black wig...again. So he'd sat with her for an hour, his job to listen and not speak, especially when it was about Liz. His job was to tire her out so it was all gone from her system by the time she got drunk. Liz would have been a wonderful mother. Liz would have been a wonderful actress. Liz would have built the first colony on the moon and performed Shakespeare for appreciative astronauts and moon rocks. She was everything and anything to Mum— other than what she was, which was dead.

Then when he finally got out of the house, and told each one of them his clue, starting at Rup's house and ending at Jen's, Steve complained that he hadn't told them all together. Now Rupesh had an advantage, he said. He had longer to plan. But Rup wasn't like that, he was as honest as it came—except when it came to copping to that brick through Strachan's windscreen. Still, he hated being on Steve's bad side—it was a real ache in the penis.

The first clue is at the pit before the lake. And you'll need to think, Countdown.

None of them asked which pit, they all knew. After the big mansion on Blythe Lane was a spooky, tree-tunnel-covered side road called Raven Way. The pit was just beyond the gate at the very end of Raven Way, close to a footpath back to the fields behind Elm Close.

And of course, now he was there, he had another problem: the bloody *balloon issue*.

He knew they were all scared of that clown in the sewer film, Rupesh in particular—his main rival at the moment. That's why he'd picked balloons. Except when he'd gone to the shop, they'd only had white ones and now Will thinks they might not be so scary after all.

And that's not even the only problem. He wanted to put all his clues on them. Tie up the balloons like they'd been in the film and write the clues on with a marker. Bonus was he wouldn't have to come up with stupid complicated clues because there wouldn't be room. He'd do them as anagrams, like the conundrums on *Countdown*. Steve couldn't shout at him for that. And he'd be so impressed by the balloons he wouldn't even mind that his clues weren't really clues but instructions. He'd even draw on that smiley-faced Nirvana logo as a sort of trademark.

Only of course the balloons in the film were bloody ghost balloons—real balloons needed helium. It hadn't even entered his mind until the first one was blown up and tied to a piece of string and the big black marker he had taken from Dad's workshop was in his hand ready to write Next Clue: I Forgot Bed, which was *footbridge*, as in the one on the path to Hampton. The one where Adeline left her clue, because it was clever to reuse—

The pit was actually a shallow indentation in the land the length and width of a school classroom, and like much of the unfinished work around the lake its original purpose was a mystery. For as long as Will could remember it had been here, and from the group Will was the longest Blythe resident by a few years, having been there longer than even Jen's family.

How long that was going to last he didn't want to think about, because the reality of it was they might be moving soon because Dad thought Mum was depressed because of Liz, and Dad had said one night that they might have to have some time apart or even get a divorce because he wanted to live by the sea where there was air and—

He tied the balloon to a rusted branch of metal jutting from the ground. When he let go, the balloon fell from his hand and landed on the dry ground where it rolled around in what breeze there was, eventually finding its way over the rim and into the pit where it tugged uselessly on its tether like a frustrated dog.

Typical he'd forgotten that the balloons wouldn't just float in mid-air. Why would they? Dad called him absent-minded all the time, often accompanied with a clip around the ear. Although it wasn't that his mind was absent. His mind was always there, occupied by one thought or the other. Only there were just so many things. Bright and colourful and sometimes frightening. It was like he was juggling them all, a bit like a clown. Only there was only ever time to focus on one, the rest were all up in—

The mud at the edge of the pit gave way beneath his feet. He lost his balance and pinwheeled his arms for a comic length of time before finally falling the few feet to the floor of the pit, where he landed on his arse.

"Shit," he said, then laughed. "Ow."

It wasn't far, it didn't hurt even. He just hoped no one had seen this rotten cherry on the mouldy cake of his day.

About to get up, his attention was drawn to a slightly different shade of soil, in the area up where the ground had fallen apart under him. He crawled closer so that the edge of the pit was at eye-level. Something was buried there, reddish brown.

From around the object he pulled away soil until it was too firm to move without great force. It was already obvious that this was the edge of some old pot.

273

He experienced a rare moment of focus, one of his conversations with Bill coming back to him.

Will looked at the pot. Then at the balloon. Then at his watch. Then he did the same thing, again and again. There was some time, forty minutes in fact, before they all left, but that wasn't really enough to get the pot out, get it home to safety, then get the rest of the clues out. His Dedication wasn't long, but it was spread out. And he couldn't take the pot with him in case he fell, or he dropped it.

He could always run back and explain, tell them all what he'd found and hope they thought it was as exciting as he did. But he could imagine their faces if they didn't understand, their disappointment. Steve's disappointment. They would think he hadn't planned anything, was making things up, the way they'd done with Rup, which would really be a shame given how much planning—

He would come back. That was it. He would lay out the rest of the clues, then come back here. Yes, it would mean the pot was at risk of being found by someone else. But it had lasted this long untouched.

Will reached over, grabbed the soil from his partial excavation and covered the pot. There. No problem. Taking his bag of balloons and marker pen, he set off to the footbridge on the Hampton footpath.

"BOY FINDS ROMAN HOARD," he said to himself. Well casual. Then he frowned. "DOG WALKER FINDS ROMAN HOARD." He needed to walk faster.

None of it took as long as he expected, and he was back at the pit in under an hour—this time with his spade. The others might not even have reached the pit themselves yet—unless one of them snuck out before they were meant to. It was a risk coming back before they had found the first clue, but one he was willing to take for the sake of getting the pot out safely before anyone else did. It actually wouldn't matter to the game, not really. As long as he got to the final place before the others.

Down in the pit, he moved the soil out the way with his hands again, then started using the spade edge on the tough soil. He was gentle, but sometimes, when the soil just wouldn't budge, he wanted to scream and smash the spade down edge first and properly do some bloody damage but—

That was the ciggies talking. He recognised their voice now, especially the longer he left it between nicks from Monks's stash. He took out the one he'd stolen that morning, one with a little extra in it, and lit the match on his fly.

Will hummed while he worked, so engrossed that he didn't hear someone approaching from the direction of Raven Way until they were at the edge of the pit behind him.

"What are you doing?" a voice said.

Will jumped, then turned.

"Why are you *here*?" Steve said. Predictably, he wore that screwed-up expression on his face, like Will was a fresh fart.

"It's okay." Will got to his feet. He held up his palms like Steve was sticking him up. "I've got the whole thing under control."

Steve sprang down. Will stepped back and the pit's wall cut into his knees, which gave way, leaving him sitting on the edge not far from his find.

"What's going on, mate? Why aren't you taking this seriously?"

"I am taking it—"

"If you were taking it seriously you wouldn't be here." He sounded a bit upset, didn't understand that Will had this under control.

"Mate, I had to come back for something."

"Don't go all Rupesh on me," he said. "Are your other clues set up even?"

"Yes. Yes, the whole thing is fine."

He shook his head. "I thought you were into this game?"

"I am," he said.

"Then get going, because this is probably against the rules. I'm not meant to see you." Still shaking his head, he added, "You made me promise to stick to the rules of this thing. And I really don't want you to get the ban."

"Don't worry."

"I am worried," Steve said. "I'm worried because you came last before, and I'm worried you're hanging out with that wanker Strachan. I don't know what's going on with you."

Will shrugged. How could he convince him about Bill in the time they had? Not that he'd listen anyway. Once Steve made his mind up that was it. He tried anyway. "He's okay really."

"Is he?" Steve said. "He was cruel to his dog. And that dog bit Obi, remember, which is probably why he ended up like he did."

"There's reasons," he said.

"There's always reasons. Hitler had reasons. He's messing with your head. Use your brain."

Will hated Steve when he was like this. He didn't hate people often, not even when he fought with his brother. Steve, though, could just be so…so unfair. *Don't talk to me like that.* He wanted to say it, and his mouth clutched the words, but they remained unsaid. He shifted his leg and it rubbed against the spade. Steve widened his eyes, which meant, *Hurry up, dickhead.*

He stood up to his full height and walked in the direction of the footpath back to the fields behind Elm Close. When he was like this it was better to walk away. Although, like Bill said to him once, some people only respond to a clout round the ear.

Deep in the maize, Will's shame and anger leaked away like so many of his more intense emotions. Like there was a hole in him somewhere. Even when things were at their worst, at their Liz worst, he wasn't able to hold on to a meaningful emotion for longer than a few minutes.

Overall it was for the best. There were emotions he had that he didn't really want. Like the ones that flooded him when he was around Jen and Rupesh these days. He held nothing against Rup, how was he to know what a bitch Jen had been to him? But she'd not been nice about what happened at the train tracks last summer, blanked him, laughed at him, not made any effort to hide her and Rup's thing. Still, even now his heart always felt like it was stretching after a sleep when he saw her.

He took a long head-spinning drag from his cigarette, then chucked it into the crops. Hey ho, there was nothing he could do about those feelings, even if they were the strongest feelings of all, compelling him to do things that he couldn't do and making him feel weak. Weak and lonely and—

The pot! Of course, what was he going to do about the pot? Not much he could do about it now, maddening as that was. He would have to wait until the game was over. And hope. Hope that none of the others did anything to it by accident. Or hope Steve didn't see it and smash it out of revenge.

He stopped walking. Should he go back and watch, just to make sure? No, Steve was mostly a good guy. He wasn't malicious. He really had got it into his head that Bill was a monster, so he was just being a good friend if you thought about it. A good, wrong friend. Yeah, he lost control of his passion sometimes, but that's what made him Steve. And unless you talk to Bill, you wouldn't know why he was so angry at things. Why his dog was angry all the time. Why—

Bill! He would know about the pot—know what to do with it to keep it safe or get it into the right hands or get the best money for it. In fact, with them all out doing the game, he could visit now and tell him. It was the weekend, so he'd be home. And if he ran he could make it in no time. He just had to make sure he got to the end before Steve did.

Bill didn't answer his door, which gave Will a little bit of time to catch his breath before walking around to the back and down to the workshop where Bill usually spent the weekends. The building was an oversized shed spread out almost fence-to-fence at the end of the garden. He rapped on the wooden door and Bill called out for him to wait a moment.

When the door opened Bill looked surprised to see him. He wore a vest and blue shorts, sweat on his forehead and his face was red.

"I think I found something, a pot, in one of the fields," he said, and Bill nodded.

He'd been doing his exercises; Will could smell that once inside. Sweat and rubber and varnish. All Bill's weights and his punchbag were set up in the far left corner. He used to be an amateur boxer when he was a kid but the doctors had told him if he got another punch in the head he'd be a vegetable. A big red beetroot. On the right was a shelf on which all his cool artefacts were displayed. Belt buckles, shards of old pottery, coins. His retirement fund, he called it; reckoned he had about twenty grands' worth of stuff all in all, things he'd found, things he'd swapped. Pretty casual all things considered, not a bad amount of cash to collect from digging around like—

Elvis, the dog, the one that used to be chained up in the front, sat on a battered old sofa at the back of the room. He'd learned to recognise Will's voice now and barely reacted to his presence. He was all right actually. Licked your hand and everything. Bill told him that his wife took him in from a rescue home, and it used to get stuff chucked at it all the time by its previous owners when it tried coming in the house, which is why it liked being outside. Stressed him out being inside.

Thing was, when his wife left him for some wanker ex-pat over in Spain, the dog couldn't go in the garden any more because like Obi, it kept running off.

"It used to wait in the garden for her to come home," he'd said, "and when it didn't it went looking for her, little idiot. Found him out by those train tracks once. Never again. That's all I've got left of her now." That was why he'd chained it up.

He wasn't any sort of hero, Bill. He called Rupesh a Paki once, and called Adeline "Jailbait" when talking about her, and he was always talking about things he'd done for Birmingham gangs when he was younger like he was making things up to show off. But that thing about the dog made Will hate what they'd done last year, and like Bill for at least trying to do right by the dog despite what his wife did.

Will found a bright side to it all, though. The dog actually preferred it out in the shed. Smelled a bit like outside but meant he didn't wander off. Win, win.

"It's probably an old bit of kit from the works they were doing up there," Bill said, mopping his forehead with a towel slung over the push-up bench thingy which he was now sitting on.

"It's well older than that," Will said. "You can tell."

"You think?" Bill considered the likelihood of this. "Want me to come out and look? Elvis is due a w-a-l-k."

The dog cocked its ear like it could spell, funny stuff.

"Can't do it now," Will said. "I'm in the middle of something."

"With your little gang?"

He nodded. Bill reached out and touched his shoulder. He touched him a lot, on his shoulder, on his side. That was really the only time he ever got the feeling Steve might be on to something. He did like to touch, which maybe Will wouldn't have minded if they weren't always on their own.

"This isn't you playing funny buggers, is it?"

"No," Will said. "They don't know I've found it."

279

"The tall lad. Does he know?"

Had Steve seen it earlier? Even if he had he wouldn't know what it was, would he?

"No, not yet."

"Good. Keep it that way. Don't trust that kid at all. Then you and me go fifty/fifty on whatever this thing turns out to be." With his other hand he reached out to Will to seal the deal. Will obliged and was now in both Bill's hands. The handshake was firm and went on a bit long, but then he let go and Will agreed to meet him out there later on, at around 5 p.m., giving him the exact location of his find.

Before leaving, he felt obliged to say, "Steve's all right, really."

It's what he'd have said if the situation had been reversed. Had, to be fair. Bill just grunted, and started punching the bag.

Will sat on one of the six concrete bollards that marked the road behind the lake's end. It was close to the railway footbridge, but Rupesh had come here before without freaking out. Although he supposed if he played the game the way Steve wanted them to he should have put his clue right on the tracks.

The slap and crunch of someone coming down the path from the lake made Will look up. Typical, it was Steve. Taking his total up to eleven. He didn't even need the points now. He sounded out of breath. Maybe he'd run. Winning probably mattered enough for him to do that.

Steve sat on the block to Will's right, both of them facing the long path back to the lake.

"Balloons," he said, nodding. "Nice."

"I was trying to fuck Rupesh because that film shit him up."

"You better hope that Rupesh isn't here next, though."

It wouldn't actually end right here if Rupesh arrived next, but Will would only be able to draw with him. But maybe Steve was right that Will needed to start worrying, he was usually right.

Will associated this place with what happened to Obi. Steve and him had always been mates, but that day with Obi had made Will realise Steve valued him in a way that he didn't value the others. He was the only one Steve asked to help bury Obi, probably because Steve once found him burying that bird out in one of the fields. Will dug the hole while Steve talked about what a good dog he'd been, though towards the end that hadn't been strictly true. The dog was always trying to bite everyone, Steve included. It had a bad attitude. Will had picked up the dog's body parts and put them in the ground. Obi's guts had fallen on his leg.

But had he complained about it once? Not at all. Not even when Steve told him to get the dog out and make the hole deeper, and wider, because he didn't want foxes digging up the body. By the time he was done the hole could have fit three or four dogs in it.

"I'll do the rest," Steve had said, and Will left him to put the soil over Obi.

Will had never buried a dog before then, but he'd buried other—

Animals were idiots sometimes—as if the exact thing Bill had worried about with Elvis had happened to Obi. Why did they even go up to the train tracks? The smells probably. Funny Strachan and Steve both had similar dog problems. Funny, funny, funny. If they didn't hate each other they'd probably be friends.

Will's connection with Steve that day, he'd come to understand, was that only the two of them had been honest enough to realise that the dog was better off dead. Steve had once joked to Will about putting Obi out of his misery on the train tracks, which went some way to making him feel better about having often had the same thought, especially when Obi had been barking at him and—

281

They raised their heads to the sound of slow footsteps approaching.

It was Adeline, the three points hers. She ambled down the path to them without a drop of sweat on her face.

"That was hard," she said.

Rupesh and Jen arrived last. They were laughing and joking together when they walked along the last stretch of the lake, concealed from the three of them by a large hedge. They all waited on a block of their own, their conversation having ended the moment they heard the others coming. This wouldn't make Steve happy at all. He'd already made it clear he thought Jen had helped Rupesh to win her Dedication. This would go a long way to confirming that theory.

When they appeared at the path's far end and saw that they were the final two, their laughter stopped. Rupesh, possibly being shoved by Jen, ran to Will, touching him on the arm on the way past. Jen didn't run. She didn't dawdle either. She sloped, almost ashamed to look at Will, because in helping Rupesh she was condemning him.

"The balloon on the bridge burst," Jen said. "We bumped into each other trying to hold it together and work out the clue."

"Can't believe you just reused my place," Adeline said.

Will shrugged.

If Steve was annoyed he didn't show it. Once they had settled down, and complimented Will on the imagination he'd shown for his Dedication, Steve recited a score update.

Steve — 11
Adie — 9
Jen — 8
Rupesh — 7
Will — 5

"Jen and me can still win," Adeline said to Steve.

"No one really *wins* The Dedication," Steve said, and while the comment was addressed to the whole group, Will caught Steve's gaze as he surveyed them all and felt a charge pass between them.

On the way home, Will, attempting not to draw attention to himself, peeled off and started back towards the burial site once the gate at Raven Way came into view. All the chatter was about Steve's Dedication, The Big One, everyone agreeing it would be hard for Will to catch up now. He didn't care about that, though. He might be rich and famous by then if the pot turned out to be—

"Where are you going?" Jen said. "You not even going to say goodbye?"

"Thought I'd slip off," he said, which sounded a bit like he was a snake so he made his arm wriggle to show them he'd meant it deliberately. Some of them laughed at this, the way they often did when he wasn't trying to be funny.

"Without even telling us? We've talked about this, Will," Jen said.

"I found something at the pit I wanted to look at."

"What did you find?" Steve said.

Shitbarn! He hadn't meant to tell him. "Might be nothing."

Steve didn't look convinced, but didn't ask any more questions. He said, "It's going to rain soon, come on." They were content to go on without him. No doubt they would all end up back at Steve's watching films anyway so it wasn't like he would miss out on anything.

The pit wasn't far, and the spade and the pot were where he'd left them—the former he'd concealed in the nearby maize. A breeze dashed loose soil against the nearby fence posts and rattled the maize in the field beyond. He was glad for that noise, because he found that when it fell silent, as it often did, it gave him the creeps. He understood why Rupesh got scared of things when it went quiet like that.

Kneeling down by the pot, he patiently broke away pieces of soil, every so often looking over his shoulder to check he was still alone. If he was asked, Will probably would have said that his pot, if Roman, was from something small like a toll house. Not a settlement. The Romans knew better than to settle *nowhere*, which is what these places were, these tiny villages around the West Midlands countryside. They were stopping points on the route to better places, or dwellings for the servants and staff that worked for whoever owned all the old mansions.

Perhaps he needed a cigarette. That might explain the shifting in his guts. It was utterly irrational, but he was suddenly possessed by the notion that places settled for a reason, and that those drawn to the places like Blythe were fundamentally wrong in some important way. That was why Monks said Dad wants to move to the seaside. It's where the interesting stuff happened, where the boats came in and brought new things, and where the people that liked new things went to experience them. Monks said the country was where people ran to escape, the way nits all run to your crown when you've covered your hair in poison.

He shuddered. What did Monks know anyway? All he did with his life was listen to music and play computer games in his room. And the latest game he was addicted to was more pointless than most; apparently all you did was walk around in an empty desert for ever and ever without finding anything or reaching any kind of—

A large chunk of earth fell away and the pot moved a little in a pocket of air. Another chunk came away then, and another after that, creating a hole through which he was able to pull the pot.

"The real fun is finding out what's inside," Steve said from behind him.

If he intended to make him jump again it didn't work, but inside he felt cold. Hadn't he been expecting this?

Without turning around he inspected the pot's contents. It was filled with compacted dirt.

"I'm going to take this home," Will said. "Now it's out I don't want to do anything that might damage it."

"Probably a good idea," Steve said, jumping down to the same level as Will.

"Where are the others?" Will said.

"I *slipped* away," he said, and made Will's wriggling gesture with his arm. "Said I left my wallet with you. But I came to find you because I had an idea."

"Well, it's out now," Will said, holding up the pot.

"What do you think it is?"

"Dunno."

"Is it valuable?"

"Dunno."

"Can I have a look?" Steve held out his hands.

Will didn't want to give him the pot, didn't trust him. "What was it, your idea?"

"It's about the game. The bookies have actually stopped taking bets on you being kicked out of the group. You know, even if Rupesh finishes last you have to finish in first place to beat him outright."

"I know. There's a good chance I'll lose," Will said. "But there's also a chance we'll draw. What happens then?"

"You don't want to know," Steve said. "But I think the fairest thing, given Jen quite obviously helped out Rupesh, and no one is really taking this seriously, the best thing to level things up would be for me to help you."

"How can you help me?"

"It's my round. I can help you win. I can't necessarily make Rupesh lose, he's all fighting talk back there. But I can make sure you have the best chance."

It was nice of Steve to offer, and yeah, now he brought it up it probably was unfair that Rupesh'd had some extra help. What was in it for him, though? Why would he come all this way back if there wasn't something in it for—

"Steve, who do you want to win?" Will asked.

The question clearly surprised him because he shifted his weight onto his other foot, poked out his lower lip and shrugged. "I don't really have a preference, Will. I just want it all to be fair. Balanced. I don't want anyone to feel cheated."

He could understand that, balance. Why he'd wanted to defend Bill to Steve. Balance. Speaking of which, Bill would soon be here, it had been ten to five when he'd last looked at his watch.

"I'm going to head back soon," he said, planning to perhaps make up a story about meeting his dad in order to get away from Steve before sneaking back here.

"Do you want to hear my plan?"

Will wouldn't like what Steve was going to say, that much he was convinced of. It would be about Rupesh. He was the only one of them that ever really stood up to Steve, even if it was in his own, quiet little way. Maybe he should just say yes to whatever it was, then come last anyway. It would be funny, even if no one else found out. Especially if Dad really was going to move the family to the seaside soon. And pissing Steve off would have its own appeal.

"Yeah, but I should probably get this back. I'm worried if rain gets on it."

"Really? What is it you think this is? It's a bit of rubbish. Fine, take it home, then come to mine."

"Yeah, will do."

He held out his hands again. "Can I at least see this wonder of the world then?"

Will didn't hand over the pot. He pulled it closer to him. Steve frowned. "Just let me hold it, mate. Two seconds."

"I can show it you once it's been cleaned off."

Steve rolled his eyes, then took a step towards Will.

"You need to take no for a fucking answer," Bill said, coming over the stile behind the pit. He was using a voice that made all those gangster stories he told suddenly a lot more believable. Will felt relief and fear; he'd not wanted this meeting to occur but at least he didn't have to hand over the pot.

"What's it got to do with you?" Steve said. He didn't sound as sure of himself any more. Will hadn't heard that before.

"There's a word for kids like you. You're a bully, and I've no truck with that sort."

Steve laughed at this, forced and loud.

"I told you before, you're on eggshells with me," Bill said. "I wouldn't go pushing your luck. Why don't you hop it? I want to see what this is all about."

"I don't have to go if I don't—"

Elvis burst out of the cornfield and ran around the pit barking, then he jumped down into the pit and charged at Steve, knocking his leg out from under him and causing him to fall onto his side.

"Elvis," Bill said, and the dog ran to his side.

Steve got up, looked down at his dirty jeans, then at his hands. There was blood on one palm. He held it up to Bill with a grin.

"That's probably enough to have him put down," Steve said.

Bill only glared, sizing Steve up. Would they fight? Would they actually fight? A part of Will was curious to see it happen. Who would win? Strachan was strong, sure, but the thing about—

287

Steve jumped out the pit and started backing up in the direction of Raven Way. He pointed at Bill.

"*You're* on eggshells with *me*," he said. "That dog's on death row. It should have been put down years ago. Will, you coming? You don't want to be out here with him, on your own."

Will paused, not knowing how to get out of this without picking a side. "I'm all right," he said. "I've got to show him something anyway."

Steve didn't know how to react to this. His face tried on a number of fierce expressions before settling on dismay. He shook his head, threw up his arm and walked off, muttering something about the dog.

Will didn't like that at all. No, not one bit. Maybe a physical fight would have been better. At least then there was a winner and a loser. Before this things had been balanced, now Steve would want revenge. He had let the wallet thing go, had wanted to move on to other things. Now it might all start again.

He hadn't noticed that Bill was admiring the pot now. He made the same give-me gesture Steve had earlier given him, only this time Will handed it over.

"You've done well here, mate," he said. "I think you might actually have something good. Do you mind if I show it to a few people?"

And strangely he didn't mind at all.

"Do you think that kid was serious, by the way, about Elvis?" Bill said. "You saw he didn't touch him."

"I'm meant to go see him later," he said. "I'll try and talk him out of it."

"If he comes for him I'll kill the fucker. You can tell him that."

A little speck of spit had flown from his mouth when he'd sworn and it landed on Will's cheek. He wiped it away. Bill looked like he really meant it. And once more all those stories he'd told Will about the past felt like they might actually be true.

Winter, 2015

The afternoon has given way to the evening by the time Dad and I are set free from the waiting area of Marlstone Hospital and allowed to enter the ITU. New Year's Eve is only a few hours away.

Mum's head has been shaved and bandaged. The surgeons have done what they can, and the tones they've spoken to us in are hopeful though the story their eyes tell is grim. Mum doesn't look like Mum at all, and perhaps that is a good thing. It's a stranger in the bed.

Dad looks tired and he has been continuously mumbling to himself since my arrival. He insists on staying at the hospital all night—in the waiting room if necessary. Needing a break, needing air and space to understand, I offer to return to the house to pick up some things for him. He isn't hungry, but he asks for his toothbrush and his puzzle book.

Out in the ambulance bay I turn on my phone. It buzzes and flashes with messages of concern. From the fragments displayed in the bar at the top of the screen most of them are from the others, worrying, wanting updates, wishing me well. One is from Xan, an order to call him because Jon has made a decision. It's a message from another lifetime, a parallel universe.

I call Steve, on standby since dropping me off that morning, and he dutifully picks me up and drives me back to Elm Close.

"Thank you so much," I say as we pull onto the drive. I lean over and kiss him on the mouth. He offers to come with me but not knowing what I'll find in the house, I suggest he waits in the car.

Inside is oddly calm given the events of that morning. Still, I'm anxious. What if Mum had heard someone downstairs that night?

A semicircle of blood marks the carpet at the foot of the stairwell, not much, but it brings to mind the scene that must have greeted Dad: Mum's slack face beneath her blood-soaked hair. I kneel down by the patch, can't resist touching it, though it's hardened and leaves no mark on my fingers.

"I'm sorry," I say. I'm crying, not because the anger has suddenly drifted away and given way to deep love, rather because all at once it occurs to me that our relationship might now be a finite thing. That it will be forever broken, forever stuck as it always had been, had always meant to be, a child and her child. There will be nothing more to it.

I've gathered all Dad's things, and am preparing to leave, when I notice another envelope on the kitchen counter. ADELINE is written on the front beneath a smiley face with crossed-out eyes. I open it, and as I read my hands begin to shake. Then I'm running out of the house, to Steve's car, and he takes me into his arms and reads the letter over my shoulder.

"We need to get the others together," he says.

Friends,
   You weren't meant to find me yet! So now the game has changed.
   NEW RULES: I have someone. Play along and they'll live.

Consider it a reboot, Adeline; a new Dedication, Steve; opening night, Jen; the cure to what ails you, Rupesh.

Tomorrow trace the paths of your original Dedications. There will be items left along the way that you will need to present to me at the end. Bring me them all and the girl can live.

ADDITIONAL RULES: Anyone doesn't play, calls the police, gives up: I'll come for you. And I won't stop there. I'll come for your friends, your families, your pets. I can get a lot done before I'm caught.

Ask Adeline's mum if you don't think I'm serious?

The order of your Dedications tomorrow:

Trashcan, Please, Resist, Strain.

Each anagram belongs to just one of you: perhaps it's a secret, a memory, a moment we shared. The only way you'll know whose is whose is to take a walk down memory lane. Get to know each other all over again.

I'VE WATCHED, I'VE LISTENED, I'VE LEARNED.

Now it's your turn. Start early tomorrow, I suggest 6 a.m. It will be a long day. My final location will be revealed at the end of the final Dedication.

Love, Will X

Jen is the last of us to read the note, a side of childish writing on an A4 sheet. Done, she puts it down on Rupesh's coffee table. She is next to me, and reaches over to touch my arm.

It's so soft I don't notice straight away, and when I do I smile weakly. I'm trying hard not to throw up again, my hangover not entirely gone and now reacting with the adrenalin in my blood.

"Obviously we go back to the police," Rupesh says. "But we need to think for a second."

"Sure," Steve says. "What about this person he has? I mean, you read what he said. If we don't play this sick little game of his... And then there's our safety if we don't do what he says..."

"We're not sitting around solving clues and doing our Dedications again?" Jen says. She's determined, almost angry. She's not making eye contact with anyone and appears embarrassed to be here.

"No, I just meant what Rupesh said," Steve says. "That we need to think about it."

"Well, I just meant that we need to get our story straight," Rupesh says. "Are we going to tell the police what we've done? Are we going to tell them about breaking into Will's house? About your visit to Derby? They're going to want to know how we got his address."

Once more, Rupesh is thinking about himself.

"Exactly," Steve says. "We need to consider this carefully. All of it."

"The longer we wait the more questions they'll have about our timeline," I say. I've decided already, did all my thinking on the journey to the hospital and back taking Dad his things. "It's already been an hour since I found the note. I think we should just come clean. About everything. There's too much potential for messing up if we start lying to them. They might already have a report on Jen somewhere that they'll link to this. I want them to take us seriously now, I want Will caught and I want this over with. We don't even know he actually has kidnapped anyone."

"It's a trick," Jen says. "To get us alone out in the fields."

This is exactly it. Who knows what will happen once we are all out there, in the dark, sleep-deprived? Everything is in focus now, the murders, the smiley faces. I try to recall that innocent night in The George, and how we'd stumbled right into what he wanted, unprompted. Except there had been a prompt, all those years ago in the fields behind Blythe. He'd known even then that telling us what he did would become the very thing for which we'd remember him. And all it took was not showing up at a reunion.

"We have to assume he intends to kill a third person," I say. "If it's not this person he has then it must be one of us. Or all of us. This is a total unknown."

"The morality isn't clear here," Rupesh says.

"This again," Steve says.

"We don't know what Will's planned or, like Adeline says, if he even has a person kidnapped. All I'm saying is if we do go to the police then it's not the same as pulling the trigger on this girl's head."

"Your old friend will take us seriously now, Steve," I say.

"I don't know," Rupesh says. "What if they think we're pulling some prank to get them to look into—"

"My mum's in a fucking coma, Rup." For a while no one speaks. My words have extra weight. "We have to go to the police."

"Steve, you said you were worried for our safety," Rupesh says.

"Of course I am," he says. "He could be outside this place right now. He could have mic'ed up this place and be listening to us." Steve gestures to the letter. "He implies he'll be watching our every move. Suppose he sees a police car pull up here, then how do we know he's not already waiting to go after your parents?" He looks at Jen. "Or Adeline's dad? And what do you think happens once we're done with the police?"

No one has an answer to this, so Steve continues. "They're not going to give us armed protection, are they? We'll walk out of the police station and be at his mercy until he's caught. I mean, he's not going to be hanging around that flat any more, is he? He'll be hiding out, seeing what we're doing."

It's a good point, and one I haven't considered. Those boxes we'd assumed had not been unpacked might actually have been *recently* packed, ready for moving at a moment's notice.

"Or it's all bluff," Jen says. "Either way the answer isn't actually doing his stupid game, is it?" No one answers, so she says again, "Is it?" Her jaw quivers.

"No," I say. "No, it's over. It doesn't stand up to this much thought. We go to the police, we tell them everything. Now."

We leave Rupesh's separately—Will can't follow us all. Steve and Rupesh drive straight for the police station in their own cars, while Jen goes home to make sure her parents are out of the house for the rest of the night, somewhere public, at least until the police can advise us on our next steps. I drive to the hospital to tell Dad I've booked us both into the same hotel where Steve is staying, and that he's to remain at the hospital until I return. For tonight at least, the plan is to stay together, strength in numbers.

When I arrive at the police station, the straight-faced receptionist takes me through to a stuffy side room where the other four are already seated beneath the harsh strip lights. Jen and Steve have both given statements, and they've apparently sent officers out to the address in Sparkbrook.

"They've gone to find someone else to interview you and Rupesh," Jen says. She still seems twitchy, keeps brushing her hair over her ears.

"So they're taking us seriously?" I say, relieved. Jen shrugs.

294

"They keep saying they're looking into it. I don't think they know what to make of us."

After ten minutes, the receptionist offers to make us drinks and apologises for the delay, remarking on the lack of officers in the building and its relation to budget cuts.

"I don't think he's planned everything, you know," Steve says when she's gone. "This note, the attack...I've read up about this stuff. This is a textbook behaviour pattern. He's losing control. Serial killers often do when they're nearing the end of their spree and they want to get caught."

"Yeah, I remember that killer in Ipswich got interviewed on the telly before they caught him," I say.

"I read once, Dahmer I think it was," Rupesh says, "he was inviting victims over to his place while his other kills were— Well, you get the point."

"I think they'll catch him," Steve says. "That it's over now." From the seat beside me he reaches over and takes my hand.

Like he can't bear the quiet, he asks, "Anyone thought on those clues in the note? Maybe they'll help the police?"

"Let's not," Jen says.

"First one was Trashcan, all one word," Rupesh says. "I've been trying to work it out. I can't help myself. I used to watch *Countdown* with him sometimes." There's real emotion in his voice.

I make a brief attempt to solve it in my head but too much is competing in there for my attention. I take out my phone and find a website that decodes anagrams.

"Nothing useful here really. I mean, Cash Rant, Arch Ants, Can Harts."

Most of us latch on to this distraction, and next we try *resist* as *sister*, and after mulling it over Rupesh asks the rest of us if we know Will had a sibling that died before. None of us do.

"So that one could be me?" Rupesh says. "I only found out by accident one day. He never talked about it."

"I've got no idea if we're on the right track or not," I say. "They're so vague."

"He's playing head games," Jen says. "This is stupid. All that stuff about us getting to know each other. He's hoping we'll confess *all* our secrets while trying to work out these *real* meanings."

"Why would he do that?" Steve says. "Do we have that many secrets?"

"To get us to turn on each other. Or make us vulnerable, I don't know." Jen is breathing quickly and looks pale.

"*Strain* could be *trains*," I say.

Something shifts in Steve's manner, his hand rises to touch his forehead. A soft little creak sounds from deep in his throat.

"This might—no, this one *has* to be mine," Steve says. His face hardens, battling with something in his head.

"What is it?" I say.

"It's nothing," Steve says, staring at the far wall. No, through the far wall. Is it Obi perhaps? "Just something that...Something happened between me and him up at the train tracks, really late on that summer."

"What?" I say.

"I never told anyone because...I felt so guilty. We'd been arguing about Strachan a lot. He'd been spending all this time with him and I was getting annoyed about it, and—"

"It's Strachan," Jen says. We look at her. "Trashcan. I think it's *Strachan*."

"Strachan. Of course," Rupesh says. "Well, that could be me too."

"You again?" Steve says.

One side of Rupesh's mouth turns up just slightly. "Well, it was me that threw that brick through his windscreen."

"Fuck off," I say.

He shrugs, no big deal. Although to me it is. At the time it had been so shocking. Not to mention painful, being parted from Steve prematurely in the aftermath. And I've always assumed it was Will, and a large part of what made him a loose cannon in my head was this incident.

"I wanted to do something to make up for falling asleep the night you all left that note about his dog, do you remember?"

"You fell asleep?" Steve says.

"I was trying to make it up to you. And in my drunken mind I thought it couldn't be any worse than the hoops you'd make me jump through to get even. Then when the police started sniffing around I didn't take the credit. Bloody stupid really." He shakes his head. "Will was the only one I ever told about that."

"Well, it might be me too," I say. "I don't know if you all knew about my mum and Mr. Strachan—that I caught them having an affair?" I look to Jen.

"Well, actually, *Please* might be me, too," Rupesh says. "Could be *asleep*, as in the night of the note again. Will definitely knew that."

"I don't think that's you," Jen says.

The door opens and PC Clarke and PC Massey enter and begin apologising. They've been to the house in Sparkbrook and no one was answering.

"So what's the plan?" Steve says.

"Well, I think for now you need to be vigilant," PC Clarke says.

"We did that," Steve says, "and now this has happened. Have you gone in his house?"

"We need a warrant for that, which can take time. And we need the rest of your statements—"

"Are you taking us seriously?"

297

"Yes, we are," PC Massey says. She glances over at Jen. "But there are complicating circumstances."

"So do we just leave?" I say.

"The idea some of you mentioned was good," PC Massey says. "Getting a hotel tonight together to look out for one another. We'll be in shortly to do the rest of these interviews, but we ask you please to just bear with us on this."

When they are gone Jen sighs and stares up at the ceiling.

"This is ludicrous," Steve says.

"I'm sorry," Jen says. "It's my fault."

"What's your fault?" Steve says.

"I got into a muddle in my interview," she says, and now her face is like a wet flannel being wrung. "I'm sorry, guys. I'm sorry." She begins to cry. Rupesh gets up and sits by her, tries to put his arm around her. She won't have it and pulls away from him. He holds up both hands and goes back to his seat on the opposite side of the room to give her space.

"We said we were going to tell them everything, okay," she says, "so I did. I told them that I drew the smiley face in my shower."

Silence. No, not quite. I can hear the hum of the heating system in the walls. An emotional sinkhole opens and down, down, down we fall.

"Why would you do that?" Steve says.

"I made it up. But please listen. I was convinced it was him, okay? *Asleep*, that's a clue about me. I fell asleep on his lap by accident this one time. I woke up later, like hours later, and he was still staring at me. And he had this erection, and it really disturbed me. Like what had he done while I slept? I never forgot that, and it's been in my head this whole time. And when you two found out about Will being dead, I thought you were all going to give up. That's how it felt. But I knew it was him, I knew it and I was right, but I was worried we would walk away. So I wanted to just keep you all..."

She trails off. Rupesh has cupped his mouth with both hands. Steve is biting his top lip.

"I didn't do the first one. The first one was probably Will, I don't know. But Adeline, I'm sorry I put that first letter in your parents' post box, too. I drove it over before you picked me up."

None of us can speak. I can't unpick what this means. How much of our decision-making has been tied into those messages? We'd perceived them as direct threats. And where did this leave us? If she set up those faces, why not all of it?

"I told the police this, and they understood," Jen says. "But then they asked me if I thought anyone else in the group might be responsible for what happened to Adeline's mum. And I panicked because I thought they were trying to imply it was me, but it wasn't, Adeline, I promise. So I said you, Rupesh. I said you because I left a smiley-face note in your tea jar the day I told you about the one in the shower. And when I stayed at yours last night I'd just assumed you'd not found it, but then when I looked this morning, before the others arrived, it wasn't there. And I didn't know what that meant, because why wouldn't you tell us you found it? Why would you have kept that hidden?"

"Oh, Jen," Rupesh says. "You've just told us you set up half of the stuff we've been basing this whole thing on and you're suggesting *I'm* in some way involved? We were together last night."

"I don't know? I was asleep last night. I heard you get up. You live around the corner from Adeline. It all made sense this morning. I just, I couldn't lie to them."

I look at Rupesh, sitting with his hand still on his face, head shaking. Why hasn't he told us about that note? The Nessie figurine, the cabin up in Scotland, not to mention that cold medical utilitarianism he'd shown about Mum: these could be questions that need answers now. And what of all the odd hostility he'd barely been able to contain around Steve and our past at his house that first morning after The George?

But what to make of Jen? Why let her derail us from the obvious? God, she left all those smiley faces, and now I'm supposed to believe she didn't leave the one about Mum? The police had the notes now, we couldn't even compare the handwriting. They could, of course, but without being sure it was Jen I didn't want to distract them unnecessarily—nor implicate Jen as a plausible suspect by throwing my own doubts about her into proceedings.

"Jen," Rupesh says, his voice calm but firm, "I didn't tell anyone about what I'd found because I suspected it was you, and I didn't want to embarrass you. I could see from the way you were acting and I was worried. I had a suspicion you'd done the others too, but I always believed you were being genuine about everything else. That's why I went with this lot and broke into that bloody house, for God's sake."

"I did not do the first face," she says, outraged.

"I was worried you were out of control and I wanted to be certain before saying anything. And I watched your reaction every time we met up, the way you expected me to tell you all I'd found something. Then your disappointment when I didn't. I'm sorry, Jen."

Steve turns to me. "This is insane. Anything you're holding back, Adeline? Did you happen to kill anyone and not mention it?"

"No," I say.

"Well, that's something. Fuck, guys, fuck."

"I'm sorry, I thought it was the right thing to do," Jen says.

"No wonder they're not beating down his door," Steve says.

Jen's tone shifts abruptly. "At least I did something. I didn't just sit back like you two and watch all this like it's another film you can pick apart."

She's talking to me and I am gobsmacked. Where has this come from? I don't know how to react, and immediately Jen is withdrawing into herself at her outburst. "Sorry," she mutters, and closes her eyes.

We sit in silence until PC Massey comes in and asks to speak to the next person. I am grateful for the break, but before I follow the PC we all agreed that now would be a good time to leave, sort out our respective affairs, then meet back at the hotel.

My interview with PC Massey is short. She asks me if I think Jen might have attacked Mum, and I tell her no. She asks if I think it is anyone else, I say no. But then I tell her I haven't a clue what the hell is going on any more and that I am desperate for it to be over. On this latter part she agrees with me.

I drive to the hospital to collect Dad and take him to the hotel, telling him the same thing Jen is going to tell her parents: that an unstable friend has made a number of non-specific threats online, and that, while it is probably nothing, we need to be careful until the police find him. Dad nods knowingly—that's the problem with all this *Facespace*, he tells me, the mistake deliberate to highlight how proud he is to be an old fuddy-duddy. "Some of these people you're never meant to see again. You're supposed to leave them behind."

He's compliant enough, and the hotel *is* closer to the hospital than home. When he asks me if any of it might be related to what happened to Mum I can't lie.

From the hotel Rupesh, Steve and I head out to Elm Close to

pick up belongings together, while Jen agrees to wait with Dad. Her parents weren't concerned enough by her story to leave the house, and with her sister present they feel they have safety in numbers. More than likely they suspect the whole thing is part of whatever breakdown she is having, which is why they want her home that night, which she has agreed to.

I'm only a little alarmed about leaving Dad with her, although what could really happen to him in such a public place?

It's nearly 9.30 p.m. when Rupesh, Steve and I come back through the doors of the Premier Inn.

Steve's part of the furniture here now. "Do you ever have a night off?" he says to the teenage receptionist with gaping tunnels through his earlobes. The kid smiles and forces a laugh.

We find Jen in the hotel bar.

"Where's Dad?" I say.

"He went to bed," Jen says. "He'd had enough by the time I got in this."

There is already a bottle of red on the table. And why not? We all deserve a drink after the night we've had. Everyone looks knackered, Rupesh particularly, the dark marks beneath his eyes like warpaint. Like he hasn't slept for days really. I resist initially, my head still in recovery from the night before. Then when Steve gets in another bottle, I have just one glass to help me sleep. To rest my mind. And this wine is actually nice, so I have another. And before we all part company, there is a little laughter between us, not much, but enough to remind us we are more or less on the same side still.

Jen's parents arrive to collect her. She still looks shell-shocked. Steve, who has barely been able to look at her all night, gets up and hugs her before she can leave.

"We'll come out of all this stronger," he says. She smiles at this. It's a nice touch.

We head to bed. Rupesh leaves Steve and me in the lift on

302

the first floor. He looks utterly defeated, perhaps finally having let go of the hope that he and Jen might still have something in the future despite her problems. Seems unlikely now.

Steve and I have only booked one room. I know it will be trouble, but can't resist having another mini-bottle of red before the tentative kissing starts. It's been a long day.

The sound of banging on the door wakes me for the second day in a row. I squint from the light coming through the curtains. Fuck, another hangover—I might even have to throw up again. This poisonous drinking needs to stop, it hasn't been this bad since sixth-form college.

"Steve," Jen says through the door, her voice high and agitated.

Steve jumps out the bed, groaning, and goes to the door.

"Is Adeline with you?" she says, barging inside. I sit up, holding the quilt to my chest. My head feels like it's been stuffed full of rocks and holding it up is an effort.

"I'm here," I say. "It's okay."

"Rupesh isn't answering his door," she says.

Why the hell is she here at the hotel this early?

"What's the time?" Steve says. "He said he was going to go into work?"

"I know. It's nine," she says. "I couldn't sleep, and…I wanted to talk to him again before. I feel so terrible about it all. Steve, what if it's Will?"

"It won't be Will," he says. "There'll be an explanation."

He gets dressed, and he and Jen leave me in Steve's room, alone. I stand up and struggle into my clothes. It's not quite as bad as the day before, though once more I can't bring to mind the exact chain of events that had led me to drink this much. Had we slept together again?

I find Steve, Jen and the teenager from the front desk at

Rupesh's door. Steve's clearly spun some sort of fiction to get access to the room because the kid is asking, "Can you die from a diabetic coma?" while he inserts the key card into the slot below the handle.

The door opens and the three of them step inside. I follow, trying to resist reaching out to the walls to prop myself up so I don't appear like a complete wreck.

I should have checked on Dad. Once this is over I need to find out if he is okay. He's in the hotel but how had we left it last night? Did I take him to his room?

Jen, Steve and I are lined up, looking down at the bed. Steve turns to the teenager and says, "Phew, thank God for that. Looks like he's gone out after all." I can hear it in his voice: he's lying again.

Letting out a deep sigh, the kid says, "Close call."

"You didn't see an Asian man leave earlier?" Jen asks.

"I didn't, but I don't see everyone come and go, like I said to the gentleman. He could have gone out through the fire door. It brings you out onto the car park."

"Do you have cameras here?" Jen says.

"I don't know if the one on the car park still works." Then, the kid adds, "Is that a tip on the bed?"

I stand beside Jen. On the immaculately made bed an envelope is propped between the two pillows. It's not a tip. This envelope has been addressed to us.

Steve, 1998

It was going to be a wonderful day. The sun was out, the air was fragrant with cut grass and barbeque smells, and if all went as it should, he might not have to listen to Rupesh's endless negativity for the rest of the summer holiday—all of a month still despite having lost the last week to Jen's family's holiday in Portugal. Providing Will didn't mess everything up, that was.

Steve strolled down Blythe Lane, passing the mansion on the way to the river that he often fantasised about one day buying and dividing up into a little commune for the gang—fat chance of that now his dad had decided to make the move back to London despite his work in the garden. This was probably the route Jen took for her round, the one Rupesh actually won. There was no way Rupesh could have won without her help. As if they thought he wouldn't know. They were the worst liars ever.

Never mind, it almost helped him now. It had changed the moral spirit of the game, set the precedent for him to influence the outcome. Game rules should be obeyed, of course, but when someone else was cheating you were surely allowed to take action to make things fair again.

In Steve's hand were his clues, four gold envelopes he'd found in Mum's box of stuff under Dad's bed, behind the porno mags. He often rummaged through the box, reading through her old travel brochures and notebooks. It wasn't so much that he missed her—those emotions had dried up years ago along with a clear picture of how she looked—it was more he felt these objects held the past within them in some important way, and that by touching them he was connected to all the past versions of himself. That was important to Steve, because without evidence of his own past self he would be stranded on an island of the present, forever doubting himself the way people demanded he did.

The thing was, he'd told his parents that moving away from London would cause them to split up. And although it was never admitted out loud, that is what had happened, wasn't it? They could pretend Mum was working abroad, and that their occasional phone calls and even less occasional meetings were the functions of a normal, if a little modern, family. But she lived in America now. Lived with another man who was obviously not just her friend from university.

And he'd been right about all the other things too: that he'd die inside a boarding school, that Dad would claim he'd be around for the holidays but never would be, that when Obi died no one would even notice. Yet every time he'd given his opinion, they'd told him that they appreciated his input, but that he didn't have the life experience to have a *good opinion*.

"Your brain hasn't developed fully yet," Dad said, "you're capable of opinions but not good opinions. That takes time."

When he'd been about seven they'd been holidaying in a remote North Wales farmhouse. Steve had seen a weather report the day before forecasting rain, and told his dad, with some pride, that it would be a bad idea for them to go walking after lunch. Mum had been out shopping, and Dad grew angry when Steve wouldn't accompany him, insisting they'd get soaked.

Eventually he gave up trying to shout Steve into putting on his wellingtons, and simply picked Steve up and took him to the area at the back of the farmhouse.

"It's a clear day," Dad said, "but no, you always know better."

He practically threw him over a low wire fence that ringed a small empty grazing field and walked off. Steve knew what this meant, because electric fences had fascinated him every time they came away to the countryside, and Mum always pointed them out and warned him to be careful.

"What if the fence is on," he yelled, panicked, "what if the fence is on?"

"You can work that out," Dad shouted back. "You know everything, don't you?"

He hadn't known that, no, but when Mum came home she found him shivering and crying beneath the very downpour he'd tried warning Dad about. And though she hugged him, she did also find it funny, because the fence hadn't even been on and even if it had the gate itself wasn't electric.

He never claimed to know everything, but time and time again he was right. And what the hell was a good opinion if not a right opinion? If they'd listened to him and not moved away from London the first time, everything would have stayed the way it had been. But they didn't listen. And now, irony of ironies, Dad's moving them back there.

The river was now within earshot, about half a mile down the unpaved section of Blythe Lane. Steve quickened his pace.

No one bloody listened, no matter how many times you were right.

That was why sometimes you had to show people they were wrong, people like Rupesh, who was happy to come over to his house and watch his films, but couldn't just get involved with the stuff Steve did for the benefit of the whole group. Always fighting against Steve and what he was trying to do for them all.

Maybe it would take something like the humiliation of coming last and being kicked out of the group to make him realise its value. And would it be that bad if Rupesh's whining wasn't part of his final month there? That was if the others would even go along with it, which he doubted they would when it came down to brass tacks. He'd try, though. And he did have sway over the farmhouse.

But it wasn't just Rupesh who had bothered Steve lately. Something strange was going on with Will. Will, who he had always admired for being a bit different, a bit open minded, was now suddenly obsessed by this pot and Mr. Strachan. He'd completely lost interest in the game and had been brainwashed or *seduced* by the closest thing Steve had to a nemesis. Obi would still have been here if it weren't for Strachan and his fucking dog. But Will didn't seem to care about that any more.

Strachan had shown Will's pot to a friend at some Birmingham museum, and they'd got very excited about it. They reckoned it was significant, that it changed local history. They found two coins inside all the packed mud, too. The local paper wanted an article about Will, and Will had said he'd only do it if his friends could be in it because he'd not have found it without them. That had been a nice touch: their final summer, immortalised in print.

At the bridge over the river, he crossed from the left side of the road to the right, then peered over. The river was low enough to see the gravelly bed in places. It still ran through the three main tunnels, but the two smaller overflow tunnels on either side, each the size of a car tyre, were dry. One was right beneath him. Steve vaulted over the bridge wall and down to the riverbank a few feet below.

He crouched, the sewer stink from inside the opening making him grin and grimace. This will be awful for them. Especially for Rupesh.

This clue would turn Rupesh back for certain.

The overflow tunnel's shining exit was only four metres away, but the combined light from either end wasn't enough to illuminate the central part.

"Good luck," he said, and threw in the first gold envelope. It landed about two metres inside, a perfect distance. They would need to go in. Adeline would give him shit for this one, but he would warn her to wear jeans in advance. Fuck it, maybe he should just tell her all the answers and where the final meeting was, too? No, she wouldn't like that at all. And if he let her see he was happy bending the rules now, she might guess that he was sabotaging Rupesh.

The clue in the tunnel read:

If the lake is an eye, what is the pupil? Your clue lies here, hope the water's not too cool.

He jogged back up towards Blythe, then turned right at Raven Way before the mansion. After twenty minutes, sweating and out of breath, he reached the lake. After a quick warm-up (Mum used to warn him about the idiots who died cramping up in cold water like this), he stripped down to his boxer shorts and left two remaining envelopes on the shore. With an envelope in his mouth, he swam on his back out to the overgrown islet in the middle of the lake. Bugs and rubbish floated past him, and the water was freezing. But it was worth it, because no matter how awful this was for him, it would be ten times worse for Rupesh. Once on the islet he found everything was covered in bright white bird shit. Not wanting to tread on it with his bare feet, he left the envelope under a nearby rock and swam back.

He dried himself with the towel he'd brought as the sun began to dip. Having gone to all this trouble, it was a shame he wouldn't get to watch Adeline strip down to her pants and bra when the time came. While they'd done a lot of kissing, and their hands were unafraid to wander, he hadn't seen her even close to naked. No matter how intimate they got, they could never quite make it to the next part. He wanted it to happen, and no doubt they weren't far off, but whenever they came close they always stopped. But then they'd laugh, and after a long silence he'd always change the subject to avoid the awkwardness.

He dressed and walked to the railway bridge where Will had ended his Dedication. The remaining two clues in his hands were the first and last. At the bridge he jumped over the fence and onto the ballast. This was where he first saw Adeline, standing in a Green Day T-shirt. He'd gone and found out as much as he could about Green Day, trying to get beyond his superficial knowledge of the band to impress her. It was obvious he hadn't needed to do that, looking back. She liked him in that same instant he liked her.

At around the point where he'd found most of Obi's remains he turned to face the opposite bank. Checking both ways for trains, he sprinted across and up a faint path in the embankment foliage. He followed the path into a wooded area that then gave way to a clearing in which an electricity pylon stood like a giant robot. Long grass and saplings grew around the clearing's edge. This was where he'd wait for them. The pylon sizzled above him, like Rice Krispies in a bowl of milk. At night it was even louder, maybe from the moisture. They would think he was cruel for coming here, a place only accessible by crossing the train tracks. *Oh my God*, he would say, *I'm such an idiot.* Only Jen would truly object, and fuck her opinion after what she'd done to Adeline.

This was where it would all happen. Where Will would meet him having pretended to solve all the clues, where Rupesh's fate would be settled, and where the idea he had way back last year would climax. It was eerie even now, in the dwindling daylight. Silence peppered with crackles, not far from that place where he'd tied up his faithful, bad-tempered, sickly dog to the track to end both their suffering.

When he got back to Elm Close Strachan's van was still on his drive. What he'd had to do to Obi was all Strachan's fault. Steve had been too afraid to tell anyone about Obi's bite when it happened, too afraid that if he went to the vets they'd put him down. It had been a stupid decision given how much pain he'd been in afterwards, and given what he ended up having to do. But it wasn't just Obi that made him loathe Strachan. There was Adeline, too. She'd told him all about what she had witnessed in her lounge, and how her mum pretended like nothing was wrong. He was so angry for her. Wanted to out the whole thing to expose Strachan. That wouldn't help Adeline, though.

He looks down at his hand, at the fading scar there from his altercation with Strachan after Will's round. He wouldn't report him for it, because no, he wanted any revenge he took to be sweeter than that. The police wouldn't take him seriously anyway. Strachan would wriggle out of it unless he had real proof.

He hadn't given up on the idea that Strachan was the one out trying to pick up kids in his van either, and that maybe he could catch him out. Another failed attempt, this time in Kenilworth, was in the news just last week. He wasn't as convinced of his idea as he'd been earlier in the summer, but the night of the supposed attempt Steve knew for a fact Strachan was out. He'd been scouting his Dedication that night, wanted one of his clues to be on Strachan's property—a final tribute to poor Obi. He only went over there because he'd seen Strachan's van wasn't on the drive.

Because Strachan was in, Steve would have to leave the clue right before The Dedication started, much later that evening when the twat was hopefully asleep.

The farmhouse was empty when he got in. He took a pizza from the fridge, the third one that week, and turned on the oven. He searched the immense stack of videos piled behind the television and popped in a film. The pizza and film were both done by 8 p.m. He tried calling Will first. The phone rang out. It didn't matter too much, their plan was set in stone anyway. So he called Adeline, bringing the others into the conference call one by one.

"Why do I have a bad feeling about you calling this late?" Rupesh said.

"You have bad feelings about everything," Steve said. Rupesh didn't sound daunted, though, which unsettled him. Even more so because Will still didn't pick up the phone when he tried to bring him in. Unlike the others, Will had even been tipped off as to the time Steve would call.

"Okay, well, I'll just give you the information and keep trying Will. Basically, you can't leave your individual houses until midnight. But the clue is: *Avoid our old enemy's lights, stay out of his sight, at the end of his garden, a prize awaits at midnight.*

"You must be—" Rupesh said.

"We have to go in his garden?" Adeline said.

"I can't say any more," Steve said.

"This isn't fair on Will, what about Will?" Rupesh said.

"Why are you worried?" Jen said. "Concentrate on your own game."

"I'll go over now and tell him," Steve said. "I don't want him losing by accident."

"You and your bloody—" Rupesh began, but Steve hung up before he could finish.

Rupesh: every time they spoke he complained and fought.

312

So irritating. He stormed out of the house, towards Blythe Lane. All the lights were off in Will's house. Steve rang the doorbell and banged the knocker. Nobody inside stirred. Were they out? Will never went out with his family. If such an event was in the diary, Will would have mentioned it when Steve was prepping him for his Dedication. Although now he considers it, Will hadn't exactly expressed gratitude for Steve's help. He'd talked more about how upset Rupesh would be if he lost. Maybe this was his way of sabotaging everything. Oh, sorry, Steve, I just forgot my parents had this thing. Acting the dippy prick when he was no such thing.

Steve banged on the front door one last time, then went home. It would probably work out. Will would just show up at his house at one in the morning as planned, and they'd go to the pylon together. Worst-case scenario he might just go straight to the pylon. Nothing to worry about.

Steve sat shivering on the concreted area at the foot of the pylon. It was 2.30 a.m. A half-moon floated in the clear sky, illuminating the clearing. Beyond that light everything was shadow. Now and then a *snap* or *shush* from the overgrowth would make his skin creep.

It was taking too long. Will should have been here now. He hadn't planned to be alone this long: practically two hours. It was all falling apart.

Every now and again the sound of a passing cargo train filled the night. It should have brought him comfort, the way it used to before Obi. Not now, not after that afternoon.

A scream rose from the direction of the tracks. He was sure his heart would burst with fright. The sound was not mechanical or electric, it was a woman, in pain perhaps, coming towards him. He heard the approach of footsteps and grass giving way beneath feet.

313

Steve stood and watched the edge of the clearing. The screams turned into squeaky, bubbling laughs. A tightness between his shoulders relented with recognition. Then Adeline and Jen both appeared at the same time from two different points at the edge of the woodland. They spotted one another, then both raced to reach him.

It was going to work out anyway. Rupesh couldn't win. At best he could only finish third now. *Third.* Not good enough. Not—

Someone shoved him from behind. He cried out, terrified, turning around just before Adeline and Jen crashed into the back of him.

Rupesh stood beneath the pylon, hands on his knees, shoulders rapidly rising and falling. He was staring at Steve with triumph, the white teeth of his grin shining in the moonlight.

"Fuck. You," he said, and raised his middle finger. "Fuck. You." Then he turned around, and threw up into the grass.

It couldn't be. How had he got behind him? He would have heard.

Jen said, "You are a fucker, Steve Litt." He turned and she slapped his arm. Hard. Then she went to Rupesh and rubbed his back. "You found the short cut okay?" she said to Rupesh, sounding smug. "You should have seen *his* face."

Jen's attack deflected his rage.

"Why am I a fucker?" he said.

"No Will yet, then?" Adeline said. Her hair looked wet below the shoulders and she had her arms pulled tight across her chest.

"No," Steve said.

"Well, we didn't see him," Jen said.

"What do you mean, *we*? You came together?" Steve said. Jen's eye-roll riled him further.

"Well, given it was quite dark and scary," Adeline said, "we might have helped each other out a little bit."

"But—" Steve went to protest.

"We knew it was important, though," Adeline said, casting glances at Jen and Rupesh. She was handling him, telling them to keep out. Usually he didn't mind being handled by her. It was nice, always affectionate. Not now. Now wasn't the time.

"But…"

"All the envelopes were sealed," Jen said. "We knew Will wasn't ahead of us each time, and we waited for him at the start and he didn't show up. So there wasn't any point in doing it separately."

"It was fair at the end," Adeline said. "We had a foot race from the lake to the final clue. Rupesh won this fair and square. It was more fun that way."

Steve sighed, disappointed now. "The point… The point is to show your dedication. To the cause. To the gang. You can't just change the rules when you feel like it." His voice sounded whiny, but it was out of his control now.

"Fuck off," Rupesh said. His voice was serious, tinged with acid. "You designed those clues to fuck me."

"No I didn't," Steve said. "I didn't think about you at all."

"A bloody lake? Midnight? Train tracks?" Rupesh said.

"Well, you did it, didn't you?" Steve said.

Rupesh glances to the other two, then nodded.

"I honestly forgot," Steve said. "You've been doing so well recently. Sorry. Well done. I think you deserve to have won the whole bloody thing for that."

He held out his hand and Rupesh gripped it with his own. It was shaking.

He meant it. He would rather Rupesh was in the group now than Will, the fucking useless knobhead.

"Let's go," he said, and started walking in the direction of the footbridge. "Rupesh, will you be okay going back this way?"

"I don't have a choice, do I?"

"We have to wait a bit longer for Will," Jen said.

"I'm freezing, Jen," Adeline said.

Steve swivelled to face them all. "Will?" he said to them. "He's dead to us now. Someone can tell him we'll do the draw at mine tomorrow." He resumed crossing the clearing, hearing their reluctant footsteps behind him.

The morning before they came over he brooded while watching films on his own. It didn't matter really, what Will had done. None of it, in the scheme of things. Whenever things got like this you needed to zoom out and look at things from above. He would be gone from this place soon. Perhaps it was never meant to be with this lot—strangers thrown together by the decisions of their parents. Whoever heard of anyone important still being friends with the kids they grew up with? All those movies about gangs of kids having big adventures never showed you the sequel, about them all being adults together. Because it didn't happen.

In London he could start over again and pick a new set of friends from the new school. And while he would miss Adeline—there was more to their relationship than chance alone—it would be a relief to be out of her orbit. While she was close by it was hard to put her out of his mind.

At some point he needed to tell her. But for now it was best that none of them knew.

She was the first one to arrive at the farmhouse, at which point he already has the three forfeits written out on scraps of paper and laid out on the coffee table for everyone to inspect.

BAN
FILMS
NOTHING

316

He'd brought down three more of the gold envelopes and when the others turned up he explained he would put the clues inside. Will avoided looking at him, even at the point he held out the three envelopes to him.

"I thought the winner was meant to choose," Will says.

"You do it. I don't want anyone accusing me of cheating."

He picked the middle envelope, opened it up, and smiled.

"It's 'Films,' isn't it?" Rupesh said.

He shook his head and held up the piece of paper.

Ban.

With a nod at Steve, like it was all understood, he turned and left. They all watched in silence, staring at the closed door once he was gone until Adeline said:

"Are you going to go and get him?"

"Get him?" Steve said. "Why would I do that? He made me promise to stick to it. You lot have to decide what's right, I can't make you. But I think the fact he didn't even try very hard makes me think he actually wants to be banned."

Will hadn't even come to apologise, or explain why he hadn't stuck to their plan. He didn't want to waste any more time on Will now. He'd shown his hand.

When the others have gone he burned the envelopes in the fireplace. The elementary sleight of hand he'd used to swap *Films* and *Nothing* with two more pieces of paper reading *Ban* would never be known now.

Steve bided his time, watching Elm Close from the window. Occasionally they would stand around on the road in small groups, never all four at once. He caught Jen staring at the farmhouse one day from the end of his drive.

Dad came and went without Steve seeing him, leaving behind a full fridge—the food fairy.

He didn't want to lose Adeline. But equally what was the

point of anything, any of their last few summers, any of the effort he'd made, if he just gave in now? All of it would have been for nothing.

He didn't believe in God, but if there was one he or she would at least understand Steve's point of view. They would be in his head and know how hard he tried for them all.

It was so unfair that Will wouldn't just accept his fate, was probably moping around looking for sympathy votes. It actually made Steve angry. The ban wasn't enough really, when it came to it. He'd really fucked up everything after he'd given him an out on a plate.

While overdosing on films, his mind occupied, some deeper part of his brain reached an important conclusion: they actually can't do anything without him. They needed this place. Jen's parents were never away long enough to go to theirs, and Adeline never wanted anyone around at hers for long because of her mum. And there was no way they would hang out at Rupesh's or Will's.

He just had to wait. They would eventually come back. And if they didn't, he'd just find Will and speak to him. Tell him to deal with the consequences of his actions.

It was Rupesh who came over first.

"Not seen you in a while," he said, sheepish. He waited for an invite before sitting down.

They watched a film. Later that day Jen came around, under the guise of looking for Rupesh. They both made themselves comfortable, snuggled up out of sight, and watched another film, although they constantly tried to bring the conversation back to Will. He made them drinks and got a fire going when it got cold. He was patient with them, but always managed to avoid falling for whatever little softly, softly plan they'd cooked up.

"Are you going to be part of the photograph when it happens?" Jen said that evening. "Or will you still be having a hissy fit?"

Steve resisted the urge to lay into her, took a breath, and as he'd planned, said, "I'm going to be part of it. I just don't think Will should be."

"Well, you can't stop him being in it," Rupesh said.

But, yes, he could if he wanted. And he did want. Will needed to know. Very calmly, and very rationally, he explained how he felt. How Will didn't try in any of the rounds, regardless of the last one. It wasn't like he was being unreasonable. If Will had just phoned him that afternoon, told Steve he couldn't make it, everything would have been okay. Steve could have postponed it. But he hadn't, despite Steve going out of his way to help him beat Rupesh.

When he finished, they shook their heads. The word harsh was thrown out more than once. And though neither of them agreed or disagreed with what he said outright, and made noises like what he said was in some indefinable way wrong, neither of them left. And neither of them disagreed outright with the notion of suggesting Will bow out of the photo.

"So really it's up to you," Steve said. "But you know, you lot can still see him if you want. You don't have to come over here to mine all the time, do you?"

But the next day, they came over again.

A week after his round Mr. Strachan came to see Steve. It was early, before the others had come over and before he had even showered. He didn't hold back once Steve opened the door.

"Your dad in?" he said.

"No," he said with a tone to let him know it was none of his business really. Seeing a change, a glint in the old man's eye, Steve knew he'd fucked up.

Strachan pushed the rest of the way inside and pinned Steve

up against the back wall of the entrance hall, his meaty arm and all its grey hair wedged under his chin. Steve bit his tongue and he tasted blood.

Eerily calm, Strachan said, "My mate Will tells me you're trying to stop him being in the paper. That right?"

Where does he start? Can he start? Is this man capable of understanding? He smells of booze.

"And before you speak," Strachan said, "I'm just giving you the one chance here, okay?"

What the fuck did that mean? He didn't know, but tries to say, "It's complicat—"

His words are choked off by Strachan's arm pushing into his throat and lifting him from the floor. He was being hanged. Strachan raised his eyebrow, disappointed, then lowered him back down.

"Yes," Steve said.

"That's not happening, you understand?" he said. "Whatever little power trip you're on, it's not worth it." He raised Steve off the ground once more and a sound he'd never heard himself make before squeaked from his mouth. Placing him back down, Strachan said, "Whatever command of yours he's disobeyed, you say sorry to him. He's a good kid and I know you're trying to get in his head. If I see he's not in that photo, you're fucked. Okay? Fucked."

He let Steve go and he collapsed to the floor and watched Strachan leave, calmly closing the door behind him. He touched his tongue, and when he saw his bloody fingertips his eyes welled with tears.

Winter, 2015

After dropping Dad back at the hospital, I drive straight to my parents' where Steve is already waiting. Jen arrives not long after. The three of us sit in my parents' lounge. I cradle a black coffee in shaky hands. It's nearly lunchtime.

We haven't told the police that Rupesh is missing because we already know where he is and how we can get him back. Also because the latest note from Will explicitly forbids it.

Friends,
Rules aren't made to be broken. So now...
Just one Dedication, yours Steve, the big man, but the stakes are so much higher.
You're playing for Rupesh. And this will really strain you.
If you: haven't started by 10 p.m., aren't with me by midnight with all the clues I leave for you, don't visit every stop of Steve's Dedication, even think about the police again...
I can make it painful, for you and him.

Tell the police you'll be at the hotel tonight then be at Adeline's from 2 p.m. where I can see you all but you won't see me. That'll come later.

Do as I say and you won't come to harm. This is meant to be fun.

The big reunion.

Love, Will x

At the bottom of the note is the dead smiley face again.

Jen finishes reading it and Steve says, "Does anyone think we should tell the police?"

He tries making eye contact with us. Jen shakes her head, her eyes wet with tears. I can only look at the floor. It's obvious, to all of us, that if we do, there is no guarantee that the police won't decide it's better to sacrifice Rupesh for the greater good. Charge in regardless once they know where he will be and when. But equally there's no guarantee Will won't kill all of us once we are out there on our own along with Rupesh. No guarantee he'll keep his word.

"It feels like a trap," I say. "He wants us to think we've got control over what happens to Rupesh when we don't."

"And if we do?" Jen says. "He could have killed us already. He could have killed us last night. Could have done it any time before."

"He's got something planned. Some grand *finish*," Steve says. "It might not necessarily mean he plans to hurt us."

"We won't know that going out there," I say. Just hearing it aloud, the very idea of us stepping into the night with Will out there waiting for us, is dreadful enough. How has it come to this? Things hadn't been perfect in London but I'd been safe there. I had things to look forward to, so many of them. Why can't I just walk out the door and forget all of it? Go back to what I'd been doing before.

Steve leans down and grabs his head with his hands. "*Strain,* that clue again."

"What?" Jen says.

With a sigh, he says, "The more this has gone on the more I remember how angry I made Will at the end of that summer. I'd come here sort of worried about how everyone would remember me because of how I used to be, but mainly it was Rupesh. Because in my head it was him that I'd always been so disappointed in all the time. I mean, shit, I remember designing my round of The Dedication so that Rupesh would lose. If I'm honest, maybe the whole game was designed to get him back for always being so half-arsed. But when Will came last, I turned on him really bad. Do you remember? And now he keeps mentioning this *Strain* thing. I think if he's going to harm anyone, it might be me."

"What do you mean?" Jen says.

"Why is this *my* Dedication he's making us do? Why is that clue he wrote us connected to what I saw at the train tracks?"

I can't remember exactly what did happen after the game, outside of those events at the campfire. So Will was banned from Steve's house, but it had all been sorted. Steve and Will had patched things up, hadn't they?

"What is 'strain' then?"

Steve shakes his head and his voice softens. "I went to see Will after we kicked him out. Do you remember? You made me, Adeline, because he wasn't right. You were worried about him. And I found him walking around the fields. He wouldn't talk to me, but I walked with him around the lake, trying to convince him it would all be fine, told him he could rejoin the group if he wanted, that I was only doing it because he'd asked me to make sure the rules were obeyed no matter the outcome."

"I remember," I say.

"But he just kept walking and babbling, but not in his usual way. Really weird shit, about the afterlife and his family. I think he was high, and I was worried, especially when we ended up at the train tracks, and he told me he'd not been able to stop thinking about Obi and the trains. And what it must have been like for Obi, whether he knew anything about it or not.

"That's when he said he thought he could lie under the train and it would go over him. And I laughed, same old Will, right? I told him the suction would pull him up and he'd be torn apart like they tell you at school and he told me Mr. Strachan and him had been talking, and that he thought it was a myth. So he went and lay between the tracks. I told him he was going to die, that he'd die and fuck me up in the process, and he started laughing and said that wouldn't be such a bad thing. And he didn't move. I thought any second he'd get up, joke's on Steve, but also I sort of *knew* he wouldn't because of how strange he was acting. And he stayed there. He even closed his eyes. I saw the real Will then, the one we'd missed because we'd been too busy laughing at him.

"I started telling him to move, swearing at him. I tried dragging him off but he was so strong, grabbing the rails. I knew a train would be there any second and so I ran. I ran away and just waited down by the bollards at the lake. I was bloody shaking down there, and when I heard a train go by shortly afterwards I didn't know what to do. Had it hit him? Wouldn't it have stopped?

"About ten minutes later he just walked on up and sat down with me. He said, 'Told you.' I didn't believe him. And he just shrugged. It was weird because then I did believe him. I believed that I'd upset him enough to do that."

"That can't—" I say, because it's impossible. No one could survive such a thing, could they?

"Of course he made it up," Steve says. "But at the time, and for a long time afterwards, it haunted me that he had done it, and that I'd just…let it happen. And it terrified me so much, how nonchalantly he walked over to me after. I kept saying to him,

'It's impossible, it's impossible.' I looked it up once. What he did, whether it could be done. Recently enough that YouTube existed. The videos there are likely fakes, but some people on forums reckon if you're strong enough, and there's nothing dangling underneath, it's possible. Unlikely, but possible."

Now I vaguely remember Steve coming back from that meeting with Will all those years ago, acting distant and uncommunicative. I had taken it personally, of course, without a clue as to what had just happened. What had *really* upset him?

"I think this clue refers to what happened then. That's why I think it's me he's focused on," Steve says.

"But why would he want to get back at you?" Jen says.

"I don't know," Steve says. "Maybe he holds me responsible for how his life turned out for his own batshit reasons. You didn't see how he was with me the other night, but that's how it felt." He looks at me for reassurance and I nod. "He calls me *the big man* in his note, like we're all sixteen again. Maybe he never forgave me for kicking him out of the group. Maybe he's angry I left him at the train tracks. Maybe he thinks I'm the reason Strachan decked him. I don't know. But I need to go out there tonight because everything here suggests that whatever his grudge, it's specific to me. I'll understand if you guys don't want to come. But if I'm right about this, and if anything happens to Rupesh because of it… Well, this is what I came back for really." He looks at me and I want no part of this, and like a coward I stare at the floor again.

Will's 2 p.m. deadline is fast approaching, which forces us to act without making a definitive decision about what to do later. For now we'll play along. We agree to head to Marlstone and return together in one car. If we're parked outside mine all day it might draw in any passing police patrols checking Elm Close. I drive to the hospital to see Dad first, while Steve heads straight to the hotel. Jen goes to her parents, the idea being

Steve and I will pick her up on our way back to Elm Close once I've ditched my car at the hotel.

I find Dad conducting his vigil at Mum's bedside. I sit with him, holding his hand. Mum's face has swollen since the day before, a combination of the drugs she's on and the injuries she sustained. Purple marks have appeared on her face and around her eyes. She'll remain in an artificially induced coma until her brain has healed sufficiently, the doctors say—should it heal.

"You can talk to her," Dad says. "I have been. I read it helps."

"I should think I'm the last person she'd want to hear from," I say, unable to think about anything but the night ahead, barely present.

Dad smiles. "She thinks a lot of you."

I force a smile back when he bumps my shoulder for a response.

Dad leans in without looking away from Mum, and whispers, "She's got a drawer about you."

"What?" I say, the peculiar sentence pulling me into the moment.

"A drawer full of clippings, from the *Guardian*, from the *Radio Times*. All your Cambridge stuff. She'd never tell you, wouldn't want you getting a big head, and she doesn't think I know about it, I shouldn't think. But there you have it."

He's being sweet to me, and to Mum, even though he must be so worried himself. I lay my head against his arm. He has no idea what she's really like. No idea what she did to him, and the position she put me in, box of clippings or not.

"I never really forgave her for moving us from Marlstone," I say. "I always thought she did it to spite me."

"Well, it was my fault we ended up in Blythe," Dad says, never taking his eyes from Mum. "I was worried about the shop at the time, and the mortgage we had. I was having to work so hard all the time, never seeing either of you. Your mum didn't want to go. She was worried you'd be bored and get into trouble, but I thought the opposite. And you soon made all your little friends, didn't you? It was just so pretty there, and for what we were paying elsewhere..." He grips my hand and only after a moment do I squeeze back.

I tell Dad I'm feeling unwell, which isn't a lie, and that I'll probably sleep for the rest of the day, which is one.

"Go straight to the hotel, Dad, okay," I say. "Don't wake me up if I'm not around. Just stay in your room and I'll find you tomorrow. Hopefully the police will have some information for us soon."

I get up, dread like rocks in my belly, and kiss his head.

"Happy New Year," I say.

Then, perhaps just for his benefit, but perhaps not, I kiss Mum's head too.

Back at mine we sip tea and pick at biscuits, barely speaking to one another as the 2 p.m. deadline comes and goes. Jen turns on the television, but we only watch the clock. Both Steve's and my phones ring. We let them go to voicemail. It's PC Massey, telling us not to worry, that she is only checking in with us. Being vigilant. Steve calls her back and tells her we are fine, and that we'll be safely tucked up in at the hotel again tonight.

The afternoon passes and I have to turn on the lights. While never committing to anything, we begin discussing what we *might* do *should* we go—all hypothetical, of course. About how we should prepare for the worst, arm ourselves as best as we can. We go through the drawers in the kitchen, picking out possible weapons and leaving them out on the counter. It's probably this more than anything else that moves us beyond the hypothetical.

Steve runs through each part of his round of The Dedication— though we all remember it too—estimating that we'll need a good two hours at least.

327

"Obviously," Steve says, "being a bastard when I was sixteen, I made my round hard to try and put off Rupesh. It's only fair that I do all the hard bits. Adeline, we need a towel for the lake—"

"No, Steve," Jen says. "I need to contribute something. After what I—"

"It's fine, I'm doing it. End of. We have to check every place and be prepared for any outcome."

Steve is taking control. It would be just like the old days, just like Will wanted, if not for Steve's wan face and wavering voice giving away just how little he wants this role now. He tells us to charge our phones, and to run in different directions and call the police if anything goes tits up out there.

"Just try to get to the nearest safe place," he says. "Run all the way to Knowle if you have to. And for fuck's sake, if he tries anything, don't hold back." It's the last thing anyone says for a long time.

It's nearly 9.30 p.m. when I step inside my parents' bedroom and look through Mum's drawers. If I'm going to die tonight, I might as well die knowing the truth. And just as Dad said, in the bottom drawer beneath some bed clothes, I find a box full of newspaper clippings and computer printouts, all about my recent successes. It would feel good now to cry, and I often wish I had the knack, but I don't.

Downstairs Steve is on his feet. "I don't think we can leave it much longer," he says. "Whatever you lot want to do, and I'll understand, I'm going. If I'm right that this is about me, then I think I can still stop it."

The atmosphere on the walk to the fence behind Mr. Strachan's old garden is businesslike. Before any of us can do the same Steve leaps up to the top of the six-foot fence in one bound and jumps down to the other side, no shed there now to hide behind. Something cracks in the woods nearby, loud enough that Jen and I look at one another. When Steve reappears, he is holding a balloon. SHOW is written on the white rubber in black marker above a smiling face with two crosses for eyes.

"Does it mean something? Is it an anagram?" Jen asks.

We walk to the bridge over the river next, and I somehow end up leading the way. I'm in an oversized synthetic coat of Dad's and a light rain taps its hood.

We pass the pub on the main road, The Centurion, renamed thanks in no small part to the pot Will found out by the lake. A healthy New Year's Eve crowd are celebrating inside. Shortly, we pass the walled mansion on the right, unchanged since we were children. Then we are at Raven Way. Over in the direction of Balsall Common a firework explodes in the sky, scattering multicoloured sparks. What I'd give to be there, or in the pub, instead of here.

A pavement has finally been added to this section of the road, and we follow it along the right-hand side until we reach the bridge. Like starlings we cross the road together without speaking. The river is swollen, so wide that it's running through all of the overflow tunnels.

Jen peers over the bridge's edge, shakes her head, then lies over the wall on her belly, gripping the edge to stop herself plunging headfirst into the water. Her legs bob up and down as she tries to see inside the tunnel where Steve once left his clue. "Someone grab my hand and I can get a bit lower."

"Fuck, Jen, be careful," Steve says. He gets closer to her. "Let me, I'm taller."

Jen straightens her body and looks behind her to check where Steve is. Then she gives Steve her hand. "I think there's just some rubbish in there."

The headlights of a car coming towards us from the direction of Balsall Common illuminates the bushes a little further down the road. We continue searching on the bank until the car, a police car, reaches the bridge. When it crosses the headlights are blocked by the wall but cast their light on the tree hanging over us.

It would all be over if I simply yell something now. We could get in the car and tell them everything. Will won't know. He can't be watching our every move.

From our position down below the road we all see the balloon tied up on the branch of the tree.

The police car appears to slow down but we are well concealed, and once the lights disappear into Blythe Steve retrieves the balloon by climbing the trunk and along the branch. He brings it over. ME is written on the white rubber in black marker, another Nirvana face below.

It's apparent now that these aren't anagrams. He is keeping things simple, spelling it out to us. SHOW ME... what?

We keep talk strictly navigational on the twenty-minute journey to the next stop, the lake—now the centrepiece of a luxury golf course. The area has changed so much, all the dirty paths are proper roads, the pits and mounds of earth all flattened and overlain with trim grass. A giant club house and car park have been built at the end of the path, obscuring the lake. There are no cars, and all the lights are off.

The eighteenth hole has its own island, connected to the main course by a thin strip of grass on the lake's west side, and it's as close to the islet we can get without getting in the water. We walk around to the green and approach the water, Jen crying out when she thinks she sees someone standing by some bushes watching us. It's just a tree, though, and she apologises.

"I hate this," she says. "I keep seeing him everywhere."

In the moonlight, the islet appears to have survived the redevelopment but for a large sign asking golfers not to disturb the wildlife.

"Better just get this done," Steve says. He puts down the towel bag he's been carrying and pulls his jumper and top over his head. "Like ripping off a plaster."

"Steve, it's freezing," I say, knowing he will do this anyway.

"Like a plaster." Steve runs to the shore and jumps in, disappearing into the black water before emerging again several tense seconds later. Agitated ducks honk over on the islet. Steve crosses the ten-metre stretch and exits the water unscathed.

"I should have stretched," he shouts.

It's cold for me just watching. How must it be for him in his boxer shorts, his bare feet on the uneven, stony surface? I know all too well how that water feels, because I'd gone in on behalf of us all the last time we'd done this.

He's carrying another balloon when he re-enters the water. "The clue is YOUR," Steve says, then plunges into a breaststroke, the balloon floating behind him.

SHOW ME YOUR...It gets us no further in understanding what it is Will wants us to see.

Halfway across, Steve stops swimming and cries out.

"You okay?" I say.

"Cramp," he says, and starts to laugh. Only then the lake is filling his mouth and he's going under while trying to say something through all the water.

"He's fucking drowning," I say, but just stand there watching. He vanishes completely until only the rain disturbs the surface of the lake. He's not coming up. After all this, the promise and the terror, it will end in such a stupid—

I throw down the knife I'd brought with me and yank off my top and jeans. Only when I am in mid-leap do I notice Jen jumping too. Then I am under, the water clamping my body. With great effort I kick against the paralysing cold and break the surface. My hamstrings cinch, my calves are rocks. I'm close to panic, but I fight. I take a breath. And another. And another.

A hand emerges from beneath the lake a few metres to my left. I swim over, gasping, and beneath me warm hands grab my legs. Then they are tugging, and I am going under again, and I try to scream but now the water is in my mouth. I'm drowning too, I'm fucking drowning. I'm one of those people in the papers who swim in quarries despite people dying that way every year. The people you think must be idiots to take such risks, the cautionary tales of the world.

The hands stop tugging, and I buck, gasping in what air I can once I'm above the waterline. Jen is yelling my name, but I ignore her and reach out with my left leg while moving my right to stay afloat. But then hands are on my arm, and I take the hands with mine and pull. Steve's head appears in front of me, his hair plastered against his skull except around the little bald patch that is no longer hidden. I manage to wrap my arm across his body to keep his head up above the surface, trying to pull him by the armpits and not put pressure on his rapidly moving chest.

"Fuck," he says. "My legs just went."

The green's edge is sheer, but he manages to pull his upper torso out while I push the rest of him to safety from beneath. Jen helps me out of the water, then clambers out herself having retrieved the balloon. She ties it to the other ones, which are weighed down by her jeans, away from the lake.

"We need to go and get dry properly," I say.

Jen picks up her phone from where she threw it down. "It's nearly eleven," Jen says. "We can't risk it. By the time we get back and dry off it'll practically be midnight. And we don't know what else he's got planned for us."

"We keep going," Steve says, rubbing his legs, shoulders bobbing, shaking his head.

So I put on my top and pick up my knife, reassured by its handle in my palm once more.

*

A six-foot wire-mesh fence separates the golf course from the old footpath linking the far end of the lake to the road. Once we have climbed over, we kick our way through dense weeds to get to the six concrete blocks at the road's end.

More fireworks burst in the sky, not just from Balsall Common now but from every direction. I again fill with that ache to be somewhere else, at some non-specific New Year's Party that isn't here. It's stupid really, because usually I hate New Year: too much liberal drinking, not enough discerning sex. Yet there it is, a yearning for something I don't even like. Nostalgia is an illness, that's what Rupesh said. Another twinge of longing strikes, even more ridiculous than the first, because now I miss a conversation from just last week.

Steve stands and faces us when we reach the railway bridge.

"Let's stay close," he says. "Everyone keep your eyes open. I'll go first."

We help one another over the still dangerously low railing and onto the ballast at the track side. We run across, and only when we reach the embankment does it becomes clear the foliage is so dense we can't find the old path.

"Didn't Rupesh find another way to the pylon?" Steve says. "Isn't that how he won my round of The Dedication? He came up behind me."

"Yeah, I told him to use it to surprise you," Jen says. "I found it when I was messing around here once. With Will. It's probably as high down there, though."

Steve leads us along the tracks away from the footbridge. It's hard to walk as the ballast is steep here. The pylon is visible to our left, a steel skeleton against the night sky, crackling now as it did then.

"Hold on," Steve says, thrusting out his right arm. I jump.

Another balloon, dripping with rain, lies in the grass on the embankment. Steve walks over and grabs it with one hand. With his other hand, he picks up something wrapped in a plastic bag attached to the balloon by a piece of string. It's an envelope. He opens it and reads the message while we all watch. Steve begins to nod his head. After a moment, the balloon bursts in his clenched hands.

"What did it say?" I ask.

Steve throws down the remnants of the balloon and the envelope, then descends the ballast. He crosses to the furthest track, and turns to face us. He pulls the strap of his bag over his shoulder and throws it over the tracks.

What the hell is he doing?

"This is what he wants," he says, "just like I said."

Now I understand. He gets down on his haunches, gazing at the rail before him, the threshold between our world and Will's insanity. Or was our world ever sane? How could it have been if it led to this? Our childhood games created Will Oswald and this moment.

"Steve, what's going on?" Jen says. "Tell us your plan." Her voice is stony. A teacher's voice.

"There's no other way," he says. He bites his top lip. "I have to get on the tracks."

"Stop being ridiculous," I say, but because he sounds so serious. Jen retrieves the balloon remnants and brings them over. We can see the D and the ATION in amongst the smiley face, and can work out the rest.

SHOW ME YOUR DEDICATION.

I don't wait to read what's in the envelope. I throw my knife down on the floor and run to Steve. I try to grab him but he pushes me away, hard. The force is terrifying, his determination palpable.

"Tell me how else we do this?" he says. "Did you read what he wrote?"

Jen arrives beside me with the envelope. The black ink on

white paper is just about visible in the starlight. I can guess what the clue is but I read anyway, fast, because a train could come at any moment.

Dear Steve,
   Impossible's what you said?
   You didn't stick around to see.
   But now you get to find out.
   Look up at the stars and trust me.
   Prove to yourself it can be done.
   Nearly there now. So don't let us down.
   If you fail, he'll be dead before you get here.
   Love, Will x
   PS And hurry, midnight's coming! See you at the pylon.

"You lot need to move away," Steve says. "Just in case. I think I can feel one coming in the tracks."

A hum fills the air. I turn in the direction we came from and see the lights of an approaching freight train, high speed.

"This is fucking idiotic, Steve," I say. "You're not actually thinking of doing this?"

"He wants me to prove myself, that's what this has always been about, to humiliate me the way he thinks I humiliated him. It's this or Rupesh dies, right?"

"If he wants one of us to lie under a fucking high-speed train then the rules have changed," I say. "You think Rupesh would be here doing the same for you? No, he'd be spouting some shit about the moral responsibility not being black and white or being more complicated than our brains can handle. And he'd be right, because this is—"

335

"What do we do then?" Steve says, still staring at the tracks.

"Phone the fucking police," I say. "Like we should have done before."

"No," Jen says. "We can't. Not yet. We do that, he'll definitely kill Rupesh."

The shearing sound grows louder so quickly.

He stands, and he is not looking away, in profile he appears so determined.

"I'm not losing you now I've found you again," I say.

The train is nearly on us, the driver sees us and blasts the horn. The noise isn't only loud, but invasive somehow. It slices into my head.

Steve reaches out and grabs my hand, and for an insane moment I am convinced he is going to pull us both into the train's path. Instead, he squeezes, then allows himself to be dragged to the embankment again where all three of us stand, breathing hard, waiting for the train to pass. The driver will surely phone the police now.

"What now?" Jen says. "What the fucking hell do we do now?"

Steve is staring over at the opposite embankment, at the foliage near the top. It takes a moment for me to understand something is wrong there; that is why he won't look away, why he won't answer Jen.

"I swear, I see someone," Steve says.

Jen gasps. "Where? You sure? Shit, I think I see."

"Don't stare. It's him," Steve says. I look up to where shadows that could be people move from side to side. "He's watching us. Just...Shit. He's seen me." He jumps the first track. "Come on, before he gets to Rupesh..."

Steve runs towards where he saw Will, across the second rail and up the embankment. We follow, and I retrieve my knife on the way. At the top, the scrubland between the tracks and the pylon is taller than us, but Steve leads us along a faint path through it. I've never brandished a weapon like this before, out in front of me, ready to use.

I concentrate on every step, Jen in front of me, whining "no" but pressing on regardless.

Jen says, "I think I heard someone." But she's panicking, it's impossible to hear anything with us all brushing up against the scrub surely?

"I heard it," Steve says.

"He's near us," Jen says, her voice shrill, jammed up in her nose, making everything worse.

Then I hear something, ahead of us and to the left. A rabbit running away? A fox? Will throwing something at us?

I speed up. It's claustrophobic, worse than the maize fields, perhaps because these plants aren't meant to be here. They are wild, thick, untended. If someone is in amongst them, someone unafraid of this place, I want to be out in the open as soon as possible.

"Keep going," I say, bumping into Jen with my shoulder. My grip on the knife tightens.

We walk quickly, for less than a minute, even though it feels longer. Once out in the clearing at the foot of the pylon, Jen turns to us.

"He was there. Shit. Shit," she says, her breathing laboured.

"Keep going," Steve says.

We move through shorter grass towards the concrete base to the right of the pylon. Only then Steve stops abruptly, a whimper escaping his lips. The suddenness is awful, and I'm of all things angry. I don't want to be scared any more. I resent it. Want it over now.

Then I turn and see what he is seeing.

Someone is sat at the bottom right leg of the pylon, twenty metres away from where we stand. The body is slouched and still, around the head a plastic bag that tapers at the neck.

"Is it him?" Jen says. "Is it Rupesh?"

There is a second body, a plastic bag around the head, lying at the feet of the first. I recognise the cagoule on the body slumped up on the pylon. Jen runs over to the prone form at Will's feet, calling out Rupesh's name. She begins tearing at the bag on his head, tugging it apart from the top because the bottom had been attached to his neck, too. She cries out, "He's breathing. I think he's okay."

The same can't be said for Will, though. He isn't moving and something about the way his body has come to rest—has folded—is unnatural.

I step closer, Jen's one-sided conversation with Rupesh becoming louder, though I'm not listening. Steve tries to hold me back but I shrug him away. I want to understand. Is it over? Is this it, Will's final message?

Once near enough to Will, I see that there is a balloon tied to his wrist, frantically trying to escape behind him on the wind. Eventually it turns so I can read the message, an anagram, two words in black marker pen.

Dead Edict.

His chest isn't moving, but I don't want to touch him to feel for a pulse. I already know he's dead. At his feet is an open but empty Evian bottle.

Rupesh is starting to make noises, and Jen lifts his upper body onto her lap and strokes his hair. I feel Steve beside me and this time let his arm come around my waist and pull me to his shoulder.

"Why has he done this to us?" Jen says, her cry like an infant's.

I can't reply then. But later, when we are waiting for the police, I understand Will's last message to us is not only an anagram, it is the answer.

Dedicated.

Part IV

All shadows, behind us, waiting.

Adeline, 1998

Everyone settled back into an uneasy rhythm of hanging out at Steve's, including Adeline. As much as Steve was being a cock about the outcome of The Dedication, she couldn't fight that she still found herself wanting to see him. She tried to avoid things getting physical, wanted to be angrier for Will. But turning up to watch the occasional film with the others, pretending like everything was normal and that at some point she could convince him to let Will back in, soon led to more kissing. And not long after the other stuff followed. It was amazing, and unsettling, to discover that she could compartmentalise the good and bad of Steve almost at will.

Once, they had come close to going all the way, one television-illuminated evening when Jen and Rupesh hadn't been over on the sofa having thumb wars and kissing, and she ended up straddling his lap without her underwear on. His trousers and boxers were down to his knees, only then, as always seemed to happen, they stopped. She fell into a brief and frustrated sleep on his bare chest, then woke up, still confused. Instead of asking him why he kept stopping things, she started a fight about Will. Told Steve she thought he was being a prick.

It was stupid, though Adeline believed everything she was saying. When Steve wouldn't even listen to her points, she

341

threatened to leave but couldn't find her knickers. That's when he told her that he was moving back to London at the end of the summer. She ignored him, thought he was saying it to be spiteful.

She stormed off in a rage, knickerless, her earlier excitement feeling like it belonged to an entirely different summer.

One afternoon she noticed Will outside from her bedroom window. She'd seen him around once or twice in the week or so since The Dedication, although felt awkward about saying hi in case Steve saw. He was ambling in the direction of the farmhouse and the fields, head down and gait more stooped than usual. His feet slipped off the edge of the kerb every now and again and he would stumble into the road. Was he drunk? That was a worry.

By the time she reached the road he was already turning down Dead Man's Alley. She followed him, holding back so that he couldn't see her. She didn't want anything bad happening to him, but she wasn't sure she wanted to speak to him like this either.

He vanished into the first maize field. She followed, and once inside, when the path straightened, she realised he wasn't in front of her. She stopped to listen; perhaps he had taken a sideways path into the stalks. She bit her thumbnail without thinking, then shook her head. She needed to stop this stupid habit. Her nails looked—

"Aghhh-deline."

She screamed. Hands settled on her shoulders from behind. She spun around, ready to lash out on behalf of her thundering heart, but now he was laughing, and when she saw his red eyes, that sound became a mournful donkey bray that filled her with pity.

"I couldn't resist," he said, smiling in a way even goofier than usual. "Oh, I need to sit down."

He fell backwards and landed on one hand, then settled onto his arse.

"Are you high?" Adeline asked.

"Yeah," he said. "I've got more if you want?" Will reached into the pocket of his coat. The badges on his lapel rattled together like castanets.

"No, Will. I'm okay."

He shrugged and started rolling another spliff on his leg. She sat down with him.

"How are things?" she said. "I haven't seen you in a while."

"Why would you?" he said. "I'm out of the group now, aren't I? And to be honest. I can't be bothered with it all. We might be moving anyway. And, you know, it's not even like we're all going to the same sixth form."

"You reckon you'll get the grades?" He nodded and lit up his droopy spliff. "Even more reason we should all see out this summer the way we started it. Send it off with a bang."

He took a long drag this time, and the glowing end ate up over half the length of the cigarette. He held his breath, and after nearly twenty seconds he broke into a coughing fit.

"Shit, Will. You're going to kill yourself."

He chuckled. "Maybe I should. Or maybe Steve."

Adeline watched him, waiting for his punchline.

"Steve thinks he's doing what you want, you know?" she said. "Sticking to the rules because you insisted he did. That's what's fucking dumb about all this. He is doing this because he respects you."

"You think he'd be doing this if you'd come last?"

How to reply to that? No, if she's honest, probably not. He'd have concocted some bullshit to change the rules somehow.

"You know what he's like," she said. "There are no rules in his life, so he sort of grabs onto the ones he finds like they're really important. Like how sentimental he is about birthdays and Christmas. It's because of his parents, you know that. It's not personal."

"Boys without rules turn into donkeys."

"*Pinocchio*," she said. "Yeah, he's fucked up."

"He's annoyed at me because of Strachan," Will said.

"Maybe he is," Adeline said. And rightfully so; Steve was probably on to something about Strachan. "We all find that a bit weird, to be honest. I don't think it's connected."

"You've got him wrong," Will said, shaking his head. "Strachan's no worse than any of us. He reminds me of Steve sometimes. You can love him and hate him depending on what he's doing. Some people are like that, though, aren't they? No middle. I don't know whether the world needs those people to make things interesting, or if it's a shit place because of them."

Given he was so fucked, there was something to that, enough that it made her smile.

"Also, if this is just about the game, why is he trying to get me out of the photo for the pot?"

"What do you mean?"

"Jen and Rupesh are rubbish liars," he said. "They've been saying I shouldn't go along as it will be stressful, trying to make out it'd be better for me. They just don't want Steve to ban them from the house. Fair enough."

"You found that pot," Adeline said. "If anything we shouldn't be in the photo, you should. This is getting ridiculous."

He shrugged. "None of it matters really. Do you ever think about time, Adeline? That rhymes. Ha! Sometimes, when I drink a lot, I can't even remember that I'm upset. Is it really all that...all that...*ghostly*, all this stuff we do, that it can just vanish if we forget it?"

"Well, the rest of us all remember it," Adeline said. "So we can put it all together later to make it whole."

"Patchwork quilt. Hmm. And if you didn't remember?" Will

picked up a stone from the ground and held it in front of his face, his eyes crossed, and said: "Sometimes I can see what it is we really are. Not memory, not bodies—all shadows, behind us, waiting…"

Will wasn't good, worse than she'd feared coming out here. He'd done the mental equivalent of her bike coming off its chain.

Surprising her with a sound that made Adeline nauseous, Will turned and threw up.

She wanted to walk Will home but he wouldn't have it. So instead, she went to the farmhouse and let herself in. The other three were sprawled around the television. None of them looked up to acknowledge her entrance.

She marched to the television and switched it off to a chorus of protest.

"I just saw Will," she said to them, and they went quiet.

"How was he?" Rupesh said.

"So high he threw up." She looked at Steve. "We need to talk about the photograph again."

"It's already been decided," Steve said without even looking at her.

"No, it hasn't, Steve," she said. "Because I think everyone here has been too polite to call you a dick to your face, which is what you're being about this. The game was supposed to be fun, a laugh. I didn't realise we were literally supposed to be showing our dedication to *you*."

Steve's face remained unmoved, though he did finally look at her. No one else spoke. Instead they all stared like cattle.

"Can we speak in the kitchen?" he said.

"No," she said, hating the way he was trying to control the situation. "We all need to decide this. I don't think any of us knew how serious you were about kicking—"

"Please, Adeline. Can I just talk to you in the other room?"

The revolution she wanted to spark depended on her remaining here in the lounge, with the others. They were looking away from her. Were they embarrassed?

Steve stood up from his chair and walked to the kitchen. Asserting his control. His power. No choice now, she followed.

When she walked through the door she was ready to unload on him. Maybe even break up with him if necessary, not that either of them had ever called what they had anything as formal as boyfriend and girlfriend. Steve was far too fucking cool for—

"What?" she said. But his cool demeanour had shifted into something softer. Gone was his straight back and severe glare from the lounge; it was replaced by a slight hunch and big eyes. Something else became apparent in the harsh light of the kitchen, a red mark across his neck.

"I'm so sorry, Adeline," he said. "You were right, I realised that when you left the other day after our fight. I'm going to go and speak to him, okay? I was waiting for Rupesh to speak to him first for me, just to soften things, you know? And then I was going to tell you."

"So you're going to lift the ban?" she said.

"Yes," Steve said. "I just…Got carried away. I was so pissed off with him. I'm going to find him now. Where did you last see him?"

All this doubt, all this thought. Where had this boy been the other day? In any of the days since his Dedication? She wanted to touch him, wanted to smile, because suddenly the boy she liked was here again. As if a button had been pressed.

"I'm not going to make an excuse," he said. "I just always try and be in other people's heads and sometimes when they don't try and be in mine I get upset and lash out."

He came towards her and touched her arm. She didn't move away. "Also, you know, I'm leaving soon. And I realised that I want to make the most of you while we're here. I don't want everyone at odds."

"So you're really going?"

He nodded. When he went to kiss her she pulled back her head slightly. Was he letting Will off the hook because he knew it was wrong, even insane not to? Or was he just performing, having realised that perhaps Will's exile wasn't quite as important as remaining on her good side?

There was an important difference here, one that she wanted to think about. Only then his lips were so close, and thinking didn't matter that much any more. So she kissed him back.

Whatever Steve said to Will had done the job, although when the two of them returned nearly two hours later Steve didn't look entirely happy about it. It went unspoken that it had all been resolved, but Steve's downcast eyes when he entered—how defeated he looked—told some other story. He was pale, and for the next hour he barely spoke. When it turned cold later he poured far too much petrol onto the wood while gazing off into the middle distance, then nearly burned his face off when he lit the match.

About the conversation with Will he said nothing at all, and even left them all in the lounge and went up to bed because he wasn't feeling well. He clearly resented doing it, but at least he'd done the right thing.

The photo shoot was arranged for the following week, the day after Adeline's birthday and the week before GCSE results. Steve now had the date of his move back to London brought forward by his dad, and it didn't give them as long as they'd hoped together.

Mr. Strachan, the idiot, had let a bonfire at the bottom of his garden get out of control and set fire to his shed the night of Adeline's birthday. It had needed a fire engine and everything, and the whole street came out to watch: quite the birthday present.

Adeline's mum told her that Mr. Strachan kept a lot of valuable things in that shed, and suspected he hadn't shown his face because he had just accidentally blown his retirement fund. Everyone but Will found it funny. He still hadn't quite got back to his old self, although neither had Steve really—two things that were surely connected given the way they barely spoke to one another.

Once the photo shoot was concluded—the photographer taking all of a minute before informing them that, being perfectly honest, the article might not be large enough for a photo—they lugged large chunks of wood from Steve's house to the base of the pylon over three trips, and built a campfire there in the fading light. Despite his shaking, Rupesh insisted that he was fine when the five of them began sharing out the booze; he needed to keep challenging himself, he said, and it really was a great place for them to keep out of sight.

Will started smoking, and was almost instantly on better form, his confidence buoyed. Jen handed around a bottle of awful-tasting liquor called Pernod, which none of them were able to sip without squinting. Steve was still acting a little distant, but was doing a better job of hiding it, even if he couldn't stop staring at Will.

"Dad reckons that The Nag's Head were thinking of changing their name soon, and they think they might make it something Roman related," Jen said. "How cool is that?"

"The Bored Centurion," Will said.

"Why is he bored?" Jen said.

"I don't know. Because he was stuck in Blythe."

They all laughed, and Will gave a sly smile and took a drag on his extremely large spliff. He offered it to the others, but they all declined.

"It's all a bit silly, isn't it?" Will said. "History."

"What the hell does that mean?" Jen said. "You love history."

"When you think about it, that pot might have been something he didn't want. Maybe it was his bog or whatever. He leaves it behind and then time happens and then—suddenly it's the most important thing in the world. I could do a shit in those bushes, then millions of years later it's worth a gabillion pounds."

"Gabillion?" Jen says with a laugh tinged with disgust. "That's not a word."

In Adeline's experience, with Alexa and her other old friends, when drunk and excited and sad, the empty promise of meeting up again would always be chucked out at times like these. But this time it didn't happen, perhaps because all of them had always known that their friendship was situational, a semi-permanent arrangement. The closest they came to such a thing was when the fire was dying, but no one was quite ready to leave yet. Jen asked the group now they were all sixteen, what did they think they'd be doing in another sixteen years' time.

"I hope I'm an astronaut," Will said.

"Really?" Rupesh said.

Will shrugged. "Dunno. I don't really like heights."

"What *will* you be doing, then?"

Will gave this some thought, then turned the question back on Rupesh.

"Dad wants me to go into medicine like him." He shook his head. "I've got on to do science at A level so that's probably my whole life decided."

"A good, safe choice, Rupesh," Steve said.

"Yeah, well, I don't know really," Rupesh said. "I've got two years and science keeps my options open. What about you, anyway, Steve? I suppose you've got it all planned out."

He nodded. "Astronaut." Once the laughter died, he said: "I don't know. At school everyone talks about the City. Going to the City. Working in the City. I don't like cities, so maybe I'll just move back here and do something like write film reviews."

"You bloody *like* everything," Adeline said. "You'd be giving *Scooby Doo meets the Boo Brothers* five stars."

"Fuck off," Steve said. "I have excellent taste."

"Maybe you could write me a nice review," Jen said. "I wouldn't complain."

"Is that what you want to do, then?" Adeline said.

She nodded. "I wasn't sure, but that A star for Drama made me think it was possible, you know?"

"An actress?" Rupesh said.

"What? Don't you think I could?"

"Of course you could. It's just really hard, isn't it? More luck than anything else."

"I think you can do it," Steve said. "You make your own luck by trying harder than anyone else."

"You would say that," Rupesh said. "But some people have better luck with luck than others."

Jen was shaking her head, smiling defiantly. "Thanks, Steve, at least you believe in me. I'll prove you wrong, Rup. You'll see. Just don't come crying to me for backstage passes to the Oscars."

"What about you?" Steve said to Adeline.

"I'm not being a fucking astronaut," she said. "That's what I do know. It's a bit of a waste of money, isn't it, space, when there are people starving in Ethiopia?"

"Not if the moon is made of cheese," Will said.

"Good point," Adeline said. "Basically, I don't know what I want to do. I think you can't know really, and anyone our age who says they do know exactly what they want to be is a liar. I know what I don't want to do, though, and that's a start."

"Be an astronaut?" Steve said.

"That. And I don't want to be just married with kids living

out in the middle of fucking nowhere doing some boring thing I hate. Something *conventional*. I don't ever want to be doing anything that didn't feel like a choice."

"You'll do something cool," Jen said. Adeline couldn't read her tone. "I just know it."

Against her better judgement she smiled at this, unexpectedly touched.

For a while they all sat in silence, for so long a crack from the dying fire made them jump. Then they all laughed together.

"Okay, I've decided what I want to do when I'm older," Will said. He was wasted. "You need to kill at least three people to be a serial killer, right? So that's what I'll do. There you go, good plan right?" He paused, thinking. "Maybe it won't be exactly sixteen years, but at some point in the future..."

They all listened while Will outlined his plan in disturbing detail.

When he was done, there were such fits of hysterics that Adeline assumed all of them were in on the joke. Only when she wiped her eyes, neither Will nor Steve were laughing. They just stared across the fire at one another.

And when it was quiet once more, Will said: "Or maybe I'll be a DJ."

A little while later, as the laughter died down, Adeline had the unsettling feeling that they were being watched. All of them did—a passive high from Will's drugs perhaps. Steve even got up at one point and ran after someone he thought he'd seen in the bushes. He was gone for a while, nearly five minutes. Probably taking a piss. Adeline hadn't seen anything, but they were all convinced they'd heard something out there that wasn't just the wind in the weeds.

When he returned he was shaking his head. He looked straight at Will.

"It was Strachan," he said. "I swear it was him. I saw his hair and his moustache."

Although how he'd seen anything in the dark she had no idea. All of them were sufficiently spooked, though, and when they walked home they did so close together.

"What the hell is he up to?" Adeline said.

When they arrived back at Elm Close she went back to Steve's. He'd given her a CD on her actual birthday the day before, the new Bad Religion she'd wanted. But he said he had one more present for her. Perhaps tonight would be the night they took things further. She hoped so.

Instead, he told her to wait downstairs and vanished up to his room, coming down after a short while with one of those gold envelopes he always used. It wasn't sealed, whatever was inside wouldn't fit. He'd probably shoved it in just now as an afterthought.

She reached in and took out a brown wallet, Strachan's wallet, and had no idea how to respond.

"When you told me about your mum and him I changed my vote," he said. "Happy birthday."

"You never took it back?"

"No."

She stared at it, and given he was so into birthdays, she thanked him.

"You don't sound convinced," he said.

"I just...don't know what to do with it?"

"Oh right," he said. "Well, shall I just ditch it for you? It's a symbolic gift really."

"Yeah," she said. "Would you do that?"

"With pleasure," he said. "I hate that guy, you know. Hate him."

They kissed on the sofa, but without much commitment. Earlier than she usually would, she went home.

New Year, 2016

The first days of the New Year are a blur of questions, travelling and endless searching for places to charge a phone. The police take my preliminary statement on New Year's Day, as they do with the others, including Rupesh, who spends just a few hours recovering at the hospital before discharging himself despite frostbite and hypothermia. I return every day to answer further questions. Massey, Clarke and the more senior officers I speak to are unreadable: possibly angry at us for going out there alone, possibly wanting to make amends for not taking us seriously.

To me, having lived through the whole thing, I'm in no doubt about what happened. It is so obvious that Will committed the crimes I don't understand some of the lines of questioning they take with me. Sure, they need to do their job, but their repeated unsubtle questions about my relationships with the others begins to grate. They're more interested in when I last saw Rupesh and Steve than when I last saw Will. Twice they ask about the person we'd seen running away from us, and whether that could have been a different person to Will. Which, of course, it could have been. It *could* have been Lord Lucan. But of course, it wasn't, was it? The third time they ask I respond with a question of my own: "Do I need a lawyer, do you think?"

They ask for my patience. Thank me for my cooperation.

Could I have been mistaken? they ask. Because the way in which Will died would not have been sudden, so it's doubtful it could have been Will that we'd seen.

Things happened at a frantic pace that night, but yes, I think I am sure.

Yes, it could have been someone else. It gnaws at me, makes me want to discuss it with the others. I suppose it could have been Rupesh. Perhaps he ran off fast enough to then set up the scene they'd found. Yes, there are lots of things about him that have made me wonder if he had been behind it all, but what motive did he have? He liked Will, always had. Jen is the one in the group that hated him the most, but she was with Steve and me the whole time. It hadn't even been her that ran after Will on the embankment—that had been Steve. But he had been with me both the night Mum had been attacked and the night Rupesh had been kidnapped.

Which only left one other possibility. Mr. Strachan, the option we had only dismissed because Will had turned out to be alive. I tell the police this, and they don't seem interested, dismissing it as too tenuous given what they already have in front of them.

"This whole thing is a total mess," PC Massey says to me in the corridor after another interview, sounding like she might go home that night and start looking for a new line of work.

Surely at this point they're just tying up loose ends. Despite mentioning Strachan, I know now it was Will. It was always Will. I don't know how long forensic stuff takes, but I suppose they have to establish whether he was alive or dead at the time we found him. It took the police a while to reach the location and the body had been outside of course, but it couldn't have compounded things that much.

Both Xan and Jon try to call me repeatedly, and finally I text them both to let them know what has happened. I tell Dad everything too; the police also question him between his after-noon and evening stints at Mum's bedside.

Nothing anyone says dissipates the paralysing confusion. No one can truly know what it is that we all just went through. That is why I text the others, hoping one of them will suggest meeting up, a debriefing, even a shared phone call of the sort Jen showed us all how to do once upon a time. Rupesh doesn't reply. Jen sends a simple message to let me know she is okay, but suggests nothing more.

Steve is still solid, there for me every time I text with his gallows humour and his continued flirting. He has to commute back and forth to Oxford for work so I see him just a handful of times. He comes to the hospital to see me, brings me coffee one afternoon when I'm on the verge of losing it completely. Perhaps he'd been right when he said it had always been just the two of us back then. Still, after everything we went through it's sad.

"They're ignoring me, too, if it makes you feel any better," he tells me on the phone. "You know, at sixth form I had this little group of skaters and wannabe-intellectuals, but after col-lege we never saw each other again. At uni too, I had all these friends into films. We had all these plans to be film-makers, and all star in each other's films, and talk each other's films up in interviews."

"Like the Bloomsbury Set."

"Yeah, or the Actors' Gang, or like Kevin Smith. I don't know. After Emily and I split, I had a big go at contacting all my old friends, because I sort of sensed it coming and wanted to feel like I hadn't wasted my whole life with her. That I had other friends. I heard nothing from anyone…It was pretty lonely. Humiliating, actually. When Jen got in touch and it just…meant a lot. Like all the other friendship groups had been stand-ins for you guys. But maybe I imagined that." He sighs. "Or maybe they need time."

The following weekend Steve books a room in Marlstone again, so he can be closer to me, he says. We get drunk in the hotel bar. Afterwards we walk over to the hotel he'd stayed at before, wanting to retrace what happened. We hypothesise about how Will must have taken Rupesh that night. We find a fire exit near Rupesh's room that leads down to a staff car park, and a road behind where he could have kept a car running. The teenage receptionist with earlobe tunnels is smoking up against the wall, and he shares an I-won't-tell-if-you-don't look with us. Over his work uniform he is wearing a black hoodie, the word Nirvana is emblazoned on the lapel. Seeing him down here by the cars, it's entirely plausible it was him that left that first smiley-face logo on the back of Steve's car. How strange. I'd probably smile at this under different circumstances, but just seeing anything to do with Nirvana now chills me.

We drink more in Steve's room. We fall into bed and have sex of sorts, but I don't even think he comes. Lying naked beneath the bedsheet afterwards, watching Steve take off the condom, I'm a little embarrassed. He'd been tense and unyielding, broken kisses before I'd been able to lose myself in them. His touch had been unassured, bordering on clumsy.

He gives me a soft smile, then walks over to the bin in the corner of the room. I let my gaze linger on the parts of him that I really enjoy on a man, his backside, the triangle of muscle where his torso joined his legs. It hadn't been bad exactly, just, well, disappointing is the word—even if that sounds harsh. If I am honest, none of the sex so far has exactly clicked, but it is obvious why, and Steve nails it when he says: "Imagine when we can do this and all the other stuff is out the way."

"Yeah?" I say, and put enough of a lilt on the word to imply it was myself I doubted, not him.

"You know I got something I probably shouldn't out of this young PC," he says, sitting down beside me. I practically flinch at the sudden shift in conversation. He pats my leg three times. "They apparently found a laptop in the house at Sparkbrook and managed to crack it. It's pretty revealing, they say. Looks like he'd been planning this a long time, like years."

"Oh right." It's not that I'm not interested in this, but timing is everything. Now I want him to just be quiet and hold me.

"And they found a burned-out car in a field behind the pylon. Turns out it had been reported stolen not far from Will's place."

I stay the night, but my insomnia returns. In a fug I drive to Elm Close around 5 a.m. I get into bed and fall asleep instantly, able to grab another few hours before taking Dad to the hospital, a comforting routine we've fallen into amidst the chaos.

At the hospital my phone is off, but when I turn it back on that afternoon the two messages on WhatsApp are like quick punches.

Jen has left this group.
Rupesh has left this group.

By the start of the following week Mum has been taken out of her induced coma but remains unresponsive. There is no telling what might happen, no timeline the hospital can give that might allow me to decide what to do next. It could be months before they know more, it could be days. We are waiting for some response, good or bad, but Mum is giving nothing away.

Dad insists I get on with life for now, that he'll keep me posted by phone if anything changes and I can come back straight away. There's nothing here for me to do, he's right. I can't bear to leave him, though.

Eventually, he says, "I think I need some time alone with her to talk her out of it; you know how stubborn she is." And I get he's not just giving me permission.

357

On the drive away, the evening becoming night outside, I'm relieved I won't have to see the hospital, or any antiseptic-scented public building, for a while. The police haven't been in touch for a few days, which hopefully means they won't need any of us any more. Can they even bring a dead person to trial? And if they can't, would they bother reopening up the old suicide cases?

Steve has heard from his source that they're working on a theory that Will tricked the other two girls into a convoluted suicide pact while at Wallgrove. While it sounds unlikely, it accounts for the fact he seems to have been lying about having had a third victim already kidnapped. How Steve is getting this information is beyond me—no doubt flirting and charm are involved.

It feels strange just leaving for my old life without at least trying to say goodbye to the others. While packing things at my parents', still nervous about every creak and shadow in the empty house, I text Rupesh and Jen with the same curt message:

I'm heading home now, I hope you're okay. I'm fine. If you're ever in my neck of the woods come have a cup of tea. x

It's such an inane thing to write, but at least it's normal, human behaviour. Not like how they—

My phone rings. It's Rupesh.

"Hi, Adeline," he says. "Before you go do you think we could speak? Face to face."

"At yours?"

"Yeah."

"What do you want to speak about?" Over a week later, and finally he wants a fucking debrief.

"Steve," he says, rendering inert any irony or sarcasm that I might otherwise use to shield myself. "We should talk about Steve."

Steve, 1998

There had been anger before, but not like this. Strachan assaulted him. In his own house, and was forcing him into a climb-down over Will that would make him look weak and useless in front of the people he thought the most of.

Yet his mind was clear and composed when he stomped through the fields to find Will in the place Adeline said she'd left him. He knew exactly how he would balance things again. Like competing against an idiot chess player, his next move, the killer move, had simply opened up in front of him following his opponent's. Strachan had unwittingly made things easy now.

Will sat on the stile before the footbridge looking weedier than the last time he'd seen him. Sickly. He watched Steve approach through the final section of maize with what looked to Steve like fear. That was good, because he could deal with fear. No one liked to be scared. In his hand was a spliff you could smell a mile away, accounting for the redness of his eyes and the dopiness of his expression.

"We need to sort this out," Steve said. Of course he shrugged. Of course. "The others aren't happy. I'm not happy. You don't look great, mate."

Another shrug.

"I'm sorry," Steve said. The hardest bit really, because he wasn't sorry for any of it. But the time for treating Will like an equal was over. "I don't care about the photo. Or the ban. I was only holding it up because you said to make sure I did."

"I know," Will said.

"I want it to all go back to how it was before. I really do. And the others do too."

"Can't it, then?"

"Yeah," Steve said, trying to burn his smile into Will, calming the pet before the painful injection. "There's a reason they sent me. Honestly, they want you back, I want you back. But I suppose I still feel a bit pissed off. So while you'd be back in, it wouldn't quite feel the same. I'd be resentful, I suppose. You're one of my best mates, but I just don't think it can really be the same unless I understand why you didn't do our plan that night."

"I just thought it was slack," he said. "On Rupesh." He knew he was wrong, couldn't sustain eye contact for more than a few seconds.

"See, that's it. I understand that, sort of. But Rupesh wasn't taking it seriously, was he? I thought you agreed with that. And then you left me out there on my own for ages, a sitting duck for anyone lurking about."

"Sorry." He sounded about as enthusiastic as Steve had felt when delivering his apology. Will was trying hard to appear unaffected. His spine was straight despite it obviously causing him problems.

"I just don't believe that, though, mate. I want to. But you never even tried to explain that to me after. And that just made me feel like you were all, *Fuck Steve, I prefer Rupesh.*"

He shrugged. "Sorry." This time it sounded more like he meant it. "I didn't think of that."

Steve let that lie for a moment, watching his upper body wilt. His elbows take their rightful place on his knees.

Then: "Do you want the ban lifted then?"

"Yeah," he said, without any hesitation. "If you're okay about it."

"I will be," he said. "But if I'm going to be cool about this I need to know if you're cool first. I want to feel like I did when we buried Obi together—that we understand things the same way."

"Okay," he said, cautious.

"I need you to show me you understand about Strachan."

Will sighed. "He's harmless."

"You see…" Steve said. "Is he? You know he came over to my house this morning. He forced his way in and choked me. Up against the wall. Said I had to let you in the group again or he'd do worse."

Will frowned. "Serious?"

"Yeah," Steve said, enjoying this part. Enjoying Will beginning to comprehend. Beginning to see that Steve had once more been right. "Your mate. That's also why I need to let you back in. Because otherwise he'll batter me, Will. I don't know what you said to—"

"Nothing, mate," he said. "It's him. He just assumed it was you and I didn't say it wasn't. I didn't tell—"

"It's fine," Steve said. "I know it's not your fault. He's not right. I've always said that, haven't I?"

Will nodded.

"But I need to know you understand. And I need to make things right again. Balance things." He reached into his pocket and pulled out a pair of white cotton knickers with a heart on the front, stolen from Adeline the last time they'd come close to doing it for real. He'd had to stop it again, the timing and the context for that milestone still not right. His mind had been too focused on obtaining what he needed for this moment, too. He held them out to show Will.

"What are they?"

"Underpants," he said. "Girls. I found them in the back of his van."

"No way," he said.

"Yeah. I followed him this morning after he attacked me, lost my mind and went to see if the house was empty, try and break into that shed and see if it's got like a dungeon in there, some evidence. But his van was on the drive, the door open. I saw him walking back into the house, and I waited. He'd forgotten to close it. So I looked inside, and these were inside a plastic bag in the corner. Like he was hiding them."

"I don't know, man," Will said. His spliff was down to the dregs and he chucked it behind him. "Could be loads of reasons that's in there."

"Like?"

"Dunno." He shrugged. "Found them."

"You really think?" Will didn't answer. "If you want things back to normal I need to know he hasn't brainwashed you. Otherwise how can I be sure you won't say something else to him that'll bring him back to my door? I want you to put this back on his property sometime next time you are over. And then I want you to call the police and say you found this. Then they can run some DNA tests or whatever and find out once and for all what he's up to. Maybe search that shed of his."

"I don't know, Steve," he said. "That shed's just got a load of his workout shit in it. That and his museum. I've been in it."

"So you're saying no, then?"

"I just don't think he's a paedo," Will said.

"Mate, do you not get it? That doesn't matter. The police can decide that for themselves. I just want Strachan to know he can't get away with stuff. That there are consequences. And I need something from you."

"Yeah, but..." He sighed again. "If he's not a paedo, then it's well harsh. Might ruin his life."

Steve wanted to yell at Will now. The kid was so dense at times. Couldn't help it, the comprehensive education system was a lottery. And his parents obviously weren't the brightest. Still, why didn't he want to make things right again? The point was to fuck Strachan. The point was to fuck Strachan like he'd fucked them, and Obi, and him.

Instead, a new idea, fresh and exciting, occurred to him. He wasn't attached to the plan to call the police anyway. Too much risk there, bringing the police into things again, leaving it up to their competence to get things sorted. Paedophilia was a nasty thing to accuse someone of if you didn't know for sure. And who knew what Strachan did if and when he kidnapped kids? He just wanted to know Will would have done it, that was what was important.

"What's his museum?" Steve said.

"All the old stuff he's found," Will said.

"Is it valuable then?"

"Yeah, really valuable. He reckons he can retire on it. Use it to buy a motor home on this camping site he loved as a kid in Cornwall."

"Cool," Steve said. Having become momentarily enthused, Will now realised that he had made a mistake and his expression conveyed a fearful gloom once more. "Very cool. I think I have a new plan."

He didn't give Will all the details, just enough to get him to agree to show up at Mr. Strachan's with the understanding it was this or planting the underwear. Going over it now, marching back home along the footpath with Will somewhere behind him, he would have to make sure to get it right, get there early to set things up, make sure Will would have to make a decision.

Not tonight, of course, that would be too obvious. But soon, the night before the photograph perhaps. That would be Adeline's birthday night. And when he got back to the farmhouse he couldn't appear as happy as he felt. He had to make sure he looked defeated. That it took all the guts in the world to do what he'd done in letting Will back in the group. Heroic actions really, just not quite in the way they'd assume.

Only Will and he needed to know the truth.

New Year, 2016

It's surprising that there are two cars instead of one on Rupesh's drive, and even more surprising that Jen's battered Ka is one of them. Jen is sitting on one of the sofas in the lounge so I occupy the furthest seat of the empty sofa, wary.

"Listen, Adeline," Rupesh says, sitting beside Jen, "Jen and I have been talking, a lot actually, since what happened, and there are some things that we really don't understand. And it's led us to some odd conclusions."

"Like what?" He's in consultation mode. My mouth is suddenly dry.

"Well, I suppose we could sort of beat around the bush, couldn't we?" He looks at Jen, who nods. "Because there's not really an easy way of saying any of it, other than just, you know, saying it."

It's like my heart and lungs are lead-lined. I need to breathe, need to swallow, to shift my weight.

"And given how close you are to Steve we know how this will—"

"Just tell me."

"It's my fault," Jen says. "I should have—"

"It's no one's fault but his," Rupesh says, turning to Jen. Their private little bubble of reassurance is maddening.

"What about Steve?" I say.

"Jen told me the story Steve gave you about the train going over Will. About Will being suicidal. Thing about it is, that never happened. I actually know what *really* happened that day, because Will told me at the time. He practically bragged about it."

"We're taking Will's word now, all of a sudden? Okay, what did he say happened?"

"Do you remember you made Steve go and find Will in the fields to sort things out, but when he did he accused him of moping around so we'd all nag Steve to let him back in the group? He told Will he needed to be a man and accept he lost, and basically ordered him to come back to the farmhouse, tell all of us that Steve had tried to convince him back, but that he had ultimately decided to abide by the rules of the game and leave. Only Will refused, and Steve tried getting physical with him. So Will just smacked him one in the face. Will told me that when he saw Steve lying there on the floor, saw his expression, he realised how much stronger he was than Steve. And that if the rest of us wanted him back in, there was nothing Steve could do about it really. So he said all that to Steve, and Steve had no reply."

"So Will bragged to you about this and none of the rest of us?" I say, addressing Jen now because she was clearly the one fuelling Rupesh's madness here.

"He told me," Rupesh says, "because the reason he never showed up to the final Dedication was because he'd found out Steve had planned it specifically so I'd lose, which I think we all knew really. So he lost The Dedication deliberately because he didn't want me kicked out of the group."

"Will hitting Steve like that sounds like a loser's fantasy," I say. "I saw him that day, he was broken. He wasn't fighting anyone."

"More of a fantasy than a train running over Will?" Rupesh says.

"Steve never said that happened. He said Will claimed it happened."

"Then why wouldn't Will tell me that? *Ha, ha, check out this trick I played on Steve.* Look, I remember that conversation better than most things from then because it was a selfless thing he'd done for me. I was touched. And I'd have remembered if Will was suicidal. We talked a lot, I was probably closest to Will out of any of us. He was upset about how Steve was acting, and about his parents fighting, about his sister. But suicidal? So the next question is: why did Steve lie?"

"I'm not sure he did. I remember Will being really, really upset."

Some sort of trick is being played on me here, the way I sometimes feel on the podcast when one of the others has made a distracting non sequitur to try to win the argument. I need to be *that* Adeline now, because Rupesh is up to something, I'm sure.

"So Will's a reliable source now?" I say. "And Steve's isn't?"

"Believe Steve if you want," Jen says, "but there's more, Adeline. Let us finish." She's hard now in a way that's upsetting.

Rupesh takes his cue. "When I woke up in the hospital I couldn't remember much. I barely remember going to bed that night in the hotel. But I had a few very fuzzy memories when I must have come around as the drugs wore off. And one of those, one of the clearest, was of someone looking down on me, closing a door down, like a car boot, you know? Now I've had bloods done and they think I was dosed with Rohypnol—probably in the wine Steve gave us. And then again via injection, because I have a needle scar. I could have been hallucinating, of course, it's a side effect. But I kept thinking why could I remember this one thing and nothing else? It stuck with me, but I was going to let it go up until I spoke with—"

"You're saying that the someone you saw was Steve?"

"I know how it sounds. But undoubtedly, yes."

I smile. Shake my head. Smile again. What can I say to this? It's fucking absurd. This is Rupesh's grudge against Steve taking some sort of monstrous form outside of his warped mind, and no rational response will do. There are so many obvious reasons it isn't Steve where do I start? The fact he was the one urging us to go to the police. That he was with me most of the last few weeks. That both Jen and Rupesh make so much more sense as possible suspects if that was the door being opened.

"I think you've both gone mad," I say with a mirthless laugh. "I'm sorry. If, and I say *if*, Steve lied, then that doesn't mean he…he…You were drugged. He didn't even organise this stupid reunion, *you* did, Jen. I could understand if you…"

I trail off because Jen is grimacing, shifting in her chair.

"What?" I say.

"I did email everyone, Adeline," Jen says, tears quick to cover her eyes. "But I think he played me. Before I sent that email to you all I actually saw Steve. It was at the local Co-Op near Mum and Dad's in Marlstone, early December last year. And when we were talking about old times, he said to me how he'd love us to do a reunion."

"So he *suggested* a reunion to you?" I say.

"No, Adeline, wait. He actually said to me that he'd love a reunion, but didn't think anyone else'd come if he organised it because people might not like him after how that summer ended. He thought Rupesh and you might hate him."

"Me?"

"Yeah. Said he was a bit embarrassed of the past or whatever. About how he used to be. And I fell for it, because then he suggested I organise the reunion, because everyone *loved* me—oh Jen, you were always the most popular, the peacemaker, all this. He even got me—and this is how gullible I am—to agree to tell" you all we'd not seen each other in case you thought Steve was getting me to organise it on his behalf. Which I was. I feel like such an idiot.

"And I'd never have thought of mentioning this if Rupesh hadn't questioned Steve's story about the train. It's funny, I just thought it was a random coincidence seeing him there. I was back for Mum's sixtieth, and I think he said he was back seeing a friend or something. Now I'm thinking, who does he know round my mum and dad's way? Did he *follow me* there?"

"Jen," I say, biting the inside of my cheek, "can we just have a reality check? You placed notes around the place pretending to be Will."

"Only so we'd not stop, Adeline. I explained that." She is practically shouting.

"So are you saying you think Steve did all of this? Will, my mum, those girls?"

Jen and Rupesh look at me, then at each other. Is this some twisted bonding ritual?

"So in your minds Steve somehow made Will pack up his life and leave the internet after telling us he was coming to the reunion?" I say. "I mean, Will was crazy when we saw him, put a knife to Steve's throat. But you think it's *Steve* that killed Will? And left his body at that pylon like that? How does it all work, I'm just—"

"I know this sounds mad," Jen says, "but the more you think it through the more things make sense. So, like, Will was part of our group emails, wasn't he? And we know he replied to me initially, so it was definitely his account. So if Steve really did it all, how did he know Will wouldn't just *keep* emailing us, then just show up at the reunion? Would sort of ruin the whole vanishing-for-a-year thing, especially after Steve went to all the trouble of arranging those two suicides. But Adeline, it was Steve that gave me Will's email address in the first place. And it was just a Googlemail account—he could easily have set it up, then sent Will's first and only response. To hook us."

"Remember, Will said he didn't even get Jen's email when we saw him," Rupesh said.

"The worst thing of all," Jen said, "is that I said to Steve do we have to invite Will? I didn't really want to see him, was glad when he didn't show up that night. But Steve said that I had to, for old times' sake. But, and get this, Steve said Will probably wouldn't show anyway because he'd had trouble contacting him. Steve knew that Will had gone off grid even then."

"So we think Will initially did his vanishing act of his own volition," Rupesh says, "and Steve noticed and it triggered him into action. I think he kept tabs on us all, including Will, and knew about his situation somehow and took advantage of it. The night we saw Will did you not get the impression he was acting towards Steve like he'd seen him more recently than sixteen years ago? He said something regarding being *clear last time*, about not wanting to see him again."

I remember, but to me it had been the ramblings of a mad man with an ancient grudge. Of course his ejection from the group would feel fresh if he is the sort of person that can kill two—

"And Steve also made this comment about having seen Will at some point," Jen says.

"I think he set Will up," Rupesh says. "He found out about Will's decision to go *AWOL from life*, as Will put it, chose victims connected to him through Wallgrove, and then killed them in the ways Will had described."

"Maybe he even worked at Wallgrove or knew of it?" Jen says. "He said something about working in health management."

"And Will even mentioned Steve doing *therapy* when we saw him," Rupesh says, overlapping with Jen saying: "And Steve was so elusive about his job in general when we asked."

"And if he works regularly in hospitals he'd also have access to drugs," Rupesh says.

"Why would he actively let us go and confront Will?" I say. "Will could have mentioned he'd seen Steve before in front of us."

"Oh, he wasn't keen on us going, was he?" Rupesh said. "But I was the one that insisted we get it over with, so he came, his bluff called. And he was confident, too confident, as always. He probably banked on Will not wanting to stick around too long once he saw him. And I bet he had some bullshit prepared should it come up too."

"You believe this?" I said, desperate to halt this torrent of madness.

"He told us he knew PC Clarke to stop us going back after our first visit. We asked PC Clarke and he'd never seen Steve before. Was mighty interested in Steve lying about that too."

This stumps me for just a moment. "He never said he knew him for sure. He said he thought he might know him." That was what he said; I'm certain of it.

"Really?" Jen says.

"You're just finding links because you want to now," I say. "This is cherry picking, it's not scientific." Only Steve has been vague about his job, that is true. And he had been reluctant to go after Will that night. If this were Will we were discussing, how quickly would I be rushing to *his* defence?

"Just play that night again in your head," Jen says. "The way he led us, Adeline, think about it. The way only he saw Will watching us. None of *us* really saw anything."

"You did."

"I was seeing figures everywhere," she said. "I was terrified."

I need to get outside again, get some air to help me think. Force myself into critic-mode. It's impossible that Steve is involved, this has to be coming from Rupesh and his—

Something hits me then, something I wish I'd told the police, and it's surprising how much relief it brings with it.

"I heard Will out there," I say. "We all did."

"We can't have," Jen says. "I thought I did too, but then I also remember Will's body. I was right next to it. Did that look like a sudden death to you? It looked—"

"It was too dark—"

"—like he'd been there a while, posed like that. Steve could have been throwing stones to make it sound like someone was ahead of us."

"Bullshit," I say. "Bullshit. So you think he planned this out in all this detail, and yet made all these stupid mistakes at the very end? PC Clarke, the train story."

"I think he got carried away and sloppy," Rupesh says, "just like he told us killers do when they're coming to the end of their sprees."

I don't have an answer to this.

"Another thing killers do is obsess about other killers, by the way," Rupesh adds. "I don't think we were meant to ever find Will in Sparkbrook. He underestimated us, like he always used to. So he panicked, tried controlling it again, went after your mum and hoped everything would fall into place just like it usually does for him. I mean, think about it, this whole thing, another Dedication, bringing us all back together, games in the night. That's Steve, not Will."

I flare with anger now, recalling just how vulnerable Steve had been with me. How trapped he'd seemed by the version of himself they'd all had in their heads.

"You're basing all this on the Steve you remember from being a boy. A lonely, messed-up child," I say. "That's what this is about, Rupesh. Your ancient shit with Steve. And now you've decided he's a fucking murderer."

"I think he played us all, Adeline," he says. "He was a very

372

clever and very manipulative child, and now as a man...well, he's grown up and learned to hide it better."

"You think he controlled your mind?" My laugh is more of a yap, but I've heard everything now.

"I think he played my weaknesses, my competitiveness with him, my concern for Jen, all at the exact right moments, yeah."

I shake my head in the absence of knowing what to do next. It must look to them like I'm broken it lasts so long. "You know I was with him on some of these nights and mornings he's in your mind running around pushing people down stairs and executing them at pylons. I mean, how do you explain all of that?"

"We've got lots of questions too," Jen says. "But every time we come up with a doubt we can think of a way around it. And that's the thing really, in a way you're his only real alibi. And the police tell us an alibi is pretty strong in court. Which is why we wanted to ask if you're absolutely sure he didn't, you know, go out the room for a bit, or leave you sleeping, maybe drugged."

"This is fucking stupid," I say.

"Why? We know drugs are involved in this, because of Rupesh," Jen says. "And the police told me that Will probably took some sort of overdose and then suffocated in the bag. It was tied to his neck by an elastic band. But maybe Steve drugged him first? To get him out there."

"They can tell that on an autopsy, surely?"

Rupesh shrugged. "Perhaps. Depends on a range of factors, though. It's taking a long time for the police to release the body. Might be Christmas backlog, might be something more."

"So tell me how all this happens, in your mind?" I say. "Steve was with us all on the night before New Year's Eve."

"But he wasn't, though," Jen says.

"I think he drugged you and me that night," Rupesh said. "Then took me to his car, or the stolen one they found, once you were asleep, drove out to Will, drugged him, then either left us at Will's or in the massive boot of that Octavia he drives. If he stayed with us until near-morning, he could have topped up the drug long enough to incapacitate us until you all split up the next morning."

"And getting you out to the pylon? And all the things we saw and heard that night?"

"Again, implausible but not impossible. It's Steve, remember? King of planning. I think he dosed me up again and left Will to die. Whatever you think you heard or saw out there was what Steve was trying to make you see and hear."

Nothing left, I ask the most important question of all: "Why would he do all this?"

"To bring us back together," Jen says.

"He certainly did that then, didn't he?" I say. "Even Will's here, down the local morgue."

I stand up, ready to leave now; I've heard enough. This is how it happened before, how we'd turned up at the police station thinking they had a case when they clearly didn't. How Jen had turned up at the poor Kuzmenski brother's house to crack the fucking case. They were being convinced by their own conviction. They'd learned nothing at all about themselves from anything that had happened.

"What if I turned around and said I thought it was you, Rupesh?" I say.

"Okay," he says. "Why would you think that?" He gives Jen an askance glance, but appears apprehensive.

"You could equally have done any of these crazy things you're accusing Steve of. Maybe you pretended to be kidnapped, maybe you played head games with all of us. You just said you knew Will the best. And you were alone the night you were kidnapped. And Jen couldn't vouch for you the night my mum was attacked. And I'm sure if Steve has access to drugs, you certainly do, Rupesh. And what about when you suggested, rather weirdly, that I kill my mum?"

"That isn't what happened, Adeline," he says.

I know that, and I despise the sensation of myself spiralling. But I can't stop. I'm stuck in my own momentum. "But isn't it fun that I can make it all sound like it did if I want to? His cabin near Loch Ness," I say to Jen. "Do you know about that?"

"Fine," he says. "What's my motivation?"

"What's *Steve's* fucking motivation?"

"He wanted to be king again."

"Well, I think you wanted to dethrone him. That's your motivation. You never got over Steve being hard on you when we were kids so you decided to set him up."

"He told us he couldn't wait for this reunion," Rupesh says. "He was in an odd place, he said, and was over-investing in the reunion or something. And he knew the likelihood was we'd all meet up, have a nice polite evening, then go back to our lives. But that's not what he wanted. He wanted everything as it was, the ones that survived The Dedication, his three disciples. That bag on my head had holes in, Adeline. And what better way to get revenge on the one person who spurned him, who wasn't dedicated, and even humiliated him by punching him in the face."

"No." I take a giant breath and my composure returns. "I think you two need to talk, and think, and then think even more about what it is you're saying here."

"And I think you do too," Rupesh says.

"No, I'm not sure I do," I say. "You know, I'm actually done thinking about the past."

The car is packed up and waiting on my parents' drive. I get behind the wheel, hands trembling so much I can't hold the steering wheel.

So I go for a walk, one last time, to pay my respects to the childhood I won't be able to visit again. I walk by Mr. Strachan's old place and down Dead Man's Alley. And childhood has come to meet me here, because while there are dark clouds far away on the horizon, the sun hangs over me uncovered once I am out in the open and my hair soaks up the heat just like it always did in those summers.

I reach the little wooden bridge over the stream down in the trough between two fields. I run my hand on the wooden rail to the right-hand side and my fingertips brush scratches that might be letters. Beyond this bridge is where the fruit farm had been. Then it was fields all the way to Hampton. From here, the feeling of being trapped used to slip away, replaced by the promise of Birmingham and trains beyond.

If it hadn't been for the friends I'd made, God.

Steve's face, somehow both the teenage version and the adult version at once, projects in my mind.

Capability, Opportunity and Motivation—COM-B, that's what Steve said it came down to. And yes, *his* motive is so clear now, clearer than anything we could ever come up with for Will. I can hear him in the hotel that night. *I just always wanted a gang, you know? Like the kids in all those films we watched.*

Or what about when he'd said, *All the other friendship groups had been stand-ins for you guys.*

I laugh. I clap. I even shiver at how delightfully it all comes together. I'm Diane Keaton in *Manhattan Murder Mystery*. I'm nuts to think this. Nuts.

Oh, but he had the capability too. He has the cash and the car to get up to Loch Ness and back. Didn't he say his job was incredibly flexible? And the opportunity! Yes, if the others were right about Wallgrove and his connections to the health service. Because it had been weird the way Will reacted to him that night. Like he'd seen him before somewhere. And if he knew Wallgrove, maybe he knew those two women? Had them confide in him. All off the record, all completely untraceable. Made a note of them, and their connection to Will, for later use.

Charmed them, drugged them, killed them.

I take out my phone, and after bringing up his name and hesitating, I call Steve. I need to speak to him, because I'm frightening myself. On some level the things they'd said about him chime with something I've been feeling about Steve. Something I've been trying to ignore. Like how nothing had yet quite clicked between us. How he is still sort of distant, in that way he always used to be and that I'd forgotten. How the sex hasn't really—

He answers. The reception is crackly.

"I can't hear you brilliantly," he says. "Are you okay?"

His immediate concern eases my anxiety and makes me want to throttle the other two. Who else in my life cared that much about me that it's the first thing they ask?

"Sorry if this is weird," I say. "I need to ask you something."

"Where are you?" he says.

"I'm actually out in the fields. In Blythe. I needed some air, and I'm down on that wooden footbridge before the beehives. Steve, that night we met Will, he said something really odd that's been bothering me, and what with everything that's been happening I'm having all sorts of stupid thoughts about—"

"God, Adeline, you don't have to tell me. I've had all sort of—"

"Will acted oddly that night," I say. "The knife night. Like he'd seen you more recently than just when we were kids, you know?"

"Uh huh." The line goes quiet.

"I thought he'd been talking about the pub, but, what did Will mean when he said, *if I didn't make myself clear last time?* Which last time?"

His silence is much longer this time. Then he sighs. "I told you I'd seen him around over the years." He pauses. It's not a pause I like. I recall him saying that, on the first night, but he'd made the encounters sound brief. Positive. Not the sort of thing that might end with Will having to make himself clear about something. "He probably meant that."

"Right." What else can I say now?

He needs to tell me more, and he must realise this because he says, "This is a bit awkward, isn't it? I can explain, though."

My abdomen prickles with unease. "Okay, that sounds important. What makes what awkward?"

"I briefly studied in York. I mentioned that to you."

"Right. I don't remember that, but—"

"I did. I told you that everyone had connections to York, back when we found out the victims and Will were all from York."

Someone had said that, but had it been Steve? I can't recall. Hadn't it been Rupesh?

"I did an M.Sc. there for a year," he says, "about a year after Emily left me. And one of the modules was based on a mental health facility, not Wallgrove, but in York."

"You met Will?"

He sighs. "Yes."

"Jesus, Steve." The pace of my heartbeat quickens and now I'm aware of how alone I am out here in the fields.

"Bear with me, Adeline. Please. He was an inpatient, which I didn't realise until I asked him where he worked and he kind of said he didn't. And so we started talking about stuff, you know? Both of us a bit embarrassed at first. I told him what I was doing and he seemed interested. I gave him my number and I thought that it was nice to see an old friend, but you know, I never expected to hear from him again."

"So wait," I say, "when was this?"

"When I saw him it must have all been around the time of

his band kicking him out, but he never mentioned that to me. Basically he called me up months later, he wasn't a patient at this point, and we went for a few drinks. And we talked about old times, and I mean, he was just like he was that night, said he couldn't remember stuff. But as we talked he recalled some bits and pieces, increasingly so. Without me really realising they became actual therapy sessions for him, that's how I think he viewed them. But the more we talked, and the more he found out about where I was in my life, the more I think he got jealous and a bit resentful. He got angry with me and started to say things like he thought the reason he got into drugs and couldn't trust people went back to things that happened that summer. That some of it I was personally responsible for. And I don't know, maybe I was? And maybe that's why I kept insisting we meet to talk about it because then I felt guilty, even though looking back there were other things going on in his head that had nothing to do with me or us or The Dedication.

"Anyway, one day he didn't show up to meet me and when I finally spoke to him he said he was starting afresh and wanted a clean break from everything. He'd already told me he'd fallen out with his family, now he just needed to walk away from it all. I tried talking him out of it, because I thought it was probably good he'd actually been facing his past for the first time. But, well, you heard what he was like. He told me to get out of his head, that I was a snake. All that."

"I still don't—"

"Wait. Please. That's why I was so convinced it was personally about me. You know, this is the thing, I've known this all along. All this time we've been doing this I had all this additional information, and you know, I'm relieved I get to tell you now because it perhaps explains why I've pushed for certain things at times. What he told me made it a lot easier for me to believe he might have committed these crimes. Some of his views on women, and mortality. And looking back I worry that perhaps I even triggered all this by making him think about the past."

"But why the actual…? Why have you lied about it?" I'm trying to be calm, trying to remember that Steve had almost put his life on the line up at the train tracks, and is meant to be the hero of this story. There must be a reason.

"I didn't lie, I just didn't mention it because of patient confidentiality," he says. "You know, I felt I'd be betraying his confidence. I knew you could all find out about his drug abuse and his mental health problems without me having to betray his trust. Especially at the start when we were all just toying with the idea of him being a murderer still."

I laugh. That is fucking delightful. "Confidentiality? After the argument we had with Rupesh?"

"Well, maybe you can see it like that, yeah." He sounds pissed off. "But there's a difference between looking on a system for an address that any old person who pulls on an admin badge can access and actually divulging clinical information."

"Well, okay, but Will wasn't actually your patient, was he?"

"No, but that's how he viewed it. I wanted to respect that, given we'd met in a clinical setting. He thought I was a therapist, and I probably didn't bother to explain my actual research interests."

"So you knew about York and all about what Gaz told us before we went? All his mental health issues, too?"

"No. It had been two years or whatever so I didn't know where he was in that time. I didn't know about any of the stuff Gaz told us either, just Will's side. Like I said, more and more Will wanted to talk about the past not the present. He never mentioned a band. When we went to his parents' on Christmas Day we were all in the same boat in most ways. His old mobile didn't work when I tried it and he hadn't been in touch on the emails."

I find that I want to believe him, because it could be true, couldn't it? Everything he said follows logically, and sounds reasonable when he says it. I can even imagine once he'd committed to protecting Will's confidentiality, how strange it would have seemed just to suddenly betray it—and how bad it might have appeared to us.

"You there?" he says.

"Yes."

"I'm sorry I didn't tell you before," he says. "I've told the police all this, and I asked if it would have made a difference to how seriously they'd have taken us if I'd told them before and they said no."

There were so many things I wanted to ask, the train track story for one, but without betraying Rupesh and Jen how could I? I opt for: "Why are you telling me now?"

"Hello?" he says. He can't hear me, the line's dreadful again apparently. All of a sudden. "Reception at my flat is awful."

Is he going to fake hang up now? I look at the bars on my phone: it flits from one to two. Maybe it's me? I give him the benefit of the doubt again.

"What did you say before?" he asks.

"Why are you telling me now?"

"Honesty," he says. "I don't want Will coming between us going forward."

Even now, even though my heart is slamming against my chest wall, the words "us going forward" give me some base thrill.

"Well, it's great you can be so honest when someone catches you out."

"Adeline, I could have bullshitted you. Said I didn't know what he was talking about," he says. "Listen, I think you need to get up and see me soon. I miss you and want us to spend time trying to get back to where we were before all this. I feel like I want to talk to you in person to make sense of this. I know how you must feel, because all the police questions have made me think some really weird things lately."

"Are you serious?" I ask.

"Of course I am," he says. "I can't imagine what you must be thinking. I need you to see my face. I need to see yours. Tomorrow. The day after. As soon as fucking possible, Adeline," he says, then laughs.

I don't know what to say. He is doing exactly what Rupesh says he does, yet I want to see his face. Because that will be the only way I can tell for sure. Although, even then, we'd seen Will's face, and that hadn't helped alter our convictions about him one bit. When it comes down to it, can you ever really tell if there's a killer standing in front of you? Is it their eyes, their manner, their voice? Their past?

"Steve," I say, "I don't know how to feel about this. Can you understand that?"

"Are you still at the bridge?" Steve says.

"Yes?"

"Good, will you just check something? Maybe it will help with how you feel. Underneath the step at the end. I think I left something there a long time ago and it occurred to me it might still be there. I left it as a sort of present. For you, from past-me. I imagined one day we'd go out there and find it."

"What are you talking about?"

"Hello. I'm struggling to hear you, Adeline. Let's talk when the line's better, but look under the bridge, okay?"

When he's gone I stare at the screen. I feel out of touch with myself and out of control. But my critical faculties are so instinctive that when they're absent like this it usually means there's nothing to criticise. Only thought and time would allow me to process what he'd just told me.

Begrudgingly, I step off the Hampton end of the bridge and kneel down. The crevice is no doubt filled with spiders and woodlice, but I want to put my hand inside because it does look like something is back there, deep in the shadows.

At first I find only mulch. Then my hands close on something smoother and more substantial. Hoping it isn't the ear of some subterranean animal, I pull it through the opening.

It is a wallet, wrinkled and filthy. I open it, knowing it once belonged to Mr. Strachan even before seeing his name on the cards. Steve had been supposed to return this. Only he hadn't. A present to me, he'd said. I'd told him to get rid of it, and this is what he'd done. Like he knew one day he might need this to convince me of his character, and would bring me here to show me this time capsule. A true relic from our childhood. That is stupid, I know that really, yet here I came and here it is. Either it is romantic or it is really fucking sinister.

I close the wallet. I want to believe him, and that in itself is odd. I rarely *want* to believe anything. I like beliefs to happen to me, their truth undeniable.

But there is some plausibility to the notion that I might have been allowing myself to believe this Steve-is-the-murderer story a bit too readily, too. That can't be dismissed. Allowing it because us having no sexual chemistry isn't a dramatic enough ending to the romantic dream I've been harbouring these last few weeks: *Nostalgia Crush* Host Hooks Up with Childhood Sweetheart After Years of Bad Romance.

Knowing my own doubts can't be resolved until I see him, I put the wallet back. It will stay there until either the bridge falls down or the world ends. Some future human, or an alien, might find it, and like Will's pot all those years ago it will obtain significance and value. Even though the only difference between the wallet now and the wallet then will be that it is old. Old is all it is.

Will, 1998

He wasn't stupid, he knew what Steve wanted him to do. Steve reckoned he was quite cool, able to hide things from other people, but he was about as subtle as the Blackpool illuminations.

The thing was, Will knew which of the pieces were valuable, and which weren't. Knew which ones he could take without doing the collection too much damage, might even be able to take a few without him noticing, sneaky does it.

What Steve would do then he didn't know. If he could convince him not to smash them up, then maybe he could keep them. That would be all right. Then at least all this would come to an end and they could just get on with the rest of the time they had together. The main thing was giving Steve something so he didn't go too far.

At the end of Dead Man's Alley he turned left, then in the woods leaped up over the back fence into the dank space behind Bill's shed. Bill was in, the van on the drive. Midnight was a few minutes away, and he knew he'd be in bed, up early for work the next day.

"Hey," Steve said. He couldn't see him yet. "You ready to make this right?"

"Uh huh," he said. "You going to pick the lock or something?"

"No." This startled Will, because he thought Steve was to

his right. He was behind him. Will turned around and he was so close Steve's soapy scent briefly overpowered the other, much more powerful stink that reasserted itself once Steve took a step back. Petrol. Yeah, it smelled like petrol.

"Did I scare you?" he said. There was a *scritch* sound, then the dark was pierced by a flame that floated towards him.

"Take this," he said.

Will reached forward and took it obediently, only on doing so feeling any kind of concern about petrol and flames being near each other.

Another *scritch*.

"I'm making this simple," Steve said. "I've already chucked a load of petrol on the roof. I want you to throw your match up there, and if *you* don't, I'm throwing mine."

"What?" Will said. "You can't."

"This is what we agreed. So don't think about it. Just do it."

"The dog's in there, Steve," he said.

"So? Don't think about it."

And now Will understood that Steve was wrong. Wrong all the way through in a way that he'd probably known the day he'd asked him to help bury his dog.

"He killed Obi," Steve said, even though Will knew for sure now that Steve had killed Obi. "What do you care? Anyway, I know what you do. I know about all those animals you kill. I've seen you burying them around the place. Adeline's seen you. Throw the match, Will."

This was unfair, totally unfair. How did he even know about that?

"That's not what I do," he said. And it was true. He only buried the dead animals he found. The rat down by the bridge, the bird in the maize field. Jen's cat out on the main road, which had been hit so hard and so many times it was barely recognisable as an animal any more, something he'd wanted to keep from her, because it would have been so awful. Better to have her think it wandered off. He'd read a book, a lovely book about a man that thought all living things deserved a funeral. And he agreed with that. Everyone deserved a funeral, every living thing.

"Your match," Steve said. It was one of those paper matches, and they burned faster than the wooden ones. It was nearly out.

"He'll know it was you," Will said.

"Not if you, his best friend, say you were with me," Steve said. He'd thought it all through.

Will waited. His hand was actually shaking. "Let's get the dog out first."

"It'll bark."

"I'm not killing it."

"Why does no one listen to me?" Oh, the rage in his voice. Burning harder than both matches, than all matches that had ever burned. "Throw it."

"No," Will said. "Fuck off."

The match in his hand went out. Now only Steve's match burned, illuminating his face. A ghoul. A demon. A killer. The danger was real, and he'd been under their noses the whole time.

"Fine," Steve said. And then the apparition before Will was gone. Steve had thrown his match.

The shed roof ignited, orange light spilling into their hiding place.

"You were with me," Steve said. "That's all you have to say." He leaped up onto the top of the fence, and Will saw he was carrying the petrol can from the farmhouse. "You coming? No? Fine. See you."

Now alone, he knew the best thing to do was to follow Steve. But the fire wasn't quite out of control yet. It was too far gone to stop, but there was time to get into the shed. To get Elvis out. He ran around the side, the heat intense enough to make him pull his head away. Once around the front he could see that Steve hadn't just petrolled the roof, he'd petrolled the front window panels too. Tongues of flame reached up and around the glass for sustenance.

Will took out a Swiss Army knife from his pocket, and approached the door. He tried the screwdriver, the knife, the corkscrew, none of them would go into the lock. And now his shoulders were getting hot, and the fire was reaching to taste him. From inside he could hear the dog's claws on the bare floorboards like hail on a glass roof, and the low sound of its whining from inside the muzzle Bill tied tight around its mouth to stop it barking. He kicked the door, but it was sturdy. No flimsy shed this, top of the range. Will kicked again, harder. Kicked again.

It was too hot now. He stood back. His hands ran through his hair; his legs carried him from the shed porch to the magnolia tree in the centre of the garden again and again. He could wake Bill up, say he'd seen it from the road. No, that won't work. Not one bit. And Elvis, it would be too late for him. He could hear him scratching at the door, imagined he could. Over in the flowerbed was a spade. He pulled it from the ground and hurled it through the window of the shed, wanting to let the air in to help the dog. But this only invited the fire inside, and the flames were reaching in now, reaching in—

"Fucking hell!"

The sight of Bill behind him was as much of a relief to him as breathing in the smoke-free air away from the shed. He charged at Will, changed direction, then charged at the shed.

"Fuck. *Gah*. Fuck. What have you done?" He was up at the door, trying to put a key into the lock, but it was too hot and he was having to let go. He tried again, and again, then gave up and started to kick the door. One, two, and in, clumsily though a large hole where the wood split. Ghosts of smoke poured from inside the shed.

Will wanted to say it wasn't him. He stopped himself, though. Couldn't betray Steve. Not after Steve had asked him not to. It would be fine now, Bill was here. He would—

Out he came, in his arms the dog, lying with its head much too far back for everything to be okay. He placed the dog down on the grass away from the shed, metres from where Will stood paralysed. The dog wasn't moving. The dog wasn't moving. The dog wasn't—

"Did he do this?" Bill said, stare fixed on Will now. Will wanted to hide from that look. Knew bad things had happened to those that caused that look in the past. "He did this, didn't he?" His mouth didn't open very far when he spoke. He was nodding the way Steve nodded, to get him to agree.

"No," Will said, his voice coming out of some other person standing on a distant planet in some other galaxy.

"Will, tell me it was him."

"No."

"You wouldn't do this," he said, and put a palm on the dog's still chest.

Oh, the time that flowed while they stared at one another was like syrup and he was drowning in it. Then wood cracked, and part of the roof fell onto the shed porch.

Will turned, and he ran. He ran and ran. And by the time he got home he could hear the sirens approaching down Blythe Lane.

Even at that point, as always seemed to happen to him, the strongest emotions from that night were beginning to fade. Pretty soon he was hungry, and though he'd dream of fire and smoke that night, he would sleep.

*

Steve left Blythe and the farmhouse stood empty.

Jen and Rupesh both swanned off on holiday again after GCSE results, their parents allowing them to miss the opening of sixth form to take advantage of the cheaper flights. Typical. Before Rupesh left he asked Will why he didn't show up for Steve's Dedication, and Will told him the truth, about how Steve wanted to rig it so Rupesh lost. Wasn't much point in lying about that bit. He didn't tell him about the other stuff, though. About the fire. When Rupesh asked for details about what had happened when Steve wanted him back in the group, he told him he'd punched Steve and told him to let him back in. Not a bad lie, although one based on something he'd occasionally wished he'd actually done more than once since.

Adeline spent a lot of time in Marlstone now, hanging out with some people she knew from her old school that she met on an open day at Marlstone College. Nice for her, he supposed.

So Will walked the fields on his own as August became September. Sometimes missing them, sometimes not, but always making sure his destination was some previous haunt of theirs. At the railway tracks that sleepy afternoon with Jen drifted through his head, along with it a sense of shame he didn't understand. Whatever: when he started college soon there would be other girls, and Jen would become a thing of the past. He started finding pictures of fit girls in Mum's catalogues and Dad's magazines, cutting them out and sticking them up on his wall, reminding himself that other girls existed. Jen wasn't everything. Since he'd started doing that, though, Monks had begun sneaking into his room and drawing things on the women to make him laugh, moustaches and beards—poking holes in their eyes, too, and worse, holes in places that weren't even that funny when you—

He'd expected Steve to mention the fire again, but he never

did. Not the day of the photo shoot, nor the night up at the pylon, nor any of the few times they'd met up at his before he went away. The time at the pylon had been one of his better nights. He'd joked about becoming a serial killer, stupid really, but he'd made the others laugh. Monks had shown him a documentary on serial killers recently—he was really into them—and Will hadn't known before that the magic number of victims was three. Mainly, though, killers were on his mind because Jen had been over to pick his mum's brains about acting that morning, and all that obsessing over *making it*, which really meant getting famous, had made him think about how if they really wanted fame, a much quicker way to it would be to kill enough people to become a—

He'd even made himself laugh that night, something he hadn't done much of recently. But not Steve, no... he didn't laugh. And with Steve's eyes boring into him, it hadn't seemed that funny any more. Then they'd all got spooked anyway, thinking someone was out there in the bushes, watching them.

He'd been expecting Bill to come for him, or to send over the police. Sometimes he glimpsed a shape out in the fields he thought might be him, but it was always so easy to imagine things out there. No one did come, even though Adeline said that Elvis was dead and the entire shed and all the back fence was ash. Bill was telling people it was his fault. That a bonfire caught the roof. He had a burn barrel back there so it was a good lie. Poor Elvis, though. Poor Elvis. He'd been an all right dog, despite what Steve thought. Some nights he dreamed of them both. In them he managed to save Elvis, pick him up from the burning shed floor, the dog licking his face, only to get outside and find Steve there. He would demand the dog from him. And while he would fight him, he would always end up giving him the dog. And then Steve would do something terrible. A different fate each time but one that would mean Will woke up crying, even if it was only for a minute or so. Had he overheated, or just breathed in too much smoke? How would that feel, to breathe that in, and would it hurt?

Will was out in the fields one September afternoon, just when it was starting to get dark. He only got as far as the footbridge when he realised it was time to turn back. When he did he saw a shadow moving down the path towards him. Drifting to begin with, then he could see a sort of wonkiness to the movement, and at the same time the general shape of this person's upper body was familiar to him.

"I thought I'd seen you," Bill said. His words were a bit wonky too, his mouth not closing down around the words properly. "Come back to mine." Will nods. "To talk."

He didn't really like it, the way Bill sounded, it was the way Dad and Mum sounded when they were on the plonk. He followed Bill, though. When they got to the end of Dead Man's, Bill walked Will out to the middle of the road. In the orange streetlights, he could see giant sacks under Bill's eyes. And the dim glint of kindness that sometimes looked back out at him wasn't there any more. Nothing was there any more.

The two of them stood facing one another, and Bill said, "I was out there listening to you that night. I heard what you said. About killing people." He shook his head. "You're a nasty lot, aren't you?"

Will shrugged because what could you say?

"Still can't believe it was you, though. The shed. You can tell me. It were him, weren't it?"

Will stayed silent. He knew about gangsters and grassing. Knew Bill would think less of him even if he told the truth.

"You know I lost the lot. You know I lost him." Still Will said nothing. "You telling me you did that?"

"Sorry."

Nope, he won't fall for it. And Bill got it, because his shoulders sagged and he closed his eyes.

"Wait here," Bill said. "In that spot."

So Will did, and Bill went into the house for a good five minutes before coming back out. Bill's breath stank of whisky when he spoke, and mmmm, wouldn't a whisky be nice now?

"I've called the police. You understand, I'll tell them I did it. But you understand my life was in there. You know that, don't you?" He reached out and touched Will's shoulder. Something black is wrapped around the knuckles on that hand.

"But you can't take the blame for it," Will said. "It wasn't you."

"It was."

The pain in Will's head didn't register until he opened his eyes to see the concrete surface of the road just centimetres in front of his eyes. By that point it was almighty, all down his neck and on the insides of the actual bones in his head. And God, some tearing agony pushed behind his right eye, and the road was wonky now and—

Another blow struck the top of his head.

And another straight away.

Then Will could just make out the edge of Bill's shoe coming towards his face, then he had to shut his eyes.

This was what he'd been waiting for.

This was his punishment.

This was his—

New Year, 2016

"You know I love this film," I say, "it's hilarious, the writing's great. Other than when he's bothering Sigourney, Bill Murray is hilarious. Even more so on a big screen where you can see him improvising with his face when he doesn't have a line."

"You're still going to put it in the crusher?" Jon says. He's watching me from across the table in the studio with the usual mix of disdain and amusement.

"She won't," Xan says. "You won't."

"But. Buuuut... You can't avoid the fact that *Ghostbusters* has a really, really bad attitude towards government regulation and environmental protection," I say. "Walter Peck is more evil than Gozer the Destroyer. He sneers and bullies and cajoles, and can't even be bothered to say the whole of the word ghost sometimes, so beneath him is what the *Ghos-s*busters are doing.

"But the bloke is just doing his job. And these pricks were kicked out of university for having *sloppy methods*, they're shooting things with unlicensed nuclear weapons that are *at best* unwieldy. Walter Peck works for the Environmental Protection Agency. How can they be the bad guys? You know, this is the standard, Randian individualist stuff—"

"Oh Christ—" Xan says.

"—that lurks in the dark heart of eighties American comedies.

We've talked about it before. Sinister government regulation in the way of the beautiful, progressive force of the free market. Well, I call bullshit. The Ghostbusters are an out-of-control vigilante group that are more of a danger to New York than the ghosts. They need controlling, they need some rules, they need mandatory fucking training on health and safety."

"Still, in the crusher?" Xan says through laughter. "The original *Ghostbusters*?"

I hold up my palm, a wry smile on my face. "Sometimes, you like something because you like it. And other times you like something because it symbolises or embodies *something else* that you *really* like. Only you don't know that. So you hear a song in a club, 'Saturday Night' by Whigfield, and you get off with some boy and it's your first kiss and you go home and think about that boy and all of it's really good. The Whigfield song is terrible. Sure, it's in tune and it's in time, but the song sucks. It just does. But you think you like it when it comes on because it fills you with all those happy memories again."

"Bloody hell," Jon says, trying to catch his breath. "So *Ghostbusters* is 'Saturday Night' by Whigfield."

"*Ghostbusters* is a classic," I say. "It's not terrible, obviously. It's brilliant—that's not the point. But, listen, I'm appalled by the way Bill Murray treats Walter Peck in their first meeting. *Mr. Pecker?* Just fucking rude. And that is what this podcast was always about, separating what we actually like as grown-ups from what we just like because it reminds us of nice times we had as kids, back when our brains hadn't developed enough to have proper opinions about films. So yes, despite its brilliance, free-market propaganda piece *Ghostbusters* is getting crushed. I'm voting to put it in."

I lean back in my chair and cross my legs. It's gone well despite my concerns that we had overdone the number of podcasts recently. *Ghostbusters* was number ten of ten. I am trying to appear cool, but am loving that the other two are still giggling about my closing monologue even though the recorder is now off.

"Well, at least we're going out on a high," Jon says.

"Our best batch maybe," Xan says.

"You think?" I say, though on the whole it might be true.

"Everyone here sure about the choices they've made?" Jon says.

Xan barely acknowledges the remark, only giving himself away with a smirk and a minuscule shake of his head. They're through the worst of it now. Xan is preoccupied both with his break-up from his boyfriend and with the new podcast he's planning to do with Rose Hamlin, a former criminal lawyer turned podcaster who'd made a small name for herself three years before with a podcast about white-collar criminals. It's not been long since Christmas, but already things are moving on. Jon and I were waiting for the final details of our BBC contract, and the events from Christmas are already starting to seem like they happened years, not weeks, before.

"When are you seeing him again?" Xan asks while we pack up the tiny studio. "Cusack?"

I've not been entirely honest with them about how things ended. About the doubts still niggling away at me. I've given the impression that we are taking it slowly, which if I look into his eyes tonight and believe him might turn out to be true.

"Tonight," I say. "I'm driving straight to Oxford now."

Nothing has become any clearer since the New Year. Steve's been difficult to pin down, vague about meeting up. It's annoyed me. But then I've been busy, so it hasn't been entirely his fault. It doesn't mean anything necessarily. I need to go up there like everything is normal, like we really are going on an actual first date again. Give him a chance to convince me.

That the police haven't been in touch since makes me assume they really do think that Will was responsible, which makes me more confident that it can't be anything to do with Steve. Every time I try to run through all the things the others told me in my head I can't see what scared me so much that afternoon.

Rupesh occasionally tries to call, but I don't answer. I assume he and Jen still want me to firm up their story and I don't want anything poisoning my judgement.

Once we have packed, the three of us stand at the door of the empty studio.

"It looks like an abandoned film set now," Jon says. "Just another functional space."

"Xan," I say, "are you absolutely sure you don't want to come with us?"

"Yeah," he says. "You two go and give those endless super-hero films hell. You don't need me for that."

"Enjoy your life of crime...solving," Jon says.

Xan raises his hand. "See you on the other side then, Ray."

"Nice working with you, Dr. Venkman," I say, and with that, he walks away.

The days are just beginning to grow longer, the very worst of winter itself the stuff of nostalgia for another year. When I drive into Oxford it's just getting dark. I only ate toast between the *Howard the Duck* and *Ghostbusters* podcasts, and my stomach is making noisy complaints.

Once off the motorway, my satnav guiding me closer to the city centre, it's obvious Steve is doing all right for himself. Whatever he gets paid it befits the private education for which his parents forked out, although he probably got a fair bit of inheritance money too.

I pull up in a two-hour parking bay that expires at 6.30 p.m. Steve assured me it would be safe until 10 a.m. the next day, hinting at how he imagined the night might go down. I'm nervous, and I calm myself by rehearsing my excuse to get away should I need one: Mum. She is still in hospital, Dad home alone. I'm quietly optimistic about her. The doctors are being cagey, and she is still unconscious. Her body is still living, though, even without life support, and there have been signs that both Dad and I think indicate that there may be more to come by way of recovery. She's been moved into a private room and Dad plays her Roy Orbison albums and puts on her favourite films, like *Casablanca* and *The Wizard of Oz*. Dad remarked one day on what he'd do with all Mum's royal family memorabilia if she passed, and as a joke I suggested eBay. Mum then groaned, which made us laugh, and then cry, even though the noise was most likely involuntary.

I walk up a large gravel drive filled with expensive cars and Steve's Octavia, then descend a set of stone steps and ring the bell on his front door. His flat is in the basement of a four-storey town house. The only one without a shared entrance, he'd told me.

He answers with a grin, dressed in tight blue jeans and a blazer buttoned up over a red T-shirt. When he pulls me to him I get a nose full of his spicy aftershave.

"You smell nice," I say. He does, and it's distracting.

"So do you," he says. "Hold on one second." And he goes back inside, closing the door in my face.

"Okay," I say to no one.

He returns with a coat in his hand and says, "Just in case." He steps outside with me and turns to lock the door.

"Do I not get to see the abode?"

"Sure, later maybe," he says. The door locked, he bounds up the stairs and gestures for me to follow. I oblige. "It's just I've told the others to get to the restaurant for five thirty, so I don't want them thinking we're not going to show up."

I'm confused. Have I misunderstood?

"The others? Who else is coming?"

"The gang. Although I hoped we'd get some time to catch up first, but obviously you didn't beat the traffic. Did you come the way I said?"

We walk out onto the main road. "Uh huh."

"Are you okay?"

"Well, I think I must have got the wrong end of the stick," I say. "I thought it was just us two, actually. The way you made it sound. I didn't know the others were coming."

"It might be just us. Neither of them got back to me to confirm." He looks at his phone like it might provide him with answers. "Us at a table for five," Steve says.

I'm not paying attention, and the number only strikes me as odd after I replay the words I caught in my mind and work out what he must have said.

"Five?"

"Maybe you think it's dark, but I thought a chair as a tribute to Will, well, the Will we once knew, might be appropriate. Obviously we couldn't really rock up at his funeral."

"Oh right," I say.

The restaurant is an Italian chain on the high street. After persistent badgering from the waiters about the whereabouts of the rest of our party, Steve and I are moved to a window seat for two where the night I'd been preparing for begins, albeit visually only.

He'd given no hint of a group gathering in the things he'd said, in the suggestive way he'd spoken. What the actual fuck is he playing at? He hadn't even asked if I wanted to see the others. What planet is he on that he thinks they are interested in seeing him, unless something has transpired that I don't know about?

398

"Don't be cross with me," Steve says. He grins, straight teeth beaming, skin around the eyes crinkling.

Fine, he's handsome. But he is fucking weird. That's the bottom line. How have I forgotten this about him?

But somehow he manages to pull it back, charming me with his ability to listen and repeat back the important parts of what I say, nodding along in the right places and generally being nice. I'm more aware that this is what he does now, but it doesn't make him any less appealing. And that shocks me. I'm so nervous I'm letting him convince me.

"This is a really good date," he says. "It probably should have been this all along." He gives a small grimace, then a sideways glance at the window, letting me know that he knows he fucked this up a bit.

Am I any wiser about how I feel about him? No. I need to banish my nerves. I order a glass of wine, but don't give in to his hectoring. I need to be able to drive away at a moment's notice.

"Have you heard anything about Will?" he says.

"No, I try not to think about it."

"The guy I've been speaking to, he basically admitted, after I'd kept him talking a while, that the consensus is there are suspicious things about the suicides that were overlooked by the various departments, but I got the feeling no one wants to reopen old wounds for the sake of something they can't take to trial."

"So they can't convict him posthumously?"

"Maybe it's for the best." He looks out of the window.

"You think?"

"What will the families gain in reality? You know, in the cold light of day. It won't bring their daughters back. And if they're happy with the story as it is, why bother? Those girls *were* suicidal, after all."

"What about truth and justice and all that?"

"I'm sure there are more easy and productive avenues to bring those things about if that's what you believe in. Maybe that sounds a bit cold, a bit *Rupesh*, but I suppose my job has sort of made me hone my idealism a bit."

"Yeah, it does sound cold. I mean, my mum still might die. She might come out of her coma a fucking vegetable, Steve."

"Sorry, Adeline," he says, wide-eyed with shock. "I just... You know, I didn't even think. Just, I thought you hated her. But of course, she's your mum."

I don't know what to say. What am I doing here with him?

"No, seriously, sorry," he says again, gazing down at the table. "I'm a bit nervous and I'm fucking everything up tonight. I'm actually a little distracted that the others didn't come, a bit sad."

I don't have it in me to just walk away. This is Steve Litt. I have to see it through to the very end.

Steve, 1998

From his dad's window he watched the arrival of the fire engines and the slow emergence of Elm Close's residents from their slumber, out onto the streets. Just like the gang had come out after hours to witness his first strike against Mr. Strachan, now most of Blythe was here to see his final strike. The one that Strachan would remember.

If Will told he would bring him down with him. He'd watched him run from the property long after he'd made it through the fields and home. Long after Strachan's lights had all come on. No doubt he was found at the scene.

Even if he did tell, it would be easy to get out of. His dad would lie for him when it came down to it. Would say that he'd been with him all night. Sure, he'd be angry at Steve for being involved. Might even believe he'd done it. But ultimately, with them moving, he wouldn't want the hassle.

No one could really do anything to him any more. Nothing at all. He'd found a place within himself tonight into which self-doubt could be crammed and sealed. It meant it didn't matter if others didn't understand that he knew best. They didn't have to. What mattered was that the things he was certain about came to pass, that no one stood in his way. He could see balance and harmony the way bats could sense cave walls—a new sense that others didn't have. He'd brought about the magic of this summer, had known just what to do. And now he knew how it had to end.

The more he watched the chaos on the street below, the more convinced he was that Will wouldn't tell. He felt powerful. A bit godlike, if he was honest. And if Strachan caught Will, he was sure he wouldn't come for him either. His only concern was the dog. He knew it was in there, but he worried Will might have got it out in time. The dog needed to burn. An eye for an eye.

He saw Adeline out on her drive with her dad. He wanted to meet up with her right now. Wanted them to finally make love—not fuck—was ready to let it happen. But he couldn't with everyone around. He could wait, though. The important thing was ready finally. Everything felt perfectly balanced.

New Year, 2016

We are on his driveway. He asks me in. Having not brought it up himself, I force the issue.

"I'd love to but I do have to work tomorrow, and, you know?"

"What?"

"What are we doing here, Steve? I mean, really? I'm fucking clueless, I'll be honest. One second we're on a date, the next you want the whole gang together and I'm just part of that for you. One minute we're sleeping together, the next we're apart for weeks. Then you're saying weird things and lying about Will, and you don't even bring it up like it's important."

"Adeline, I thought I'd explained all that. Forget the others, you're right, it's always been about you. For me, without you there is no gang."

"You see—" I want to say, *What the hell does that mean?* That's what I would say with any other man. But. But. Still I'm standing there staring at his lovely face.

"Why don't *you* write something?" those message-board haters always said. It's easy to criticise. Well, here is my chance; write *my* ending. Write the ending that I want to see, the one where the main character isn't some useless idiot who can't walk away from a man who is seriously fucking weird.

"I can explain again," he says. "If it will help. Just come inside."

And the horrifying thing is I wanted to come here and be convinced. I understand that now. That's why I can't leave yet.

"I'll just have a cup of tea," I say.

"Brilliant," he says, and even though I made it sound like I was in charge, it doesn't feel that way.

Inside it's cold and damp. The ceilings are high, and when he shows me into the lounge we pass through a tall archway in the wall. He turns on the light and gestures for me to sit on one of the sofas positioned around a television in the corner. Magazines and old newspapers lie in cluttered heaps around the room. Nice of him to make an effort. As a boy he'd been so neat. What has happened to him?

"Sorry, it's a bit messy. I'll just go and put the kettle on."

He leaves me staring at this monument to Steve Litt's adult life. It is hard not to take in the walls with a mixture of amusement and genuine shock. I walk past a frame in which nearly fifty gig tickets are assembled into a collage. Names like Green Day, PJ Harvey, Garbage all jump out. I am hard-pressed to find any artists who weren't also playing gigs during the 1990s, even though the ticket dates are all from 2000 onwards. He is a man of great consistency, that is certain. Next to this are framed movie posters: *Stand By Me*, *The Goonies* and *The Usual Suspects*. Along the back wall are vinyl records, postcard collages and even more posters. On the shelves are more movie and music paraphernalia, mugs and models, books and CDs. Even a selection of tapes. There is a dog collar on the wall, one I think might belong to his childhood dog. It was on his wall back in the day, as was The Nag's Head matchbook next to it, pinned to the wall in the middle exposing a mostly full set with three matches missing.

This is how his bedroom used to be. He'd been so secretive about that room, had even said something about it being an insight into who he really was. Which was why even though we had free rein of that farmhouse all summer long, even his dad's bedroom, none of us were allowed into Steve's room. Then, when I finally saw it, just the once before he went to London, the insight wasn't particularly insightful after all. So what, he liked films and music?

But now there is insight. Insight into who he has become and how that compared with the boy from my childhood. Is there even a difference?

I can't imagine a date returning to this place and not being a little thrown. Is *this* why he's still single?

Enough, what does it matter that he hasn't changed? Adulthood is a social construct, right? In a way it's surely sweet. The part of me that always felt a little tenderly towards Steve, had felt sorry for him tonight even, cries out in protest as I judge him. Jon and Xan's places are both just like this. And my own place has one or two movie- and music-related bits and pieces on the walls. Just because I can make that connection between then and now doesn't mean there hasn't been growth. That inside his soul he hasn't refined the décor. No danger in a little bit of nostalgia, you'd be an idiot if you didn't take some things with you from the past—the best bits.

I move to sit on the sofa, but the cushions are cluttered with printouts and magazines. One is a healthcare journal called *Health Psychology International.*

"So your job," I say. "Can you explain it to me properly now?"

"It's a real yawn." His voice floats in from another room.

"Yeah, so you've said. Still. Bore me."

"Do you want any kind of special tea? I've got Earl Grey or herbal—"

"Normal breakfast will do. And your job?"

"Okay, so I specialised in a relatively new field called behavioural economics after I got my first degree. I worked in public sector commissioning for a while, then did a Masters and started a one-man consultancy to advise on how to better create interventions for chronic diseases using knowledge of human psychology. So you know, I design a lot of choice architecture stuff, make sure it's easier to make healthy decisions. Like hiding impulse items from the checkout, and putting fruit and veg there instead, that kind of stuff."

I opt against sitting down, and place my bag on the sofa before walking over to the bay window that looks out onto a brick wall and the stairs down to the flat.

"You're not one of those nudge guys, are you?" I say. "All that *people are completely irrational so let's trick them into being healthy.*"

"And there you go, that's why I never mentioned it before. Always the critic."

"I'm sure those things have their place. It's good to know, it explains a lot that you're in the business of mind control."

"Technically behaviour control, but you know, it's for the greater good. It balances the universe. Health inequalities."

On one of the shelves is a stand with a wide circular base and a single pole jutting upwards, on which hang a number of brightly coloured fabric bands. I step closer. They're festival bands in various states of tattiness, about fifteen in total.

Green Man 2010, Reading '99, Secret Garden 2007.

One near the top, bright red, reads *fest*. I reach over and lift another band out of the way to confirm it says Manifest.

A sensation like déjà vu washes over me. When I spin this band around, it is going to be from last year. Somehow I know this, like I've been through this moment thousands of times before. Steve is going to have a wristband from last year's Manifest.

I'm smiling, no grinning, madly, while inside things are freezing: my muscles, my lungs, my thoughts.

It doesn't necessarily mean anything if it is from last year. It could belong to someone else. Perhaps he collects them and a friend of his…

Everything in the room is his. This is him. And whatever that wristband says, it belongs to him. But of course that could be a coincidence, too. Just because he was at Manifest last year doesn't mean anything either. Lots of people go to festivals. Just like lots of people lived in Yor—

A spoon tings against a mug in the kitchen.

Oh yes, that other lie. That other fact he forgot to mention. Only being around Manifest at the same time Will supposedly went—although had the police actually found any evidence of that yet?—is a different thing entirely. He wouldn't be able to wriggle out of this one using—what bullshit thing had it been?—*confidentiality*. This placed him at a murder scene.

I turn to the archway, just to check he isn't there, but only the men in the *The Usual Suspects* poster are watching me now. How fucking perfect.

With a quick movement I reach up to the stand once again and spin the band, confirming what I already know.

The walls of the room feel miles away, my brain pulling off a Hitchcock camera trick. I want to laugh, as my mind protests that this could mean anything. It could mean anything at all.

But no it can't, because I can see it all now, strapped helplessly to my chair in the cinema of my mind: the camera spins around Steve and Will while they sit in the corner of a dingy York pub. Will tells Steve he is putting his past behind him, then walks out. Steve is crushed at first. But then he's angry. His face screws up in hatred. So typical of Will. Rejecting him once again. Just like when he'd not tried enough during The Dedication and finished last.

A plan begins to solidify in his head. He remembers Will's murder spree, because in morbid moments he's hoped Will might really do it one day, because if it happened it would

dramatically reunite us all. The ones that mattered. The dedicated. Because something dramatic like Will's murder spree…
that would bring them back under different circumstances than
just coffee or a meal. There would be intensity. There would
be drama. The bonds would hold.

So why wait for Will? What if he just commits the murder
spree, in exactly the way Will said he would? Sets it all up so
that they discover Will's crimes together. He knows Will won't
show up, will be difficult to find. It would be perfect: the gang
would be together again, solving puzzles, hanging out. And he
would have his revenge on Will.

Now I see a close-up of myself at a computer, committing to
the reunion, and it begins. He finds patients in York that Will
might also have come into contact with, ones at risk of suicide.
Two people who want to die anyway—he's being helpful, even.
Maybe he charms them into it, a suicide pact. Or maybe he
just arranges to meet them somewhere, drugs them, then kills
them himself? Yes, it requires a lot of planning. Getting the victims to Loch Ness and into Manifest. But for Steve Litt, archi-
tect of our childhoods, planning is second nature. Maybe he
even made that film of the Manifest body, or left some of those
comments on the message boards Jen found, scattering clues
across the internet for us to find and keep us going.

Too many images are rushing through my head now. It's hard
to focus on one.

Was killing Will always part of the plan, or had he tacked it
on afterwards in addition to framing him, as revenge for holding the knife to his throat? Or had he just lost control when it
looked like the gang would part ways—just as Jen had done?
A penny for his thoughts at the time she started making her
intervention.

He must have made up the train story, just as Rupesh said
he did: and the reason why is obvious now. All that needless

self-sacrifice; all that bravery in the face of danger. And what had he said that night in the hotel?

But you can't force that kind of thing, can you? Force someone into seeing what you mean to them. And Mum; God, no, Mum. He probably thought he was doing me a favour by attacking her. Two birds with one stone: a sick romantic gift and a display of intent.

But how had he got the bodies to the pylon? Well, possibly the same way he made sure I hadn't woken up. Because yes, Rupesh and Jen, how tired I had been those very nights things were meant to have happened, and how sick had I been in the mornings. And how strange had that awful hotel wine tasted? I see him pulling out some baggie with his back turned—because it's always a baggie—and dropping it in. Special wine from the bar—none of that mini-bar rubbish.

It is all so believable, not least because of what he was *like* during it all. So calm, so composed, until the end when he was so sure. In my memory the colour of him is still red, but now it's a dangerous, keep-a-safe-distance red. And okay, so that might have been because he knew all the things Will told him in private that he supposedly couldn't share.

Only it hasn't worked. Unless I, even as a consolation prize, am enough for Steve. Because he must love me, in some strange, crazy way. Our relationship is important to the whole story, the King and Queen of Elm Close.

"What do you think of the place?" Steve says from somewhere behind me.

I've loved films long enough to know this is the bit where I jump and spin around and fail to hide how flustered I am. So I keep looking forward at the wrist bands, the matchbook, the nostalgia. And oh, what's this? A fading newspaper cutting from the *Marlstone Times*, with four of us posed behind Will, who stands at the front of the picture holding up a Roman pot. How happy we look.

Breathing deeply, I turn and face Steve. His smile is shy and warm; those adorable little crinkles are back at the edges of his eyes. I don't really believe he killed those women, I *can't* really believe it. Can I?

He holds out a cup of tea. There's concern in his face. "I hope I didn't put too much milk in."

"I'm sure you—" I stop crossing the room, stop talking. I am no longer looking at his face but at his T-shirt, the design of which is no longer concealed by the buttoned-up jacket.

"It's cool, isn't it?" he says, looking down at his chest.

The screen-printed square at the centre of the otherwise red fabric depicts Shaggy holding a terrified Scooby Doo, both looking behind them at three ghosts emerging from a Grandfather clock. *Scooby Doo Meets the Boo Brothers* is printed above them all in white bubble letters, the two Os in Boo form two eyes.

"I wish the others could see it," he says.

"It might be one for the crusher," I say.

He laughs at this, then says, "You were looking quite intently at that wall. What did you see?"

"I just don't think I'd ever seen that newspaper cutting." The front door is so far away from where I'm standing, and Steve fills up so much of the archway between it and me.

"Maybe I should take it down now," he says. "Or blank their faces out."

I take a step towards him, wanting to at least close the distance between me and my way out. I take the tea and he stretches out his hand to lean on the archway wall to his left. To seal my exit completely.

"I think I left a very important part of myself behind back then," he says, feral eyes working me out.

"Yes, I think you did."

"I think I need to let it go sometimes."

"That's always healthy." I'm worried he can sense my fear. I try changing the subject. "Where's your loo?"

He pauses to think, like he doesn't know where the toilet is in his own flat. Like he's forgotten where he is. That's it, yes, like he'd been drifting to another place. He stands aside and points to a door on the opposite side of the flat. He lets me pass. I hand him my tea to occupy his hand, then walk right by the front door. It's the size of a cupboard, just a bright white sink and a bright white toilet, the colour scheme making up for lack of windows.

I can't call the police. He'd hear me. Can you text the police? Instead, I text Rupesh and Jen. I tell them where I am, that I believe them now, and that I need them to help me. That I need an excuse to get out the flat. I flush the chain then leave, hoping the text sent.

"I should probably think about going."

He hands me back my tea, touches my shoulder and puts his forehead to mine. I resist the urge to pull away.

"Please don't," he says. "We could do a marathon. Films from Our Past."

"That would be fun," I say. Now I step away, wondering if the tea is hot enough to throw at him should it come to it. I sip, but it's lukewarm. "*Grosse Pointe Blank.*"

"Exactly." His gaze is hungry: more, more, more.

"*Men in Black,*" I say.

"Yeah." He closes the gap between us once more.

"Uh…" He's an alpha wolf, trying to decide if I'm part of his pack.

My phone rings. Loud, obnoxious, beautiful.

I bring it out, glance at the screen, and act the shit out of looking concerned. "It might be about Mum."

I answer it. "Hi, Dad." I force my mug over to Steve again.

"Adeline, are you okay?" Rupesh says. I hope to God Steve can't hear me.

"Hang on, Dad, I can't hear you." I bring the phone to my chest and say to him: "God, you were right, the reception is *terrible* here."

Without hesitation, like ripping off a plaster or jumping into an ice-cold lake in order to fake getting cramp and drowning, I bring the phone to my ear and make for the front door. I reach up for the latch. "Give me a sec, Dad."

I wait for the hand on my shoulder, the arms around my waist, the sounds of pursuit. But the door opens, and fresh air blesses my face. He doesn't stop me walking through the door. He doesn't stop me walking up the stairs. He doesn't stop me walking down the end of the drive, by which point I am both out of danger and, surely, out of earshot.

"Fucking hell, Rupesh," I say. Looking back I see Steve's Octavia parked to one side of the building. Such a big car for a single man. With such a big boot, too. How new it had smelled. Like he'd bought it recently. Like, just before we all met up again. "Fucking hell."

I tell Rupesh everything while making my reaction look as much like a concerned daughter as possible. He is calm, tells me that I just need to get out of there first, then get to a police station, preferably Marlstone if I feel safe doing so—all without Steve knowing what I've seen.

"You call me and let me know you're on the road," Rupesh says. "If I don't hear from you in ten minutes I'm calling 999."

I hang up and walk back down the drive. I yell down: "Steve."

He appears in stairwell looking up at me. Waiting inside the door for me to finish. Listening, maybe.

"I need to leave now, Mum's taken a bad turn. Dad's in a right state."

"Oh no," he says. "Do you need company?"

"No." Then it hits me. I've left my bag in the lounge. My car keys are in there. "Could you just grab my bag?"

"Where is it?" he says. "Why don't you just come and get it?"
He stands aside, making it necessary for me to walk right by him in that tight space.

"It's in the lounge," I say.

"Won't it just be easier—"

"Steve, can you just get it for me. I don't want to lose signal in case he calls again." He doesn't move. He's actually glaring at me. "She might be on her way out."

This painful lie apparently sinks in, and slowly he turns and goes back into the house. He takes his time. He must know I've seen the band. He must be working out how he can turn things back. Or maybe not. The level of arrogance required to even leave it up on display suggests he is so out of his mind that—

"Here," he says, holding up the bag by the straps. He wants me to collect it from him. Down where no one can see us.

"Can you bring it to me," I say. "You're being a bit weird."

"Am I? I think if anyone's being weird—"

"The reception. Steve, my bag."

He sighs. He glances into his flat again. For a moment I wonder if he is going to go back inside with it. Make me come for it. I won't. If he does that I'll run.

I won't have to. Step by agonising step he brings me the bag. When I take it he offers no resistance. I have it in my hand. I'm pulling it up to my shoulder, my head turned for just a second, when he grabs my shoulder. I jump. No, he's not grabbing it. He's only touching it gently.

"Are you okay?" he says. The wolf is gone. Now Steve Litt, concerned and a little hurt, has returned to say goodbye. "I do love you. You know that, don't you?"

And even now I feel something like tenderness towards him. Just for a fraction of a second, but it's there nonetheless. Some insane biological, pheromonal coup attempt, or perhaps some trick of nostalgia, one to which I should have an immunity by now.

"Thanks, Steve," I say. "I really need to go."

And without looking back, I walk as calmly as I can to the end of his drive, then out of sight I run to my car. I sit inside for a moment, stunned, out of breath. I slide the keys into the ignition, then place my shaking hands on the steering wheel, noticing the length of my nails: when did I stop biting them? I get the car moving and head straight for Blythe, and when I finally arrive, the winding roads behind me, I'll never be more grateful to see it.

Adeline, 1998

They lay spooning in Steve's bed facing the window, his arms around her chest. The curtains were open. Not that she cared right now, her body still trembling with excitement and shock, hot all over despite it being cold in the farmhouse. It could never be cold again.

She turned and kissed him, and he kissed her back. Facing the window again, she looked up at all the stars.

"Can you always see this many?" she said.

"There's no light pollution. That's why I leave the curtains open."

His hand moved down to stroke her stomach just below the belly button, exploring. Funny there'd been a time she worried and fretted about whether she needed to do anything to the hair there. Worried about whether he would expect it to feel like it did? That thick, that coarse. Now that was just idiotic to her, his own, similar hairs all pressed up against her bum.

"Did you see *Men in Black*?" he said. "The Will Smith film?"

Not the most romantic topic, but right now he could talk about anything and she wouldn't care. Everything was right, balanced, complete. Even in this room, that smelled of old socks and had a dead dog's collar and a matchbook pinned to the wall between two of the various movie posters on display.

"We watched it together last summer."

"So you remember the ending? When it zooms out and the earth is a marble?"

"And the aliens are playing with it. Of course. I always think of that when I look at the stars. It makes you realise just how small we are in the scheme of things."

"And how pointless it all is, really." Steve kissed her shoulder.

"Yeah," she said. Although was that what she thought? In the philosophy books she had started reading they mentioned that feeling of insignificance, but one of the philosophers had made a clever argument that challenged the idea.

"Actually, no. I think it makes you change your idea of significance," she said. "Maybe significance is all in the eye of the beholder, you know? Like, to those big aliens we are insignificant, but then to us they are insignificant. So why should another's idea of significance have any impact on ours?"

"I suppose I just liked the idea of nothing mattering really, because it makes me fearless. Makes it feel like the world is there for the taking."

Steve was silent then. Was he annoyed? He kissed her shoulder again, so probably not.

"Do you think we'll ever see each other again?" Adeline said. "The gang, I mean."

"Probably not," Steve said. "It's easier being in gangs as kids. We've all got a lot in common because we've not really done anything yet. Adults just pair off and don't seem to have friends any more, just work colleagues."

It was true enough, Adeline's parents had a smattering of people they called friends but they rarely saw them outside of birthdays. Or funerals.

"If we all met up in the future," he continued, "we'd have completely different lives and probably resent interrupting

416

them with a stupid reunion with people we don't know any more. Sad, really."

"Well, maybe Will can do his murders, that would certainly bring us together," Adeline said.

His snort of amusement tickled her back but barely made a sound. The room was quiet for the longest time. Then Steve said, "Yeah, that would probably do it."

Later

It starts with rumours, concerned comments in passing of the not-sure-if-you'd-heard-this type from the few friends and family members that knew about what happened.

And she's able to dismiss them at first.

She doesn't search message boards and forums where similar rumours will also be spreading. She doesn't call and worry anyone. No, such rumours are too ridiculous, too awful, to give any thought to.

Only then, a year from when she first heard the rumours, Jon tells Adeline that they were true. It is a Friday in the run-up to Christmas, another afternoon recording at the BBC done.

"I didn't want you finding out by accident," he says.

Fragments of what she has tried so hard not to think about all these years glimmer beneath the erratic light of her attention during an otherwise numb tube journey home that she will never remember.

Once home she asks her boyfriend for space, then lies on her bed with her phone, and finds the podcast everyone has been trying to tell her about.

For a long time she stares at the ceiling before eventually pressing play.

The first voice she recognises belongs to Xan. In the years

that have gone by since she last saw him his podcast has raised significant doubts about two separate men's murder convictions, with retrials on the cards. Those first two seasons have gained two million and three million downloads respectively, although this is the first time Adeline has listened. Xan himself showed no interest in keeping in touch with her once *Nostalgia Crush* was done.

Xan's familiar voice, that once comforted her, dredges up all the details of the case for nearly half an hour, and for the most part he gets things right. How his new subject has only been convicted of the murder of Will Oswald, but how rumours surround a host of other crimes that haven't been brought to trial: two women who supposedly killed themselves; a man named Bill Strachan who was found burned in his house in what was suspected to have been an accident; the subject's own mother and father.

"You can call me Steve if you want," he says, and though Adeline has been expecting to hear his voice, it breaks over her like a wave in a winter sea. "Steven reminds me of my mum. Can I call you Xan?"

No, it's an actor, surely—doing an impression that sounds just like Steve Litt.

Oh, how unfair that he's allowed a voice in this way, how fucking unfair that no process is in place to stop him reaching the ears of millions. Or perhaps Xan has simply bent the rules somehow to allow this, high on his own success.

And when Xan brings up her name for the first time, she hears in his voice that this isn't all about justice for him.

"My own interest in this has a personal dimension," Xan says, "I worked quite closely with one of the individuals that testified against Steve Litt, and she was part of the events that occurred in Blythe on the night of Will Oswald's death."

Adeline tries to keep calm, tries to focus on the light fixture above her, concentrate on the implications of everything she hears. But it's hard. She hates Xan for this—far more than anything that she feels about Steve Litt.

"So, do you want to tell me what's on your mind?" Xan says.

"Just like that?" Steve says, apprehensive. "Okay, fuck. This all feels so intense. It's a little bit *Dead Man Walking*."

Xan comments alongside the interview that Steve is charming, and how *Dead Man Walking* is his favourite film, and that Steve's uncanny empathy might be evidence both for his guilt or for his innocence.

Adeline wants to scream then—that no, this isn't fucking empathy. Steve will have looked it up, listened to the old podcasts and heard Xan say this. Steve Litt will have done his research so that he can charm—no, flirt—with Xan to win him over.

But she needs to keep things in perspective: no matter what Xan uncovers this series, there's surely no way that Steve can challenge his conviction. On the other hand, this is episode one of eight—what is still to come?

Perhaps she will receive a phone call from Xan, asking for her side of things at some point. Maybe he will have already called Jen and Rupesh; if not, she'll need to warn them.

Steve reiterates to Xan a lot of what the courts have already heard: that he was with someone the nights he'd have had to pull off all the things he was supposed to have pulled off, and that the timelines for him doing everything don't make sense.

"I think about this a lot," he says, sounding lost and vulnerable—committing to his part. "But I decided the jury were convinced by this idea of me being a master manipulator because I have a background in behavioural science. And then, the other thing was the testimony of the others. How can you respond to that, three people that know you? Oh no, they're basing their idea of me on what I was like as a kid."

The way he speaks... oh it's easy to see why Xan is so taken by his case.

Xan asks Steve about the post-trial chatter around his other supposed crimes. Steve continues to claim that the Manifest wristband he bought at a market was a tribute to what they had all been through that Christmas, albeit a grim one. And he claims he has never even been to Scotland.

But Xan plays a role too, that of the impartial host—a somewhat strange task in a show called *Beyond Reasonable Doubt*, that has a perception of righting miscarriages of justice. What about the police having an alibi for Will Oswald for at least the Manifest death—a prostitute who'd been with Will for many of the weekends that year, and who specifically remembered the Manifest weekend because her sister was there? He also asks about Steve's DNA on the laptop in Will's attic, and about the fake email address in Will's name that traced back to an IP address in Oxford. Not to mention the samples of Rupesh and Will's hair found in Steve's car boot.

There is a silence. Then Steve, resigned, says, "I can't answer everything. I know how those things look and I can't say I wouldn't have convicted me if I'd have been on the jury. I can't even be angry about it now. I'm just... You just realise so much of what is really important is entirely in your own head. I still miss those guys, too, even though I'm only here because of them."

"You're not angry?"

"No. Sometimes."

Oh, Steve sounds so fucking honest, so defeated: the charming young man done wrong by his friends and the system.

Adeline imagines it then with chilling clarity: Steve duping the world the way he did her. How plausible it seems.

Only she won't allow it, she will fight him again. She needs to allow the past to flood back so she can crush him once more.

There's so much to remember, though. Likely she'll need to write it all down before starting.

Xan asks another question in that fake-journalistic tone: how would Steve go about finding the real culprit then? "I mean, it seems pretty clear it can't have been Will, so in your mind, who did do it, Steve? It has to be one of the others, right?"

Adeline can almost hear Steve shaking his head, so troubled, so deeply upset. "I just can't even think about that, you know. I have to think about how it's going to be perceived if I just start pointing fingers and getting it wrong. I still think maybe they messed up about Will. I keep coming back to the first night, where it all started. The atmosphere, his face, the way he phrased things. I was scared by him.

"Maybe it was a completely unknown person. Someone who Will gave orders too. I don't know. A while back I'd have probably suggested Mr. Strachan, this guy that caused us problems back in Blythe—but they tell me he died."

Then he says: "I know that this will sound crazy. I mean—" He cuts himself off, creating a dramatic pause the editors won't even need to embellish. "I mean, Rupesh had it in for me. But he'd never do it. But then, you know, I think to myself, why did he lie about seeing me when he was unconscious? Unless he hallucinated, I suppose. But I wasn't there, that's what I can say. And then I'm like, what about his cabin in Loch Ness?"

"What cabin?" Xan will be hooked. The audience will be hooked. Adeline feels sick.

"The one where he went to spread his dad's ashes the same time that girl died. You heard about that, right? I mean, I'd be interested to know what they might find up there. You know, he told me once there's a safe under the floorboards. What's in that?"

And then Steve is asked to tell the story. The whole story as he remembers it. At that point Adeline starts mentally composing hers.

"Where do you want me to start?" Steve says.

"Would it be too obvious to say the beginning?" Xan says.

"Okay. I'll do my best."

Adeline can hear his smile then, can picture him there in prison, still looking every inch the washed-up but gracefully ageing film star.

She will not let this happen. No, this will not fucking happen. Xan wants justice—it is supposed to always prevail—but he's looking in the wrong place. Adeline knows where the right place is, though: Sara Kuzmenski, Ellie Kidd, Bill Strachan, Mum.

Will Oswald.

Time alone will never make things right; justice needs provocation.

She finds a pen and a pad. She starts to remember.

Her boyfriend knocks on the door, asks if she's okay.

"I'm fine," she says.

"Do you need anything?"

"I just need time."

On the podcast there is another pause. Then, just before she turns it off, she hears Steve say:

"All of this started the night Will told us he was going to be a serial killer."

Acknowledgements

Firstly, thank you for reading my book. In a world with so many great novels and authors, I'm grateful you chose to spend some of your reading time here with me and the gang. And if you haven't read the book, and just like reading acknowledgements sections, I'll try as hard as possible to make these, at the very least, an adequate set.

It seems appropriate that following a book all about groups, I should admit that writing a novel is really a group effort—this book in particular—and I feel really lucky to have had an amazing team of generous and kind people guiding *The Killer You Know* along its way. No acknowledgement section would exist for me to write without my brilliant agent Joanna Swainson and my fantastic editor, Lucy Dauman. Thank you both for your endless patience and wisdom, and your belief in both the book and me. And an extension of that thanks to the brilliant teams at Hardman & Swainson and Sphere; thank you all for making me feel so at home in both stables. And a very special thanks to my US editor, Bradley Englert, and all the team at Redhook for bringing the gang from the lost United State of the West Midlands to the real United States.

I had some incredible first readers who all contributed so much: David Cox, Helen Brewster, Sarah Fairfield, Anni D, Hilary and Niall, Ann-Marie, Andrea, Tim, Celia, Gilly, Cara, Phoebe, and J. J. DeBenedictis. Thanks for all your hard work. And I asked a lot of questions (plenty silly) and am hugely grateful to those that provided me with answers. For all things medical and veterinarian, Jessie, Steph and Sanjey; for all things police-related, Matthew and Rebecca; for all things legal, Ezra and Helen B; and for a miscellany of random things, Vèronique, Niall Spooner-Harvey, Beasty, and social media friends for various ideas when I needed inspiration. To all of you, thank you so much. They tried their best to help me, and any errors that slipped through are entirely down to my own shortcomings.

I owe a few people from before this book was written a drink or two, especially those from the world of short fiction and music. Thanks to Rob Redman, Bruce Bethke, my AW forum buddies (Michael Wehunt, Sam, Kristi, Danielle, Fi to name but a few), John Joseph Adams and Daniel H. Wilson, Grundy, Dan, Tom W and Steve W. Thanks to the amazing Doomsday writers, for moral support and daily inspiration. Vicky McKee and Giovanni—gone, but I'm thankful for your influence every day. And thank you to Jack and the HHB crew for nourishment at the start of this journey.

Mom and Dad, thank you for continuing to put up with and love your baffling first child, and for setting up that caravan on the drive as a makeshift writing studio for me when I was a boy. Thanks to Nanny Bet Bet for too much to mention, but also for typing up ten-year-old me's stories on a typewriter. Andrew and Toppy, thanks for indulging me as both a kid and as an adult— I really did fall out of a spaceship though. Ade and Helen B, Sarah and Richard, thanks for being the best parents who aren't actually my parents. And thanks to my amazing childhood friends, who never tried to murder me, not even once: DaN McKee, Sarah T, Craig and Sarah O. And finally thank you so much to my best friend, wife, editor and soulmate, Helen, who convinced me this writing malarkey wasn't a silly dream—and for being an amazing mother to our son Joe, whom I'd also like to thank for arriving, and keeping me company, during edits. Love you both!

meet the author

S. R. MASTERS studied philosophy at Girton College, Cambridge, before working in public health and health behavior for the NHS. He is a regular contributor to UK short fiction anthology series published by The Fiction Desk, having won their Writer's Award for his short story *Just Kids*. His story *Desert Walk* was included in Penguin Random House USA's *Press Start to Play* collection, and he continues to have short fiction published in a variety of magazines. He grew up around Birmingham but now lives in Oxford with his wife and son. *The Killer You Know* is his first novel.